Some LIKE IT Hotter

Andrea Simonne

Sweet Life in Seattle - Book 3

Some Like It Hotter
 Published by Liebe Publishing
Print Edition, February 2019
ISBN: 978-1-945968-00-6

Edited by Hot Tree Editing
www.hottreepublishing.com

Cover Design © by LBC Graphics

Interior Design & Formatting by Perfectly Publishable
www.perfectlypublishable.com

Liebe Publishing
liebepublishing@gmail.com
www.liebepublishing.com

Chapter One

~ Never give men what they want because then they won't want it anymore. ~

"WILL YOU MARRY me?"

Lindsay's brows arch up with surprise. "What?"

"I want you to be my wife." The guy sitting across the table from her leans in closer, devotion in his eyes as he speaks in a thick German accent. "I love you!"

They're sitting outside having dinner at a restaurant in Berlin's trendy Friedrichshain district, a hip part of town with plenty of bars and clubs.

"I don't know what to say," she murmurs, trying to decide the best way to let him down easy. "We haven't known each other very long, Dietmar, um, Dieter." *My God, what's his name again?*

He chuckles. "You are so funny with your American humor, and so beautiful too. This is how I know you are the woman for me."

She smiles, though her eyes flash toward the sidewalk traffic along Simon Dach Strasse, wishing she could escape into the crowd. She's been in Berlin for two and a half months now, and this is her third marriage proposal. A record, even for her.

Why are all these damn Germans so eager to get married?

He leans toward her again, an adoring expression on his broad, handsome face. He's wearing a short-sleeved blue T-shirt with the name of the nightclub he co-owns imprinted on the front. There's a colorful trail of tats running down his right arm.

In truth, he's exactly her type—an industrious and talented bad boy who secretly wants to be tamed.

"You must come to my family home and meet my parents, *ja*? I am excited for them to meet the mother of their future grandchildren!"

Lindsay fingers her glass of beer just as her phone buzzes on the table. She glances at the display though she doesn't recognize the number. Tempted to answer it, she decides she isn't heartless enough to take a phone call in the middle of a marriage proposal.

"We can stay in Berlin for now," he continues explaining his plans. "But I would like us to move to my family's dairy farm soon after the wedding."

"Family farm? I thought you were from Berlin."

"*Ach nein*, I grew up outside the city. Trust me, you will love it there. Lots of cows and goats *und meine Mutter* makes the best sauerkraut you have ever tasted!"

She digests this new piece of information about him. "That sounds wonderful, and I'm sure your family is great, but don't you think this is kind of sudden?" Her phone starts buzzing again, the same number from a few seconds ago. Definitely not a local number and not from Seattle—her hometown—either.

"My family will be so pleased to meet you. I have told them you are an artist, and they say you will have plenty of time for your art after the chores are finished. Maybe even more time on the weekends."

She mentally chokes on her beer as she imagines herself working on a farm milking cows every day. "I'm flattered by your proposal—truly—but I can't possibly marry you Dieter . . . er, Dietrich."

He holds up his large hand. "I thought you might say this, but do not decide now. I am not in a rush, though *meine Mutter* says she cannot wait to be an *Oma* and hold a grandchild in her arms."

He smiles at her with big white teeth.

Lindsay sighs and takes a sip of beer—both bitter and strong. It's been one of her favorite things about Germany. So far, she's enjoyed a lot of things during her stay as part of an artist in residence program. The food has been excellent and the people are friendly, although the men are too overeager. She's used to male attention, and takes pleasure in it, but they all keep falling in love with her.

It's getting downright annoying.

To make matters worse, she's been in a sexual funk for months. None of the guys she dates are doing it for her. Lindsay hoped coming here might get her mojo back, but so far no dice. She hasn't slept with a single guy. Not one. She's kissed a few toads, but no princes yet.

At least Berlin has a thriving community for *Künstler*—artists, and it's helped bring her goals back into focus. She wants to finish her degree and get her teaching certificate. Her life has been crazy up to this point, but she's thirty-three now, and it was time to start thinking about her future. Hell, she's not exactly getting any younger.

"What is going through that beautiful head of yours?" Dieter asks, still gazing at her with adoration.

"I was just considering your offer." *I never should have kissed him.* It was only a few kisses and she didn't think much of it, but clearly it made a stronger impression than she intended. "Marriage is a big step," she explains.

"If we marry you will not have to worry about anything. I will take care of you."

In truth, she's already been married—not once, but twice. A mistake she never intends to repeat.

"I didn't want to have to tell you this." She fiddles with her glass. "But I'm sort of seeing someone back home," she lies.

He looks surprised. "What is this?"

"I have a boyfriend."

Dieter appears to ruminate on her words, and Lindsay hopes it's enough to squash any further marriage desires.

"If it weren't for him, believe me, I'd be interested in your offer," she says quickly, not wanting to hurt his feelings.

"Is it serious with him?"

"I'm afraid it is. We've had our ups and downs," she decides to spin it for realism, "but I do love him."

"You kissed me."

"I know, but only because I had a moment of weakness."

He smiles at her. "Maybe you will have a moment of weakness again."

"I'm afraid not."

"But this boyfriend of yours, he lets you run off alone to Berlin? And does he call? Does he write? What kind of man is he?"

She drinks the rest of her beer while Dieter rants on about how her boyfriend doesn't deserve her. He's so convincing, Lindsay is starting to think her boyfriend is an asshole, but then remembers he's fake to begin with.

"You're right." She gives a helpless shrug. "He doesn't deserve me, but I'm still committed. That's just the way I am."

"You are too good for him!"

"I'll tell him you said so."

Dieter grumbles as he pays the bill, and the two of them head out of the restaurant toward her studio a few blocks away. He insists on walking her home and Lindsay decides to let him, hoping he'll calm down with all this marriage talk.

Her studio is in a colorful building that dominates the block and contains artists' work spaces which double as apartments. Because she sculpts, her studio is a larger unit on the first floor. Each artist gets a space to live and work in, though they have to share a bathroom, as there are only two per floor. For Lindsay, it's been the only real drawback. Two bathrooms between ten people is like some kind of endurance test.

"Lindsay!"

She turns her head to the sound of a male voice calling her name as they arrive at her building.

Hellooo, what have we here?

A big blond mountain of guy is walking down the sidewalk toward her.

Now there's some peaks I'd like to climb.

She can't pull her eyes away. With all these desperate boys clamoring for her attention, something tells her she's finally looking at a man.

Nice.

But as he gets closer, she realizes something else. He looks familiar. Biblical sense kind of familiar.

Shit.

"Giovanni?"

The mountain grins. "Lindsay, I've been trying to reach you all evening."

"What are you doing here?"

Before Giovanni can answer, Dieter steps in front of her. "Who is this? Another boyfriend?"

Lindsay opens her mouth, not sure what to say. Giovanni isn't her boyfriend, but he's not exactly a friend either.

"*Arschloch*!" Dieter starts cursing at him in a mixture of German and English. "Bastard, you don't deserve her!"

Giovanni holds his hands up. "Look, I don't know who you are, but you need to calm down."

"Do not tell me to calm down!"

"This is not my boyfriend," Lindsay tells Dieter, who ignores her, continuing with his German tirade. She turns to Giovanni. "I don't know why you're here, but just leave, okay? This isn't going to end well."

Unfortunately, Giovanni's ignoring her too. "You've got it all wrong," he says to Dieter. "I'm only here to talk to Lindsay."

"I know what you want, but you can forget it. I won't let you have her!"

"That's ridiculous!" Lindsay raises her voice.

Dieter shakes his head and turns to her, eyes blazing. "You do not have to protect him. I do what I have to. I want to win you as mine!"

"*What*? That's stupid. He's nobody to me!"

Dieter doesn't reply and before she can stop him, he shoves Giovanni.

Giovanni is pushed backward, but quickly rights himself, his expression thunderous. "Listen, you bastard. Unless you want to eat this goddamn cement, I suggest you back off."

"*Fick dich*!" Dieter spits out.

"Walk away, Giovanni," Lindsay begs. "Please, just do it now."

He looks at her like she's crazy. "Who is this asshole?"

But before Lindsay can answer, Dieter takes a swing at him.

Giovanni ducks but Lindsay can see he's ready to battle. The next thing she knows, Dieter has thrown himself at Giovanni and the two men are grappling, both of them cursing.

She watches with panic, desperately searching around for some kind of help. It's late and there aren't many people out. A couple walks past on the sidewalk, but they seem more amused than alarmed by the two men wrestling with each other like schoolboys.

Lindsay wishes she had a garden hose and could spray cold water on them both.

"Break it up, you idiots!" she yells, but neither of them listens to her. "I don't want *either* of you! Do you understand?"

Giovanni is bigger than Dieter and seems to be gaining the upper hand, but then Dieter shoves his head into Giovanni's shoulder, throwing him off balance. Giovanni corrects himself and the men are back to grappling again.

Lindsay continues to watch for a few seconds before pulling her phone out to check the time. It's almost nine thirty.

She sighs with annoyance.

The men are still wrestling. Giovanni has Dieter in a headlock, though Dieter manages to squirm out of it.

This is ridiculous.

She stifles a yawn.

Finally, she decides to go upstairs and take a nap.

To be honest, this isn't the first time two guys have fought over her.

And it won't be the last.

Chapter Two

LINDSAY'S HOUSE RULES

~ Men live for the chase, whether they know it or not, so let them chase. ~

THERE'S A SHARP knock on the front door.

Lindsay opens her eyes and lets out a huff. *What now*? She was finally drifting off to sleep, trying to get a short nap in before she goes out later. She decides to ignore whoever it is by burying herself deeper under the covers.

The sharp knock turns into a pounding.

"Open this door, Lindsay!" A guy's voice comes through from the hallway outside her studio.

Dammit.

Annoyed, she flings back her duvet and reaches over to turn on her bedside lamp. She's only wearing panties and a T-shirt but doesn't bother covering up with a robe. When she swings open her front door, it's no surprise who she finds on the other side.

Giovanni.

It figures.

"What do you want?"

He walks right past her. "I need a glass of ice, a clean dish towel, and vodka." He glances around for a moment then heads straight toward her small kitchen.

She closes the door, but doesn't make a move to follow. "You should have taken my advice and left. There was no reason for you to fight him."

He's over by the kitchen sink. She watches him turn on the tap, test the water, and then put his hand beneath it. "I presume you heard me," he says.

"Glass of ice, clean dishtowel, and vodka?"

"That's correct." He's still holding his hand beneath the running water but looks over at her.

She's leaning against the front door. Pushing away from it, she walks toward him. His eyes take her in, drifting over the T-shirt that barely reaches the top of her thighs then down to her bare legs.

Lindsay decides to be nice and grab the items he requested. First the dishtowel from a drawer, then she pulls a bottle of vodka out of the freezer along with an ice cube tray. She fills a short glass with ice.

By now, he's turned off the tap and has dumped ice into the dishtowel, carefully wrapping it around the knuckles of his hand. His scent drifts toward her—clean male sweat with a hint of adrenaline. It's delicious and she lingers for a moment to get another whiff.

Giovanni is her brother-in-law. The one she accidentally slept with.

Oops.

Instead of putting the vodka on his hand, he takes everything over to her small kitchen table and sits down, pouring a splash of it into the glass.

Her older sister Natalie married his younger brother Anthony about a year and a half ago. In fact, they just had a baby, a cute little boy named Luca. Unfortunately, before all that happened, Lindsay had a one-night stand with Giovanni—not that she's seen him since. He's a pediatric surgeon who works somewhere in Africa. That's basically all she knows about him. He was supposed to be Anthony's best man at the wedding, but had some complicated reason why he couldn't make it.

What kind of asshole misses his only brother's wedding?

He tosses back the shot of vodka and pours himself another. He doesn't drink it though, but studies her instead. "I can't believe you went to bed."

"What do you mean?"

"Do you usually go to sleep when there are two men outside fighting over you?"

"Oh, *that*." She shrugs, leaning her hip against the kitchen counter. "I've learned you guys will fight whether I'm there or not. It makes no difference."

"After I punched him, he told me he has plans to marry you. Is that true?"

"Yes, Dietmar . . . um . . . Dieter, proposed earlier this evening."

He raises an eyebrow. "You don't even know his *name*?"

"Of course I know his name. It's Dieter." She bites her lip. "I'm pretty sure, anyway."

"When is the wedding?"

"There won't be a wedding. I'm not really the marriage type."

"It figures." He takes the ice off his hand, which appears red and slightly swollen. "You're like catnip for men. I knew it the first moment I laid eyes on you."

"*Catnip*?" Lindsay scoffs, tossing her long brown curls over her shoulder. "Try one hundred proof whiskey, motherfucker."

Giovanni chuckles as he examines his hand, bending his fingers, testing each one. "A siren singing her seductive song. The last thing sailors hear before they crash against the rocks."

She frowns to herself. The comparison isn't exactly flattering. She watches him move his hand. "Is anything broken?"

"No, I don't believe there's any real damage."

It occurs to her that he's a surgeon and his hands are probably important to him. "At least it's your left hand."

His blue eyes flash to her. "I'm left-handed."

"Really? Well, that was seriously stupid. Why didn't you punch him with your right?"

"I forgot." He seems annoyed with himself. "It's been a while since I've had to hit anyone."

She can't help but smirk. "Don't forget next time."

"Next time? Is that what it's like to be with you? I'll be forced to punch other guys?"

"You're not going to be with me."

A smile plays around the corners of his mouth like he knows something she doesn't.

Arrogant ass.

"What are you even doing here?" She walks over, slides into the chair opposite him, and reaches for his glass. Taking a swallow, the vodka is strong and bracing.

"I happened to be in Berlin, and Anthony mentioned you were here, so I thought I'd drop by."

"Why? We barely even know each other."

"We know each other."

"Ah, I see." She puts the glass down. "Just because you fucked me once you think you know me."

His eyes are steady on hers. "I'd say I knew you before I fucked you."

Lindsay holds his gaze. There's some truth in his words. Even though they'd never met before, she thought they connected that night. That there was a spark of something honest between them. But then she woke up alone in a hotel room. She'd had the occasional one-night stand before, but had certainly never woken up alone.

"So you decided to come by for a second helping?" She leans back in her chair and gives him a pitying look. "If only you'd been better in bed, I might be tempted."

Instead of being insulted, he considers her with amusement. "You really are catnip, aren't you?"

"No, I'm not. And I'm doing you a favor by sending you away. Trust me."

"I didn't come here to sleep with you again."

"Well, *that's* a huge relief. Then what do you want?"

"Are you always this hostile to the battle's victor? It sounds to me like you should be grateful I got rid of that guy for you."

She doesn't reply. Instead, she stands up and saunters over to the cabinet to get down a glass for some water, conscious of the way his eyes stay on her body. She doesn't mind. In fact, she makes a point to stretch up for a glass on a high shelf so he can get a nice, long look at the body he'll never touch again.

Nobody leaves me alone in a hotel room.

"I thought we should clear the air between us," he says.

She pours some water in her glass from a bottle she keeps in the small fridge. "Oh?"

"We're family now. Seeing as your sister is married to my kid brother and they just had a baby."

She brings her glass over and sits opposite him again, sipping her water. In truth, Giovanni is having a peculiar effect on her. She remembers it now from when they were together before. He feels familiar. It's like a tiny part of herself wants to let down her guard and trust him, to curl up on his lap and tell him all her secrets.

It must be the doctor thing, she decides. They probably try and foster this sort of response from people. Always giving off the impression they're capable and in command and deserving of your trust.

"I never would have slept with you if I'd known those two were going to get married," he continues.

"Okay."

"Okay, what?"

"Consider the air cleared. You can go." She waves her hand toward the door.

She expects him to get up, but he doesn't move. Instead, he fiddles with his glass, still watching her.

"Good night," Lindsay tells him. "Or should I say, *Gute Nacht*."

"Clearly, we're not done here."

"Oh, we're done all right. We're as done as it gets."

He shifts his large body in the kitchen chair, and she can't help admiring it. He's big, yet well-made. Her eyes trail down his shoulder to his muscular arms, and she imagines sculpting his likeness. It would be a real pleasure.

Despite what she said earlier, Giovanni was fantastic in bed. A one-night stand, but a memorable one. They met at a party, and the attraction between them was so hot they left after barely a half hour to check into a hotel. It was more than just physical though. They talked and laughed, ordered room service, playing with their food when it arrived. He smeared melted vanilla ice cream on her nipples and between her thighs before carefully licking it off. He told her she was beautiful at least fifty times that night, whispering it in her ear as he moved deep inside her. It was the way he said it too, like it was more than her appearance he was talking about. She could barely believe it when she woke up alone. There's no way sex that good was only one-sided.

She studies his face. He doesn't look that different from when she last saw him. He's handsome, but not in a pretty way like his brother. There are lines etched near his eyes and mouth, a small scar near his left brow. He's tan, probably too tan for someone with blond hair and blue eyes. Though he's Italian, he doesn't look it. His hair is short and wavy, and if it were longer, she suspects he'd have ringlet curls.

"You're angry," he says in a thoughtful tone. "Is it because I never called you? I thought you understood the situation." His expression goes earnest. "I was on a plane to Kenya less than a week later. I would have wanted to see you again otherwise."

"Is that so?"

"Yes, I really liked you."

In amazement, she recognizes what he's doing. He's letting her down easy. She's done it herself a million times.

He continues to fiddle with his glass as he tries to appear sincere. "So you see, I wanted to call, but I couldn't."

Except I wrote the book on this maneuver, asshole.

Lindsay studies her lap for a moment as if she's struggling for composure then takes a deep breath and pretends to be distressed. "Was it just meaningless sex for you? Is that it?"

"What? No, not at all."

"Because I thought we shared something special. How could you leave me like that?" She leans forward, curious to hear his answer. In truth, she had been a little hurt at the time, though mostly she was pissed.

"I didn't have a choice. My job takes me all over the world. As much as I liked you—and believe me, I did—I couldn't let myself get attached."

"You broke my heart," she tells him, putting a dramatic quiver in her voice. "I cried for weeks."

His eyes widen. "I . . . did? You *did*?"

"Of course. What do you take me for? Some kind of hussy?"

He squirms a little, and Lindsay smiles to herself.

"I thought you were trustworthy," she says, laying it on thick now. "I can't believe you would *use* me like that."

Giovanni seems agitated. "Look, it was just one night. A great night, but I don't think I used you."

"It was magical, admit it. A magical night!"

He blinks. "Magical?"

And that's when she sees the first glimmer of suspicion in his eyes.

"I can't live without you," she tells him, trying to hide her smile. "I've been waiting for you all my life. You're the wind beneath my wheels."

He stares at her. "Don't you mean *wings*?"

"Oh, yeah . . . right . . . *wings*." And that's when Lindsay bursts out laughing.

He seems taken aback, but then a grin appears on his face. "Damn, you really had me going there."

"I know, but come on. Telling me how much you *really* liked me. Is that the best you can do?"

"I *did* really like you."

She rolls her eyes. "Spare me the bullshit, okay?"

Giovanni doesn't say anything. He appears to be taking her measure, and she lets him. She leans back in her chair, meeting his gaze.

"All right," he says, slowly. "No bullshit. I had fun with you. You were great in and out of bed, but I wasn't looking for anything more."

"Neither was I."

"I guess the air is cleared then."

"It looks that way." She considers pointing out to him how rude it was when he left her, how he made her feel like a hooker, but decides not to bother.

He'll never have me again anyway, so what does it matter?

"Great," she tells him. "You can leave now. We're finally done for real."

"Why are you so anxious to get rid of me?"

"Because it's the middle of the night."

He glances at his watch. "It's barely after ten. You don't strike me as someone who goes to bed early."

"You don't know anything about me."

"I know a little." His eyes rest on hers. They travel from her hair to her face, then downward. "I have to admit, you're still very beautiful."

She glances around the room in boredom. "Thanks."

"I mean it."

"Whatever. It's not going to happen again."

Something flickers in his eyes.

She realizes it was the wrong thing to say to a man like him. Like waving a red cape in front of a bull.

A smile pulls on his mouth. "Catnip."

She lets her expression go completely flat, hoping to end this conversation.

He swigs down the rest of his drink then stands, unfolding his large body from the chair. He's too big for her kitchen, her apartment—and, she suspects, her life. She likes bad boys, and has tamed a few in her time, but overbearing men like Giovanni are usually more headache than they're worth.

She can't help enjoying the look of him though. Her eyes roam over his body, lingering for a moment at the bulge below his belt. He was big all over, as she recalls.

Her mind flashes back to the night they shared. The way his hands felt on her. Hot and sensual. Somehow, the warmth of them had gone deeper than her skin.

Annoyed, she pushes the memory away.

He was also arrogant as hell. Clearly nothing has changed in that regard.

Giovanni doesn't make a move to leave, just stands there studying her like he wants to speak.

"What is it?"

"I want to talk to you about something." He doesn't say anything more, simply stares at her, deep in thought. Finally, he shakes his head and looks away. "It's weird, but you kind of remind me of someone."

"Who?"

"No one. Forget it."

"I remind you of no one? I'm flattered, truly."

He lingers like he's still waiting for something.

"Gosh, I don't mean to be rude, but please don't let my front door hit you on the way out."

"Have you seen pictures of our new nephew lately?"

Lindsay softens. She Skypes with her sister Natalie at least once a week and gets to see little Luca every time. "Yes, he's quite the cutie." The baby looks a lot like Anthony, though she sees some of her family in him too.

"I'm glad for those two." He glances around her studio for a moment. "I was surprised when they got married, but they seem genuinely happy together."

"They are. It's a good marriage, and they've managed to make it all work." Both her sister and Anthony came into the marriage with a daughter from a previous relationship. "You missed a great wedding."

Their eyes meet, but he doesn't say anything.

"A lot of people were disappointed when you didn't make it."

"Were you one of them?"

"Me?"

"Seeing as I'm the wind beneath your wheels." His voice is dry.

She tries to hide her amusement, but can't quite manage it. "No, but your brother, your parents, and a whole bunch of Italians straight off a plane from Rome certainly were."

He opens his mouth to say something, but there's a knock at the door.

"Dammit, what time did you say it was?"

He glances at his watch. "Almost ten thirty."

"You need to leave. I have to get ready."

"Wake up, sleepyhead!" A feminine voice with a German accent drifts through the door.

He turns his head toward the sound. "You're going out?"

"Yes, I am." She stands up and pushes past him, disturbed by the spark of pleasure at his nearness. "It's open!"

Her friend Dagmar comes in. "I'm almost ready," Lindsay tells her as she heads toward her bedroom area to find some clothes. "I just need to get dressed."

"Someone told me there were two men outside fighting in front of your building—" Dagmar stops talking when she sees Giovanni. "Who is this?"

"Nobody important. Just ignore him."

Dagmar eyes Giovanni with curiosity.

"He's leaving now."

"That's a shame. He's handsome." Dagmar smiles at him with approval. "Who are you?"

He steps forward to introduce himself. Irritated, Lindsay notices the way he's smiling. Dagmar is blonde and cute, and a lot of men smile at her like that. *She can have him. Be my guest.* Though Dagmar already has a boyfriend. Lindsay notices he's icing his hand again. She wonders how much it's bothering him.

"I'm going to get dressed. When I come back, *you* need to be gone." Lindsay throws a pointed look in Giovanni's direction.

Pulling on a robe, she grabs her clothes, leaving the two of them alone in her studio. She walks to the bathroom at the end of the hall, praying it doesn't stink. Unfortunately, her prayers go unanswered. The stench of beer and bratwurst farts is as thick as a napalm cloud.

Lindsay holds her breath as she quickly slips into dark jeans that accentuate her long legs and a silky black tank top, which shows just the right amount of cleavage. She's not particularly well-endowed but knows how to work it. And "working it" is exactly what she'll be doing tonight.

She takes shallow breaths. Trying not to breathe in the stench, she fluffs out her long dark hair, then puts on fresh eyeliner and red lip gloss. Lindsay grabs her purse to check the bankroll she pulled out from its hiding place earlier.

There's a fat wad of euros, two thousand to be exact.

Hopefully, I can double that.

The most she's earned in a single night was fourteen hundred. It depends mostly on the guys and whether there'll be a few donks, especially if they're drinking. Inexperienced, drunk, and throwing around money—that's her favorite kind of man right now.

Finally, she flings the bathroom door open and rushes outside, breathing in sweet clean air with relief.

Time to go to work.

Chapter Three

~ All men like to be the hero, so sometimes you must be the damsel. ~

"WHAT ARE *YOU* still doing here?" Lindsay stares at Giovanni with irritation when she gets back to her studio. He's sitting at her kitchen table with Dagmar. They're both drinking, Dagmar leans toward him giggling like a teenager.

"He's an intense one, that's for sure. I invited him to come along tonight."

"*What*?"

"He told me he is a doctor—a surgeon." Dagmar smiles at Giovanni as if he's being a naughty boy. "Is it true?" She glances over at Lindsay. "Or is he only making fun with me."

"Fun *of* me," Lindsay corrects her. "And yes, it's true. In fact, I'm sure he has *many* important doctorly things that require his immediate attention."

"Come on," Dagmar insists. "I say we bring him along as a bodyguard. He said he used to be a bouncer."

Lindsay's eyes flash over to Giovanni, wondering if there's any truth in it. He's certainly big enough to be a bouncer.

Dagmar reaches across the table and wraps her fingers part way around one of his muscular biceps. "I'll bet you can handle yourself *everywhere*." She smiles and then glances over at Lindsay. "And you like men who can handle themselves, don't you?"

"I don't need a bodyguard."

"It's not such a bad idea." Dagmar releases his arm. She leans back and takes a drink from one of the glasses, making a face at the strong taste. "Some of those guys can become real pests."

Giovanni, who's been watching this conversation in silence, finally speaks. "Where are you two headed exactly?"

"You didn't tell him?" Lindsay asks with relief.

"He didn't ask." But then Dagmar leans toward Giovanni again. "Lindsay and I are going to Spielbank Europa."

"Dagmar . . ." Lindsay tries to stop her friend from saying more. "He doesn't need to know our business."

"What's Spielbank Europa?" he asks.

"Nothing," Lindsay says quickly, but Dagmar won't shut up.

"It's a casino."

Giovanni's brows draw together. "Is that where you meet men?"

"Yes." Lindsay moves in swiftly, taking away both of their glasses and dumping the contents into the sink. "And unless you want to meet men, I'm afraid you won't find it very interesting."

Dagmar smiles. "We go there for more than that." She stands up. "Come on, Mr. Bodyguard, let's go have some fun."

It's a warm summer evening and the smell of fried food drifts toward them once they're outside and headed to the nearest U-Bahn, Berlin's subway system.

"What hotel are you staying at?" Lindsay asks, still hoping to get rid of Giovanni. "We wouldn't want you to take the wrong train back."

"The Regent," he tells her.

"Oooh la la, that is a good hotel. Very fancy." Dagmar comes up, walking on her left.

"That's in the Mitte, right?" Lindsay questions.

"Yes, he'll need to change trains at Stadtmitte. But don't go right away." Dagmar looks over to Giovanni. "Come have fun with us first."

"I'm sure he has a very busy schedule, Dagmar."

"Not really." He shrugs.

"Now, don't be polite on our account," Lindsay says. "I know your work is important, and we wouldn't want to keep you out all night."

"You're not—"

"And I'm sure you're *exhausted* from all this traveling you've been doing. You should go back to your fancy hotel and get a good night's sleep."

"I'm touched you're so concerned for my welfare."

Once they're on the train, Dagmar peppers Giovanni with questions about his recent travels, trying to pull Lindsay into the conversation.

"He has been working in Africa, isn't that fascinating?" Dagmar says to her.

Lindsay doesn't reply. She knows what her friend is up to. She's trying to play matchmaker again. Lindsay made the mistake of telling Dagmar about the loss of her sexual mojo, and she's been determined to find her a man ever since.

"So, where have you been working in Africa?" Dagmar asks him.

"A few different places, mostly central Africa." He names off a few countries.

"Those are not exactly tourist destinations."

"No, they aren't," he agrees.

They're standing in the middle of a crowded train, holding onto one of the center poles. Lindsay pulls her phone out and tries to ignore their conversation. However, she can't stop herself from listening as Giovanni explains how he's been working for an organization that brings doctors and other medical relief workers to some of the poorest and most dangerous places in the world.

"And you are a surgeon?"

"Yes, a plastic surgeon. I work mostly with children."

"*Mein Gott*, you are so noble!" Dagmar gives him a dazzling smile then turns to Lindsay. "He is like a saint! Don't you agree?"

Lindsay scoffs. 'Saint' isn't exactly the word she'd use to describe Giovanni.

"I wouldn't go that far," he says, quickly. "Though it can be rewarding work."

"But it is amazing what you are doing. There is no reason to be modest!"

Lindsay tries not to laugh.

"How long will you be in Berlin?" Dagmar purrs, flipping her hair to one side. "I hope it is a nice long stay."

"Not long. I'm flying to Rome after I leave here. I have an apartment there."

"You do? This is wonderful news!" Her blue eyes widen with delight. "I *love* Rome. You should invite us there for a visit!" She looks over to Lindsay. "Wouldn't that be fun?"

Dagmar starts telling him how Lindsay is a talented sculptor and would certainly enjoy all the amazing art in Rome.

His eyes go to her, but she stares down at her phone, pretending she didn't hear. If this were any other guy, she would have already figured out a way to dump him, but unfortunately, he's not just any other guy. Plus, despite everything, she feels bad about him hurting his hand in that fight.

"You must leave your number with us tonight," Dagmar insists. "Lindsay and I would be very happy to show you around Berlin."

The train suddenly veers into a tunnel and before she knows it, Dagmar has hurled herself to the side, pushing Lindsay right into Giovanni's arms.

"Hey!" Lindsay yells.

"Oops!" Dagmar laughs. "I lost my balance!"

Lindsay is pressed firmly into Giovanni's chest, his arm wrapped around her back. "Are you okay?" he asks with a smile as he looks down into her face.

The whole thing is so comically orchestrated, she knows he sees right through it. "I'm fine," she insists, righting herself. He's tall and well-muscled, and a part of her is reluctant to pull away.

"Oh, my goodness, excuse me!" Dagmar laughs again. "It is so nice to have a big strong man here."

Lindsay can't help laughing as she rolls her eyes. She knows Dagmar means well, but can be over enthusiastic when she gets an idea in her head. They met not long after she arrived in Berlin. Dagmar is a fellow artist, a painter who's well-connected in the local arts community. She paints large, alien-looking flowers with oil on canvas. She also holds weekly dinner parties—her *Künstlersalon,* or artist's salon, as she calls them—and has been an incredible resource in a foreign city.

Dagmar starts quizzing Giovanni about his favorite places in Rome, still trying to draw Lindsay into the conversation. She ignores them both as she scrolls through her phone, checking e-mail. Their train is still rumbling underground when something catches her attention, and she glances up at her reflection in the dark window. With surprise, she sees it's Giovanni.

He's standing beside her talking to Dagmar, but his eyes are intent, watching her in the glass.

Lindsay doesn't move or look away and for a long moment, they study each other. Both of them traveling into the Berlin night.

When their train arrives at the station where Giovanni should separate, he doesn't leave. "I've decided to come out with you two," he announces. His eyes linger on her again, but Lindsay looks away this time.

"That is wonderful!" Dagmar shrieks.

"Yeah, wonderful," Lindsay mutters.

As the three of them board the final crowded train to Potsdamer Platz, Lindsay grabs Dagmar's arm and pulls her back. "I know what you're doing, but I'm not interested in him."

"Are you crazy? He is a handsome doctor and I can tell he likes you!"

Lindsay doesn't have a chance to reply as the train doors close. Dagmar's eyes light up when she sees someone she knows, saying she'll be right back. Meanwhile, Lindsay is pushed right next to Giovanni again.

Neither of them speaks. She notices him holding the center grip with his right hand and feels a twinge of guilt. She glances down at his left, but it's hidden from view. He's wearing a gray button-down shirt with a white T-shirt beneath it. His pants aren't jeans, but some kind of dark corduroy material. He's turned slightly away from her and, in profile, his features are serious, intense even. Between his gold coloring and the determined set of his jaw, Giovanni looks like a Viking warrior ready to battle his way into Valhalla.

"I can't believe you're Italian," she says.

"Yes, I know. I get that a lot."

His lips are nice, she decides, when he turns back toward her. Full and even, with a sensual dip at the corners. She tries to remember if she ever licked that little dip. "Your mother should have named you Olaf. It would have made your life a lot easier."

A smile pulls on his mouth. "I'll tell her you said so."

"Please do. I'm sure Francesca would enjoy that."

He shifts position, studying her with interest. "That's right, I forgot. You've met my mom, haven't you?"

Lindsay nods. She met her at Natalie and Anthony's wedding. His mother was rich, beautiful, and expected all of her commands followed to the letter. She worried Anthony's family would disapprove of her sister, but that turned out to be wrong.

She glances down. "How's your hand?"

"It's good."

Lindsay arranges her face into one of concern. "Maybe you should go back to your hotel and ice it some more."

"I'll do it on one condition—if you come with me."

"Back to your hotel?"

"That's right."

She stares at him. "And be like, what? Your nurse?"

"No, be yourself. I just want to talk to you."

"What do we have to talk about?"

He licks his lips and seems slightly uncomfortable. "I want to ask you something."

"What?"

He shakes his head. "Not here."

Lindsay gives him a look. "If this is your strategy to get me into bed again, it's seriously pathetic. I'm surprised you can't do better."

"I'm not trying to get you into bed. I just want to have a conversation."

She's almost tempted to go with him. Not because she wants to sleep with Giovanni again, but because it would be the perfect way to get rid of him. She could drop him off and leave.

"I believe this is territory we've already covered, and like I said I'm not interested in any 'conversation.'" She makes air quotes with her fingers.

Giovanni doesn't say anything, only studies her. Finally, he speaks, lowering his voice. "Do you remember the ice cream?"

"The *what*?" Her pulse jumps.

"The vanilla ice cream."

"I don't know what you're talking about."

"I think you do."

Lindsay turns away and does her best to ignore the pleasure rolling through her. The tingling between her thighs as she imagines him licking it off her again. She remembers how he brought just the right amount of patience to the task.

But then she also remembers how he treated her afterward and the tingling stops.

"I'm sorry, but there's no more vanilla ice cream for you. Not now. Not ever." She turns back to him. "I hope it wasn't a favorite flavor."

He shrugs. "Luckily, there are so many flavors to choose from that I don't have to settle for only one."

Lindsay snorts softly. "My philosophy exactly."

The casino is housed in a large building with a two-story glass front. The words 'Spielbank Europa' are displayed in big blue letters. Lindsay is pleased to discover a crowd of tourists standing out front and hopes there are more inside. At the door, they show their passports and pay the entrance fee.

"I am going to find Werner," Dagmar tells her over the noise. "I'll see you at the tables later."

Lindsay heads directly for the cage. Unfortunately, Giovanni is still at her side. "Why don't you go play slots or something," she tells him. "There's roulette and blackjack upstairs."

"Forget it. You're not getting rid of me that easily."

She tries to ignore him and when she sees Varik, the pit boss, heads directly over. He's a handsome Turkish guy in his mid-thirties who's balding a little on top. He hugs her and she's immediately enveloped in his spicy cologne. Varik knows everything and everybody.

"How are you tonight, sexy lady?"

"I'm great." Lindsay puts her mouth to his ear. "I saw a group of tourists out front. Please tell me there are more."

He smiles knowingly. "Part of their group is still here, but I think you'll have better luck at table five."

"Hmm, thanks. I'll check it out."

He eyes Giovanni lurking behind her. Lindsay doesn't introduce him, and Varik doesn't ask any questions.

She goes to the cage and chats with Petra, the woman who's working behind the glass tonight, as she buys a couple thousand euros' worth of chips.

Giovanni studies her hefty stack. "You're here to play poker?"

"It looks that way."

"So you're not here to meet men after all."

She shrugs. "Who says I'm not here for both? There's some hot guys who play cards."

He doesn't say anything, but much to her irritation follows her over to the poker floor.

"Look, despite what Dagmar said, I don't actually need or want a bodyguard. I'm just here to have some fun. Why don't you go do the same?"

"I don't gamble."

Lindsay bites her tongue before she tells him she doesn't either. Skill is foremost in poker, though a bit of luck certainly doesn't hurt. "You're going to be very bored then. Why did you bother coming with us at all?"

He glances around. "I wanted to see what kind of trouble you were up to."

"What are you, my keeper now?"

"No, but I suspect you need one."

She moves to one of the empty cocktail tables in back which gives her a nice view of the floor. It's crowded, but not overly so, and she sees plenty of tourists mixed in with a few of the regulars.

Her eyes go to table five and immediately sees what Varik was talking about. There's some heavyset guy with glasses playing on tilt. He's drinking too much and talking too loudly. There's a large stack of chips in front of him—by her estimate, a few thousand euros—and she suspects those aren't his winnings.

As she watches the floor, Giovanni is watching her again. He might only be trying to get her in bed again, but her spidey senses are tingling.

Classical music plays from his pocket, and he digs his phone out. His tense expression becomes worse.

"Something wrong?"

He doesn't answer her but goes quiet, listening to a message.

Lindsay continues her careful analysis of the floor, trying to decide what her best play is here. The guy on tilt is at a table with no openings, and she's not sure if she should wait.

When Sabine, one of the waitresses, walks past, Giovanni flags her over and orders a beer. Lindsay orders her usual mineral water.

After a short while, he puts his phone away. "How often do you come here?" he asks.

"Only occasionally."

"You seem to know everybody."

"Oh, that." She shrugs. "I like to be friendly."

When their drinks arrive, she picks up her glass, still keeping her eye on table five. She's decided she's going to wait it out.

"Wasn't your dad some kind of famous poker player?"

She sips her water. "Famous is a strong word, but yes, he played cards." In truth, her dad—who's no longer alive—was once a world-class player. He won a few bracelets at the World Series of Poker and even won the Main Event one year. Unfortunately, he also had an addiction to both gambling and women.

"What was his name?"

"Why do you ask?"

"Because I want to Google him."

Lindsay frowns to herself. She doesn't want Giovanni nosing around in her business.

Suddenly, she sees someone getting up to leave table five. There's finally an opening, and it's not just any opening—it's the Jesus seat right next to the guy on tilt.

"My table just opened. I have to go!" She quickly grabs her tray of chips along with her mineral water and heads over as one of the regulars tries to swoop in like a vulture. She gets there just in time too.

"Excuse me," she says breathlessly, as she slides into the chair. "I'd love to join the game."

The table is all men, which is typical for Berlin. Most women here seem to prefer tournaments over cash games. What she's found is that male players usually eye her with desire, annoyance, or indifference. The indifferent men being the ones to watch out for, as they're typically the real card players.

The men who are annoyed by her are often chauvinistic assholes, but she's learned to use that to her advantage. Men who try to show her up or teach her a lesson typically don't play well and will often find they've lost all their money to her.

At this table, she sees the men are mostly looking at her with desire, though one of the regulars is displeased. Lindsay nods a greeting at him, and he grudgingly nods in return. She's played him a few times. He's one of the chauvinistic assholes who used to make snide remarks about how she should go play the slots, how poker isn't a game for women. That is, until she cleaned his clock a few times.

He doesn't say that anymore.

The guy on her right, the one drinking too much and playing badly on tilt, is giving her a lascivious grin.

"*Guten Abend,*" he leers.

Lindsay smiles. "*Guten Abend.*"

"Oh, you are American?"

"Yes, I am."

"I like Americans." He leans closer and lowers his voice. His breath is strong enough to kill a cockroach. "Especially beautiful American women."

She resists the impulse to gag. "Thank you."

Her usual poker calm comes over her as she sets up her stack of chips and mineral water. They're playing Texas Hold'em—her favorite game. The same game she played with her dad at the kitchen table as a little girl. She adored him when she was growing up. He'd swoop in like a handsome prince, and everything was wonderful. Her sister was smart enough to stop trusting him early on, but it took Lindsay a long time to get to that point. Just like their mom, she always believed his lies.

The cards are dealt and she spends the next two hours in concentration, playing her best game. Cockroach Breath bemoans every lousy hand, losing one large pot after another. He makes a 'tsk tsk' noise toward her every time she raises and tries to offer unsolicited advice.

"Big mistake," he tells her when she raises after the turn, which brings a king. Happily, her hole cards are pocket cowboys. "You are going to lose a lot of money playing that way."

Lindsay only nods politely. She's pretty sure he has a pair of sevens, which he's dumb enough to think is the best hand at the table.

Somewhere after she wins her third large pot, Cockroach Breath starts to eye her with suspicion.

"What is this? Beginner's luck?"

She shrugs innocently. "I guess so."

The other new players, the ones who figured out it wasn't beginner's luck, have already left. A couple of the regulars drift over and take their place. One of them tries to outplay her with kings over nines, but her instincts tell her he's bluffing, and she's right.

So far she's up fifteen hundred and is really in the zone. Her best night ever.

A waitress, one she doesn't know, brings her a fresh mineral water. Lindsay sips it as she glances around, wondering where Giovanni went. She saw him wandering through a little while ago, but doesn't see him anymore. It's possible he finally went back to his hotel.

Maybe I'll get lucky and he won't mention any of this to Anthony.

The problem is she doesn't believe much in luck.

Eventually, Dagmar comes over and stands beside her for a short while, smiling. She leans closer and whispers in Lindsay's ear, "You are having an amazing night! And this guy next to you is almost giving you his money."

Lindsay doesn't reply. In truth, she's starting to feel a little sorry for Cockroach Breath, despite the way he keeps grabbing her leg under the table and pinching her thigh. She's been shoving his hand away for the last hour and finally had to kick him hard enough to make him yelp. Unfortunately, he's been telling her his whole sad-sack story, how his wife left him for another man recently.

"I saw it coming," he bemoans. "I begged her on my knees to stay, but she still left me."

"Love isn't worth the heartache," Lindsay informs him. "Trust me, you're better off alone."

"You are wrong. Love is everything." He picks up his drink, bleary-eyed, and takes another large swallow.

Lindsay shakes her head, surprised to hear such a romantic sentiment coming from him. Apparently, he's been on a two-week bender with no end in sight.

Not that this stops her from cleaning him out. Or almost cleaning him out. When he's down to his last few hundred, Lindsay folds her cards intentionally and tells him maybe he should just go home and sleep it off.

"*Nein*," he says, shaking his head. "I have to win my money back first!"

"Just leave while you still have some money left."

"You think you can beat me?" He stares at her with bloodshot eyes. "No dumb bitch ever beats me. Never!" He snarls something at her in German, probably calling her a bitch again.

She glances around at the other guys at the table. Two of them shake their heads, but nobody says anything, and they all keep playing. At least the casino has stopped serving him liquor.

Eventually, Cockroach Breath loses it all and throws his cards aside angrily. He tells everyone to go to hell then stands, swaying on his feet.

Lindsay, who still feels sorry for him, grabs a couple hundred euros' worth of chips from her stack and tries to hand them over to him.

"Here, take these. Then find a cab out front and go home."

"Fuck you! You think I want your money? Keep it, you stupid whore!" He shoves her hand away.

She tries to hand the chips to him again. "Take them, you dumb ass!"

Finally, he grabs them from her and staggers off. Instead of leaving, though, she watches him go right up to another poker game.

"Forget him. He is a lost cause," some guy with a Russian accent says beside her.

She turns and discovers somebody new has already taken the place on her right. A muscular guy with short dark hair. He studies her with black eyes and an interested smile.

She stays to play another hand. The guy on her right keeps asking her questions about herself in a thick Russian accent, trying to make eye contact, but she only answers them politely. The vibe coming off him is unsettling.

Just as she decides to make this her last hand, she senses someone behind her shoulder, surprised to discover Giovanni.

"I thought you left."

"No." He leans in close and puts his mouth to her ear. "But you're leaving."

She turns to look at him. "Excuse me?"

"You heard what I said." His face moves close to hers. "You're finished here. I want you to fold."

"I don't take orders from you!"

"Tonight, you do."

She ignores him and lets her breath out in a huff. *Who the hell does he think he is?*

"I mean it, Lindsay. I'm going to stand here until you leave with me."

She glances at her cards. Obviously, she was already planning to make this her last hand, but is so annoyed she's tempted to stay.

The Russian guy, who's been coming on to her, glances at Giovanni, then leans in. "Is all okay?"

"It's fine."

He nods slowly.

Her eyes flash down to the guy's hands for some reason. His left is resting on the table, and he has some kind of elaborate black Cyrillic tattoo webbed on all his fingers. She's had a lot of boyfriends with tattoos, and has some ink herself, but has never seen anything quite like this guy's.

The dealer lays the flop, and Lindsay calls. After the turn, she's in line for a ten-high straight and doubts anyone else will beat it. She considers raising. She already has four hundred in, but then Giovanni's mouth is at her ear again. "I want you to end this *now*."

She grinds her teeth. When it's her turn, she hesitates, but does what he tells her and folds. For a split second, the Russian seems surprised but quickly hides it, and she realizes he's a skilled card player.

She announces she's calling it a night. All the men at the table watch her as she gathers her pile of chips together, tossing the dealer a generous tip.

Giovanni follows her over to the cage so she can cash everything in.

"I hope you're happy," she mutters. "I don't know why I listened to you."

He doesn't reply, just watches the pile of bills being counted out to her.

"I would have won that hand. You just cost me a lot of money."

"Stop complaining. I did you a favor."

She scoffs. "How?"

But he only shakes his head and scowls. “Let’s get out of here. This place is giving me a headache.”

Lindsay’s not sure why she’s going anywhere with him, but follows him out front. On the way, she sees Dagmar and her boyfriend, Werner.

“I’m going to tell Dagmar I’m leaving.”

They go over to where the couple is standing at a table with drinks in front of them.

Dagmar grins when she sees them. “How did you do?” She reaches for Lindsay’s arm to draw her in closer, then whispers in her ear, “And I see the doctor is still here.”

“I did okay tonight.”

“It looked like you were winning a lot! That is so great. You will for sure have enough money saved before you leave.” Dagmar knows all about her plans to go back to school in the fall.

“What is all this?” Werner asks politely.

Dagmar turns to him and speaks in rapid German, telling him about Lindsay’s productive night.

“Good for you,” he says. “You must have quite a large bankroll now.”

Lindsay doesn’t say anything. Werner is not her favorite person.

“Oops, I have to go.” Dagmar is staring down at her phone. “My tournament is starting in a few minutes.” She’s only been playing poker about a year, but in the same way she’s helped Lindsay navigate her way around Berlin, Lindsay has been helping her improve her game. Dagmar comes from a wealthy family and doesn’t actually need to play poker. She leans in to kiss Werner good-bye and then turns back to Lindsay. “I’ll call you tomorrow and we can go over our hands.”

“Sounds good. I should get going now too.”

“No! You and the doctor must stay and have a drink with Werner,” Dagmar says. “Get to know each other better.”

Once she’s gone, Lindsay already sees the shift in Werner, who always acts like a gentleman in front of Dagmar, but is actually a sleaze. She knows he’s using Dagmar but is unable to convince her friend otherwise. For the life of her, Lindsay can’t figure out what she sees in him to begin with since he literally looks like a rat. He’s pale and sweaty, and has this strange haircut that’s long and thin in back, yet short and spiky on top. Plus, he wears dark eyeliner, which he thinks makes him look tough.

“So how much money did you earn tonight?” Werner asks, picking up his drink as his rat eyes flicker over her.

“Like I said, I did all right.”

“How much?”

“Enough.”

He smirks. "Don't be shy. You can tell me. We are all friends here. Is it more than you would earn out in the back alley giving blow jobs?"

She feels Giovanni stiffen beside her and wishes she had a drink she could throw at Werner. "Fuck off."

He laughs as if this is the funniest joke in the world. "Something tells me you would make more money with the blow jobs!"

"You're a disgusting maggot."

"Hey, I'll be your first customer!"

Giovanni slams his fist on the table, startling her, and making Werner jump. "What in the hell is wrong with you?"

The rat blinks but doesn't say anything as he stares at Giovanni with wide eyes.

"I'm not going to listen to you speak to her that way. You need to apologize!"

Lindsay's brows go up, and she enjoys watching the rat squirm with distress. His eyes flash over to her. He hesitates, but then finally says, "I am sorry if I offended you."

"You're goddamn right it's offensive," Giovanni growls. "And it better not happen again." He turns to Lindsay. "Let's get out of here. I've had enough of this place."

They exit the casino into the warm night. Like always, there's a long row of shiny Mercedes taxicabs lined up in front. Unlike a typical cab back in the States, the ones in Berlin are clean and comfortable inside.

She follows Giovanni to a brown Mercedes still thinking about the way he ripped into Werner. What a wonderful display. The driver holds the door open for them so they both climb into the back. Lindsay figures they'll drop her off first, but when the driver asks where they're going, Giovanni tells him, "The Regent."

"What? I appreciate what you did back there, but I'm not going to your hotel with you."

"Yes, you are." He leans back in the seat as the cab starts moving and closes his eyes for a moment. "And don't bother arguing. I don't want to listen to it right now."

She bites her lip. She still has to make sure he doesn't tell Anthony about her playing poker tonight. "Listen, how often do you talk to your brother?"

"You need to get some new friends," he says, ignoring her question. "That guy is a serious douche bag."

"Are you kidding? That piece of rat shit isn't my friend!"

"Not to mention the other one I had to punch earlier. Who the hell are these strange people you've hooked up with?"

She gives a laugh. "A better question might be who the hell are *you*? And what are you doing here?"

Of course he doesn't answer.

They're sitting close to each other in the back of the cab, but she's careful not to let any part of her body touch his. It's not easy either. To her annoyance, her physical attraction to him is so strong it's like fighting gravity.

The car radio plays bouncy Europop as they continue to drive through the city. The driver is talking to someone in German using the cab's Bluetooth.

Her eyes go back to Giovanni. "You know, in this light, you almost look Italian."

"I appreciate that." He seems mildly amused, but when he turns to her, his expression changes. "You're beautiful," he says, studying her. "And it's not just the light."

"Thanks," she murmurs but doesn't say anything more, just turns to watch the traffic outside.

"Why is it every time I tell you you're beautiful, you act insulted?"

"That's ridiculous. I'm not insulted."

He considers her, nodding slowly. "I get it now. You must hear it a lot."

"I suppose." She shrugs. It's not even vanity. The fact is most guys find her attractive. It's always been like this. Men focus on her appearance, and nothing more.

"Get over yourself, Lindsay. You're not *that* beautiful."

"I'm not?"

"Remember who you're talking to here." His eyes roam her face, examining her, before he nods. "You could be improved upon."

She blinks in amazement. "Wow, you're a serious asshole. And I'm sorry, but I don't think that's something that can *ever* be improved upon."

"Maybe so, but at least I've given you a *real* reason to be insulted."

She crosses her legs away from him. "If you're trying to get me into bed again, you're sure going about it the wrong way. This is like the *worst* seduction ever."

He snickers.

"I could write a book about how bad this seduction is."

"I'm not trying to seduce you. I already told you I didn't come here to sleep with you again."

"Then why are you hanging around?"

He doesn't say anything.

"You came all the way to Berlin to tell me how ugly I am?"

Giovanni gives a weary laugh and rubs his forehead. "God, what am I going to do with you?"

As he's saying this, the cab slows down and she sees they're pulling up in front of what must be his hotel. Everything's lit up, and there are more taxis and people waiting out front. It's the middle of the night, but Berlin is the city that never sleeps, which suits Lindsay just fine.

The cab driver turns around to tell them the meter amount and Giovanni digs his wallet out.

"I'm going back to my studio now," she informs him. "I'll pay my own cab fare."

He hands the cab driver a credit card. "No, you're coming inside with me."

"I don't think so." She leans forward. "But the next time you talk to Anthony, would you mind not mentioning this evening to him, or at least not the part where I was playing poker?"

"Why?"

"It would be best all around."

"We can talk about this more upstairs." The cab driver hands the card back and Giovanni puts it in his wallet. He opens the car door to get out.

Lindsay doesn't budge.

He leans in. "Look, if you want me to be an accomplice, I'm going to require an explanation."

"There's nothing to explain. And you're not an accomplice."

"It certainly sounds like I am. And unless you want me to call Anthony right now, I suggest you get out of this taxi."

"Come on, Giovanni, don't be an asshole."

"I'm already an asshole, remember?"

Chapter Four

~ You may catch more flies with honey than vinegar, but trust me, some men prefer vinegar. ~

GIOVANNI LETS HIS eyes slide down the back of Lindsay's black jeans, which are currently doing incredible things for her ass. He enjoys women—way more than he should—but has to admit Lindsay is in a class by herself.

"I can't believe I'm in another swanky hotel with you." She turns to him in the elevator. "This is too much like the last time we were together."

"It's our destiny."

"Hardly, and I'm not sleeping with you either. I'm only here to *talk*—that's it." Her brown eyes flicker with anger.

He doesn't blame her for being pissed since he basically strong-armed her into coming inside with him.

I'm handling this all wrong.

Giovanni's intention was to fly to Berlin and speak to Lindsay, hopefully convince her to go along with his plan—the situation he's trying to help fix—but so far, he hasn't had a chance. First, that crazy asshole in front of her building was there picking a fight with him. The next thing he knows they're at a casino. Absentmindedly, he flexes his left hand, notices a little bruising still. He should have used his right, or better yet, not have hit him at all. *That was completely idiotic.*

Before he flew out here, Anthony told him Lindsay was an artist, and that her lifestyle was unconventional, but he had no idea it was this severe.

"And you cost me a bunch of money tonight," she's still carrying on. "That was no favor you did me. I had four hundred euros in that pot."

"You're lucky I intervened."

"I would have won that hand."

He shakes his head. "Do you know who that guy was sitting next to you?"

The elevator doors open and he lets Lindsay walk out ahead of him. They head down the hall toward his room, the thick carpet nearly silent beneath their feet.

"Which one?"

"The Russian guy eyeing you like a steak dinner."

"Are you kidding? That was nothing. I handle guys like that all time."

They get to his room and he pulls his key card out to open the door. The nightstand lamp is on when they enter, and he sees the maid has turned down the bed. The room smells fresh like some kind of floral-scented cleaner.

Lindsay walks in and looks around with approval. "Dagmar was right. Ooh la la. This is very elegant."

He doesn't say anything. He barely even notices the room. It's just another place to sleep as far as he's concerned.

Lindsay's of a different mind as she continues her exploration, taking it all in. His eyes follow her movements. Unfortunately, her body in those jeans is putting too many thoughts in his head, thoughts that shouldn't be there. As much as she doesn't believe him, he really didn't bring her upstairs to try and seduce her.

She goes over to the large window, where the colorful lights of the city twinkle and glimmer outside. "Look at this magnificent view. I hope you're not taking this for granted."

He sits down on the bed, amazed he'd forgotten what powerful appeal she had. He remembers it all too well now. They'd met at a party a couple of years ago, right after his brother won a science award. The attraction between them was immediate and white-hot. He took her to a hotel downtown where they spent the night together. She was more than he expected in every way—sexy, fun, and beautiful. The elixir that helped bring him back from months of living on adrenaline, chasing away those demons. He'd needed her that night, and she'd been perfect.

He closes his eyes and tries to ground himself, still too keyed up. He hasn't been sleeping well. The air-conditioned room feels surreal compared to the dry heat of central Africa.

In his mind, he still sees his colleagues back at the small hospital he left only a few days ago. The armed guards who drove them there every morning. A civil war raged, but both sides agreed to allow medical workers through unharmed. Unfortunately, the attacks grew closer every day.

It was never easy finding his way back from the constant rush of danger, the intensity of living on the edge.

"Did you notice that guy's tattoo?" he asks her.

Lindsay turns back toward him from the window, thinking it over. "The one on his hand?"

"They all have that mark. He's a Russian mercenary—part of a particularly vicious group."

"I agree he was weird, but it was only a poker game. You don't think maybe you're overreacting?"

Images flash in his head of the time he spent in North Africa last year, some of the horrors he saw there. "Those guys don't care who they harm." His eyes drill into hers. "They're paid killers who enjoy it. I've seen the damage they do firsthand."

Lindsay grows quiet.

"I know you think I was being a dick, but I wasn't. You don't want to get on the radar of a guy like that, trust me."

She nods. "Okay, maybe you were right."

Giovanni lets his breath out, relieved she's not going to give him a hard time about this anymore. He thinks about that mercenary. Sometimes, the laws that protect people are protecting the wrong ones.

"Are you okay?" She moves closer. "You seem out of sorts."

"I'm good."

She points down. "Is it still bothering you?"

He glances at his left hand. "Not really."

The room's air conditioner hums in the background. Various floor noises thump from the room above his. Even the regular sounds here seem incohesive and strange to him. Nothing like the nighttime quiet punctuated with distant gunfire he'd somehow grown accustomed to.

The most surreal thing of all is Lindsay. He still can't take his eyes off her. He's too aware of her, of how soft she'd feel beneath him, how her cries of ecstasy would soothe him and bring him back to normalcy. A part of him wants that because he knows it would work. It would do the trick like it does every time. He wonders if she'd give him that gift again, but then stops that line of thinking, shakes it off.

He licks his lips. "So, how about you explain the poker to me. Anthony told me you were an artist."

"I am an artist."

She starts describing how she's in Berlin as part of some artist's program, but he cuts her off. "Give me a break. You're obviously a professional poker player."

"No, I'm not. I just told you I'm an artist."

"A card shark might be a better description," he mutters.

"That's ridiculous!"

"I watched you tonight, so don't lie to me."

She moves away from him and sits down in the chair, starts examining some of the objects on the desk. "I was only having fun. It's a hobby."

"You bled that poor bastard dry. The whole table was losing to you. Were you cheating?"

"Of course not!" She glares at him. "Could you be more insulting? It's one thing after another with you. I don't need to cheat to win."

"Then how did you do it?"

She doesn't answer right away. Pulling out a piece of hotel stationery, she folds it in half, then shrugs. "It was mostly luck."

"Come on, do you really think I'm that dumb? You purposefully cleaned that guy out."

"Hey, I always play a straight game. It's not my fault he was playing on tilt."

"What does that mean?"

She sniffs. "It means he was emotionally compromised and making poor decisions."

"And that's your rationale?"

"If it wasn't me winning against him, it would have been somebody else. I didn't cheat."

"Maybe not, but you were obviously working some angle." He thinks back over the evening. "And it's clear you hang out at that casino all the time."

She tosses her hair over her shoulder. "Like I said, it's a hobby. And if it earns me a little extra money on the side, so what?" She meets his eyes. "I *am* an artist. A damn good one."

"So, why did you ask me not to tell my brother about you playing poker?"

Lindsay considers him for a long moment, probably trying to figure out the best way to play *him*. Her beautiful features grow thoughtful.

He still can't believe the crazy thing he said to her in the cab—how her face could be improved. He doesn't even know what possessed him to say something so asinine.

"I don't want my sister to find out I'm playing cards," she finally admits. She tears a piece of the stationery off, starts manipulating it.

"Why?"

"It's a long story."

"Give me the condensed version."

"You were right about my dad." She avoids his eyes. "He played cards professionally. He also had a gambling addiction."

"Do you have a gambling problem?"

Lindsay looks up at him. "No, I don't."

"Then why would it bother your sister so much if she found out?"

"I don't normally keep secrets from Natalie, but this is different." Her voice lowers. "We didn't have the greatest childhood, and I don't want to bring it back for her."

He tries to imagine Lindsay as a child. She would have been clever, smart-mouthed, and hard to contain. Just like she is now. There's a reckless quality to her. A part of him wants to protect her, but at the same time he wants to lecture her.

"All right, you have my silence."

Her brows go up. "I do?"

"Yeah, but do me a favor. Stay away from that casino for a while."

"Look, you can't just show up here and tell me how to live my life."

"Of course I can. I just did."

She rolls her eyes. "This must be part of that God complex people are always saying surgeons have."

"Just stay away for a few days at least."

She opens her mouth like she's going to argue, but then closes it. "All right, fine."

He wonders if it might be a good time to bring up the reason he flew to Berlin in the first place. "Listen, I want talk to you about something else."

"What now?" She glances up from the paper she's still fiddling with and gives him a wary look.

He shifts position then leans forward with his forearms resting on his thighs. He's almost ready to say it, but then, just like earlier, something stops him. It's not every day you ask a woman this kind of question, and he feels nervous, though it makes no sense.

"Forget it." He sits up again, noticing the purse Lindsay's still wearing across her body. "So, how much money are you carrying around in there anyway?"

She hesitates. "A couple thousand."

He suspects it's more than that, but decides not to give her a hard time about it. "Maybe you do need a bodyguard. Is it all poker winnings?"

Her only reply is to rise from the desk chair, come over, and stand in front of him. She's tall for a woman, slender and athletic, like a cat burglar or a thief. It's not hard to imagine her staking out the Hope Diamond in a black leotard. The thought makes him want to smile for some reason.

"Hold out your hand," she tells him.

"Why?"

"Just do it."

Giovanni holds his left hand out.

"Not like that." Lindsay lays her cool fingers over the top of his hand and turns it over, so his palm faces upward.

Her scent drifts toward him. She's wearing some kind of light perfume, but it's her he smells beneath it.

Desire stirs. He doesn't want it, tries to stop it even, but it's happening against his will. A cobra slowly uncoiling itself within him. He wants her, but for all the wrong reasons. He knows she'd calm him, bring him down from the danger high he's been on these past months.

I'm done using women like that.

He told himself he was going to stop, and he meant it. It wasn't healthy, not in any way.

Lindsay places a lightweight object in the center of his palm. It's the hotel stationery, except she's folded it into something else. "What's this?"

"I made you a fox."

He lifts his hand and sees that she's turned the paper into a simple origami fox with triangular ears and a pointed tail. Its face is blank, but it appears to be watching him nevertheless.

Giovanni studies it for a long moment.

There are places inside him, places wound so tight he can barely breathe. He's convinced himself it doesn't matter, but to his surprise as he studies the little fox, some of those places relax.

"I'm leaving now," she tells him. "I'm going back to my studio."

He pulls his eyes away from the paper fox and up to Lindsay again.

It would be so easy to reach for her. Touch her soft skin, feel her breath on him. Taste her. Because she wasn't just any elixir. She was exactly what she said she was—one hundred proof. The hard stuff.

"I'll take you back." His voice sounds hoarse as he places the fox gently on his nightstand.

"That's not necessary. I'll just grab a taxi."

He snorts. "Christ, it's almost two in the morning. I'm not letting you run around alone at this hour."

She cocks her head. And he knows from the expression on her face that she runs around alone at this hour all the time. "That's very gallant of you."

They head down to the lobby and Lindsay has to admit she's a little surprised Giovanni didn't try to seduce her. For a moment, it almost seemed like he was considering it, but apparently he was too busy insulting her.

"How much longer will you be in Berlin?" he wants to know.

They're standing in front of the hotel, waiting for a taxi to unload its passengers who, by all appearances, have come back from a night of partying.

"Only a couple more weeks."

"And then you're going back to Seattle?"

"Yes, then I'm going back home. Why?"

"Just curious."

"How much longer will you be here?" she asks.

"Not long. I have a meeting tomorrow, and then I'm flying to *Roma* to visit family."

"But what about all those relatives in Norway? Aren't you going to visit them too?"

Giovanni raises an eyebrow. "I don't know anybody in Norway."

"Sure you do. Your real parents, Sven and Greta? I'm sure they miss you."

He shakes his head. "You think you're so damn funny, don't you?"

"Hey, I'm not the one pretending to be Italian. Though, let's face it, I look more Italian than you do."

He leans closer and lowers his voice. "*Penso che tu sia abbastanza sexy per essere italiana*."

Lindsay's breath catches, swaying toward him. She recovers quickly though and feigns curiosity. "What's that strange language? Some kind of Norwegian dialect?"

Giovanni chuckles.

"What did you say to me?"

"Sorry." He shrugs. "I guess you'll have to learn how to speak Norwegian if you want to find out."

Lindsay is glad to see his mood has lightened. She doesn't like being told how to live her life though. Not to mention the way he accused her of cheating at cards or said that her face could be improved? *Seriously*? *Who says shit like that?*

But then she thinks about the way he ripped into Werner and has to smile. *That was nice*.

He leans toward her as the cab driver waves them over. "What I said was 'I have a particular weakness for brown-eyed brunettes.'"

"Really? Well, I'm sure you'll find one if you look hard enough."

She hears him chuckle some more as they climb into the back of the taxi together. Like last time, Lindsay is careful not to let their bodies touch, though she can't stop her eyes from enjoying how muscular his thighs look beneath those dark corduroy pants. She's always liked nice thighs on a man. There's so much fuss made about a guy's chest, and she certainly enjoys a nice chest, but strong thighs are under appreciated. Though, as she recalls, Giovanni had a nice everything.

She wishes she were less attracted to him. Almost wishes she could lie to herself about it and take a free pass, but she never lies to herself.

I need sex, that's all. Real sex.

She desperately needs to get her mojo back. To rid herself of this chronic dissatisfaction. It's not that she's lacking in male attention either—three marriage proposals have proved that. She already knows the problem isn't with men at all—it's with her. It's like something within her has changed and none of the guys she dates are turning her on anymore.

They all seem like boys, but she doesn't want a boy.

I need a man.

In the meantime, she's been taking care of things herself, though her vibrator is getting worn out from overuse. She's pretty sure she heard it complaining last time. *Give me a break, will you, lady? I'm exhausted.*

"Did you really just fly here from Africa?" Lindsay asks to distract herself from leaning over and trying to get a better look at what he has going on between those muscular thighs.

"Yes, I arrived yesterday afternoon."

"That must be a weird transition, traveling between two places so different."

"It is," he agrees. "Very weird."

He goes quiet again like he did back upstairs, wearing that same tense expression. There's strain on his face, the lines around his mouth pronounced. She realizes he's different than the last time she saw him. He's still arrogant and overbearing, but there's something serious beneath it all.

It occurs to her that he's seen things far beyond her ordinary life. Terrible things. Things she probably doesn't even want to imagine.

"When was the last time you slept?" she asks.

"It's been a while. I don't always sleep well when I'm transitioning back from an assignment."

For a moment, his gaze is so weary that a part of her wants to comfort him. The mighty Thor can swing a hammer, but he's not invincible, as much as he likes to think he is. She's glad she made that fox for him. She suspects Giovanni could use some whimsy in his life.

When the taxi arrives in front of her building, he gets out and holds the door open for her. She slides over and climbs out too, but then stops and stands in front of him. He's watching her, the same way he's been watching her all night.

"It was interesting seeing you again." Lindsay glances toward her building. It's late enough now that the streets are quiet, though there are still some cars on the road.

"Same here. I can't believe I'd forgotten what you were like."

Her eyes go back to him. "And what am I like?"

"Unique."

"Hmm, I can't tell if that's a compliment or an insult."

"A little bit of both, I think."

She gives him a flirty smile. "Lucky for you, my ego can handle that. I am an artist, after all. Now, aren't you going to ask what I think of you?"

"I'm not sure I want to know. My ego might not be able to take the hit."

"Come on, we both know your ego is the size of Norway."

His lips twitch. "Okay, so tell me, Lindsay, what do you think of me?"

She pauses to consider him. "I think you're the kind of man who tries to do the right thing, though you often suffer for it."

Giovanni blinks. Seems startled even. Apparently, it wasn't the flippant answer he was expecting.

And while she still has him off balance, she steps closer. Being an artist isn't the only thing she's talented at and decides to leave him a reminder.

Silently, she puts her palm out to touch his face. His skin is warm beneath her fingers, rough with stubble. She's surprised how good he feels.

He goes completely still, like an animal struggling with something. She can see it in his eyes.

He doesn't move, so she goes to him. She slips her arms around his neck and presses her body against his, enjoying the solid feel of him. His masculine scent drifts over her like musky incense. Luckily, she's wearing heels, but even with her high-heeled sandals, she discovers it's a stretch to reach him.

At first, she only licks his lower lip, her tongue running along the edge where it's smooth, then lower to where his skin is salty and rough like sandpaper.

His breath hitches.

She licks him again, and he shudders.

Lindsay draws back. Giovanni's mouth is open slightly, but his eyes are closed. There's something undeniably raw in his expression. Unguarded. It stirs a place within her, beckoning like the mysteries of a deep ocean.

"It's only a kiss," she whispers.

His eyes open at her words. They're dark—inky blue. His hands grip her waist, and this time, it's Giovanni pulling her close, his mouth slamming down hungrily on hers.

She gasps at the need rolling off him. The bruising way he's kissing her. She shouldn't want him, but the pleasure rolling through her won't stop.

They break apart only because the cab driver is yelling at them in German.

"I can't invite you up," she tells him, her voice shaking, though she tries to hide it.

"I know." His gaze is hot, lingering on hers, but then he looks away. "It's a bad idea."

They're in agreement, though neither of them makes a move to separate. Finally, Lindsay forces herself to break contact and pull away.

His eyes, still dark, go back to her.

She's not sure what to make of his intensity. A part of her is tempted to explore those waters, but then she remembers what happened last time she swam in them. How she felt like a prostitute afterward, abandoned in a hotel room.

No one is allowed to make me feel like that. Ever.

It could be years until their paths cross again—it's possible they never will.

"Have a great life," she says. It's one of her standard lines, and she uses it with most men after she's done with them.

He nods. "You too."

She hopes Giovanni does have a great life.

Far away from mine.

Chapter Five

~ Enjoy men, but never forget they are a different type of animal than you. ~

LINDSAY DOESN'T WAKE up until noon the next day and lounges in bed for a bit before deciding to spend some quality time with her vibrator.

Of course, it complains again, grousing just like last time. The damn thing is barely vibrating at all.

"Come on, seriously?" She fiddles with it, shaking it around before hitting it against the mattress.

Lady, you need a man, not an appliance.

You think I don't know that?

She finally gets it to work, but then all she can think about is Giovanni. She doesn't want to think about him, but he won't leave her alone, still harassing her even in her vibrator sex fantasies.

It's the way he felt against her last night—solid and strong, as big as Thor with those muscular thighs. And, of course, she already knows what he has going on between those thighs. A big cock, and if memory serves, he knows exactly how to use it.

I refuse to have sex fantasies about Giovanni.

But it isn't just those thighs and the memory of that large package that has her going. She keeps seeing his face, the raw emotion on it after she kissed him. The need.

God. Her breath grows shaky.

The need is what's getting to her. The way he looked at her, like a sinner finally offered salvation. It was lust, but something more too. What would it be like to assuage him? Intense, that's for sure. It was intense last time, but something tells her this would be even more so.

Okay, she sighs and makes a bargain with herself. *I'm going to allow one sex fantasy about Giovanni, but only one. That's all.*

Afterward, Lindsay throws on jeans that fall low on her hips and a white T-shirt before wandering down the hall toward the kitchen, stopping to say hello to a few people. Most of the artists who live in the building leave their doors open during the day while they're in their studio working, which creates a nice atmosphere of camaraderie. Someone's boom box is playing foreign rap music, and the sound echoes off the walls.

Unsurprisingly, the communal kitchen is a mess. She cuts off a chunk of German rye bread then grabs cheese and cold cuts from the refrigerator to make herself an open-faced sandwich—a classic German breakfast.

She takes it back to her studio where she has an electric kettle she uses to heat water for her French press. When the coffee's done, she adds a splash of condensed milk, then takes everything over to her sculpting table, eating while she studies the polymer clay mask she's currently working on.

She's always found masks interesting—the mystery of them, the way a mask allows the wearer to hide in plain sight. As an attractive woman who's been judged by her appearance her whole life, she wanted to explore what's beneath the surface. Her masks are all doubles. You lift the outer mask to see the one below. The true face.

There are ten of them now. One is still a work in progress, two are here in her studio, and the rest have all been sent to different galleries, both in Berlin and back in the States. She has an art agent who handles the business side of things.

Hopefully, she can sell the whole series. That along with her poker money should be enough to keep her in the black for a while.

Lindsay's eyes flicker over to the bag of clay where part of her bankroll is currently hidden. She has hiding places all over her studio. It turns out Berlin is the poker capital of Germany. *Who knew?* She wasn't planning on playing cards at all when she arrived here, and had obtained a temporary work visa which allowed her to take a job in a cafe the first few weeks, but then her money started running low.

She'd gone to Spielbank Europa mostly as an experiment. They had tournaments, and she played in a few before discovering she could make far more playing cash games. It would have taken her a month of waitressing to earn what she could in one good night of poker.

She thinks about Giovanni's accusation, but she would never rip anybody off. Although she did feel bad taking Cockroach Breath's money, despite the way he called her a whore and couldn't keep his hands to himself. It was what he said about his wife. *Love is everything*. People seldom surprise her, but a sentiment like that coming from such an unlikely source did.

I must be going soft. Way too soft.

The fact is she beat him fair and square. She may not be as talented as her dad, but she plays a clean game. Straight up. Always.

I don't need to cheat to win.

"What's wrong?" Lindsay asks her sister, Natalie. It's early evening and they're Skyping with each other. She has her laptop set up on a chair near where she's been working all day.

Natalie looks frustrated and tired. Her blonde hair is pulled back, though strands of it have come loose. She's holding little Luca at her breast, nursing him. "I just found out Anthony is leaving for an observing run in Chile. He'll be gone for two weeks."

"When is this going to happen?"

"Not for a couple months, but he just came back from Keck a few weeks ago. How am I going to juggle work and a baby?"

"I wish I were there to help you. I never should have come here."

"No, you need to live your life too. I'm glad you went to Berlin." Luca's little hand pats Natalie's breast as he nurses, and Lindsay can't help but smile. There's an ache inside her, a hollow place she knows can never be filled.

Natalie is smiling at him too. She strokes his dark hair. "I wish I could keep bringing him to work with me, but I can't have a baby around hot ovens."

"What about daycare?"

"I looked into it. There's no daycare that keeps baker's hours."

Lindsay's not surprised. "Well, I can help when I get back."

"I know, but I don't expect you to do it every day. That's too much. Plus, I know you're starting classes."

She's been glad for the opportunity to come to Berlin, but a part of her feels guilty she left Natalie right after Luca was born. "What does Anthony say?"

"He thinks we should hire a nanny."

"A nanny!"

"I know." Natalie laughs. "Can you believe it? I guess he and his brother had them growing up."

"Can you guys afford a nanny?"

She shrugs. "I think so. At least part time. Obviously, I have the income from the bakery, and Anthony does okay now that he's made tenure."

"Are you seriously considering this?"

"I am. I've already gotten the names of some agencies."

"Listen to me." Lindsay sits up straight. "I'll be home in a couple weeks. Please don't hire anyone until I get back and can help pick them out."

"Why?" Natalie appears mystified. "What do you know about hiring a nanny?"

"Nothing. But I know men, and I need to help vet this woman so we can avoid any potential problems."

She unlatches Luca, switches him to her other breast, and takes a moment to get him settled. "What are you talking about? What potential problems?"

"Nanny problems, that's what. Haven't you ever noticed how many married men fall under the nanny spell?"

"Nanny spell?"

"Yes, look at all the tabloid headlines. Men are constantly having affairs with their children's nanny."

Natalie rolls her eyes. "That's silly. I trust Anthony completely."

"Yes, I'm sure that's what all those movie star wives say too, but think about it. It happens all the time."

"Anthony is not going to cheat on me with the nanny!"

Lindsay puts her hand up. "I'm not saying he would. Anthony is a good guy, but let's face it, he's still a man."

Natalie shakes her head in amazement. "You're serious about this, aren't you?"

"Hey, why put temptation in his path?" Lindsay's never understood why all these wives would bring a beautiful young woman into their home. It's like they know nothing about male psychology or something.

"You don't trust anybody, do you?"

"I trust you."

Natalie sighs. "That's something at least."

"Listen, when it comes to men, I know what I'm talking about. We need to find you an unattractive nanny who's at least a hundred years old."

"A hundred!" Natalie laughs. "Don't you think that's too old?"

Lindsay reflects for a moment. "Possibly two hundred."

"Where am I going to find a two-hundred-year-old nanny?"

"Oh, they're out there. In fact, I'm sure they're in high demand." She imagines all the smart women are snatching them up as fast as they can.

"I have a great idea," Natalie says. "Maybe we could resurrect an Egyptian mummy to be our nanny!"

Lindsay laughs with approval. "See, now you're thinking outside the box."

"You're crazy. Plus, Anthony is surrounded by college girls at the university. I can't let myself worry about stuff like that."

"That's different. Those girls aren't in his home, right under his nose every day."

Natalie sighs. "I've already been cheated on once, remember? I trust Anthony. He's not that kind of man."

"Just let me help pick out the nanny. What's the harm? I have good instincts about people, and you can't deny that."

"All right, fine." Natalie unlatches Luca and pulls her shirt down again. "I'll wait until you get back before I hire anyone."

"Thank you."

"So, what else is new?" Natalie holds a now sleeping Luca in her arms. Lindsay can almost smell his sweet baby scent through the computer screen.

"Not much. Giovanni showed up here last night." She picks some clay out from beneath her fingernails.

Natalie's mouth opens in surprise. "Really? I thought he was in Africa. What did he want?"

"I don't know." She relays the night's events to her sister, starting with the marriage proposal from Dieter, but leaves out the part about playing poker and kissing Giovanni.

"Wait a minute. You've had three marriage proposals since you've been in Berlin?" Natalie laughs with amazement. "You never told me that!"

Lindsay shrugs. "I didn't think it was worth mentioning. I mean, it's not like I accepted any of them. I don't plan to marry ever again."

"You might change your mind for the right guy."

"No. That's not going to happen."

Natalie studies her, but doesn't say anything. "So, what happened with Giovanni?"

"Nothing. I have no idea why he came here."

Her sister appears to think this over. "Anthony must have given him your address, though he never mentioned it to me. I'll ask him about it." She looks worried. "You didn't sleep with him again, did you?"

"No, of course not."

"Are you sure?"

Lindsay raises an eyebrow. "Don't you think I'd notice if I had? Although I did sort of kiss him."

"You kissed Giovanni?"

"A good-bye kiss, that's all." Lindsay thinks about that kiss and the weariness on his face. "He's changed since the last time I saw him."

"Changed how?"

"I don't know. He seems more serious."

"I've heard stories from Anthony. You should stay away from him."

"Stories?" Lindsay was picking clay from her nails again but looks up at the computer screen. "What kind of stories?"

Natalie shifts position to get more comfortable with the sleeping baby. "Apparently, he's cold when it comes to women."

"In what way?"

"Anthony says he goes to these crazy dangerous places for months at a time. When he comes back, he sleeps with all these women, but never wants to see any of them again."

"Just like the one-night stand we had," Lindsay murmurs.

Natalie nods. "Apparently, that's typical. And it sounds like it's only gotten worse over the years."

Lindsay takes this in. Her instincts were right about him. He is more trouble than he's worth.

"Anthony's tried to talk to him about it, point out how it's no way to live, but Giovanni refuses to discuss it."

"I guess I'm not really surprised he has issues."

"Don't get me wrong, Anthony loves his brother. The work Giovanni does is amazing too. Some of the children he helps . . . it sounds like he brings hope to places that are hopeless."

"A real saint." Lindsay echoes Dagmar's words from yesterday.

"In some ways, he kind of is, but apparently not in others."

Lindsay shrugs. "Whatever. I've got no reason to see him again."

After they finish their conversation, Lindsay reflects on what Natalie told her about Giovanni, how he was cold. He certainly wasn't cold in bed. It's true he was afterward, though. Her stomach goes tight. Even now, it still bothers her the way he left. They had a great time together. It felt like they'd known each other for years, and when she woke up alone, it was like a slap in the face.

He's damned lucky he didn't leave money, even for cab fare, because I would have hunted him down and made him eat it.

She grabs her phone as it starts to play "Born to Die in Berlin" by the Ramones.

"Just calling to see if a certain doctor made a house call last night," Dagmar says with glee.

"No, I'm afraid there were no house calls."

"Why not?" There's disappointment in her voice. "He was so nice, and I could see the way he was looking at you. He would have been perfect to help you with your problem."

Lindsay takes her phone over to the bed and lies down, tucking a pillow beneath her head. “The truth is the doctor already made a house call with me in the past.” She snorts softly. “Or more like a booty call.” She decides to go ahead and spill the whole story.

“But maybe he has changed,” Dagmar insists after hearing everything. “That was a while ago. People change.”

Lindsay sighs. She’s not surprised Dagmar is so forgiving since she tends to see the good in people even when it doesn’t exist. It’s her biggest flaw playing poker. She’s too easily bluffed. “Did Werner happen to mention anything about last night?” she asks instead.

“No, why?”

“He said something really rude to me, and Giovanni got angry at him.”

“Not this again.” Dagmar lets her breath out in a huff. “You just don’t like Werner, but there is more to him than meets the eye.”

Unfortunately, Lindsay once made the mistake of admitting she thought Werner looked like a rat. It was after a few glasses of wine, and ever since then Dagmar thinks she’s only against him because of his appearance.

“He’s horrible. Honestly, Dagmar, you could do so much better.”

“Forget it.” Her voice takes on a chilled note. “And Werner is my boyfriend, so please do not talk about him that way. He has had a hard life, but he still takes care of me.”

Apparently Dagmar met Werner when he defended her against some guys who were hassling her at the casino, and now she completely romanticizes him to everyone. She thinks he’s some sort of misunderstood prince from the wrong side of the tracks. Lindsay knows for a fact he isn’t taking care of her either because from what she’s seen her friend pays for everything. Unfortunately, arguments about Werner have become pointless.

“You’re better than he is,” Lindsay can’t resist adding. “A lot of nice guys would love to be with you.”

“I have a guy! He is only stressed about some things right now, but he is good to me. If you gave him a chance, you would get to know the real Werner.”

Lindsay wishes that were true. Her initial impression of the rat has never wavered even once.

“Let’s not talk about this anymore,” Dagmar says. “Do you have your notebook? Should we go over the hands we played last night?”

“It’s right here.” She reaches over to her nightstand to grab her small poker notebook and a pen in case she needs it.

They do this regularly, analyzing the poker hands they played the previous night. Lindsay initially started doing it to help Dagmar, but has discovered it’s helping her too. She remembers how her dad always kept a notebook when she was growing up.

Lindsay opens hers and they discuss each game, trying to decide if they made the best play. Afterward, Dagmar wants to know what time they should meet later, but Lindsay tells her she's staying in.

"Why? You had a very good night last night."

"I did, but I'm taking a break. Oh, that reminds me. I wanted to warn you about something." She tells her about the weird Russian guy and to steer clear of him.

After they hang up, Lindsay goes back to work on her mask. The current one is a laughing face, slightly contorted, and done in a lavish style. It's on a hinge, and when you lift it you discover a sober, serious face beneath it.

She stays in for dinner and winds up in the kitchen with the one other sculptor on her floor. He's from Japan and creates elaborate wire figures. They share a beer and talk shop for a while.

Eventually, she heads back down to her studio, surprised to find Dagmar and Werner standing by her closed door, waiting for her. The two of them couldn't be more mismatched. Dagmar with her long blonde hair and charming features could be singing in a *Heidi* musical, while the rat is hunched beside her with all the charm of a heroin addict.

"What are you doing here?" Lindsay stares at Werner with dismay. Dagmar's never brought him here before, and she's not happy to see him. He's wearing black eyeliner, and his strange spiky haircut appears freshly groomed. There's a smug expression on his rat face that's making her uneasy.

"We came to see if you would change your mind about going out tonight," Dagmar says. "We're going to the Spielbank over in Neukölln for a change."

Lindsay considers it, since it wouldn't be breaking her promise to Giovanni, but then dismisses the idea. "I appreciate the invitation, but I'm staying in."

"Also," Dagmar sighs and glances over at the rat with disappointment. "Werner admitted to me how he said something very rude to you last night and wanted to apologize again."

"Is that so?"

"I am very sorry for my joke," the rat says in his nasally voice. "I did not mean to offend you."

Lindsay studies him.

"I hope this doesn't affect our friendship," he continues. "I was surprised by the strong reaction your doctor friend had. It must be a cultural misunderstanding."

She rolls her eyes. There's no culture on Earth where his blow job joke wouldn't be offensive.

"I hope you can forgive me," he says.

Whatever.

"Are you certain you don't want to come with us tonight?" Dagmar asks. "You are leaving Berlin so soon. We need to make the most of it!"

"Not tonight. I want to continue working."

"Could we come inside and see some of your art?" Werner glances at her door with interest. "Dagmar has described it to me, and it sounds fascinating."

Lindsay's bullshit detector spikes into the red zone. There's no way he's interested in her sculptures. "Sorry, there's nothing to see right now."

"That is too bad." He's still eyeing her studio door.

"I am so glad you two have settled things! See?" Dagmar beams at them both.

Lindsay wonders what Werner actually told her he said last night, certain it wasn't the truth.

"We will talk more later, okay?" Dagmar leans in to hug her good-bye. Lindsay hopes the rat doesn't try to hug her because he's going to get a kick in the nuts if he even gets close.

He doesn't try and instead gives her a polite smile. Except she doesn't like that polite smile. Somehow, it makes her more uneasy than all the sleazy ones he's given her combined.

That night, Lindsay sleeps with a piece of wood firmly wedged in her door so it can't be opened from the outside, even with a key. It's a trick she learned years ago.

Just a little extra precaution.

Chapter Six

LINDSAY'S HOUSE RULES

~ Domineering men are like a rich dessert—tempting, but best avoided altogether. ~

BY NOON THE next day, Lindsay's still in the creative zone, hard at work, a cup of cold coffee by her side. She's piecing an elaborate beadwork pattern into an outer clay mask and is so involved she doesn't even notice there's an Asgardian mountain standing in her open doorway until it speaks.

"So, you really are an artist."

She looks up, an unwanted jolt of pleasure running through her at the sight of Giovanni. "What on Earth are *you* doing here?"

He doesn't reply but walks over the threshold toward her. He's wearing tan corduroy pants, a gray T-shirt, and brown shoes that appear to be a cross between sneakers and loafers.

Her eyes linger on his wide shoulders, indulging before they progress downward. He's big, but not lumbering like some large men she's known. He moves with sure-footed ease.

Those muscular thighs are calling her name.

Unfortunately, she was weak-willed this morning and had another vibrator sex fantasy about him.

"I thought I'd stop by and say hello. You're the only friend I have in Berlin."

"I'm not your friend."

"Family, then."

She turns back to working on her mask and doesn't bother hiding her irritation. "I told you to have a great life, remember?"

"I remember."

"So, go away and live it."

He ignores her rudeness and comes closer, wandering around the large space near the front windows where she works. "I didn't even notice all this last night." He picks up an origami elephant, studies it for a moment, and seems pleased by it. There's a whole menagerie of origami animals she's created, lined up like they're ready to board Noah's Ark.

He puts the elephant down and takes in the rest of the space. "This is a real artist's studio."

"Don't act so surprised. I already told you I'm an artist." She turns her sculpting table a little to get the angle she needs then locks it in place again.

"An artist who plays poker."

She tries to stay focused on the project at hand, but can't help her annoyance. "So what? For your information, my sculptures are in galleries internationally. I've also had commissions from both the public and private sector."

"No need to give me your Curriculum Vitae. I believe you." Next he wanders over to the wall where two of her masks are hanging and examines the first one. The outer face is a wolf. He lifts the hinge to see the true face is that of a little girl. "These are interesting."

She acts nonchalant, but when he doesn't offer more, can't resist asking, "Why do you say that?"

"I like the symbolism. One face for the outer world, one for the inner self."

Lindsay nods her approval that he gets it.

"I've always found masks to be fascinating," he continues. "Historically, they were like an early form of plastic surgery. People used masks to hide deformities—not just for the face, but the body too. There's evidence of it dating back thousands of years."

She picks up her cold coffee and takes a sip.

"Are all your sculptures masks?"

"No." She puts the cup down, realizing she should be polite and offer Giovanni something, but doesn't. "This is the first time I've made any."

"Why did you choose masks, then?"

She shrugs. "I don't know. They sort of chose me."

He's still studying them, and she can't stop herself from studying him, admiring his rear view. The way his pants hug his body in all the right places. The way his back muscles move beneath his T-shirt. Her eyes greedily roam over him, taking his measurement. When it dawns on her that she's only memorizing him for future sex fantasies, she tries to stop.

"What exactly are you doing here?" she asks, irritated with herself, though she still hasn't stopped staring. His thighs look every bit as good from the back as they do from the front. *And we won't even discuss that ass.*

When he turns to her, his blue eyes are intelligent—too intelligent. Giovanni doesn't miss much, and she can't decide whether she likes this quality about him or if it bothers her. She's used to dealing with men who are easier to manipulate.

"I've decided there's a price for my silence," he tells her.

"A price?"

Her first thought is he wants something sexual from her. Even though it's absurd and she'd never agree to it, a small part of her—the part that's been using him as vibrator fantasy material—suddenly perks up and wags its tail.

"Now that I'm your poker accomplice," he continues.

She gives him a saucy look. "What is it you'd like me to do?"

His licks his lower lip, and there's the hint of a smile on his face. "It's not what you're thinking."

"I'm sure it's not."

Giovanni is quiet and appears to be wrestling with a dilemma.

For a second, Lindsay wonders if he really does want sex. *Wouldn't that be something?*

Of course, I'd say no.

Her eyes drift down toward his thighs again, but she forces them back up.

"I'd like you to show me around Berlin today," he informs her, leaning against the table and folding his arms.

"Like a tour guide?"

"Exactly like a tour guide."

"Um, I know Dagmar offered you that, but as you may recall, I didn't."

"I don't care what Dagmar offered."

Lindsay blows her breath out. "Seriously, you'd be better off going on a tour without me. I don't speak German very well, and there are lots of great tours that can show you the city and tell you the history."

His expression grows impatient. "I already know all that, but I want *you* to show me the city."

"What makes you think I even know where to take you?"

"You've been here three months. Surely you've done some sightseeing." He frowns at her. "Haven't you?"

"I guess."

"Great, then you can show me around today."

"Why?"

"Because that's my price." He unfolds his arms. "Take it or leave it, Lindsay."

"You're completely serious, aren't you?"

His eyes flicker down over her camisole and low-slung jeans, both of which are covered with clay. She notices they linger a little on her bare midriff. "Go take a shower and get ready. I'll wait for you."

She bristles at his bossy tone. "Look, I haven't agreed to any of this. I happen to be in the middle of a project right now."

He appears to think it over. "On second thought, I'm going to leave for a short while. I saw a Starbucks down the block."

"Are you hearing a word I'm saying? I'm not going anywhere with you!"

"If you want my silence you'll do exactly as I tell you." He heads toward the door. "Now, get ready while I get us some coffee."

"Hey, maybe you could also go *fuck yourself*. Better yet, go find an espresso machine and fuck that!"

There's a smirk on his face as he glances over his shoulder at her. "Stop pouting. I expect you to be showered and dressed when I get back."

The first place Giovanni wants to go is the Reichstag. The city's most famous government building, and the seat of Germany's modern parliament. On the way there, he asks her about the tour offered, but Lindsay tells him she's never been to the Reichstag. He seems surprised, and when he asks her about a few other historical places he has in mind to visit, she tells him she's never been to any of those either.

He stares at her in amazement. "What have you been doing here this whole time?"

"I came to Berlin for the art, not to look at government buildings," she grumbles.

The truth is she hasn't done a whole lot of sightseeing, at least not the normal kind. The kind that doesn't involve shops, nightclubs, and casinos. And galleries, of course. She's seen a lot of museums and art galleries, because happily, Berlin has tons of those.

The Reichstag is crowded when they arrive, and they mingle with the other tourists, barely saying two words to each other. She has to admit the building is impressive, with its imperial front and modern dome behind it. A part of her is glad she came, and she realizes she should have come sooner.

Not that this stops her from being pissed at him for forcing her to leave her studio. She glares at him every chance she gets.

"Are you always this childish?" he has the nerve to ask as they wait in line for the audio tour of the building's dome.

Lindsay throws her hands up. "Are you fucking kidding me? I don't even know what I'm doing here!"

"You're giving me a tour of Berlin."

She looks pointedly at the guidebook in his hand—the one he picked up while he was out getting coffee. "It's clear you don't need me. And obviously, I haven't been to half the places in that book."

"I can't believe you've been living in Berlin for three months and haven't done even the most basic sightseeing. That makes no sense."

She shrugs and tosses her hair over her shoulder. "You have your sight-seeing, and I have mine."

"You should thank me for dragging you out here today."

"Of course *you'd* say that. At least you admit you dragged me" She continues with her glaring. "Did it even occur to you to ask me if I wanted to come along?"

"You would have said no."

"That's right, I would have."

"And that's why I didn't ask."

She nods. "I see, so you prefer blackmail?"

He gives her a long, measured stare before turning away. "Go on then. Leave. I won't say anything."

Lindsay studies his Norse warrior profile—handsome, but fierce. And then she remembers the way he was with her the other night. The weariness in his gaze. The hungry way he looked at her after she kissed him. A tiny part of her softens.

"Forget it, I'm staying," she tells him. "I've already wasted thirty minutes of my life in this stupid line, so I'm taking that audio tour."

He glances at her from the corner of his eye, and she's pretty sure he's trying to hide a smile.

After they finish the Reichstag, Giovanni decides they should head over to the Brandenburg Gate, another one of the city's most famous landmarks. At least this is one part of Berlin she has been to a lot since it's not far from Museum Island, one of her favorite areas to spend an afternoon.

"The pictures of this place don't do it justice." He looks upward, admiring the gate's elaborate stone structure. "It's impressive. Just think of all that's happened here."

"It's even better at night when it's lit up."

"Really? Maybe we should come back."

She doesn't answer, unsure whether she wants to commit to that. Still following his lead, they head toward Unter den Linden.

A kid's ball rolls in front of them as they stroll down the picturesque avenue. There's no apparent owner, and Giovanni stops to pick it up.

"I wonder whose it is?" Lindsay considers the blue and white-striped ball.

A moment later, a little boy about five comes running up. He halts with large eyes when he sees them.

"It looks like we've found the owner," Giovanni says with a grin.

She watches in amazement then as he drops the ball on his foot and starts bouncing it around like she's seen soccer players do. His whole stern demeanor changes as he playfully bounces the ball back and forth so it doesn't touch the ground.

The boy's smile grows wide as he looks on. Eventually, he bounces it toward the kid, who catches it with a laugh.

After he runs off, Lindsay eyes Giovanni. "Do you play soccer?"

He nods. "Growing up, I spent every summer with my mom's family in *Roma*, so I played a lot of soccer. It's still a game I enjoy."

She envies him. She spent her summers wandering the Strip in Las Vegas with her friends, getting kicked out of casinos for underaged drinking and gambling.

They spend the next few hours going from one tourist site to the next. Apparently, Giovanni's guidebook has a top ten list, and he's on a mission to hit them all.

They talk, though it's mostly small talk. He asks a lot of questions about her life back in Seattle and seems keenly interested in her situation, though she can't imagine why. She tells him how she'll need to find a place to live when she gets back home, how she broke up with her boyfriend before coming here.

"So, you don't have a boyfriend right now? What about that Dieter guy I got into a fight with?"

"No, we're not involved."

"He wanted to marry you though."

"I told you before that was all in his head." She hasn't spoken to Dieter since that night. He left a couple messages on her phone, but she hasn't called him back yet.

As they walk around together, Lindsay decides it's a peculiar experience spending the day with someone she's had a one-night stand with. Giovanni is basically a stranger, but at the same time, she knows things about him. Intimate things. She knows he likes a lover to dig their nails into his back when they come, and that he likes a bit of teeth during a blow job. That night they spent together wasn't just a quick fuck, but a long, elaborate one.

"What about you?" she asks. "Are you involved with anybody?"

He's flipping through the guidebook pages again, determined to attack every tourist destination with the zeal of a NATO general.

"You don't have a girlfriend?"

"No, I don't."

Lindsay reflects on this. "A handsome doctor—a surgeon, no less. I'd think women would be throwing themselves at you."

"As I've mentioned before, my lifestyle isn't conducive to relationships."

"That sounds like a fancy way of saying you're afraid of commitment."

He shrugs. "I'm not afraid. It's just the way things are."

"When do you fly to Rome?"

"I don't know. I haven't decided yet."

"What?" She stops walking. "I thought we were rushing around Berlin because you had to leave soon!"

"No, I haven't even let my cousin know I'm coming to stay yet." He studies one of the pages in the book.

"Your cousin? But don't you have an apartment in Rome?"

"I do, but my cousin and her family live there. They rent it from me, so I sleep in the guest bedroom."

"You're kidding."

"Not at all. I'm never there anyway." He holds the open book toward her and points. "Let's go see Berlin's Television Tower. It has a 360-degree panoramic view of the city."

She nods in response, still taking in this piece of information about him. Trying to imagine his life, so rootless, that he sleeps in the guest bedroom of his own home.

After carefully consulting the map—and not her—Giovanni nods to himself. "This way." He starts marching them both toward the nearest S-Bahn station.

She rolls her eyes. *So much for any semblance of my being the tour guide.*

They get lucky when they arrive at the television tower. It's late in the afternoon, so the queue has dwindled. The view at the top, even through the smudged windows, is remarkable and goes on for miles. After getting over her anger earlier, Lindsay has started enjoying herself and is even taking pictures. She takes a few of the view then swings her phone around to include Giovanni.

"Smile and say 'I love Norway.'"

He turns and, to her surprise, gives her a genuine smile. Her breath catches. Just like when he was playing with that ball earlier, it changes his whole demeanor. He looks younger and lighter. It's the kind of smile you give a lover after you've spent the whole morning in bed together enjoying each other.

Her heart pounds.

A wave of familiarity washes over her, except this time there's a strong yearning attached.

"I'm getting hungry," he says, rubbing his stomach. "Are you ready for dinner yet?"

With shock, Lindsay realizes he's done what no one else has managed to do. He's cut through the fog of her disinterest.

Because she wants that smile. She wants *him*.

It's rare for her to want a man she knows she shouldn't have, so rare she doesn't even know what to do. Panic shoots through her. Her hands shake as she tries to shove her phone back in her purse.

"Hey, are you all right?" Giovanni comes closer, his scent falling on her, healthy and male.

He touches her arm on bare skin, and Lindsay's eyes fall shut. She likes his touch. It's calming her. "I'm fine. I think I just need some food. I get low blood sugar sometimes if I don't eat."

"What? I didn't know that. You should have said something earlier." There's concern in his voice. When she finally looks up at him, the smile is gone, and the tension is back on his face.

The moment is over, but in Lindsay's mind, it's still clear, the flame of it brightening everything.

~ Never be surprised by the crazy shit men will come up with. ~

LINDSAY ZIPS UP her purse and takes another deep breath. "I know the perfect place to eat, so you're going to let me lead for a change, understand? No argument."

He's still studying her with concern, but then nods. "I'm not arguing. We should grab something for you on the way though."

They leave the television tower, and when they walk near a small park, he insists she sit on a bench while he buys her some sugar-roasted almonds from a street vendor.

"Are those helping?" he asks after he sits down beside her. "How long have you had blood sugar issues? It's not a recent thing, is it?"

"No, I've had it forever." Lindsay crunches on a sweet almond. "I get lightheaded if I go too long without eating." He's wearing a guilty expression, and she figures he's blaming himself. "It's no big deal. You can take your doctor's hat off. It has nothing to do with you."

"I just wish you'd told me. I would have made sure you'd eaten something."

She's touched by his concern, though she has her own and it's much larger. It has to do with the way she's reacting to him. Every time she looks at Giovanni, there's a funny feeling in the pit of her stomach, like butterflies.

She can't remember the last time she's been around a guy who actually gave her butterflies. Probably one of her ex-husbands, though as she recalls, it was more lust with them than butterflies.

This is weird.

She's used to being in control. When it comes to men, she always has the upper hand, but with dread, she realizes she doesn't have it anymore with him.

At least it's only one day together. Thank God.

She eats a few more almonds, already starting to feel better. *Maybe this whole thing really is just low blood sugar.* She holds her bag out. "Would you like some?"

He glances up from the guidebook and takes a few.

Lindsay licks her lips. "You know, I never thanked you for the way you ripped into Werner the other night."

His expression goes stern as he chews an almond. "There's no need to thank me. That guy is a scumbag. You shouldn't let anyone speak to you like that."

"It's not like I was letting him." She takes some more almonds from the bag, but doesn't eat them right away. "The only reason I tolerate him is because of Dagmar, and just so we're clear, I *never* let men talk to me like that."

"I'm glad to hear it."

She turns to him and can't help but grin. "Thank you for setting him straight though. It was fun watching the rat squirm. He even apologized again last night, not that I believed him."

Giovanni nods but then goes quiet, studying her. "Listen, I owe you an apology for something too."

She's ready to make a joke about how he owes her a dozen apologies, but doesn't when she sees his grave expression.

"I never should have said what I did to you in the cab the other night—about your face being improved. That was uncalled for."

Lindsay looks down into her bag of almonds, rubbing her thumb along the crinkled edge of the paper. "You're right, it was."

"I don't even know what possessed me to say something so ridiculous." He lets out his breath. "You may not have noticed this about me yet, but sometimes I act like an arrogant prick."

"Oh, that." She shrugs. "I figured it was just a speech impediment."

He gives her a wry smile. "No, I'm afraid it's more serious than that. I actually *am* an arrogant prick."

"Must be all that Viking blood coursing through your veins, giving you delusions of grandeur."

He grins for real before his gaze turns thoughtful. "The truth is I think you're beautiful. I thought so the first time I met you, and I still do."

She tries to breathe. It's not like she's never heard this compliment before. She's heard it a lot. It's the way he's saying it, though. It reminds her of when they were together that night—the sincerity in his voice. Like he's seeing more than just her surface.

Now who's having delusions?

"Thank you," she murmurs. "I appreciate that."

His gaze is reflective, taking her in, but then something changes. "Wait a minute, did you say you saw Werner last night?"

"Yes, unfortunately."

He shakes his head. "So, you went back to that casino even after I warned you not to?"

Lindsay's mouth opens. "No, I didn't. I agreed to stay away for a few days, and I've kept my word."

"Then how did you see him?"

"Because Dagmar brought him by my studio last night to try and get me to go out with them, but I didn't."

He studies her.

"You think I'm lying?"

"You better not be."

She sits up straight. "Listen. You don't own me, so stop acting like you do."

"You agreed not go to back there for at least a few days. Though if you ask me, I think you should avoid it altogether."

"I didn't go back! But I can't not *ever* go back. I need the money I earn there."

"What you need to do is stop being a card shark."

"I see," she mutters. "So you're back in arrogant prick mode again."

"Taking advantage of people is no way to make money."

Lindsay rises from the park bench and throws the rest of the almonds in the trash. "Fuck you, okay? You don't know what you're talking about. I play a straight game. Plus, I already told you I'm an artist. Playing cards only supplements my income."

"Come on, you and I both know there's something wrong when you have to lie to your family about your activities."

"You don't know shit about me or my family, so let's not pretend you do." Her eyes rake over him "But I know plenty about you and yours, and let me tell you, we didn't all have nannies growing up."

"What?" Giovanni looks at her in amazement. "What the hell does that have to do with anything?"

"Because you've never had to worry about money a single day in your life."

He doesn't say anything for a long moment. She's sure he's seen terrible poverty, though she doubts he's experienced any on a personal level. Finally, he speaks. "You're selling yourself short. That's all I'm saying."

"God, you are such an ass. Next thing you'll be telling me is I should go find a nice rich man and let him take care of me."

"No, that's *not* what I'm saying!"

"I live my life on my terms and in my own way, got it? I don't need or want your judgment."

"Christ." He rubs his forehead like he's trying to ease the strain on his face. "This isn't going the way I intended at all. Every time I'm around you I can't think straight."

"What are you talking about?"

"Nothing." He unfolds himself from the bench. "Let's go. We'll get some real food into you and then maybe have a normal conversation for once."

Lindsay takes Giovanni to the food court at the KaDeWe, Berlin's famous department store. Dagmar brought her here right after they met, and for Lindsay, it was love at first sight. A food universe unto itself, and one of the places she'll miss most when she leaves Berlin.

The KaDeWe has *everything.*

It's a trek to get there, and they have to change trains a few times, but he follows her lead and doesn't complain. They don't talk much and he spends most of the time texting, and then receives a call once they're out walking on the sidewalk. He motions with his hand that he needs privacy and goes over to stand under a store awning while Lindsay window shops. She tries to ignore him, though a few words drift her way. It's mostly medical talk, along with the names of some places she's unfamiliar with.

"So, when do you go back to Africa?" she asks after he's done with his call. "I couldn't help but overhear what you said."

He glances around as they arrive at the giant department store. "I'm not going back."

"You're not?

"No. I'm changing direction entirely."

They enter the front doors and Lindsay leads them to the elevators where a small group of people is already waiting. Someone's floral perfume hangs in the air.

"So, you're changing jobs?" she asks as they board the elevator. She checks to make sure the sixth-floor button for the food court is pushed.

"I won't be working overseas anymore. I've accepted a position in the States."

A prickle of unease runs through her. "Where?"

Giovanni doesn't respond right away, and before he even speaks, she has a premonition she isn't going to like it.

"Seattle Children's Hospital."

Her mouth opens in shock. "You're moving to *Seattle?"*

"Yes, it looks that way."

"And you didn't think to *mention* this?"

"I only just found out. That's what the phone call was about. I spoke to them yesterday when they made the offer, but I hadn't accepted yet." The elevator stops moving as they arrive on the sixth floor. When they exit, Giovanni looks around. "Damn, you weren't kidding. This is impressive."

"Why would you want to move to Seattle? Wouldn't LA be a better choice?"

He doesn't reply, still taking in the enormity of the food court. "What's this place called again? I think it might be listed in my guidebook."

"The KaDeWe. And yes, I'm sure it's in your guidebook."

He stops checking out the food court and starts staring at her again. "We need to get some real food into you. Something with protein and carbs would be best."

"When are you moving to Seattle, exactly?"

"We'll talk about it after you eat." He pauses and his eyes settle on hers for a moment. "There's something else I need to speak with you about."

Lindsay's spidey senses tingle. "What do you mean?" It occurs to her this isn't the first time he's mentioned wanting to speak to her about something.

He ignores her question though and points at one of the nearby deli stations. "There's a place that serves sandwiches over there. I also see a fish place next to it. What are you in the mood for?"

They wander around looking at food while he continues to ignore every question about Seattle. She realizes she's not going to get an answer out of him until they've had dinner.

In the end, she orders one of her favorite dishes—creamed chanterelle mushrooms over thick slices of toast, while Giovanni gets some kind of German dish with sauerkraut.

"What do you think?" she asks after they sit down and start eating. She usually has to wait for a table with a window seat, but they managed to snag one right away. "Isn't this place great? I love it here."

"It's all right," he agrees, though he seems distracted. When his phone buzzes, he starts texting again.

Lindsay tries to stay calm. She needs to decide how she's going to handle Giovanni living in Seattle. Her 'have a great life' speech is obviously meaningless now, since she'll be forced to see him.

It won't be so bad. It's not like I'll have to see him very often. Maybe the occasional holiday at Natalie and Anthony's.

She hopes that's all.

When they're done eating, they push their plates aside and he centers his glass of beer in front of himself. He isn't texting anymore, but is on his phone speaking Italian.

She pulls a chocolate strawberry out of the box she bought for dessert. After licking some of the dark chocolate off the tip, she finally bites into it. *Yum.* It's tart and sweet, with just the right amount of bitterness from the chocolate.

He's watching her as he talks, sipping his beer occasionally.

There are a few guys seated at nearby tables and she senses their eyes on her, but she ignores them. Mostly she eats her strawberry and admires the view outside, listening to the melodious sound of Giovanni conversing in Italian.

Eventually, he wraps up the conversation and puts his phone down on top of his guidebook.

"Norwegian is kind of sexy," she tells him as she sucks on a strawberry. "You should teach me some words."

"What would you like to learn?"

"Something naughty, of course."

He considers this but doesn't offer any lessons. He's still staring at her and seems very interested in her chocolate strawberry.

"Do you want one?" She moves the box closer. "They're delicious."

"No, but I'm enjoying watching you eat them."

Lindsay's pulse quickens and she gives him a seductive smile. "You shouldn't say things like that to me, Olaf."

"I know." He sighs with frustration and glances away.

When his eyes come back, they stay on hers. His are dark, just like the other night.

The food court is big and noisy with people all around them, but somehow that fades into the background. All she can see is Giovanni. His potent gaze pulling her in, wanting things from her.

She lets out a shaky breath and finally turns, studying the view again, the familiar streets of Berlin lit up.

"Look at me, Lindsay." He leans forward, placing his muscular forearms on the table. "I need to ask you something important."

She goes on high alert at his tone. Her spidey senses aren't just tingling anymore—they're buzzing like a chainsaw.

Giovanni shifts uncomfortably in his chair before he clears his throat.

"What is it?" she asks.

He licks his lips. It's like he's trying to smile, but can't quite manage it. Sweat breaks out on his brow. His skin looks pale, almost green beneath his tan.

Her eyes roam over him. "Are you okay?"

He takes a deep breath. "I need to know if you'll marry me."

Giovanni lets his breath out. His stomach's still queasy. For a moment, he felt so ill he thought he might need to lie down.

What's wrong with me? There's no reason it should be so difficult this time. None whatsoever.

But as he takes in Lindsay's appalled expression, it hits him like a punch in the gut.

She reminds him of Olivia.

Not completely—only a little, actually—but enough that it's all coming back. The humiliation when he'd asked her to marry him. The shame, still fresh after all these years. She'd laughed at him for being the young idiot he was back then. In love with the wrong woman.

So in love it nearly wrecked his life.

At least Lindsay isn't laughing. Instead, her expression has changed to what appears to be fascination. Her rich brown eyes are studying him as if he were a peculiar sculpture she needed to analyze.

"Was it the kiss?" she asks, leaning toward him, still holding the half-eaten strawberry. "Is that what pushed you over the edge?"

"What are you talking about?"

"My God, I never should have kissed you!"

"Kissed me?"

"Yes, I kissed you the other night. Don't pretend you don't remember!"

"Of course, I remember."

Giovanni remembers all too well. That kiss nearly broke him in half, his self-control hanging on by the thinnest thread.

He'd gone back to his hotel after kissing her and sat in the bar for a long time. He didn't want to be alone. Not with his thoughts or the high-octane blood flowing through his veins. He slowly sipped a glass of scotch, trying to dull his senses with something artificial. When a blonde took the chair beside him, he seriously considered taking her back to his room. She was attractive and eager, kept touching him, putting out every signal imaginable. Her voice grated like metal though, and she had too many sharp edges for his taste. Worst of all, he suspected she was married.

If she'd been brunette, he doubted any of that would have mattered.

Instead, he went back to his room alone, took a long hot shower, and jerked off. He thought about Lindsay in front of the taxi, how he wished she'd invited him upstairs, wished he were with her right then. Her edges weren't sharp at all, but smooth, and beneath them he knew she was soft . . . oh so soft. She'd moan and cry and wrap her lithe body around him in ecstasy, and finally, he'd lose himself.

After the shower, he lay exhausted beneath the cool hotel sheets, the scotch and orgasm wearing him down. The little paper fox was still on his nightstand, its blank face watchful, easing him in a strange way.

"That kiss is not why I asked you to marry me," he tells Lindsay, though she appears skeptical.

"Are you sure? What else could it be?" She's still holding the half-eaten strawberry, pointing it at him like a weapon. "Is there something strange in the water here?"

"What the hell are you going on about?" It figures she wouldn't react like a normal woman. It's clear nothing about her was ever normal. With annoyance, he realizes she hasn't even addressed his proposal yet. "I just told you I needed you to marry me. Aren't you going to ask why?"

"If you weren't so humorless, I'd think you were joking. But you're not, are you?"

"Humorless?" Giovanni scowls.

"Is it the air? Something in the Berlin air causing this to happen?" Her eyes roam wildly upward.

"What do you mean? I'm not humorless."

She puts the strawberry down on a napkin. He studies her hands—even her fingers appeal to him. Surprisingly, they're not the well-manicured ones you'd expect on a woman like her, but are unadorned and a little rough.

He thinks about those clay masks she creates, her hands molding them into shape. Without trying, he imagines them on his body, the way they'd mold him too. Stroking him. He looks away from her as he tries to stop blood from rushing to parts of him he'd prefer it didn't.

He's already noticed all the men in the food court checking her out. It's been the same everywhere all day. She captures the attention of every male within spitting distance. He handles it like an Italian, glaring at each and every one of them. Luckily, it deters them all. Lindsay is beautiful, but it's more than that. She has a kind of sexual magnetism that's difficult to ignore.

Catnip for men. Except she's worse than catnip. After spending the day with her, he's more affected than ever. It's no wonder she's used to men fighting over her, all of them hoping for a taste.

His scowl deepens.

"All right." She sighs, sweeping a handful of brown curls over her shoulder. "What is this all about? You've fallen madly in love with me?"

"No."

"No?" Most women wouldn't like that, but she seems pleased. "Really? Thank God!"

This only annoys him further. Everything about her is unpredictable.

"I need you to marry me as a favor."

Her eyes narrow with suspicion. "What kind of favor is that?"

Giovanni takes a deep breath and lets it out. "It's a long story, but bear with me." And so he explains the situation. How his last work assignment was in a country fragmented by civil war. "One of my best friends was a doctor who grew up there before the recent problems began." He grows quiet, remembering Paul and how much he admired him. "He was killed twelve weeks ago."

"I'm so sorry." Her eyes are kind.

He shakes his head. It shouldn't have happened, but it did. "Paul was a widower with two kids. His brother, Phillip, contacted me recently. He lives in San Francisco and has been trying to bring his niece and nephew to the States, but he's running into problems. Political problems. Phillip has ties with the former government, so now the current government won't let him and his wife have the children."

Lindsay's eyes are focused, listening. "Who are they with now?"

"Their grandmother, but it's not a long-term solution. As it turns out, I'm in a unique situation to help. Phillip has talked to a lawyer about setting up a private adoption."

"Who's going to adopt them?"

"Me."

"You?"

He nods and presses his lips together. "I'll adopt them temporarily to get them to the States, and then hand custody over to Phillip and his wife."

"Wow . . . that's some plan."

"It should work. I've been living there for the last six months so I have temporary resident status, which fulfills one of the adoption requirements. Unfortunately, there's one other requirement I don't have."

Lindsay leans back in her chair and studies him, before fiddling with her strawberry. "Let me guess—you need to be married."

"Yes."

"But you're a doctor. Isn't that enough?"

"It isn't. No country on Earth is going to let a single thirty-seven-year-old male adopt two children who aren't even a blood relation."

She takes this in, then leans forward again. "So let me get this straight. You're asking me to commit marriage fraud?"

"Basically, though the odds of getting caught are very small." He watches her closely, can see the wheels turning as she sorts it all out.

"How many women have you already asked?"

Giovanni hesitates, but tells her the truth. "You're the third woman I've asked."

"The other two said no?"

"The first one said no, the second one said yes."

Lindsay's brows go up.

"Her boyfriend said no."

"I see."

"We wouldn't have to stay married long. Once Phillip and his wife legally adopt the kids in the U.S., we could get divorced."

"What made you think of me in all this? We barely even know each other."

He takes a sip of his beer. "Anthony mentioned you were here in Berlin, so I asked for your address."

Her eyes widen. "Anthony *knows* about this?"

"No, I didn't tell him. I only told him I wanted to look you up to be friendly. I remembered how he once told me you were unconventional though."

"Unconventional? What is that, code for weird?"

"Not at all. Just that your lifestyle is unorthodox."

She snorts softly. "I could say the same thing about yours."

"You could," he agrees.

"So *this* is why you've been hanging around," she murmurs. "It all makes sense now." She takes another strawberry out, but doesn't eat it. "Why didn't you just tell me all this the other night?"

He licks his lips. "To be honest, I was trying to charm you a bit first."

She laughs in amazement. "You're kidding, right?"

"Sadly, I'm not."

"So, all the tour guide stuff today? That was you trying to charm me?" She gives him an incredulous look.

"Basically."

"There are no words."

"I know." He glances around the food court and sighs. "Charm has never been one of my strengths."

"You can say that again."

Maybe I have lost my sense of humor.

Part of the problem has been Lindsay herself. He's too attracted to her. Forget charming her—he can barely think straight with this constant desire pressing on him.

He glances at her. She seems deep in thought.

"What's the penalty for marriage fraud?" she asks.

Giovanni picks up his beer and takes a long draw, her eyes on him the whole time. He puts his glass down and licks his lower lip. “Sometimes doing the right thing means you have to circumvent the law.”

“Tell me the penalty. You must have looked it up.”

He lets out his breath with resignation. “Up to five years in prison, along with a two hundred and fifty thousand dollar fine.”

She blinks. “Are you crazy?”

He doesn’t say anything. Years ago, Paul helped him and now it’s his turn to repay the debt.

“I’m sorry.” She shakes her head. “But the answer is no.”

Chapter Eight

~ A man can never take care of you better than you take care of yourself. ~

"NO ONE COULD ever prove fraud," Giovanni tells her. "Marriage fraud typically involves immigration, but we're both American citizens. Hell, we've even slept together. Not to mention we have close family ties."

"If we got caught though . . ." Lindsay shakes her head.

"We won't. The risk is minimal."

"I feel for this situation. I truly do." She reaches over and briefly touches his arm. "But I can't do it."

Ironically, a few months ago, she wouldn't have given much thought to the consequences. But coming to Berlin has made her realize it's time to make some changes in her life, to start thinking about her future.

"You're right." He closes his eyes and rubs his forehead. "I apologize. I shouldn't push you. Obviously, there is some risk involved."

"How many other women are on your list to ask?"

"Two more. They're both long shots. Longer than *you*, even."

"Maybe one of them will agree. Or maybe the kids' uncle will find another solution. He's still trying to get them out, right?"

Giovanni nods, though his face is grim.

They leave the KaDeWe together, the mood between them subdued. When they reach the front, she tells him she's going back to her apartment. "I come here all the time, so I know my way back."

"No, I'll take you." His tone allows no room for argument. "We'll grab a taxi together. It'll be quicker than the trains."

There's a cab stand nearby and they walk over to it. Lindsay feels bad—for the kids, for the situation—but how can she agree to something like this?

"What are you going to do now?" she asks once they're in the Mercedes cab headed toward her studio.

"I'm not sure. I didn't realize it would be this difficult. I guess I'm less desirable marriage material than I thought."

"To be honest, women don't find marriage proposals involving fraud very romantic."

"I suppose not." He glances at her. "Would it help if I bought you flowers and a ring?"

Lindsay smiles. "You're not still trying to charm me, are you?"

"Don't worry, I'll spare you that."

She thinks about that genuine smile Giovanni gave her earlier, how she wishes she could see it again. "You're a lot different than the last time we saw each other. You know that?"

His eyes go to her.

"You're far more serious. You were really cocky before." She goes quiet. "Though I guess it makes sense with everything. I'm so sorry about your friend."

He nods, but doesn't say anything.

"Is that why you've decided to move to Seattle?"

He shakes his head. "No. I've been thinking about moving back to the States for a while. It's not uncommon to reach burnout if you do what I do for too long."

"Are you burned out?"

"With being a doctor, no. I could never do anything else. But with how the world sometimes works?" He looks down at his hands. "Maybe so."

She can't take her eyes off his profile. The colorful lights of Berlin flicker across his handsome features as they drive. Despite everything—or maybe *because* of everything—a strong desire to reach for him comes over her.

She knows she should resist the impulse. There are a lot of reasons to resist it, good reasons, ones she knows will stop her if she thinks about them for even a second.

So she doesn't think about them.

Instead, she shifts position in the cab's backseat. She's been careful not to allow any part of her body to touch his, but now she lets her leg press against the outside of his thigh, her arm brushing lightly against his.

Giovanni doesn't move.

For a moment, she wonders if he even notices.

But then the air density inside the car changes, particles attract and repel. "What are you doing?" His voice is low, just above the engine noise.

"I think you know."

He turns toward her, his eyes dark and questioning.

Lindsay reaches out for him, her fingers stroking his jaw, caressing his cheek. "You've seen terrible things, haven't you?" she whispers.

He doesn't reply, but he doesn't have to. She can see it on his face.

And like the other night, she doesn't wait for him. Pulling him toward her, she slides her hand to the back of his neck to draw him near.

He's so much larger than her he could resist easily, but he doesn't, and when their mouths meet that same desperation is there. The need so powerful, coming off him in waves, pulling her under.

He stops kissing her, his mouth close, breath hot. "What's it going to be?"

Lindsay knows what he's asking. Despite what happened the last time they were together, she can't help herself. She shouldn't want him, but she does.

His eyes on hers are desperate, misinterpreting her silence. "Let me be with you tonight." His voice shakes. "Please, let me." The difficulty of pleading apparent in his gaze.

Understanding washes over her about the kind of man he is. His strength. Giovanni is the kind of man who picks up others when they fall. Who offers help when no one else will.

But who picks him up? Who helps him when he falls?

She strokes his cheek. "I want you to stay with me."

His eyes close and he lets his breath out. She assumes he's relieved, but when he opens them, she sees a glimmer of something troubled.

They exit the taxi into the warm summer evening. The street in front of her building still has a steady stream of pedestrians. They walk beside each other, not holding hands, not even touching, but the heat between them radiates.

He follows her inside and up the short landing to the first floor. Unlike the day hours, most people shut their doors at night. When they're close to her own door, he suddenly reaches for her and pulls her against him, as if he's been trying to hold back but can't stop himself any longer.

"I lied to you that first night I came here," he tells her, his hands splayed on her back.

"You did?"

"When I told you I didn't want you again." He lowers his voice. "I wanted you from the moment I saw you."

She slides her arms around his neck. "I know that."

He chuckles, then gives her one of his genuine smiles. "Catnip."

Lindsay giggles, and she can hardly believe the sound. She's most certainly never been a giggler.

They're alone and he pushes her against the hallway's long wall. The sound of a distant television show broadcasting in German drifts out. There's a lingering smell from someone's evening meal. All she can think about is Giovanni. The anticipation of having him again is taking her breath away.

He reaches behind and lifts her as if she weighs nothing. She's a tall girl, and there's not a lot of guys who can lift her so easily. She wraps her legs around his hips, moaning softly when he buries his face in her neck.

His mouth moves back to hers and they kiss passionately, clutching each other. He tastes delicious. His hands grip her ass, and she feels all of him, hard and ready, pressing at her center. Her breath catches as she remembers all those vibrator fantasies.

The real thing is so much better.

He draws back and eases her down, his face flushed. "Let's go inside," he urges.

She nods. They're next to her door and she starts fumbling through her purse, searching for her keys.

"Hey, wait." He grows still, on alert.

She looks up. "What is it?"

"Something's wrong. Don't move."

Lindsay turns and sees what he's talking about. Her front door isn't closed all the way.

She sucks in her breath. "I locked that!"

"You did." He's still staring at it, but then turns to her. "Stay here."

Before she can say another word, Giovanni has pushed her front door open and gone inside her studio.

She waits for a moment, panic rocketing through her when she realizes what's happening.

My money!

She rushes through the door and sees him standing in the center of her studio.

"Whoever they are, they're gone now." He turns to her, his eyes stricken. "Goddamn, Lindsay, I don't know what to say."

Her jaw drops when she sees how her entire studio has been ransacked. Immediately, she rushes over to the bag of clay where she hid part of her bankroll.

"Oh, no!" she moans. The bag has been torn apart. There's clay everywhere, and it's clear the money is gone. "I can't believe this!"

He strides over and stands next to her with his phone out. "I'm calling the police."

She rushes to her second hiding place behind the radiator. She shoves her hand behind it, but of course there's nothing there. "It's gone too!"

He's talking into his phone, though she's too upset to pay attention. "What's your address?" he asks her.

She frantically goes to each hiding place. They've all been found, except the one under a piece of broken wood flooring in the corner, which still has a thousand euro.

It's after that she freaks out even more because she notices her masks. The one on her sculpting table is still there, but the ones on the wall have been knocked to the floor. Broken. "Who would do this?" she cries. "Motherfuckers!"

"I need your address, Lindsay," Giovanni tells her with clipped command. His operating room voice.

She gives him her address. His expression is tense as he explains what happened to the police on the other end of the line. She realizes there's nothing they can do about the missing money. Nothing. She can't even report it stolen.

He hangs up. "The police are going to send someone out right away." She sees the way he's still taking in everything, the chaos, but when he notices the broken masks, his expression grows hard. "Why would someone do this to you? Do you have enemies?"

She shakes her head. "Not that I know of." There've been a few guys she's turned down, and there were those marriage proposals she refused. But she doubts any of them would want to rob her and break her sculptures. And that's when it occurs to her. There *is* one person who would do this.

Werner.

"Are you sure it's him?" Giovanni asks, his jaw clenching.

Lindsay nods. "It has to be. That's why the rat came here and apologized last night." She looks at Giovanni. "He's never been here before. Ever. Now all of a sudden, he shows up and my money is stolen? My place is robbed?"

"Wait a minute, what money?" He considers her. "Poker winnings?"

"Yes, and you can't mention it to the police." She has no idea what the law is in Germany regarding gambling winnings.

"How much was there?"

Lindsay opens her mouth but hesitates.

"Tell me the truth. How much?"

She turns to him, her throat tight. "Twenty thousand."

His eyes widen taking this in. "Are you serious?" But then he frowns. "And you kept it all *here?*"

"I didn't know what else to do with it. I didn't want to put it in the bank because then I'd have to report it."

"You can't keep that kind of money lying around."

"It wasn't lying around. It was *hidden*."

He shakes his head. "That's crazy. You should have put it in the bank anyway."

"Please, stop giving me shit, okay? I was just robbed and vandalized!" She waves her arms around. "Look at this place!"

He goes quiet, steps closer, and reaches for her. "I know. I'm sorry."

She lets him pull her in, closing her eyes as he hugs her, allowing herself to be comforted.

When they pull apart, Giovanni studies her. "I still can't believe you won twenty grand playing poker."

"Well, I did."

"Christ, I had no idea you were that good."

She tries to think of some wisecrack remark but fails. Her stomach hurts. She wants to cry, but she's too furious. Yes, she won that money playing cards, but she worked hard for it. She was at that casino every night, analyzing each hand, improving her game.

And now it's gone.

Those winnings were going to pay for her classes in the fall. They'd help her find a new apartment and get herself settled back home. And now it's over, her dream killed before it even had a chance to take flight.

Two police arrive. A man and a woman, both very polite and officious, as they look around her studio. They ask her a lot of questions in their heavy accents. She shows them her passport, which she luckily always keeps with her. She tells them her suspicions about Werner, but doesn't mention the money, only tells them she had some cash here—a couple thousand euros. They ask Giovanni questions too, want to see his passport as well. To his credit, he doesn't mention the money either.

The police tell her they'll open a case file on it and ask around with her neighbors to see if anyone saw anything. They take down her cell number.

Once they've left, Lindsay starts picking up all the pieces of broken clay. At least she only had two masks here, three if you count the one she was working on. She gets a broom, but then puts it down and sits in the wooden chair next to her sculpting table, surveying the mess. There's a lump in the back of her throat, making it difficult to swallow. Her instincts had been right about Werner when she wedged that piece of wood in her door last night, only she didn't realize it was her money he was after. *I should have known. How could I be so stupid?* She looks up at Giovanni. "I have to go find that bastard."

He's leaning against the back table, contemplating one of her broken masks.

"I have to get my money back," she tells him.

"And how do you plan to do that?"

She grits her teeth as she imagines getting her hands on the rat. "Squeeze his nuts until he screams and tells me where it is. Listen, you don't have to come with me. I understand if you don't want to get involved in any of this."

A grin pulls on the corner of his mouth. "It's never a dull moment with you, is it?"

"Hey, I didn't ask to get robbed! But I can't just sit here when I know very well who fucking did it."

"I know. That's not what I'm talking about." He moves closer and puts his hand out to help her up. "Come on, let's go find that scumbag."

They take another taxi while she tries Dagmar's number. "She's probably playing cards," she says. "We turn our phones off when we're at the tables."

He doesn't say anything, only watches her as she makes more phone calls. She has Varik's number, the pit boss at Spielbank Europa. He gave it to her a while ago. She's never used it, but she calls him now.

He sounds surprised to hear from her. "What can I do for you?"

"Something's happened tonight. Are Werner and Dagmar there?"

"Dagmar is here," he tells her. "I have not seen Werner. What is going on, Lindsay?"

She tells how someone robbed her and wrecked her studio.

He's quiet for a long moment. "I am very sorry to hear this."

She explains to him how she's headed over there now to speak to Dagmar and that she's already reported it to the police. She senses Varik is hesitant to get involved, which she totally understands.

When Lindsay and Giovanni arrive at Spielbank, they immediately head for the poker floor, keeping an eye out for Werner.

She finds Dagmar playing poker and goes over to stand behind her.

"We need to talk," she tells her in a low voice.

Dagmar looks over her shoulder and smiles. "I am so glad you came tonight!" She leans closer. "Though I have to admit it has been very slow."

"Where's Werner?"

"He is not here." Dagmar turns back to the table and throws in a twenty-euro chip to call. "Why?"

"Did you get my message?"

"No." Dagmar looks at her with concern. "What's wrong?"

"Someone broke into my studio and robbed me. Broke all my masks."

Dagmar's eyes widen in shock. "I can't believe it! When did this happen?"

"Today. I think Werner did it."

"What are you saying?" Dagmar shakes her head vehemently. "No, he would never do that!"

Lindsay motions over to the side of the room. "I'm here with Giovanni. We've already spoken to the police. Come over when you finish this hand."

Giovanni is at one of the back tables waiting for her, studying his phone. He looks up when Lindsay joins him. "What did she say?"

"She thinks Werner is innocent, of course. She has a blind spot for him."

He shakes his head. "What exactly does she see in that guy?"

Lindsay thinks about how some women don't want to see the truth about the man they're involved with. Her own mother was that way.

A few minutes later, Dagmar comes rushing over. "Tell me everything that's happened!"

Lindsay explains what they found earlier—her place trashed, her money gone, the masks broken.

"I am so sorry!" Dagmar's face looks especially pained at the mention of the broken sculptures. She reaches out to hold Lindsay's hand. "Thank God your other masks are at the gallery!"

"Where's Werner? I need his address."

Dagmar gives her a reassuring look. "He is not here. He went to stay with his brother in Frankfurt and left this morning. That is why I know he could not have robbed you."

"You saw him get on a train to Frankfurt?"

"No, but I know he is there. I spoke to him only a couple of hours ago."

"Where does he live?" Lindsay asks. "I want to see for myself."

"Werner was kicked out of his apartment two days ago and had to stay with me." Dagmar's expression turns sad. "Poor guy, he cannot seem to catch a break, but that is why he has gone to Frankfurt."

Lindsay stares at Dagmar amazed at her continued faith in Werner. She'll never understand why some women are so attracted to losers. "Can you call him?"

"Of course! I will call him and you can speak to him yourself." She pulls her phone out of the small leather purse she carries as Lindsay and Giovanni watch her call the rat. "Werner, *Liebchen*!" She starts talking into her phone in German, but Giovanni interrupts and puts his hand out.

"Give me the phone. I want to speak to him."

"No!" Lindsay puts her hand out. "Give *me* the phone." She looks over at Giovanni with irritation. "*I'm* the one who got robbed here!"

"Yes, but I'm more intimidating than you are."

She scoffs. "Says who?"

Dagmar watches them bicker while still talking to Werner. She lowers the phone to her chin. "He says he is sorry you were robbed, but he did not do it."

"He's lying. Give me that phone!" Dagmar finally hands it over to her. "Listen to me, you sleazy fuckwad," Lindsay snarls. "I know what you did, and I want my fucking money back!"

Werner's smug nasal voice responds. "I am very sorry you feel this way, but you are wrong. I am staying with my brother in Frankfurt, so I could *not* have robbed you."

"I haven't told the police about you yet," she lies. "And if you give me back my money I won't, but if you don't, I'm sending them right the fuck to you."

There's a pause. "Dagmar told me you had a mercenary beside you during a poker game a couple nights ago. Maybe he is the one who robbed you."

"That's ridiculous!"

"It sounds plausible to me."

Lindsay's fury takes over. "You lying piece of shit! You slimy rat fuck-stain! Urine gargling, cocksucking, motherfuck—"

Giovanni rips the phone from her hand.

"Hey!" She gapes at him. "I'm not done!"

He ignores her and puts it to his ear, his voice hard. "Werner, you made a big mistake today, and you better pray you didn't leave a single fingerprint or piece of hair behind. You also better pray you aren't stupid enough to talk on a cell phone claiming to be in Frankfurt while you're still in Berlin."

Giovanni is silent for a moment, listening, then hands the phone back to Dagmar. "He hung up."

"Of course he hung up!" Lindsay shakes her head in disgust. "He's probably sitting at a bar right around the corner. His pockets stuffed with my money!"

"No," Dagmar insists. "He is in Frankfurt. I helped him pack his bag this morning." Her eyes go back and forth from Lindsay to Giovanni. Lindsay sees how unsettled she's become and feels a little sorry for her, despite everything. "He would not lie. And he would not rob someone who is such a good friend to me!"

Lindsay sighs with exhaustion, weary beyond belief. "Unfortunately, that's exactly what he did."

The three of them leave the casino together and share a cab home, taking Dagmar to her apartment in East Berlin first. "Do you want to stay over?" she asks Lindsay. "It is probably not safe in your studio."

Lindsay has stayed over at Dagmar's apartment a few times, drinking wine and talking into the late hours after a dinner party. From the outside, her building looks sterile and utilitarian, like the former communist barracks it is, but inside it's all modern German *gemütlichkeit*—cozy and welcoming.

"No, I'll be okay."

Dagmar's blue eyes go to Giovanni then back to Lindsay, assessing. She nods, and then smiles a little at Lindsay, who knows what she's thinking.

She thinks I've hooked up with Giovanni.

When she leans in to hug her goodbye, Dagmar whispers in her ear. "I'm at least glad the doctor is taking care of you."

After dropping her off, they head to Lindsay's studio. There are people in front, and she runs into a couple of artist friends in the hallway. Apparently, since the police questioned everyone, the whole building knows what happened. They tell Lindsay how sorry they are.

She and Giovanni swing open her studio door with the broken lock on it, and nothing has changed. Her heart hurts for a moment, but then her anger eclipses it as she looks around at the damage she'll have to clean up.

Everything's turned to shit in one day.

"Listen, Dagmar's right about one thing," He says, surveying the mess. "I don't think it's safe for you to stay here tonight."

"I'll be fine. I can just wedge the door shut. Hopefully, the landlord will fix the lock tomorrow."

"No, that's unacceptable. I want you to come back with me to my hotel."

She shifts uncomfortably. "I know we had a moment back there, and if I hadn't been robbed we'd be in bed right now, but everything's changed, okay? After what happened, I'm just not feeling it anymore."

He moves closer but doesn't touch her. "That's not why I want you to come back with me."

"I'm not sleeping with you."

"And I'm not asking you to. I just want you to be safe. You can even get your own room."

She laughs. "I can't afford a room at The Regent!" But then she goes quiet. "The truth is I can't afford a room anywhere now."

"Do you have any money left at all?"

"A little over a thousand. That's basically it." She has a few hundred in a savings account back in the States.

He studies her, opens his mouth like he's going to say something, but then looks away.

"What is it?"

He shakes his head. "Nothing."

She wonders if she should stay with him. It probably is safer. She tries to imagine herself alone here tonight and doubts she'll get any sleep.

"What if I offered to give you the money that was stolen?" he says, watching her closely. "The whole twenty thousand."

She's taken aback. "Why would you do that?"

"Because I'd like you to do me a favor in return."

"What favor would that be?" But then it dawns on her. "I can't believe it. Are you fucking kidding me with this?"

"I'd like you to marry me."

Chapter Nine

~ Always trust your instincts
when it comes to both men and life. ~

"FUCK OFF!"

"Think about it for a minute," Giovanni says. "It would solve both of our problems."

"There's nothing like taking advantage of a person when they're down, is there?" Lindsay glares at him. "And you call *me* a shark."

His expression turns fierce. "I'm not taking advantage of you! I'm only trying to help a couple of kids."

"And what am I supposed to say to that? I sound like an asshole because I don't want to risk going to jail."

"Sometimes, doing the right thing means sticking your neck out, thinking about someone besides yourself for a change."

She moves briskly away from him toward the long wooden table where she keeps her tools. There's a broken mask on it, and she feels like throwing it against the wall. Instead she closes her eyes for a long moment, thinks about how much work went into creating it. "So, you think I'm selfish, is that it?"

"To be honest, after seeing how you live—yes, I do."

She whirls around on him. "So, the saint is going to kick me when I'm down and then tell me how to live? God, you really are an arrogant prick."

"The last thing I want to do is kick you when you're down." He comes over to her and rests his hand on the table. "And I'm definitely not a saint. Trust me, I'm far from it."

She starts shoving the broken pieces of the mask together like a jigsaw puzzle. She's able to make a lopsided face that should be laughing but looks more like it's pissed off. *Exactly how I feel.*

"It sounds to me like your whole life is about duty," she mutters. "That and telling people what to do."

"That's not true." He lowers his voice. "Believe me, duty was the furthest thing from my mind when you were pressed against me earlier."

"I had a weak moment, that's all. We both know it's a terrible idea."

Giovanni doesn't say anything.

She continues trying to fit the pieces together the best she can. "Believe it or not, this mask used to be smiling."

"I remember." He tilts his head. "Now it looks constipated."

"God, you're right." She laughs a little, forcing one of the pieces in a bit more. She reaches for some paste and a brush.

"The grimace of constipation. First in a new series by Lindsay West."

She glances at him. "Careful, you're in danger of getting a sense of humor." She starts gluing the polymer clay pieces together the best she can.

"I don't know why you keep saying that. There's nothing wrong with my sense of humor."

"It's strange," she muses, still working on the mask. "But I always thought Norwegians were a jolly people."

"I happen to have a *great* sense of humor," he growls, his eyes roaming her studio. "Unfortunately, not everyone appreciates it."

She wipes the excess paste and touches the mask gently to make sure it's stable enough to bake later. "Don't worry, I'm sure you have other good qualities that are hidden. *Deeply* hidden."

"I can't remember if I've ever met anyone who gives me shit as much as you do."

She snorts. "And you want to marry me."

His eyes flash to her. "Does that mean you'll do it?"

Satisfied her mask is stable, Lindsay puts the paste back and wipes the brush, taking it with her to the small kitchen sink. There's a torn box of cookies on the floor, and she picks it up to throw in the garbage. There's a bag of granola scattered too, but she leaves it, figuring she'll deal with it all later. She opens the freezer, seeing the bottle of vodka is still there. *Thank God for small mercies*. She grabs a coffee mug and pours a healthy splash, drinks it like medicine, then pours herself another.

Giovanni is still watching her from across the room. She turns around to face him and leans against the counter with her mug. "I always swore I'd never get married again, but I guess everyone has their price." She stares over at her bed with the sheets torn off, the mattress askew. "Including me."

"You've been married before?"

"Yes." She takes another swallow and shivers. "Twice, actually."

He comes over to stand beside her. "You never do anything by half measures, do you?"

She doesn't reply to that. "What about you? Have you ever been married?"

"No." He takes the mug from her hands. She thinks he's going to drink from it, but instead he puts it down.

He brushes her hair back and slips his hand to the back of her neck. Right away, she's soothed as his fingers begin kneading her tense muscles. Her eyes drift shut. Somehow, his touch is drawing away all the stress of what's happened today, if only for a few moments.

When she opens them, he's looking down at her in a way that sparks her butterflies. He doesn't try to kiss her, and instead, they gaze at each other. The depth of strength in his blue eyes astonishes her.

This isn't a man who merely talks about changing people's lives. He changes them.

"Go pack a bag," he tells her, his hand gently stroking her skin. "You're coming with me."

Giovanni stands in the kitchen, waiting patiently while Lindsay packs her things. He can tell the anger she's been using as fuel is starting to run low, as her movements are jerky and stiff. He has to admit she's tough though, tougher than he expected. Most people would have fallen apart long before now. He doesn't blame her for going after Werner either. She's action-oriented, the same way he is himself.

It's too bad they didn't find that scumbag.

She's pulling clothes off the floor and from her dresser, but then stops and glances at him. The expression on her face is so upset he walks over.

"What's wrong?"

"That rat fuck went through my underwear drawer." Her voice shakes. "He touched *everything*."

His anger flares as he stares at the colorful bras and panties strewn about. *I'd definitely like to get my hands on that slimy son of a bitch.*

"I can't wear it knowing he's touched it with his rat fingers."

"We'll have the hotel wash everything for you. I'll tell them to use extra-hot water and bleach."

She nods. "Okay."

He wishes he could take her in his arms. He doesn't want to risk changing her mind about coming to his hotel though. If she does change her mind, he's already decided he's camping out here—even if he has to sleep in the hallway.

Once she's gathered all her things into a black suitcase, he takes it from her.

"Just so you know, I'm only staying one night with you," she says. "I packed everything because I want to wash it."

"I understand." He already has her landlord's number and plans to call tomorrow and make sure her front door lock is replaced.

They don't say much to each other on the ride over, though he notices the way she's careful not to touch him in the taxi. He feels guilty about the way he finally convinced her to marry him, but he's glad nevertheless. Soon, Paul's kids will be safe in the States, and this will all be behind them. And it's not like Lindsay isn't benefiting—twenty grand is no small amount, after all.

When they arrive at The Regent, Giovanni heads straight through the opulent lobby to the front desk. It's busy despite the late hour.

"What are we doing?" Lindsay asks as they wait for the next available staff person to help them.

"We're getting you a room." When he notices her worried expression, he clarifies, "I'm paying for it, don't worry."

She only nods.

When it's their turn, he tells the clerk he needs a second room for the night. They find her one on the floor above his, but when he takes his credit card out she touches his arm.

"Don't get me a room. I've changed my mind."

"You have?" He sees how the stress of the day is wearing on her. There are shadows below her eyes, strain on her face. His instinct is to fix all this for her somehow.

She smiles with embarrassment. "I don't want my own room."

Her voice is soft, but there's no hint of seduction. It's clear she's feeling vulnerable. He puts his credit card away. "Come on, it's okay. We'll figure it out."

They arrive upstairs and, as always, the room's been freshly cleaned with the bed turned down. Unlike the other night, when she moved around with ease, Lindsay stands there looking awkward.

"You can have a seat," he tells her.

She nods, her movements a bit smoother now as she goes over to sit on the edge of the bed.

Giovanni calls down to housekeeping and tells them he needs someone to come up and get his laundry.

"Do you want to order room service?" he asks her, still holding the phone. "Maybe you should eat."

She shakes her head, but there's a small smile on her face. He suddenly remembers the last time they spent the night together in a hotel and how much they both enjoyed room service.

"I can order a cot brought up too," he offers.

She appears to be thinking something over. "Do you really think the police will come back to my studio and check for fingerprints and hair samples?"

"No." He puts the phone down. "I only said that because I wanted to scare that stupid bastard."

She nods. "Werner's probably still in Berlin though. We could tell the police how he's lying about being in Frankfurt, and they could check his phone records."

"It's worth mentioning."

There's a knock at the door, and he answers it to find the maid from housekeeping. Lindsay rises and takes the canvas bag they offer her for laundry, stuffing it with clothes from her suitcase.

After they leave, she gathers some of her things and tells him she's going to take a shower.

While she's in the bathroom, Giovanni grabs a bottle of water from the mini fridge and stands in front of the large window, gazing out at the picturesque view of Berlin at night.

What a crazy day. But then he's used to crazy days.

There's sexual tension in the air, but he can't tell if it's only coming from him. Fighting this attraction to her is taking a lot of effort.

Fighting an attraction to a woman who will soon be my wife.

The irony isn't lost on him.

He figures he'll call Phillip tomorrow to tell him the good news, and speak with the lawyer to get the wheels rolling for the adoption. He needs to start thinking about his move to Seattle too.

Eventually, the bathroom door opens and Lindsay emerges. Her long dark hair is damp, and her face is scrubbed clean of all makeup. She's wearing a white camisole with pink flowered pajama bottoms. She looks like a college sorority girl. It surprises him. He's not into college girls, but the look is a good one on her. Different than her usual seductress aura.

She comes over to stand beside him, and he still can't take his eyes off her. Without asking, she takes the bottle of water from his hand.

"Appreciating the magnificent view?"

"I am," he says.

She drinks from the bottle and hands it back. Her eyes shine like onyx. Giovanni tries to relax, to ignore the want pulsing through him, his body stirring in reaction to her.

Maybe I should have gotten a second room for myself.

He doesn't want to stare at her in that skimpy top, but he can't seem to stop himself. It certainly isn't hiding much. Her breasts are small and lovely and fit her slender frame perfectly. He tries to remember what her nipples look like, but it's been too long. A flash of memory comes to him where he's licking them, sucking each one in turn, her moaning in his arms.

Jesus.

"So, when do you want to get married?" she asks, gazing out the window, a resigned note in her voice.

"Uh . . ." He licks his lips, momentarily unsteady as he tries to recover from the memory. "I figure I'll arrange everything as soon as possible."

"Are we going to Italy?"

His brows come together. "No, what gives you that impression? I figured we'd go to Las Vegas."

"*What?*" She turns to him, her eyes large. "Why can't we go to Italy? I thought you were Italian."

"It's true I have dual citizenship, but getting married in Italy would take forever."

"Why is that?"

"Because nothing bureaucratic happens quickly in *Roma*. Las Vegas will be much faster. We're both going back to the States anyway."

She's obviously unhappy with this explanation.

"Do you have a problem with Las Vegas?"

She doesn't reply for so long he wonders if she's going to.

"I grew up there," she finally says.

"You did?"

"Yes, remember my father was a professional gambler. We split our time between Reno and Vegas when I was a kid."

"That's right," he murmurs. "Do you still have any family there?"

"No. My dad died, and my mom lives in Arizona with her second husband."

"Las Vegas is our best option."

She still appears unhappy.

"I need to fly to Italy first before we get married," he says. "I have some things to take care of with my apartment. I figure that will give you time to tie up whatever loose ends you have here."

Lindsay doesn't say anything, just gazes out the window.

"Look, I'm sorry about how all this is going down for you. I wouldn't have asked you to do this if I didn't think it very important."

"Why *are* you doing all this?" She turns to him. "I'm sure you want to help, but don't you think this is a bit above and beyond?"

Giovanni considers telling her about the debt he owes Paul, but rejects the idea. "Paul was a close friend, and I want to make sure his kids are safe. I'm lucky to have the opportunity to help."

She studies him. Her expression tells him she suspects there's more to the story, but she doesn't push it. Instead, she leans against the window frame. "Another marriage that ends in divorce. I'll be a three-time loser."

"It's not like it really counts."

"I suppose not." She sighs and glances toward the room. "I'm exhausted. Do you mind if I go to bed now?"

His pulse spikes at her words and his balls tingle. He can't help it. The cobra within him begins to uncoil. "How do you want to handle the sleeping arrangements? Should I call down for a cot?"

She hugs herself and seems embarrassed, just like she was downstairs. "Do you think we could share a bed and not have sex?"

He swallows. "I . . . yes, we could do that."

"I don't want to torture you. It's just that I don't want to be alone. It's been a long day." She takes a deep breath. "An awful day."

The cobra stops completely and Giovanni's pulse slows again. He puts his arm out. "Come here."

She hesitates at first, but then goes to him. Her arms tighten around his waist as she rests her head against his shoulder. He holds her close, stroking her back over the camisole. Her hair is still damp, and its clean scent fills his nostrils.

There's a peculiar tightness in his chest as he comforts her. He suspects Lindsay is seldom vulnerable like this. Such a tough girl, making her own way in the world. It occurs to him that, with her beauty, she could have easily married for money. Plenty of wealthy men would be more than happy to have a woman like Lindsay on their arm, but it's obviously not her style. He can't even imagine her happy in a situation like that.

When they pull apart, she gives him a brief smile and moves to climb into bed.

The sheets rustle behind him. He does his best not to think about her body as he stares out the window again and finishes the last of his water.

It's going to be a long night.

Finally, he tosses the empty container in the trash and goes into the bathroom to change. He usually sleeps in a pair of boxers, but figures he should wear more, so he throws on a white T-shirt from his travel bag.

Leaving the bathroom, the room is dark with only the city lights reflecting off the walls. He makes his way over to the bed and sits on the opposite side from her.

This is where the problem begins.

He already has a hard-on. Like an idiot, he realizes he should have jerked off in the bathroom to take the edge off. He's ready to get up and do just that when she stirs beside him.

"You kept my fox."

He nods, but then realizes she can't see it in the dark. "I did."

"Do you like it?" Her words slur a little—sounding sleepy.

"I like her very much."

"Her?"

"Yes, isn't the fox a girl?"

"I suppose." Lindsay sighs. "You needed her."

He's not sure what she means by that but realizes it's true. Giovanni lets his breath out, closes his eyes. *I need a lot of things.*

Instead of going back to the bathroom, he climbs into bed beside Lindsay. Pulling the duvet up, he tries to pretend this is all normal.

In bed with my future wife.

A surreal thought comes to him where he wonders if this is what it feels like to be in an arranged marriage. He's met plenty of people over the years who are in them, as it's still common in many parts of the world, yet he's never really considered what it must be like.

Marrying someone you barely know.

He closes his eyes and tries not to think about this soft beautiful woman beside him. Figuring he'll be awake all night, he starts going over his schedule for the coming weeks. He hates surprises and always prefers to have a plan, to prepare himself for any contingency.

"Would you mind rubbing my neck again like you did before?" Lindsay asks, her voice breaking his reverie.

Giovanni stiffens, but then he realizes she only wants to be comforted. He rolls on his side toward her. "Are you okay?"

"Not really."

"Lindsay . . ."

"I don't want to talk about it." She changes position so she's on her stomach, her face turned away from him. "That neck thing you did was really good."

He groans to himself. "All right."

Sitting up partway, he brushes her hair to the side and puts his hand to her neck, touching her smooth skin. Her neck muscles are definitely tense, so he begins to massage them again.

Right away, she sighs, and it goes straight to his dick. The scent of her skin, clean and feminine, drifts toward him. His hard-on, which never left, feels like iron now, and he figures he's going to have the worst case of blue balls in the history of man.

He tries to ignore it, concentrating instead on helping her feel better.

"I can't stop thinking about it," she admits after a little while, her voice soft. "Walking into my studio and finding it torn apart. The violence of it."

His jaw clenches as he thinks about how he'd like to tear Werner apart, limb by limb. "I'm sorry you had to experience that."

"My whole life has been turned upside down in one day."

"It's true," he murmurs quietly. "At least you'll have the money from our arrangement."

"It's not the same."

Giovanni nods. It certainly isn't the same for her. He sits up a little more and moves from rubbing her neck to using both hands on her whole back over the camisole. Her breath hitches and unfortunately, the sound only fans the flames, exciting him further.

"I know you don't think much of my playing poker," she goes on. "But there's a reason I worked so hard at it."

"What reason is that?"

She hesitates, but then tells him. "Don't laugh, but I've decided to go back and finish my degree. I just got my acceptance letter before I came here. I want to teach art to high schoolers."

He takes this in as he pulses his fingers down her spine, getting tangled in her top a little. He tries to imagine Lindsay as an art teacher. *Every boy in class will be in love with her.* "It sounds great. How much more schooling do you need?"

"A couple years, plus I'll have to get my teaching certificate."

"That's not too bad."

"I'll still be an artist, but it won't be my only gig."

"What about poker?"

She doesn't reply. Instead she sits up and, to his astonishment, pulls her top off. Still facing away from him, she lies down on her stomach again.

"There," she murmurs. "That should make it easier."

His head swims as he stares at her naked back. *Easier for who?* He swallows hard and tries to calm his lust. His eyes have adjusted to the dark room, and her skin is milky in the light coming through the window.

There are tattoos on her back. He already noticed the one on her right shoulder. It's written in a simple script and says, 'We make our own luck.' There's a lotus flower on her left shoulder and then down near the center of her back, there's an elaborate Queen of Hearts playing card. His fingers go to it, tracing the design. In truth, he has mixed feelings about tattoos, especially when a woman has skin this beautiful. In his professional experience, most people want to remove them.

"Does your Queen of Hearts have special meaning?" he asks, still tracing his fingers over it.

"Strength," she murmurs. "And that I own myself, my own heart."

Giovanni nods, taking this in. He wants to taste her—badly. Finally, he can't resist any longer and leans over, putting his mouth to her smooth skin. He drags his chin, rough with stubble, over the center of the tattoo and is rewarded with a breathy moan from Lindsay.

Taking that as a sign, his hands slide down to grasp her hips. She lifts slightly though and turns, looking at him over her shoulder. "What are you doing? Get back to work."

He chuckles, despite the need pulsing through him. His erection aching and heavy.

When he starts rubbing her back again, she lies down and sighs some more. His breath is becoming erratic. He wants to stop this lust, but it's like a train run off its rails. He keeps stroking her for a little while, trying to convince himself he can enjoy the feel of her skin without wanting more.

But he does want more. A lot more. He wants to lose himself in her. He *needs* it. It's the one thing that will help. He nearly gave in to it earlier—God, he wanted her so badly—but that was before she agreed to marry him.

Now he knows he can't use her like that.

Finally, he stops touching her, pulls away, and swings his legs over the side of the bed, ready to go into the bathroom and take care of this himself. It won't really fix it, but it's better than nothing.

Lindsay sits up too. "I think the last time a guy seduced me with a back rub was high school," she jokes.

He doesn't respond. He wants to joke, but he's far past it. *Guess I really am humorless.*

"Hey." Her voice softens. "Is everything all right?"

He's sitting with his head bent down, forearms resting on his thighs as he tries to gain control over himself. He feels like the worst kind of asshole. He should be comforting her after what she's been through today. *But it turns out I need some comforting of my own.*

She runs her hand down his back and he closes his eyes.

"It's best if you don't touch me," he tells her roughly.

Of course, she doesn't listen. When does she ever? Instead, she scoots closer until he senses her right beside him.

He swallows. "Listen, Lindsay. You should stay away from me. Let's not turn this into something it's not."

"That's what my sister told me, that I should stay away from you. She said she'd heard stories about you from Anthony."

His brows go up. He should be more surprised than he is, but it doesn't matter. He doesn't even have to ask what she's heard. "The stories are true." He licks his lips, and when he speaks, his voice sounds guttural. "The fact is

I'm not always a good man."

She grows still. "Why do you say that?"

He doesn't reply. Doesn't even know how to explain it to her.

"Is it the reason you left me alone in that hotel room after we slept together?" There's an edge to her voice, and he turns to look at her. She's naked from the waist up, and he can't stop himself from being mesmerized.

"Yes." He turns his head away. "That's why."

"I was pissed at you for that. In a way, I still am."

"You should be. I told you before, I'm an arrogant prick."

For some reason, she's stroking his back again. It feels so good he knows he shouldn't stay. He needs to get up, needs to leave this room.

"Tell me why. Is it because you feel trapped?" she asks.

His eyes go to hers. It's dark, but they can see each other well enough. "No, that's not it." And so, against his better judgment, he tries to explain it to her. He explains how, when you live on an adrenaline high for a long time, it can be difficult to come down. "It's different for everyone," he tells her. "Some people smoke or drink. They'll use something artificial to get back to their baseline."

"What do you use?"

He doesn't want to admit it—not to her, not to anyone. He's never admitted it because he's too ashamed. "I think you already know." His eyes find hers again and, to her credit, she doesn't look away. There's comprehension dawning on her face though.

"It's *women*, isn't it?"

He nods. "It is."

Chapter Ten

LINDSAY'S HOUSE RULES

~ Temptation is as sweet as sugar and as sticky as honey. ~

LINDSAY PULLS HER hand away and stops stroking the taut muscles of Giovanni's back. She knows she should listen to him, should stay away. He's right about that.

Too many women fall into the trap of thinking they can fix a man. Her own philosophy has always been that it's better to find one who doesn't need fixing.

Yet, here she is, wavering, ready to swim in that ocean.

It's his genuine smile from earlier, the way it moved her. And those butterflies. Nobody has affected her like this in a long time, and she senses he's more than a match for her.

She thinks about how much it takes to bring a man like Giovanni to his knees. *A lot. It would take a lot.* He must have been pushing himself in ways that were inhuman.

It doesn't change anything about what he's just admitted though.

"It's wrong, what you're doing," she tells him. "Using women like some kind of sexual vampire."

"You think I don't know that? For years, I've been telling myself it's no big deal." He lets out his breath. "But I know it's despicable."

"You need to stop that shit."

He snorts. "Now, why didn't I think of that?"

"Have you ever paid for it?"

"No, of course not."

She watches him closely to see if he's lying. "Why not?"

He smirks without humor. "Despite my apparent undesirability on the marriage market, I've never had any trouble finding bed partners."

"Wouldn't it be simpler to pay someone?" She's still watching him. If he sleeps with hookers, then that's it for her. Game over.

"I've known women who were prostitutes and the abuse that brought them there." He shakes his head. "I could never be a part of that."

"Not all women who do it are abused."

"I worked at a strip club years ago, and a lot of the girls prostituted themselves on the side. I saw enough to know it's not a profession anyone chooses because they enjoy it."

Lindsay is still processing his words. "You worked in a strip club doing what?"

"I was a bouncer."

So it's true what he told Dagmar. But at a strip club? It sounds bizarre and out of character for him. "How old were you?"

"Twenty-one. I dropped out of college for a while. It was right after—" He stops talking abruptly. "Forget it."

"What?"

"Nothing." He shakes his head. "It wasn't a good time in my life. That's all."

"Did you sleep with the strippers?"

"No, I just told you."

She tries to imagine Giovanni at twenty-one. Handsome, cocky, and probably irresistible. "I doubt they would have charged you anyway."

"It didn't matter. I wasn't interested in any of them." He grows quiet. "That's all in the past now. It was a long time ago."

Lindsay wants to hear the rest of this story, but there's finality in his tone, and she already knows how difficult it is to get information out of him when he doesn't want to give it.

He's still quiet. The discussion must have brought up bad memories for him.

"When you first mentioned working in a strip club, I thought maybe you were a dancer," she teases, hoping to lighten his mood.

His eyes flash to hers. "What?"

Giovanni's a big guy, and graceful too, but she can't picture him dancing. She remembers how they first met at an after-party that had a DJ, how he stood off to the side with his hands tucked into the front of his jeans, watching her dance.

"You know, like those 'Thunder from Down Under' guys."

His eyes widen. "You're kidding. You thought I *danced?*"

"Sure, why not? You have a great body."

And then, to her surprise, he bursts out laughing. Full on laughter like she's never heard from him before. It's infectious, and she can't help but join in.

"Jesus, you have no idea . . ." He finally calms down, wiping his eyes. "Try to picture Frankenstein's monster having a seizure. Because that's what I look like when I dance."

"Really?" Lindsay laughs some more. "Sounds kind of hot."

"It's mostly disturbing. People usually think I need medical attention."

"Come on, I can't believe it's that bad. You have such a graceful walk."

"Yes, thank God I can handle *walking*, at least."

"Does that mean you won't dance for *me*?" She allows her voice to take on a seductive note.

He hears it too. She sees how his body stills, the way his eyes go to hers.

She's already made the decision. It was up for debate when she came here tonight, but now it's certain. Seeing her fox on his nightstand was the first thing that swayed her. Then it was the way his hands felt on her skin, the warmth of them burning through all the stress of the day until there was nothing left but ashes.

That's why she pulled her top off.

So, despite everything—the warning bells clanging in her ears, the crazy shit he just admitted to her about himself—she's diving into those waters again.

He shakes his head. "We both know this is a bad idea. You don't want this. Not really."

"But I do."

"You'd let me use you like that?"

She wonders who's using who though. "Despite your overbearing personality, I happen to find you very sexy. I even fantasized about you."

"You did?"

"Yes, I used you as vibrator fodder."

"Is that so?" he murmurs. His voice has grown huskier, and she can tell his body is onboard even if his brain hasn't caught up yet. "You may have to explain what that means in more detail."

"I could do that." She slides her hand down his back, stroking him again, watching as he closes his eyes. "Have you fantasized about me at all?"

"Too many times to count."

She figured he had, but it's always nice to hear these things. "What's your favorite fantasy about me?"

He opens his eyes, his expression thoughtful. "What am I going to do with you?"

She smiles. "I have some ideas."

"Seriously, I can't offer you anything. You know that, right?"

"Just don't vanish on me," she tells him quietly. "That's all I ask. I don't want to wake up alone tomorrow."

He licks his lips. "I wouldn't do that."

"But you *did.*"

"We're getting married, remember? I can't."

She rolls her eyes. "Ugh, don't remind me."

Giovanni grins. "I've never met a woman like you before. In fact, I've never met *anyone* like you before."

"That's most certainly true."

He reaches out and touches her hair. "It's like unwrapping a beautiful gift only to find there's another gift inside, one that's even more lovely and unique."

Lindsay stops breathing. Her eyes sting, and she looks away.

"Do you really want to know one of my fantasies?" he asks.

She nods, still trying to pull herself together.

He shifts on the bed. "Come here and stand in front of me."

She rises to her feet, does as he asks, and stands between his open thighs.

"God, yes," he murmurs, his hands sliding over her body. "That's perfect."

He grasps her hips. She's shirtless but still has on her pajama bottoms. His arms wrap around to bring her closer, pressing her against him. She runs her fingers through his short golden waves, inhaling the light scent of hotel shampoo. He's solid muscle all over, but his hair is remarkably soft.

He continues to hug her tightly, the side of his face against her breasts. And that's all he appears to want.

The intimacy of holding her.

Minutes go by, and they remain this way, her throat tightening as she strokes his hair. Her hands glide down to his shoulders. It's like they've done this a thousand times—the warrior home from his battle at long last. But then she remembers that Giovanni doesn't really have a home, not in any true sense.

"How long has it been since you were with someone?" Lindsay asks softly, curious.

"Eight months."

Her eyes widen. "That's a long time."

"I know. I've been trying to change my ways." He pulls back a little and puts his mouth to her skin, kissing the space between her breasts. "To stop being—how did you put it? A sexual vampire."

"By going celibate?"

"I didn't know what else to do." His hands slide around to cup each breast, caressing, and molding. "Guess I'm all about extremes."

His voice is rough, breathing harsh, as he drags his thumbs across each of her nipples. Finally, he takes one in his mouth, gently sucking.

Her breath catches. With every flick of his tongue, there's a pulse between her legs.

He continues licking and suckling her, single-minded about his task. Desire floods her veins like warm water, and she's amazed at how good it feels. It's been too long since she's felt this way. Sensual and alive.

He draws back from her breast and immediately wants her mouth, bringing her to him then kissing her in a slow, involved way.

When they draw apart, their breath mingles. She senses he's trying to pace himself, how he's struggling with it.

The need coming off him is like some kind of erotic perfume, impossible to resist. She can't believe he hasn't had a lover in so long. And then there's the knowledge that she's the one who broke him.

Lindsay likes that too much, even if she shouldn't.

She decides to take the reins and goes down on her knees in front of him. Giovanni tries to stop her, but she ignores him. "Let me do this for you" is all she says.

His eyes stay on her, dark and absorbing. She sees the desire, but the vulnerability too. His mouth opens and he shakes his head, but it's not because he doesn't want what she's offering.

"Take your shorts off," she tells him.

He pauses for a second then wordlessly stands and strips off his T-shirt first, then his boxers. She admires his powerful body, runs her hands down the length of it. Especially those muscular thighs—such perfection. She grips each one, wanting to take a bite, but figures she'll save that for later.

His erection is large, jutting out in front of him. He sits down on the bed again, but she doesn't reach for it yet. It pokes against her when she moves closer to put her mouth on his chest, his skin salty beneath her tongue. She goes to each pebbled peak and does what he did to her, gently suckling and pulling.

His breath goes ragged as he slips his hand in her hair, fingers kneading her scalp.

After a short while, he urges her back up. "Kiss me again," he murmurs, his voice a low rumble. His mouth on hers is deliberately sensual as their tongues slide over each other's.

They're still kissing when she reaches down for his cock. He freezes. She's ready to pull away with concern, but then he groans into her mouth—a rough sound between desperation and relief.

A wave of protectiveness washes over Lindsay. She may be the one on her knees, but he's the one at her mercy. A heady thrill with any man, but especially one like Giovanni, and she doesn't want to abuse her power.

She continues to stroke his erection. He's big, just like she remembers. Not scary big, but long, plump, and currently hard as steel.

"Do you want me to blow you?" she asks, licking her lips, already totally turned on. She knows he wants her to, but she's always enjoyed a little dirty talk.

His mouth opens, though no words come out. Apparently, he's beyond speech. His eyes, half-lidded, are so glazed with lust she can see it even in the darkened room.

She's still using her hand with a loose grip. Finally, she tightens her fingers, leans forward, and goes down on him while his breath comes out in a long hiss.

His body tenses, a sheen of sweat developing on his skin as she uses her lips, tongue, and a slight grazing of teeth on his shaft. After a short while, she looks up at him and smiles. "Say, 'Yes, Lindsay, I want you to suck my cock.'"

"Jesus . . ." Giovanni shudders.

She lowers her voice provocatively. "Say, 'I love the hot, wet feel of your mouth.'"

He swallows, closes his eyes again, and licks his lips. It appears he's trying to gain some measure of control. "This is going to last two seconds if you keep that up."

She lets out a shaky breath of her own. His excitement is turning her on more than anything. "We have all night, don't we?"

He nods. "But I'd like to survive it."

"Listen to you," she says, squeezing the plump head, rewarded with a bit of moisture. "Making jokes in the heat of passion."

He emits a deep growl. "Come here . . . right now." He drags her up to him even though she protests.

"But I want to suck your—" He cuts her words off, devouring her, his fingers holding her still for him as he kisses her deeply.

Ohmigod.

His arousal is having a powerful effect, her control slipping as he pulls her out with him, far away from the shallow water and into the deepest part of the ocean.

"I'm taking over now," he mutters, tugging her hair to give him access to her neck where he gently bites, licking her afterward like a real vampire.

This time, she's the one who shudders.

"Get on the bed," he tells her.

Lindsay pulls back but doesn't go anywhere.

He puts his hand to her jaw, meets her eyes. "Please."

"The magic word," she murmurs.

She climbs onto the bed again, his hands still on her like he doesn't want to lose contact, and lies down on her back.

He shifts onto his knees as his warm hands continue to stroke her breasts. The city lights reflect on his face, and Lindsay watches his fierce expression as he caresses her. His eyes roaming over her like she's the first woman he's ever seen. It's all so good—unlike anything, and she wonders if there's something to the notion of a person with healing hands.

"There are a lot of doctors in your family, aren't there?" Lindsay remembers it from Natalie and Anthony's wedding, how many of his relatives were physicians or did something in the medical field.

Giovanni's breath is steadier now that he's in charge. "Yes, especially my dad's family. Why do you ask?"

"It's your hands." She smiles a little, embarrassed to admit it. "They're so soothing. I wonder if it's like a talent or something, to have a healing touch."

"Probably." He doesn't say anything more on the subject, and she can tell he's too distracted by her body. His fingers hook into the sides of her pajama bottoms. "Let's take these off."

She lifts a little, and he pulls off both her bottoms and panties at the same time, tossing them aside. When she relaxes again, his hand is on her hip before it glides down to her legs. "You're so soft," he murmurs, letting his fingers lightly graze her skin. "Everywhere . . . so soft."

Her breath comes out in a shaky rush when he slips a hand between her thighs. He groans with approval when his fingers gently slide to where she's wet and ready for him.

She grasps his forearm, watching him through slitted eyes as he strokes her very core.

Giovanni brings the fingers that were touching her to his mouth and closes his eyes. He seems mesmerized by the taste.

"You should kiss my pussy, lick me," she suggests, hooking her leg around his hip to draw him closer. "It's one of my fantasies."

He grins a little. "Mine too."

But he doesn't go down on her, simply continues caressing her skin. His fingers trail down her legs, then up her inner thigh as she squirms with anticipation. Despite his obvious excitement, it's clear he's pacing himself—a man savoring the experience.

Finally, he changes position and lies down on top of her so they're face to face. The hard column of his erection pressing into her stomach, she shifts a bit before wrapping her arms around his neck.

"Am I crushing you?" he asks with concern.

"No." He's heavy, but she doesn't mind. "I like it."

Giovanni brings his thigh up and presses it against her center. And then he starts kissing her again, one hand tangled in her hair, kneading her scalp. Each kiss is long and sinful, slowly fucking her mouth with his own. She can't remember ever being kissed like this as he goes back and forth between her mouth and neck, drugging her with his essence.

Occasionally, he tells her how she's beautiful, how much he wants her.

Lindsay's breath shakes. She doesn't know how to respond. It's too much. All this kissing and whispering is doing dangerous things to her. It's turning her on, but it's turning her inside out.

Her head swims and her stomach quivers, yet her whole body feels lighter and more alive. She's worried, though, worried her own need has grown stronger than his. Her hips move, and she wraps a leg around him as she keeps trying to reach down for his cock, but he won't let her touch him.

She's going out of her mind, and it gets even worse because he starts whispering in Italian. Finally, she pushes against his shoulders. "Can't you just fuck me? I'm going crazy."

His response is some kind of rumble deep in his throat, which she's certain is a chuckle. But then he rolls onto his back, bringing her with him.

"Let me take care of you," he murmurs. "Come up and sit on my face."

She doesn't need to be told twice as she scoots up and maneuvers herself over him. She doesn't face the wall, instead turning outward with plans of her own.

He grasps her hips, positioning her, and as soon as she feels his mouth and tongue, her eyes fall shut. The pleasure is over-the-top, and she simply allows herself to enjoy it.

Giovanni is good. Her favorite kind of man—the kind who loves oral sex. She remembers it from last time. He's deliberate and patient, and she has the distinct sense he's enjoying it as much as she is.

It doesn't take long before the first glimmer of ecstasy arrives. Lindsay has been blessed with the ability to come easily and often, so she's tempted to hold back before lowering her body over his, before taking his cock in her mouth. But she doesn't, and instead his musky scent surrounds her.

Sixty-nine.

It's been ages since she's done it, but now she wonders why she ever stopped because it's the perfect symphony of intimate and dirty.

He groans when she grabs him. "Wait," he gasps, trying to stop her.

But she doesn't want to wait. She wants him to join her on this merry-go-round, so she gives him her best effort. It's happening fast, but somewhere amid all the lust her chest goes tight, and a funny emotion takes hold of her—tenderness, of all things. Tenderness toward Giovanni. It surprises her and she realizes it's the same as when he gave her that smile earlier. She closes her eyes and gives in, lets it flood through her right before her orgasm explodes and she's out of control.

A second later, his powerful body trembles beneath her. His erection grows harder and larger as he grips her ass, groaning like he's still trying to fight it. But then he loses the battle, lost in ecstasy.

Afterward, Lindsay lies on top of him, resting her head on his thigh. "My God, I think I'm in love with you," she breathes.

He sighs deeply, chuckling a little as he tries to catch his own breath. "Me too," he jokes as both his hands slide down her body.

She swallows, tries to make sense of her feelings. The problem is she's not joking.

Chapter Eleven

**~ A beautiful smile and a big cock.
You'd be surprised how far that can take you. ~**

HOW IS THIS possible? Lindsay wonders. *It can't be real.*

She can't be in love with Giovanni because she barely even knows him.

He hands her the box of tissues from the nightstand. She sits up, cleaning herself off before turning around to lie down beside him once more. As soon as she sees his handsome face and that lazy grin, a happy sensation washes over her—tenderness, excitement, and familiarity all rolled into one.

Something that feels an awful lot like love.

This isn't happening.

'The heart wants what it wants.' It's a saying she's heard over the years, but has always dismissed as nonsense because her own heart has only wanted what she's told it to—and it's always followed directions perfectly.

So, why is it misbehaving now?

Especially for someone with Giovanni's kind of issues. That's the last thing she needs. Handling men is one of her special talents. She's seldom burned by them because she's always long gone before things get complicated.

"Hey, is everything all right?" He studies her, too perceptive for his own good. "Why are you staring at me like that?"

"I'm not staring at you."

"Yes, you are. You look pissed. Did I do something wrong?"

She snorts.

He licks his lips and lowers his voice. "I mean, I know that was quick, but I told you how it's been a while for me. I'm surprised I lasted as long as I did."

She rolls her eyes. "Forget it. I don't care about that."

"I tried to stop you from going down on me, but I'm only human."

"I told you I don't care. I did it on purpose. I wanted you to come when I did."

His lazy grin is gone and she's sorry to see it go. Instead, he's wearing his usual tense expression. "What's wrong, then?"

She rolls away from him and onto her back, staring up at the ceiling. "I think I've fallen in love with you." The words sound absurd, and she's not sure why she's telling him. Probably because she knows he'll talk her out of it.

"Is that right," he responds. "Look, Lindsay, I don't think my ego requires this much stroking, though I appreciate the effort."

"I'm not trying to stroke your stupid ego!" She glares over at him, but unfortunately, he's so appealing she turns away again. "You think you know everything better than anybody else, so why the hell would I bother stroking your ego?"

"So, you're telling me you're in love with me for real?" His tone is heavy with disbelief.

"Yes, I'm serious."

He chuckles.

"Is this how you always act when a woman says she's in love with you?"

"Come on, we barely even know each other. There's no way you're in love with me."

Lindsay likes what she's hearing and rolls back toward him. "I know, it's impossible, right?"

"I have to admit we have great chemistry, but it's only lust."

She grins. "Lust I can handle. I enjoy lust."

"Powerful lust." He draws her closer. Their eyes meet and they're gazing at each other. Giovanni smiles that crazy-beautiful smile, and her insides go quivery again.

"You've been through a lot today," he murmurs, stroking her back. "Anybody would be feeling emotional after what happened."

She nods. "You're right, that must be it." Of course, these feelings came on before the robbery, but she decides to keep that to herself, figuring maybe she's just confusing things. "Have you ever been in love?" she asks instead.

His breath stops and the hand caressing her back slows. It only lasts a second, but a second is long enough.

"Yes," he finally admits. His fingers begin lightly drifting down her spine again. "A long time ago."

"Who was she?"

He shakes his head. "No one important. What about you? Have you ever been in love?"

"Of course. I've been married twice."

"And you loved them?"

"I think so." Lindsay is trying to remember if she had these same tender, stomach-quivering feelings for either of her ex-husbands, and what's strange is she's not sure. She certainly cared for them, especially her first husband. "My first husband I definitely loved."

He seems to find her answer amusing. "You don't sound entirely certain."

"It was like ten years ago. I was really young."

"Why did you get divorced?"

"He was a musician and I kept worrying he would cheat on me."

"Did he?"

"No." She thinks back to those early days of her marriage to Josh. All the fanfare. His band started getting more attention, and there were always girls hanging around.

"How long were you married?"

"A little over a year, though we were together for a couple of years. The breakup was my fault. I just couldn't handle being married, so I ended it." Every time Josh was out late with band rehearsals or went on tour, she worried he'd cheat on her. It was like a strange kind of madness possessed her. She knows he never did, but she couldn't get past it. In the end, Josh begged her to stay, but they were trying to have a baby, and when she couldn't get pregnant, she took it as a sign.

"What about the second husband?"

"He was sort of a mistake. It only lasted a few months. I ended that one too." She married him on the rebound, a fellow artist she met in class. She tried to get pregnant with him as well, and that's when she finally went to the doctor. They couldn't find anything wrong with her at the time, though she eventually discovered she was infertile.

"Hmm, I think I'm seeing a pattern here. What about other relationships?"

"There have been a few . . . more than a few," she admits. "I'm not cut out for long-term commitment."

Giovanni watches her, considering her words. "Not exactly a great track record you have there."

"Give me a break. This from a guy who uses women like an addict searching for his next fix?"

He frowns then stops touching her, rolls onto his back, and goes silent.

Lindsay realizes she shouldn't have been so blunt. It's a character flaw she's always struggled with a bit. Despite everything, she's curious about him. His brother, Anthony, seems fairly well-adjusted, so she can't understand why Giovanni turned out the way he did.

Minutes go by and still he doesn't say anything.

"Did I offend you?" she finally asks.

"No."

She puts her hand on his arm. "Then tell me something. Why are you so screwed up?"

He closes his eyes. "I don't think the parents of the children whose lives I've helped change would say I'm screwed up."

She quiets at that. It's true. In fact, she's certain the parents of those children include him in their prayers of gratitude every night. "I'm not talking about them. I'm talking about *you*."

"I don't want to discuss any of this." His voice has that brisk note of finality she's come to recognize from him. He rolls back toward her and draws her close. "Do you know what I've missed the most about sex?"

"Lovers who ask a lot of nosy questions?"

He smirks for a second, but then his gaze softens. "Kissing."

"Mmm, I could tell." She licks her lips.

"And the taste of a woman's skin." He brings his mouth to her throat, tasting her.

Her breath hitches.

"Your scent is incredible," he whispers in her ear. "And you're right. It is like a drug."

"What else do you miss?"

He pulls back and looks into her face. "Do you really want to know?"

"I do." Her breath is coming faster now. "I want to know everything." She slides one hand down to grip his firm ass.

His expression changes, goes hungry, and his only answer is his mouth on hers, his large body pressing her into the mattress. She knows he's changing the subject, but decides to let him because this is the kind of subject change she doesn't mind at all.

I never should have told her. The thought rings through Giovanni's mind like an alarm bell. *That was a mistake.*

There's no room for mistakes in his life, and he's not used to making any.

He's still not sure what possessed him to tell Lindsay one of his deepest, most shameful secrets. He assumed it would push her away, but instead it appears to have drawn her in and now she's like a dog with a bone.

The truth is he shouldn't be in bed with her at all. *After eight months, it's only one slip*. And Lindsay is going to be his wife soon—however temporary.

He knows he's rationalizing, grasping for any reason to make this right because he wanted her from the moment he laid eyes on her. He knew she'd be exactly what he needed, and he was right. Energetic and lusty with just the right amount of seductive allure. He's always enjoyed bed partners who were confident in their sexuality.

He was surprised when she came up with the whole business about being in love with him though. At first, he thought it was her strange sense of humor because he honestly never knows what's going to come out of her mouth, and then he thought she was trying to manipulate him. When it dawned on him she was serious, he knew it was the shock of being robbed today and felt guilty for taking advantage of the situation.

Not that he's planning to stop now because he's past the point of no return. It's like being thrown a lifeline after months at sea. She tastes too good. Feels too good. He can already tell it's helping him shake off the adrenaline.

She breaks the kiss but doesn't move away, instead licks the corners of his mouth. "I like these—each little dip."

He's not sure what she's talking about but enjoys her tongue lapping at him like a cat.

"Mmm . . ." She licks him some more. "You have such sensual lips."

He feels oddly flattered. Women mostly compliment him on his size—especially his height, and then his dick when they finally see it. Which is apparently Lindsay's next stop as her hand slides down his chest, over his stomach, and lower until she's grabbed hold of him. Hard and heavy as stone again. He lets her handle him this time. She kept trying to reach for him earlier, but his control was on a hair trigger.

"Such a big, hard cock," she whispers. "Is it all for me?"

He closes his eyes as blood surges through him. Maybe that hair trigger isn't so far off.

Giovanni pulls her hand away. When she tries to reach for him again, he laces their fingers and brings their hands up near her face.

"Here's what going to happen, Lindsay. I'm going to kiss you for a nice, long while because it pleases me. Then I'm going to fuck you." Her eyes light up and her breath trembles. "But only if you're good and stop all this dirty talk. Understand?"

"God, you're a control freak."

"I haven't had sex in eight months, so you need to give me a break here."

"What's wrong with a little dirty talk?" She slides her free hand down to his ass. "It's nice to get things heated up."

He snorts. "Things are heated up enough, trust me. I'd rather not embarrass myself any further."

"You didn't embarrass yourself. Plus, you just came."

He doesn't say anything. He knows he just came, but it barely made a dent. He's already getting way too aroused.

"I'll do it on one condition." She gives him a little smile.

"What's that?"

"I want to take over."

It figures. "We can't both be in charge."

"I know, so let me have my way with you. I've still got all those vibrator fantasies I want to live out."

He has to admit he's curious about these fantasies of hers. Their eyes meet and he feels her leg slip behind his thigh. She's soft and inviting, and a part of him wants to take her right now, though at this rate he'd probably last two seconds.

"All right." He sighs. "We'll try it your way and see how it goes."

She gives him a wicked look, and he wonders what exactly it is he's agreeing to. "Lie on your back," she tells him.

Giovanni releases her hand and rolls over, trying to avoid jostling the mattress too much with his large body. When he's lying flat, he reaches back and tucks a pillow behind his head.

She's sitting back with her legs tucked under her, waiting patiently.

He decides to attempt a joke. "What now, mistress?"

Lindsay laughs then gives him another wicked look. Her long brown curls tumble forward, blocking his view of her body as she kneels before him. When he moves to brush her hair back, she stops him. "You don't get to touch me."

"*What?*" He goes still with surprise. "What do you mean?"

"I mean, that's part of my fantasy. No touching allowed until I tell you."

"There's no way I'm agreeing to that."

"You said you'd give it a try."

"Well, forget it." He softens his voice and slides his hands down her hip. "Come on, Lindsay. I have to be able to touch you."

She leans closer until she's hovering right above him. Her hair falls softly against his face, her feminine scent drifting over him, sweet and musky. "Just relax," she whispers in his ear. "I promise you'll like it."

"I don't believe this," he mutters, as she reaches down and grabs both his hands, placing them over his head.

"Don't make me tie you up." She eyes him with a playful gleam.

"You think I'd let you?"

"Yes, I do."

He takes in her lively expression. She's right. He would let her tie him up. To be honest, he'd probably let her do anything to him she wanted. It's becoming apparent how beauty is the least of her charms. He's never been involved with an artist before and has to admit he enjoys her offbeat way of seeing the world.

"Close your eyes," she tells him.

He does as she asks.

"Keep them shut, no peeking." Lindsay climbs off the bed, and he wonders what she's up to. He hears her go into the bathroom and turn on the tap.

She's in there for a short while before there are sounds from the mini fridge. Giovanni can't resist smiling to himself and with amazement realizes he's having fun.

He hears her feet padding softly on the carpet as she moves closer. "I'm impressed by how well you're following instructions," she tells him, getting back onto the bed. "I wasn't sure if you could do it."

Not only is he having fun, but all this subterfuge is turning him on. Maybe there's something to the notion of letting someone else take over occasionally.

"For that, you get a little reward." Suddenly, Lindsay is above him. He senses her body and then her mouth is on his, kissing him. Their tongues slide over each other's in a sensual dance.

When she breaks away, he opens his eyes, gazing up at her.

"Hey, no peeking." Her voice is breathy, mouth still open. A warm feeling glides through him as he remembers that this is her fantasy about *him*.

He starts to reach for her but manages to stop himself in time. "It's hard to keep my hands still."

"Relax," she says softly. "Let someone take care of you for a change."

He blinks, his throat going tight as her words sink in. He can't remember the last time someone offered to take care of him. For an instant, his body tenses with adrenaline, ready to dismiss all this as nonsense. *I don't need anybody to take care of me.*

But he knows it's a lie. One he's been living with for a long time.

Giovanni closes his eyes again.

He lets himself give in to Lindsay and all her seductive ways. Her mouth glides down to his throat then his chest, playing with his nipples for a while, using her mouth and fingers, before moving lower. Her hands caress him everywhere. All the while, there's this strange energy coursing through him, pooling in the pit of his stomach. It's mostly pleasurable, but there's an edge to it he doesn't understand.

She pushes his legs apart and moves between them, biting his left thigh hard enough to make him groan. It should disturb him, but it's turning him on even more.

Lindsay moves away for a moment and takes something from the nightstand. He hears liquid sounds and then her hand is on his cock, grasping him, fingers pulling on his length in a way that means business.

When she finally puts her mouth on him, it's warm—hot, actually—and it takes him a second to realize she's heated it. He thinks back to the tap he heard running in the bathroom. *So Lindsay is an artist in more ways than one.* The sensation is incredible, and he's trapped by the eroticism as she takes over, giving him head with her hot mouth, his whole body trembling.

He's on the verge of stopping her, worried he's going to explode, but then she pulls back, and he feels cool air on his dick.

There's panting sounds in the room, like some kind of beast, and it's him. He swallows, tries to calm down. His arms are still above his head, gripping the smooth wooden headboard.

But then her mouth is on him again, except this time it's ice-cold.

He startles. Hisses. The sensation unreal. He opens his eyes to watch her. The way she's bent over him, moving up and down with her mouth and hand. Lindsay cups his balls with her other hand—also icy.

"Jesus . . ." More than anything, he wants to touch her. He's relieved when he reaches down, and she doesn't stop him from sliding his hand beneath her hair, lightly rubbing the back of her neck.

She takes another drink from a bottle, swishing it through her mouth before going down. It's hot and he sucks in his breath. "This is . . . incredible," he manages between gasps.

She gives him a seductive smile. "I told you you'd like it."

He nods, and there's something about her expression. He can't pull his eyes away. What she's doing is base and earthy, but he can see on her face it's more than that for her, and he realizes she's doing exactly what she said she would.

She's taking care of me.

His breath shakes, and it's not just from the blow job.

Lindsay looks up again. Their eyes stay on each other for a long moment, and his whole body feels lighter. His heart pounds. "Come here." Giovanni reaches for her shoulders to bring her closer.

She rises and climbs over him, but halts at his groin and puts a knee on each side to straddle him.

It's not what he meant, but he isn't stopping her either. He doesn't want to stop her. He grasps her hips and his body tenses as she takes hold of him again, lowering herself.

"Lindsay," he breathes. His eyes fall shut against his will. He wants her so badly that he's grateful. *So damn grateful.*

She sinks onto him and slowly starts to move, and already he's losing himself. The sensations overtake him fast, like quicksand, until he's fully immersed and in over his head.

It goes on and on, the two of them together. His control balanced on the edge of a blade, Lindsay's allure so powerful as she leans over, riding him, her hair in his mouth, her scent on his skin. He can't get enough. She's noisy, gasping and moaning, but then puts her mouth close to his, sharing the same breath.

"Fuck me hard," she begs.

Her words are lightning and, for a moment, he's blinded. He growls as something primal takes hold, and in one fluid movement, he flips her so she's beneath him. A part of him is still careful, mindful of her. But it's obvious she doesn't want him careful, doesn't want him mindful, so he gives her exactly what she does want.

He fucks her hard.

Sweat breaks out on his back as he grabs one of her thighs and pushes it high. Her hands grip his shoulders then move down to scratch his back, but through the haze of hard lust, the whole time he's still aware of one simple thing.

The wonder of Lindsay—her unique magic.

And, for a split second, he opens himself to it, lets his heart experience her.

And that's when he understands the edge he's been avoiding this whole time because it slams down like a metal gate. A steel prison. He wants to fight it, but he doesn't know how, so he does exactly what he's been doing for years—the only thing left.

He stays locked inside.

It's still night, but Lindsay can see the barest hint of orange in the dark sky from their hotel room window.

"How old are you?" Giovanni asks, his voice a low rumble.

She's lying with her head on his chest, the rhythmic thump of his heart beneath her. She can't remember the last time she had sex like that, where she wanted to give so much of herself. It frightened her a little.

"Thirty-three."

"I should have known," he mutters. His words trail off. "You're the same age."

"As who?"

His breathing is slow and deep, and she can tell he's falling asleep. The exhaustion coming off him in waves.

"Who am I the same age as?"

"No one . . ." His words slur into sleep. "Forget it."

Her spidey senses tell her otherwise, and she can't let it go. "Were you in love with her?"

"Yes."

"Are you still?"

"No."

There's a twinge of jealousy, but she's more interested in the facts. "Do you still see her?"

Seconds pass. He's quiet, breathing deeply, and she figures he's fallen asleep.

"She's dead."

Her breath stops. It's not what she expected, and she feels bad for bringing it up at all. "I didn't know. I'm sorry."

He doesn't say anything more. She figures he really is asleep this time, but he's not. When he speaks, there's a bitter note in his voice, one she doesn't understand.

"Don't be."

Chapter Twelve

~ Never trust a man unless he's already taken a bullet for you. ~

LINDSAY SLEEPS HARD like she's in a coma. The sun shining through the window with bright intensity is what eventually wakes her up. It takes her a moment to orient herself, but then it all comes back in a crazed downpour—the robbery, the marriage agreement, and finally the night of all-consuming sex with Giovanni.

She rolls over, her thighs aching a little, but discovers he's not there beside her. The bed is empty. Lindsay listens to the quiet of the hotel room. There's nothing. She jerks into a sitting position, her eyes scanning for any sign of him. A sick feeling swims through her gut because she already knows the truth.

He's done it to her again.

"Son of a bitch!" She throws the duvet off and gets out of bed naked.

She strides over to check the bathroom and, of course, all his stuff is gone. She jerks open the wardrobe then slams it shut. Empty. No sign of his travel bag or clothes. He's left nothing behind. Not a single thing.

"That sneaky motherfucker!"

She can't believe he actually did it. Not after last night, not after everything that happened. She glances over at the digital clock, and that's when she sees something on the desk. It's a note along with both a credit card and the room's key card. Picking it up, she sees his handwriting, a messy right-angled scrawl:

Lyndsey,

I didn't want to wake you. I'm setting things in motion for our marriage. Use the credit card for whatever expenses you require. The room is paid for three more nights.

G.

She looks down at the credit card. *That bastard.* Her eyes sting. She takes a deep breath and pushes away any thought of crying, annoyed at her own weakness.

This one is on me. I should have known better. My reward for being stupid and believing him.

Anger grips her as she studies the Visa card with 'Giovanni Novello' typed in raised letters. She wonders what his credit limit is and decides her first purchase will be a mink coat and a diamond ring from the KaDeWe, both of which she'll give to charity. Better yet, she'll just make a hefty donation directly to her favorite kid's charity.

There's a telephone number scrawled beneath his 'G' signature. She walks over and picks up the receiver from the hotel phone on the nightstand, punching in the number.

It rings, and to her surprise, Giovanni answers right away with an officious sounding, *"Pronto."*

A peculiar longing washes over her at the sound of his voice, which pisses her off even more. She's still holding the note in her hand. "You spelled my name wrong, asshole."

"What? Who is this?"

"It's Lindsay! Who else would it be?"

"Of course." She hears the phone jostling. "There's too much noise here. I was expecting my cousin."

"Where the fuck are you?"

"I'm at the airport. My flight to *Roma* leaves soon."

Lindsay takes this in with amazement. "You're flying to Rome today and you didn't think to mention it to me? I woke up alone in this fucking hotel room, with your fucking credit card to keep me company!"

"Calm down. You were sleeping so hard I didn't want to wake you."

"Don't tell me to calm down you uppity McFuck! What is the one thing I asked of you? Do you fucking remember?"

"Stop swearing so much."

Despite the reprimand in his voice, Lindsay can tell he's in great spirits. And why shouldn't he be? He got laid fantastically last night. *I should be in great spirits too, and I would be if he hadn't abandoned me.* "I'm pissed off at you, so I'll fucking swear as much as I fucking want. Got it?"

She hears what sounds like Giovanni chuckling.

"Donkey dick, motherfucker," she mutters.

There's a choking noise before he bursts out laughing.

"You think this is funny, asshole?"

He's still laughing.

"Fuck you!"

"God." He chuckles some more, but then sighs. "I think I already miss you, Lindsay."

She feels herself soften a little. "Why the hell did you leave without saying good-bye, then? I told you I didn't want to wake up alone."

He doesn't reply for a few seconds. "I had a plane to catch."

"You're lying." Her bullshit detector swings to the red zone. "Don't lie to me. At least tell me the truth."

She hears hesitation on his end, and then, "I am telling you the truth."

"No, you're not. You think I can't tell when someone is bullshitting me? You didn't even have a flight planned today."

"Look, I just—" Giovanni's voice cuts out. "—such a big deal about it."

"What? I can't hear you." There's some kind of background speaker announcement, but then the line breaks up again. "Are you still there?"

"I have to . . . flight boarding now. I'll talk to you later."

The line goes silent and Lindsay grits her teeth. A strong desire to rip the hotel phone out of the wall and throw it across the room comes over her. *Maybe I'll get lucky and it'll break something, and they'll have to charge Giovanni for the repairs.*

Instead, she puts the receiver back and goes to grab the clean laundry she spies by the front door. The maid must have brought it this morning while she was still asleep.

She pulls out some clean clothes then takes a long, hot shower. Her whole body aches, but in a good way. The kind of ache that comes from a long night of kick-ass sex. She tries not to think about it, but can't stop the images and sensations flooding over her. The way his hands felt. The way he hated breaking visual and physical contact with her. She saw how he struggled with it, and it moved her beyond words.

And then that strange conversation later. He'd been in love with someone who died? Is that what's at the heart of all his issues?

But then she thinks about how he abandoned her and decides—who cares? Fuck Giovanni. Would it have been so difficult to wake her and tell her he was leaving? That he had decided to fly to Rome today?

Not to mention the way he left that credit card.

Payment for services rendered.

She knows it isn't like that, and she wanted him just as much as he wanted her, but it stings nevertheless. She may be accepting that twenty grand, but she needs that money for tuition. It's not for anything else.

I'm nobody's whore.

After her shower, Lindsay gets dressed and packs her suitcase with all the clean clothes, grateful Werner's rat germs have been exterminated. She wishes she could find that slimy thief and get her money back. By now, he's probably left the city for real.

I'll be leaving soon too.

It's less than a week before she flies back to the States. She has to admit she'll miss Berlin. Her stay has certainly been memorable. Dagmar is planning a good-bye dinner party for her on Saturday, her last one.

Lindsay finishes putting on makeup then stuffs her toiletries into her suitcase. She's tempted to take a cab back to her studio and charge it to Giovanni's credit card, but has decided not to use it at all—except for that hefty charitable donation, of course.

Instead, she pulls her rolling suitcase behind her, wrestling it onto the S-Bahn.

When she finally makes it back to her studio, she's surprised to discover the lock on her door has already been replaced. Her landlord must have had a fire lit beneath him.

After retrieving her new key, she spends the rest of the day cleaning up the mess from the robbery, her heart weighing heavy the whole time. It was a lousy way to leave a city that's become like a second home to her. She's even grateful Giovanni forced her to go sightseeing with him.

If he'd stayed longer, she could have shown him her version of Berlin—the art galleries, both ancient and modern. The nightclubs where the parties don't start until dawn. The fantastic restaurants, the amazing boutiques. Dagmar has shown her a lot, but she's made plenty of discoveries on her own too. She can think of lots of places he would enjoy.

But then she stops that train of thought because after what he just did, she knows she can't sleep with him again.

It's like playing out a lousy hand of cards you have no chance of winning. Better to fold early.

When her studio is finally back in shape, she sits on the bed with her computer and sends out e-mails. She contacts her art agent, Emily, to let her know what happened with the robbery, and how there will be two fewer masks to send out to galleries for now. She checks Facebook and her website, then updates her blog to announce she'll back in the States soon.

Lindsay wonders if she should mention her upcoming nuptials with

Giovanni. It's probably the smart thing to do, to make the whole thing look more real. She doesn't have the heart to act excited about something so fake, though, so all she mentions is that she has 'news' and will share it with everyone soon.

There's a sudden noise out in the hallway and Lindsay startles. She holds her breath for a second before realizing it's only one of her neighbors moving stuff. She's been on edge the whole time she's been back here and wonders how she's going to get any sleep tonight.

She could always call Dagmar and stay with her, but knows they'd only argue more about Werner.

After going pee while holding her breath the whole time, she makes a decision. It's the thought of a stink-free bathroom that finally sways her. Giovanni's note said there were three more nights on his hotel room so she might as well use them.

And it's not like I'm taking any money from him since the room is already paid whether I'm in it or not.

It's nearly nightfall when Lindsay makes it to Giovanni's hotel. She wonders whether she's going to hear back from him, but so far nothing.

By the time she's lounging in bed in her pajamas, drinking a glass of wine, and flipping through German television channels, things aren't looking too bad.

When her cell phone rings, she grabs it and sees it's her sister, Natalie.

"Sorry," Lindsay says. "I completely forgot about our Skype session tonight. Let me get my computer set up and I'll call you back, okay?"

"I'm here, but I have to go to work soon, so don't wait too long."

She turns on her computer and searches around for info that describes how to use the wireless. In the top drawer of the nightstand, she's surprised to discover a small stack of comic books.

What's this?

She pulls the stack out. There's *Spiderman*, *Superman*, a couple issues of *Wonder Woman*, plus a few others she's not familiar with.

Do these belong to Giovanni?

Eventually, she finds a card for the Wi-Fi, and a few minutes later she and Natalie are connected.

Her sister's face comes on-screen, her long blonde hair pulled back into a ponytail. She's clearly dressed and ready to leave for work soon. "What's going on?" Natalie asks. "Is everything okay?"

"Not really." Lindsay doesn't even know where to start. Finally, she sighs. "I'm all right, but something happened yesterday."

Natalie's expression turns to concern. "What do you mean?"

"I got robbed." She explains how her studio was torn apart and her masks broken. She doesn't mention the amount of money stolen because then she'd have to explain about the poker.

"That's terrible! Are you really okay?" Natalie centers herself on-screen. "Is there anything I can do? Do you need more money?"

"No, I'm okay for now. I'll be back soon anyway. I'm going to try and finish this last mask before I leave."

"Who would do something like that?"

She shrugs noncommittally. With a sick feeling, she realizes her poker secret has grown larger than she ever intended. Her sister is the one person in this world she completely trusts, and yet she's not telling her the whole story.

She'll say I'm just like dad, but I'm not.

There's some movement behind Natalie and Lindsay sees Anthony. He bends down to kiss her sister then turns to the screen. "Hey, Lindsay."

She listens as Natalie relays the news about the robbery to him. He looms in front of the computer, his face worried as he asks her all the same questions Natalie did a moment ago.

"I'm okay, really. I appreciate the concern."

In truth, she can't stop staring at Anthony as she thinks about Giovanni. The brothers do have a familial resemblance, but beyond that, they don't look much alike. Anthony, with his dark hair and eyes, looks like a classic Italian.

"Where are you now?" Natalie asks, coming back on the screen. "It doesn't look like your studio."

"No, I'm in a hotel room. I figured it was best for now."

"A hotel? Are you sure you can afford that?"

She licks her lips. "Actually, it's Giovanni's room."

Natalie's eyes grow wide. "It is?"

Lindsay suddenly sees Anthony looming over Natalie's shoulder again. "You're in my brother's hotel room? Is he there?"

"No, he flew to Rome earlier. The room is paid for the next few nights, and he left me his key card."

"I thought you weren't going to see him again," Natalie says.

She takes a deep breath and decides she might as well get this over with. It's like ripping off a Band-Aid. "Giovanni and I are sort of getting married."

Natalie's mouth drops open. "*What?*"

Both Anthony and Natalie are gawking at her with such shock it's comical. It makes Lindsay want to laugh, and she would if this whole crazy situation wasn't actually happening to her.

"Why would you guys do that?" Anthony asks. He frowns and is obviously trying to figure this out. “Are you pregnant?”

I wish. Despite years of knowing and accepting her infertility, his question is still a kick to the gut. “No, it’s nothing like that. It’s a long story.”

“I thought you weren’t planning to ever marry again. Are you two in love?” Natalie asks.

Lindsay isn’t sure how to answer that. It occurs to her how it wouldn’t be a good idea to admit their marriage is fake over the Internet. Plus, she wouldn’t want to mess anything up for the kids involved. “It’s complicated.”

“I’ll bet it is.” Anthony shakes his head. “He hasn’t said a word to me.”

“It’ll be easier to explain all this in person.”

“Where are you planning to live?” Natalie asks. “You’re not going to Africa with him, are you?”

“No, he took a job at Seattle Children’s.”

“Seriously?” Anthony starts laughing as he disappears from behind Natalie’s shoulder. “I’m calling that asshole right now,” Lindsay hears his voice trailing off.

Natalie leans in closer to the screen. “What is actually going on here? Are you in love with Giovanni?”

“Oddly, I do sort of have feelings for him, but don’t tell Anthony I said that.”

“Why not?” Natalie appears mystified. “None of this makes any sense.”

“I know. I’ll explain everything when I see you.”

Natalie considers her. “You’re not in some kind of trouble, are you? Please, tell me the truth.”

“No, I’m okay.”

Her sister studies her like she doesn’t believe it. “When is the wedding?”

Lindsay shrugs. “I’m not sure. Soon. Giovanni is going to set everything up. We’re flying to Las Vegas.”

“Las Vegas!” Natalie’s brows shoot up to her hairline. “And you’re okay with that?”

“I’m trying to be.”

“What on Earth have you gotten yourself into?”

“I’m fine. I’m sorry to be so evasive. And I promise I’ll explain it to you soon.”

Natalie looks worried. “I can’t believe you agreed to fly to Vegas at all, much less get married there.”

She takes a deep breath. “I know.”

Chapter Thirteen

LINDSAY'S HOUSE RULES

~ Men have feelings too, especially between their legs. ~

LINDSAY'S PULSE SHOOTS up when the pilot announces their plane is thirty minutes away from arrival. She leans over a bit to glance outside, but all she sees are blue skies.

Most of the other passengers seated around her are middle-aged women, part of a tour group ready to party and gamble—though judging by the amount of alcohol imbibed they've started the party early.

Instead of flying to Seattle as she had originally planned, she flew from Berlin to San Francisco. After going through customs, she's now on a plane headed for the one place on Earth she swore she'd never go again.

Las Vegas, Nevada.

She closes her eyes and tries to calm down.

To make matters worse, she's getting married. The one other thing she swore she'd never do again.

How did I get myself into this mess?

She wishes now she'd forced Giovanni to meet her in Seattle. She wasn't thinking clearly and has the nagging sense she still isn't.

They haven't even spoken on the phone, not since her angry conversation before he flew to Rome. She waited for him to call, but he never did, and there was no way she was calling *him* again.

She spent her last week in Berlin shopping for gifts to bring home for everyone and tying up loose ends. And then, of course, there was that goodbye party. It went on for two days, with Dagmar inviting nearly every artist in Berlin. They drank, ate, talked art, and played hours of poker.

A few days before she was scheduled to leave Berlin, Giovanni finally texted her the flight information to Vegas. When she texted back that she already had a flight to Seattle, he told her to cancel it and keep the money. Being that her funds were so low she was running on fumes, she did just that. Unfortunately, after the cancellation penalty there wasn't much left over.

I'll be broke in Las Vegas, just like always.

Sweat breaks out over her whole body as her stomach cramps. It's her worst nightmare come to life.

But I'm not broke. Soon, I'll have the twenty grand Giovanni agreed to pay me.

She still has his credit card too, not that she's touched it for anything personal.

"Is this your first time in Las Vegas?" the male flight attendant asks her. Lindsay has an aisle seat and he's been flirting with her most of the way from San Francisco. It surprised her because she thought he was gay. He lowers his voice. "Would you like to grab a drink together after we land?"

She tries to smile. "Thanks, but I'm actually here to get married."

"Is that right? Congratulations." His eyes flicker down her body—clearly not gay at all. "He's a lucky guy."

She grips the seat's armrests. Her anxiety skyrockets at the realization that the stress of all this has put her normally excellent instincts about people completely out of whack. It's like she's lost one of her primary senses.

Once the plane starts its descent, she's so dizzy she has to put her head down. The tour group ladies all make sympathetic clucking noises toward her. She lied and told them she was afraid of flying because it was clear she had to tell them something when they noticed how anxious she was.

"There now, see? Everything is fine," the stylish red-haired grandmother—who polished off two whiskeys during the short flight—says with a smile after they finally land. "You had nothing to worry about."

Lindsay nods, but knows it isn't true. She can already feel the grimy Vegas heat coating her skin, and she hasn't even left the plane yet.

In his text, Giovanni told her they were staying at the Bellagio. A good thing, at least, since she doesn't have any particular memories associated with it.

She figures she'll grab a taxi outside the airport, but when she disembarks her eyes widen. Giovanni is in the passenger area waiting for her. Standing there as large as Thor, he's leaning against the wall with his arms crossed. He'd be hard to miss.

A girlish excitement grips her and those butterflies come swarming back.

Instead of his usual corduroy pants, he's wearing dark jeans and a blue button-down shirt. Her first thought is how incredible he looks and how happy she is to see him. Not that she's forgotten what happened in Berlin, because she certainly hasn't.

She notices his tan has faded a bit, but there's a healthy pink flush to his cheeks as he waves and grins at her with white teeth.

To her surprise, as soon as she's close enough, he pulls her into his arms and hugs her. Lindsay knows she should resist, should push him away, but he feels so good she lets her guard down. It was terrible holding it together on that plane ride, so for one long moment, she lets herself relax and be held.

Despite all of his issues, she feels safe with him. Giovanni's the kind of man you want on your side in a crisis.

When they pull apart, he's still grinning as he looks down at her. "Wow."

"What?"

"I'd almost forgotten how stunning you are."

She rolls her eyes. "I look terrible. I just flew halfway around the world and haven't slept in twenty-four hours."

"It doesn't matter. I think you're beautiful."

She tries not to smile, but can't help it. In some ways, he's like a big kid—speaking his mind without guile. She nearly tells him he's beautiful too, because he is, but then stops herself. It's like he's already working some kind of voodoo on her. "Stop being so nice. I'm still pissed at you."

"Ah, I was hoping we were past that."

"Think again." She glances around the airport, remembering how she's returned to the one place she hates.

"Well, even though you're still angry with me, it's good to see you, Lindsay." He seems about to look away, but his eyes go back to her and roam her face, perceptive as always. "Is there something else bothering you?"

"No, it's nothing." She takes a deep breath and tries to push away her anxiety.

"You look pale. We should get some food into you."

"I'm fine," she mutters, more to herself than him.

"I'll bet you haven't eaten for hours." He reaches around to grab her bag. "Come on, I have a rental car. We can get dinner or if you prefer, room service at the hotel."

She follows him through the airport, still trying to hold it together. She feels much better than she did on the plane and realizes his presence is calming her. He's solid and in command, and as much as she hates to admit it, that's exactly what she needs right now.

As soon as they walk outside to the parking area, she gasps. There's a wall of blistering heat.

Welcome back to Hell.

It's evening and the sun is setting in an orange sky, but it's at least a hundred degrees. Even though she grew up here, it feels foreign to her, and she misses the cool green of Seattle.

She concentrates on Giovanni instead, following behind him. Admiring the way he walks, the way his ass looks in those jeans. She doesn't recognize the cut and guesses he picked them up in Rome.

Eventually, he stops in front of a plain brown four-door sedan and pops open the trunk.

Lindsay stares at it then bursts out laughing. "This is the car you rented?"

"Yes, why?" He looks at her questioningly and seems baffled by her amusement.

"This poop-brown sedan? Are you kidding? It looks like something a down-on-his-luck pot dealer would drive."

He glances at the car as if finally noticing it for the first time. "I admit it's not glamorous, but it seems to run okay."

"Why didn't you just rent an SUV or something?"

"I don't know. This seemed adequate. Plus, I was in a hurry to pick you up and told them to give me something quick."

Lindsay opens the passenger door and climbs inside the stiflingly hot car, which smells like a combination of dirty socks and vanilla air freshener. "At least we won't have to worry about it being stolen. I doubt we could pay somebody to steal this ugly thing."

After putting her suitcase in the trunk, Giovanni slides into the driver's seat. He starts the engine then fiddles with the dash panel for a few seconds to get the air conditioner blasting. "I don't know what you're talking about. This car isn't so bad."

She glances around at the plaid fabric seat covers then up to where his head brushes the ceiling. "It's hideous, and it's too small for you. We should take it back and get a normal car."

"Now you're hurting my feelings. You don't really want to return this sleek sex machine, do you?"

"Sex machine!" She laughs out loud. "There's no way anybody ever got laid in this car. Trust me."

"Is that a challenge?" He grins and holds her gaze for a long moment. The shirt he's wearing makes the blue in his eyes stand out.

"You think you could seduce me in this horrible shit-colored car? Seriously?"

"I believe I could manage it."

She smirks. "Good luck with that." *Good luck with ever seducing me again, in fact.*

"Care to place a wager?"

"You don't want to gamble with me."

He shrugs. "Sure I do, why not? We're in Las Vegas, after all."

Against her better judgment, she decides to go along with him. "All right, let's hear it." She crosses her legs and lets her eyes roam over him. "What's the bet?"

"Sometime before we leave Las Vegas, I'll seduce you while we're in this car."

"In *this* car, for real?" She points down at the faded plaid seat.

"That's right."

"And if I win the bet and you don't manage to seduce me, what do I get?"

"That depends. What do you want?"

Lindsay thinks it over. There's only one thing that comes to mind. "You have to tell me everything I want to know." She's not even sure why she's saying it, but something compels her forward. "Any question I ask you about yourself, you have to answer honestly."

His eyes widen, and it's clearly not what he was expecting. He rubs his jaw and seems wary. "I was thinking more along the lines of buying you earrings or something."

"Come on, you think I'd make it that easy?"

"No." He chuckles and glances out the window. "You're always a surprise." He turns back to her, his hand resting on the steering wheel. "What do I get if I win?"

"The pleasure of seducing me, of course. And I should tell you, after that shit you pulled in Berlin last week, it's not going to happen."

Giovanni goes quiet and appears to be thinking things over. "Here's what I want." He leans toward her. "I want you to tell your sister about your poker playing."

"What?" She stares at him with dismay. "You need to mind your own business. That has nothing to do with you."

"You're keeping a secret from someone you care about. It's a mistake. Believe me, I know. You need to tell her the truth."

"God." She rolls her eyes. "How could I have already forgotten what an egotistical ass you are? You picked me up, what, twenty minutes ago? And you're already trying to run my life?"

"You know I'm right, Lindsay."

She shakes her head and turns away from him, annoyed.

"So, do we have a wager or not?" he asks.

She doesn't say anything, reflecting on his words. The truth is she does need to tell Natalie about the poker. It was easy to hide it in Berlin, but she already knows how difficult it will be if she's hitting the tables in Seattle again. She's always had her secrets, and it was a way of life for them growing up, but she's tired of all that, and she especially hates keeping secrets from Natalie.

Then she thinks about Giovanni. How is it that a well-respected surgeon could be so messed up about women? He's been traveling and working in all these dangerous places for years, but she suspects he's been hiding in them too. But hiding from what?

"All right," she says. "I'm all in."

It's nearly nightfall, and the Strip is lit up bright and garish as always.

Lindsay tries to ignore the onslaught of emotions gripping her as they drive past some of her old stomping grounds, the casinos she and her friends used to sneak into back in high school. They'd gamble—mostly slots—until the security guards caught them and threw them out. She'd tried playing poker with a fake ID a few times, but too many people knew who she was.

When she was a kid and her father was still alive, he used to take her with him to Fremont Street, to the Horseshoe and the Golden Nugget. Old-style Las Vegas that doesn't exist anymore. Tables with stacks of chips and men drinking booze as they played poker for hours on end. Cash games with thousand-dollar buy-ins. You'd find some of the world's greatest poker players in those smoke-filled rooms, and her dad was one of them.

It wasn't a place for children. In fact, she doubts she was even supposed to be there, but she loved it. She'd hang out with the waitresses, who were always nice to her. They'd set her up with a Shirley Temple to sip on. There was always one who was particularly nice. At the time, Lindsay didn't realize it, but it was usually one of her dad's girlfriends.

"Here we are," Giovanni says as they drive past the Bellagio's large fountain to reach the main entrance.

She glances around, taking in all the glitz and glam, and the large number of tourists. They stop for the valet, and she's pretty sure she hears the guy snicker when Giovanni hands him the keys to their car.

Once they're upstairs and inside the room, she's amazed.

"Wow." She walks over to the huge floor-to-ceiling window looking out on the fountain and the Paris Hotel across the street. "I have to admit, you don't mess around when it comes to hotel rooms, do you?"

"Glad you like it. It's the honeymoon suite."

Lindsay whirls around. "It is?"

"We *are* getting married, after all."

His expression is so grim she wants to laugh at the absurdity. "Your face looks just like I feel."

"I'm only worried. I hope this still works."

"What do you mean?"

"I spoke to Paul's brother, Phillip, yesterday." He shakes his head. "Apparently, the new government is tightening things, and fewer people are being allowed to enter and leave the country. It could pose a problem for the adoption."

"What are we going to do?"

"We're going to get married as planned. Phillip's lawyer has already drawn up all the paperwork. There's no reason to give up hope, but I just thought you should know."

She nods. "I see. Okay." She studies him. "Can you tell me why you're really doing this? I know you want to help those kids, but we're getting *married*. That's no small thing."

"What Paul did for me years ago was also no small thing."

"But what was it? Did he save your life or something?"

Giovanni takes a deep breath. "In a way, he did. I don't know if I'd even be a doctor today if Paul hadn't helped. Definitely not a surgeon."

"What did he do?"

He opens his mouth but then closes it. A little smile tugs on the corners. "I don't have to answer your questions unless you win that bet."

She rolls her eyes.

"Hey, that was the wager."

"You're definitely going to lose. In fact,"—she puts her hand on her hip and glances around the room— "despite this being the honeymoon suite, you should know we won't be sharing a bed anymore. I hope that couch is comfortable."

He blinks in surprise. "Why not?"

"You already know why."

He studies her a moment before looking away. "I see. So you really are still angry."

"Why wouldn't I be?" She barrels forward. "You can't just leave me alone in a hotel room with a credit card like some kind of hooker!"

His eyes go back to hers. "It wasn't like that and you know it."

"It's how you made me feel."

He seems genuinely mystified. "We wanted each other. There's nothing more to it than that. And I left you that credit card because you admitted you were nearly broke after being robbed."

"Why didn't you wake me up before leaving?"

"I already told you. I didn't want to wake you because you were sleeping so hard."

"That's bullshit!"

The natural flush on his cheeks goes from pink to red. His jaw tenses, but he doesn't say anything.

"Don't fucking lie, okay? That's the second time you've done that to me, but it's also the last because I won't let it happen again."

He nods. His expression hard, but there's something else there, and she suspects he's upset about more than just sleeping with her again.

"It's never like this for you, is it?" She watches him closely. "You never have to see the women again and deal with their anger. But here I am, and you don't know what to do."

"I'm sorry you feel this way," he says stiffly. "But you're overreacting."

"No, I'm not." She goes over to where he left her suitcase by the desk and grabs the handle, pulling it behind her toward the bedroom where she sees a large king-sized bed. "I'm taking a shower and then I'm going to sleep. Alone."

It's dark when Lindsay wakes up, and for a moment, she's disoriented, though she senses it's still night. There's movement beside her and then someone—Giovanni—switches on the bedside lamp.

She's lying on her back and covers her eyes with her forearm. "Turn that off."

He sits beside her on the bed. "Do you remember what I told you back in Berlin?" His voice is low. "How I couldn't give you anything more?"

"I remember."

"It was the truth. I never meant to hurt you, Lindsay."

She takes her arm away and looks up at him. "Maybe not, but after everything we went through that day and then spending the night together, you shouldn't have left like you did."

"I didn't know what else to do. I haven't been in a real relationship with a woman in years." He's wearing his usual tense expression, and it's clear he's struggling with something. "I'm just not . . . able to."

"Why?"

He only shakes his head, licks his lips. "I want to. In fact, I wish I could."

His eyes stay on hers. Against her better judgment, she reaches out and puts her hand on his cheek, moving her fingers lightly up over his brow. His skin feels warm beneath her touch.

She caresses his face. So handsome, and strong too. Even in his vulnerability, Giovanni emits a kind of resilience.

"I can't let you treat me like that." She puts her hand back down. "You have to know that."

"Of course." He nods, his expression sober. "I understand."

"What happened to you? There must be something, because you're so capable in every other way. It doesn't make sense."

"That's the dichotomy, isn't it?" He lets out his breath. "But it's a long story."

"I don't mind long stories."

He shakes his head. "Not tonight."

They gaze at each other, the lamp casting their shadows across the wall. She wishes things were different, wishes he were easier. Wishes he was like all the other guys, the ones who follow her lead, fall at her feet and don't need fixing. But then she wonders if she'd want him as much if he were easy.

Probably not.

"I'd like to show you something," he tells her, a smile pulling on his mouth. "It's out in the other room."

She sits up on her elbows. Her eyes go to the drawn curtains, where there's definitely no light peeking through. "What time is it?"

"It's just after midnight."

"Are you serious?" She groans and flops back down. "No wonder I'm still exhausted. I need to sleep."

"You can, but first come see this."

"See what? Can't it wait till morning?"

"Trust me, it's worth waking up for. At least come out and meet them."

"Them?" She sits up all the way. "Who are you talking about?"

"Joseph and Sara, Paul's kids. I'm going to Skype with them in a few minutes."

Her brows go up. She climbs out of bed and follows him into the suite's living room area, noticing how his laptop is set up on the coffee table, stacked on a couple of cushions.

He takes a seat on the couch in front of the computer. "I figured you might want to meet the kids you're helping before we get married."

"You're calling them right now?"

"Yes. They're about thirteen hours ahead, so it's midday for them. I texted Joseph to let him know."

She sits beside him on the couch. "They have cell phones over there?"

Giovanni nods, focusing on his computer. "You've never done any traveling in Africa, I take it?"

"No." She watches the screen as he shuts down his e-mail and some other documents he was working on.

"Everybody has a cell phone. I've been to places so poor there's no access to clean drinking water, but people still have their phones." He shakes his head. "It's crazy."

Lindsay looks at him with surprise.

"But Paul's a physician, so his family has always lived comfortably." He pauses and grows momentarily serious. "*Was* a physician.

She touches his arm and their eyes meet. She sees the sadness in his. "You're a good friend to him, even now."

He nods, but doesn't say anything more.

She watches as he opens Skype. There's a basket of fruit on the table, and she reaches over to grab an orange, realizing she's starved. When she turns back, Giovanni has finally connected, and there's somebody on screen.

It's a young teenage boy with close-cropped hair and dark skin. He's grinning with straight white teeth. "Uncle John!"

"Hey, Joseph, it's good to see you. How are things?"

"Not too bad. It is good to see you too," he says with accented English. "I am very glad you called because I have something here you might enjoy." Joseph holds up some kind of comic book.

Giovanni opens his mouth with surprise. "Are you kidding me? Where did you get that?"

"A friend of mine gave it to me. Ha-ha! I knew you would be jealous."

"I *am* jealous!"

Joseph laughs with mischievous delight. "I can let you borrow it, so no worries."

Lindsay remembers the comic books from Berlin and realizes they did belong to him. She watches as the two of them talk and is amazed at the change in Giovanni. He's joking and relaxed, obviously in his element with kids.

"Is Sara around?" Giovanni asks. "I have Lindsay here, and I'd like you guys to meet her."

"She is here, let me call her." They both hear Joseph yelling loudly for his sister to come to the computer.

A few moments later, a pretty, dark-skinned girl of about ten comes into view. She's wearing a white blouse and blue ribbons in her pigtails. It looks like some kind of school uniform. "Hi, Uncle John!" She tilts her head as her whole face covers the screen.

"That is too close, Sara." Lindsay can hear Joseph in the background.

Sara finally moves back and Giovanni introduces her.

"Hi." Lindsay waves. "It's great to meet both of you."

"Oooh, you're pretty!" Sara says with big eyes. "Uncle John didn't tell us how pretty you are!"

"Thanks." She smiles. "I think you're very pretty too."

Sara grins and murmurs, "Thank you," though she seems shy.

Lindsay says hello to Joseph as well, and the four of them talk for a while. The kids tell her about their school and their grandmother. They mention Phillip and how they hope they'll be able to go live in the States soon. They're worried because it's taking so long. Giovanni explains how everybody's working on getting them here. He's calm and reassuring to both children.

It's not a long conversation, but by the end of it, both kids are in good spirits. Sara tells her a funny story about how her grandmother's goat ate her math book recently, and how she's happy about it, and Lindsay laughs.

Seeing and conversing with them changes everything. Suddenly, Lindsay finds she's really glad to be able to help these two.

After the four of them say their good-byes, she nods over at Giovanni. "That was great. Thank you for setting it up."

"You're welcome. I thought it might help if you met them and saw for yourself how they're not just an abstract concept, but real children."

"You're right. It does make a difference. I hope I get to meet them in person soon."

"Me too," he agrees.

Lindsay thinks about the conversation. "I'm curious about something though—why were they calling you Uncle John?"

"Oh, that. Paul and I were friends in college. I've known those two since they were babies."

"I figured that much, but why John?"

He glances at her with confusion as he shuts down his computer. "Because that's my name."

"It is?"

"Yes, Giovanni is John in English."

Lindsay's mouth drops open. "I didn't know that!"

"Lots of people call me John."

"Weird." Her eyes roam over him. "So, what you're saying is nobody calls you Olaf?"

He chuckles. "No. You're the only one."

"What name do you prefer being called?"

He takes his computer off the cushions and sets it directly on the coffee table. "Either is fine. My family calls me Giovanni, so I associate that with people who are close to me, but I have plenty of friends who call me John."

"What should I call you?"

He shrugs. "Whatever you're most comfortable with."

Lindsay considers the options. "I like Giovanni. It has a romantic ring to it, though we both know Olaf is your true name."

He smirks. "Just don't let my mother hear you call me Olaf. For her, nothing in this world is as good as being *un Italiano*."

"Also, I'm curious, do you really read comics?"

He chuckles. "Sometimes. I always keep a stack in my bag for my patients."

"A surgeon who reads comic books."

He shrugs. "I have to read a lot of medical text, so it's a nice break."

Lindsay's thoughts go back to the kids she just Skyped with. How lively they were in their conversation. "It's weird, but you'd never know Joseph and Sara lost a parent recently. They didn't seem sad or anything."

"That's not uncommon." His expression goes serious. "Losing a parent is so devastating for a child they can't take in the loss all at once. It's too much. Their grief is spread out over a lifetime."

She nods, thinking back to her own childhood. "I lost my dad when I was a kid too."

He looks at her with surprise as he sits back down on the couch. "I didn't know that. How old were you?"

"About Sara's age. Eleven."

"I'm sorry to hear that." He reaches for her hand, and she lets him take it. "Were you close?"

She nods. "I idolized my dad, even after I found out the truth."

"What do you mean?"

"All his secrets and lies." Lindsay looks down at Giovanni's hand holding hers. "He won huge amounts of money playing poker, but half the time we barely had enough food to eat. He was constantly losing it at the track or the blackjack tables. Spending it on women when he should have been taking care of us."

"Jesus." He shakes his head.

"He used to always tell me how much we were alike. He'd say, 'You and I are made of the same stuff, Lindsay.'" She takes a deep breath. "Sometimes, I worry it's true."

"Where was your mother in all this?"

"Burying her head in the sand, as usual. She was an artist who drank too much. She still does." She gazes outside at the fountain. "Natalie is the one who raised me, even though she was just a kid herself."

"I'm sorry, Lindsay. I didn't know. It sounds like it was tough for both of you."

"Yeah." She smiles with embarrassment. "I'm not sure why I'm telling you all this. It must be the exhaustion from traveling."

"People tell me things all the time. I am a doctor, after all."

He's still holding her hand, stroking his thumb over the top of hers, and even that bit of touch from him relaxes her. Their eyes stay on each other.

A part of her wants to invite him back into her bed tonight. He feels so familiar, so right. God, she's even telling him her secrets.

Not all of them though.

She wants to absorb his essence, his strength. Giovanni is a force to be reckoned with, and the fact is he's sexy as hell. But then she remembers what happened after they slept together in Berlin and pulls her hand away.

"And besides . . ." His voice takes on a humorous note. "It's not long before I'll be your husband. We are getting married tomorrow."

Her eyes go wide as adrenaline rockets through her. "Did you say *tomorrow?*"

Chapter Fourteen

~ If a guy wants to be in charge, let him. But then do whatever you want. ~

GIOVANNI'S BACK ACHES like a son of a bitch from sleeping on that damn couch all night. Fortunately, it pulled out into a bed, but unfortunately, the mattress was too short to accommodate his six-foot-three body, and his feet stuck out. Of course, the metal bar running across the center was the real cherry on top. It dug into his spine with such accuracy he's certain it was designed by military intelligence as a torture device.

He considered calling downstairs for a cot, but in the end decided it would probably be just as uncomfortable. Plus, he wasn't sure if he could deal with the embarrassment. He was seldom embarrassed about anything, but staying in the honeymoon suite while sleeping on a cot was just enough that it might tip the scales to where he felt humiliated as a man.

If only Lindsay had invited him into her bed. He hoped she would, and it looked like she was even considering it last night, but in the end, she went to sleep alone.

He knows it's his own fault. He screwed up. He doesn't know why he left her alone in that hotel room in Berlin. All he knows is when he thought of waking her, of taking that next step between them, something stopped him.

Old habits die hard.

What's crazy is he wanted to. He wanted to spend more time with her. Despite his guilt, that night they had together was incredible. He hasn't been able to stop thinking about it, and not just because it helped him come off the adrenaline. The more he gets to know Lindsay, the deeper he's drawn in.

Initially, she reminded him of Olivia, but he sees now how wrong he was. It's clear the two of them are nothing alike. *Thank God.*

"This is weird," Lindsay says the next morning.

They're sitting across from each other at one of the hotel's restaurants, eating a late breakfast before they get married.

"What is?" Giovanni speaks around a mouthful of food. He's scarfing down a plate of pancakes and sausage. Nervous energy has always made him hungry, his body burning calories at an astronomical rate.

"All of it. Our marriage will only be temporary, so why are we both so tense?"

He swallows. "Tense? I'm not tense."

"Give me a break. You're sweating even though this place has the air cranked so high it's like the North Pole."

"I don't know what you're talking about. I'm great. Better than ever."

She laughs, her expression incredulous. "Really?"

"Solid as a rock."

"Wow." She leans closer. "I don't think I've ever seen you actually scared before."

"*Scared?*" He picks up his napkin and mops his face with it. In truth, he is sweating like crazy. For a moment, he considers whether he might have contracted something before he left Africa. Malaria? Ebola? *Christ, I hope not.* He knows that's absurd though. He wasn't anywhere near Ebola, and he took every precaution possible against malaria. He goes back to attacking his food. "I'm not scared. You're delusional."

She gives him a knowing smile as she picks up her coffee mug. "All I can say is please don't ever play poker."

He polishes off the last of his pancakes and even considers ordering another plate of food, but decides to have more coffee instead. It's a treat he only seldom gets to partake of, as he requires his hands to be as steady as possible when he's working.

He flags down the waitress and holds up his mug.

"Coffee is the last thing you need," Lindsay tells him.

"I don't know what you're going on about. I'm totally calm."

She nods. "It's actually kind of entertaining seeing you so freaked out. I'm guessing it's a rare event."

Giovanni drinks his coffee and decides to ignore her silly remarks.

"Don't worry, it'll be okay. As you know, I've been married twice, and it's really not that difficult." She smiles at him, clearly pleased to be the one with the upper hand. "And it is only temporary."

He swigs down more coffee and grunts to himself. Difficult or not, temporary or not, in a few hours he'll be at the courthouse obtaining a marriage license so he can attend his own wedding where he'll then be married.

To one woman.

Legally married.

Jesus.

He licks his lips and takes a deep breath. *Maybe Lindsay's right. I am freaking out.*

"So, what are you planning to wear on this glorious day of our blissful union?" she asks with a smirk.

He puts his coffee down. "I, uh, picked something up in *Roma.* A suit."

"You did?"

He nods.

Lindsay considers him. "What about the rings?"

"I figure we can stop at a jeweler's after the courthouse and on the way to the chapel."

"It sounds like you've thought of everything."

"I'm just trying to be efficient." He prefers going into every scenario with a solid plan. Just the thought of it calms him. He consults his phone and, when he sees the time, tells her they should get going. "We don't want to miss our appointment."

On the way back upstairs, Lindsay cracks more jokes about their nuptial bliss. He keeps thinking about her childhood. Though she seemed embarrassed, he's glad she told him more about herself last night. It sounds like it was both unusual and difficult, but it also explains why she's such a tough girl, defensive at times, never wanting anybody's help.

Once they're back in the room, both of them separate to get ready. She stays in the bedroom while he uses the small bathroom off the living area. After showering and getting dressed, he finally remembers their bargain.

He knocks on the bedroom door, wearing the dark blue Armani suit his cousin Sophia helped him pick out in Rome. He wasn't planning on spending this kind of money, but Sophia talked him into it, insisting he needed a good suit. And, like most Italians, she didn't understand the concept of budget when it came to matters of style.

"What is it?" Lindsay asks, swinging the door open with irritation, but then her eyes widen and she sways a bit, gripping the door. "Wow." She seems almost panicked, but then gives him a smile with what looks like real pleasure. "Look at you. Fantastic."

"Thank you," he says, pleased by the compliment. He's holding the check in his hand, but then freezes when he sees what Lindsay's wearing. She isn't even dressed yet, still wearing the hotel's puffy white bathrobe. To make matters worse, there are large rollers the size of Coke cans in her hair, and her whole face is covered in some kind of pink goop.

"Are you kidding me?" He stares at her in disbelief. "You're not ready yet? We have to leave soon!"

"Just give me a minute."

"Do you understand we have to be at the chapel in less than two hours?"

She frowns. "Then stop interrupting me." She tries to close the door again, but he puts his hand out.

"I came to give you this. Payment for our arrangement."

"Oh?" She takes the check from him and stares down at it.

"Twenty thousand dollars, as we agreed. I figured you might like to deposit it as soon as possible."

"Of course," she murmurs softly.

He watches the thoughtful expression on her face as she studies the large amount of money he just signed over.

As he's standing there, he suddenly notices a familiar medicinal smell coming off her. "What is that stuff? It almost smells like Pepto-Bismol."

"It is Pepto-Bismol." She chews on her bottom lip, still studying the check in a distracted way.

He can't help grinning as he absorbs the fact that her face is covered in diarrhea medication. His eyes roam over the giant rollers in her hair, past the pink goop, the terrycloth robe, all the way down to her scarlet-red toes. And he realizes none of it matters. It turns out whatever new eccentricities he discovers about her, whatever craziness she throws his way, it all adds up to one irrefutable truth.

He finds her irresistible.

"And the bride wore black," Lindsay jokes, finally emerging from the bedroom. The only thing truly dressy she packed is a slinky black cocktail dress. She figured it was good enough for a quickie wedding in Vegas until she saw Giovanni in that suit. Talk about a hunk. She's never swooned in her life, but she actually felt her knees go weak.

Somebody get me a doctor.

"It's about time," he says, glancing up from the chair near the window where he's studying his phone. He took his suit jacket off, so he's only wearing the white dress shirt and a blue tie. The effect is devastating. The shirt hugs his broad shoulders perfectly, and the tie brings out the vivid blue in his eyes.

I think I need CPR.

He seems stunned for a moment when he sees her. His eyes take in her face and hair, then roam downward. "You look lovely, Lindsay. Just beautiful."

"Thanks. Sorry about the black dress." She glances at herself. "It's all I had with me."

He doesn't reply for a long moment, his expression difficult to read. "It's all right," he finally says. "I wasn't expecting you to wear a wedding dress."

He gets up and walks toward her, and she decides he looks almost perfect. There's only one thing missing. "Let's put some gel in your hair. I have some in the bathroom."

"Gel? We don't have time for that." He shoves his phone into his front pocket.

She reaches down for his hand, knowing for someone as tactile as Giovanni, it's the best way to reach him. "Come on, it'll just take a minute."

He looks like he wants to protest again, but doesn't, and instead lets her lead him into the large master bathroom. She lets go of his hand to grab the tube of gel she has in her travel bag.

"This will be just the right finishing touch," she says with a grin. "You want to look pretty for the wedding pictures, don't you?"

Giovanni seems dubious but stands in front of the mirror in that lost way men sometimes do when a woman tries to groom them. He leans forward for a second and examines himself more closely, running a hand through his golden curls. "I should have gotten a haircut when I was in *Roma*. It's starting to get unruly."

"You have gorgeous hair. What's it like when it's longer?"

"A big mess."

"Ringlet curls, I'll bet." She wets her hands with water first and pats a little onto his hair. Then she squirts some gel in her palm and rubs them together. "Come here."

He leans closer. He smells delicious, like some kind of subtle, but expensive cologne. Her butterflies are starting up again. His nearness is turning her on, but she tries to ignore it. She's wearing peep-toe platform pumps, but he's still a few inches taller as she reaches up with both hands to run gel through his soft curls.

She senses his eyes on her, and when she looks over at him in the mirror, he's watching her intently.

Her fingers continue to rake her through his amazing hair, tugging a bit, bringing some control to it. When she's finally done, she turns again to check her work.

This time, when their eyes meet in the mirror, Lindsay is struck by how right they look together. As if it's all destined somehow. As if they were a real couple getting ready for their real wedding today.

Giovanni gives her one of his genuine smiles—like a happy groom—and it takes her breath away. She doesn't even know where this emotion is coming from—this crazy longing.

"What do you think?" she whispers.

He doesn't look at his hair, keeping his eyes on her in a way that makes her wonder if he feels it too. "Lindsay . . ." is all he says, his voice low.

She trembles a little. It's like they recognize each other. Recognize that maybe at heart, they're the same kind of people. Whatever his problems are and whatever hers are none of it matters.

It's just the two of them.

I can't get pulled into this again. Lindsay breaks eye contact with him. *I won't let myself.* She steps back and busies herself with closing the tube of gel. He's still watching her, but she pretends not to notice.

To his credit, he doesn't try to touch her. "We should get going," is all he says quietly.

They leave the bathroom and he grabs his suit jacket, along with some kind of large manila envelope, before they head down to the front of the hotel and wait for the valet to retrieve their car.

She brought the check he gave her tucked away in her purse, figuring they can stop at one of her bank's branches after the ceremony and deposit it.

Twenty thousand dollars.

Every cent of her poker winnings returned, as if by magic. She should feel relieved to have the money. Now she can pay for school, pay for a new place to live, and she has a bankroll again if she decides to hit some of the poker games in Seattle. *I'm not broke in Las Vegas, not by a long shot.* The problem is she keeps thinking about Joseph and Sara.

The valet drives up in their poop-brown sedan and Giovanni takes the keys from him. The air conditioner is cranked full blast, but the car's interior is two thousand degrees.

First, they stop at the courthouse to get the marriage license. As they wait in line, Giovanni opens the folder and, to her surprise, has some papers for her to sign—a prenuptial agreement along with the adoption paperwork.

Lindsay's eyes widen as she studies the former. "I've never signed one of these before."

"Phillip's lawyer faxed them to me. He thought it was a good idea for both of us. Just standard stuff. I printed up one for you too."

She snorts softly. "I don't exactly have assets to protect."

Finally, they get the marriage license but are so rushed for time they drive directly to the chapel without stopping at the jeweler's. Luckily, they discover the chapel sells cheap wedding rings. They both pick out plain gold bands, and it all feels surreal to her.

To her amazement, he's set it up so they're getting married by an Elvis impersonator.

"An Elvis wedding?" She raises an eyebrow. "Seriously? That doesn't sound like your style."

He shrugs. "Guess I just wanted to prove to you I have a sense of humor after all."

It's clear he's trying to appear calm, though he's obviously still freaking out. The normal healthy flush on his cheeks is gone, and he actually looks pale. One of the chapel's salespeople, an attractive older blonde dressed up like Marilyn Monroe, asks if he'd like a glass of water after they pay for their wedding rings.

"I'm all right, thank you," he tells her.

"Maybe you a need a doctor." Lindsay smirks. "Or a sedative."

"We get some nervous ones in here sometimes," Marilyn admits. "You two will be fine though. You make such a cute couple."

"Thanks." Lindsay takes Giovanni's arm. "Olaf and I are just so damn excited to be here!"

He makes a strangled noise.

For whatever reason, she doesn't feel particularly nervous anymore. She knows how easy it is to get married after all. Unfortunately, she also knows how easy it is to get divorced.

Married in Vegas. Divorced in Reno.

She's never done that exactly, but there's a first time for everything.

When it's finally their turn to be married, the short, chubby Elvis minister comes out in a white spangled jumpsuit and jumps onto the small stage in front of them. Lindsay and Giovanni stand across from each other.

"Please take your bride's hand, sir," Elvis tells Giovanni in a fake Mississippi drawl.

He takes her left hand. To her surprise, his is warm and dry.

She assumes they'll recite their vows now, but instead, music starts coming through the speakers. There's some rhythm guitars and a rolling drum beat. Before she knows it, the Elvis minister is singing Lord Almighty and going on about his temperature rising. It takes Lindsay a second to recognize it's a rollicking version of "Burning Love." He stomps all over the stage in his shiny white jumpsuit, waving his hand in the air as he belts it out.

It's so unexpected that she can only stare with her mouth open. She glances over at Giovanni, who appears just as stunned.

"Woohoo!" Elvis yells as he dances around with his little pot belly, occasionally pumping his fist in the air. He seems to have forgotten most of the lyrics because he's mostly going "Yeah!" and "Mmmm . . . mm" with a few more "Woohoos!" thrown in for good measure.

Lindsay admires his enthusiasm. In fact, she finally pulls her hand away and starts clapping, and joining in.

By the time the song winds down, she's even managed to get Giovanni to join in with a "Woohoo!"

"Wow," she says when it's finished. "That was awesome!"

Giovanni nods, chuckling in agreement.

Elvis's round face is pink and sweaty. "Thank you. Thank you very much." He beams at them with a smirk worthy of the king. "Now, let's get you two lovebirds married! That's right, baby!" He mops his face with a towel as he comes over and situates himself directly in front of them on stage. Elvis is still grinning, but then his expression turns comically solemn. "Dearly beloved . . ."

Giovanni takes her hand again. Lindsay tries to pay attention as Elvis speaks the marriage vows, but for some reason, she starts thinking about that check in her purse. The twenty thousand. *Is this really what I want?*

"Stop!" she suddenly says, and everyone looks at her with surprise. She pulls her hand away from Giovanni. "We have to stop this."

His eyes widen and his mouth opens with alarm. "What do mean? What's wrong?"

"I'm sorry, but I can't marry you."

Chapter Fifteen

~ Don't let the past decide your future. ~

"YOU'VE CHANGED YOUR mind?" Giovanni's adrenaline spikes, pumping hard through his bloodstream.

But Lindsay doesn't answer, instead, she walks over to her purse hanging on a nearby chair. She picks it up, ready to go. Thoughts of the kids run through his head, helping Joseph and Sara, but to be honest, he's mostly thinking of himself and how much he doesn't want Lindsay to leave.

"What are you *doing?*" he asks, not bothering to hide the squeak in his voice. "You're not going to marry me?"

"Just give me a minute." She rummages through her purse as he watches in disbelief.

He feels the eyes of everyone in the chapel now, looking at him with pity. He's certain they've seen plenty of people jilted at the altar. Despite how nervous he's been all day, he realizes he wants to marry Lindsay. In fact, he's surprised how strongly he wants it.

Finally, she comes back to stand in front of him, bringing her purse with her.

"Is everything all right there, little lady?" Elvis asks with concern.

The expression on Lindsay's face is unreadable as she reaches down and takes his hand, placing something inside it. It's the check he gave her earlier.

"I'm giving this back to you," she says.

He lets his breath out in a rush of disappointment. "So, you really have changed your mind."

"I don't want your money."

Giovanni nods, staring down at the check with resignation.

"I can't do this for money," she says. "But I'll still marry you."

His eyes flash up to her with a surge of surprise. "You will?"

"Yes, I will."

He blinks, smiling.

And then to his everlasting relief, Lindsay smiles too.

He barely remembers the rest of the ceremony. It's nothing but a blur as he spends most of it recovering from the shock of what he thought was her ending things. He doesn't calm down until it's over.

"You've really never been to Las Vegas before?" Lindsay asks afterward, shifting position in the seat across from him.

They're sitting outside the wedding chapel in the rental car—the one she's been complaining about so much, and the one he's guessing he has zero chance of seducing her in before they leave.

Even though she's his wife now.

My wife.

"It's true." He rests his hand on the steering wheel as he tries to relax. "This is the first time I've been to Las Vegas."

Her lovely brown eyes consider him. "How is that possible? I thought you grew up in LA."

"I did, for the most part, but the opportunity to come here never presented itself."

She turns and looks out the window at the chapel they were just married in. It's late afternoon and a limo has just pulled up in front. They watch as another couple gets out and makes their way inside. The bride is wearing a white dress as puffy as a cloud.

Giovanni realizes then he should have gotten them a limousine. *Christ, I'm stupid.* He had to set up everything online from Rome, and between the airfare, wedding, and the move to Seattle, a limousine never even occurred to him.

Of course, they could have just gotten married with a justice of the peace, but when he saw the online ad for an Elvis wedding, something made him click on it. He'd hoped it was offbeat enough that Lindsay would enjoy it.

"So, what should we do on our wedding night?" she asks, turning back to him. "How about we go out dancing and you can show me what you've got."

He snorts with laughter. "Let's not scare the poor villagers."

"Come on, I want to see your Frankenstein moves."

"No, you don't."

She leans toward him. "It might help you seduce me in this car."

"I'd say it would do precisely the opposite."

"All right." She leans back and lets out her breath. "Any other ideas? I guess we could take in a show somewhere."

"I know exactly what I'd like to do for our wedding night." He gives her a hopeful grin.

She rolls her eyes. "Dream on."

He sighs to himself. Memories of their night together in Berlin flash through his mind, torturing him. He does his best to ignore them as he starts up the car. "How about we go grab dinner somewhere? I could definitely use a drink."

"That's the smartest thing you've said all day."

He starts driving out from the chapel's parking lot, headed toward the Strip again. "I have to admit, from what I've seen of Las Vegas so far, it's exactly what I pictured. Non-stop debauchery."

Lindsay remains quiet and he glances over at her. There's a pained expression on her face as she's looking out the window.

"Hey, are you all right?"

She nods. "I just haven't been here in a long time. I always swore I'd never come back."

"Do you want to go hang out in the room? We could order room service and catch a movie on television. We don't have to go anywhere."

"You wouldn't mind that?"

He shrugs. "It's fine."

She studies the passing scenery but then shakes her head. "No, let's go out. You've never been to Vegas, and we're both dressed up." She turns to him, eyeing him with appreciation. "Plus, you look amazing in that suit. I should be showing off my new husband, right?"

"Are you sure?"

She nods. "I'm sure."

"Okay, any suggestions where you'd like to go?"

She bites her lip and thinks it over. "Yeah, I know just the place. You'll like it. It's old-school Vegas, if that's okay?"

"Sounds great."

He drives following her instructions. She takes him past all the big hotels and the throng of tourists to an older part of town. The casinos are smaller, though there are still plenty of people around, everything lit up. He parks and follows her into a place called Binion's. She leads him past the casino to an elevator in back that takes them to the 24th floor.

"Where are we going?" he asks.

"A steakhouse."

When they arrive at the top, he discovers it's one of the coolest steakhouses he's ever been in. There are velvet wingback chairs and the room has crimson wallpaper. It's older and kind of worn down, but it looks exactly like the sort of place you'd imagine the Rat Pack hanging out.

Once they're seated, Lindsay studies the magnificent view which encompasses the entire valley. "I haven't been here in years," she says softly.

He gazes at her, pondering the bizarreness of this situation. Married to a woman beautiful beyond his dreams. He's already noticed all the admiring stares from the men. And yet, surprisingly it's her personality he feels drawn to the most.

He chuckles, thinking back to the ceremony and the way she sang along with that roly-poly Elvis.

"What is it?" she asks.

"I was thinking about Elvis and 'Burning Love.'"

She laughs. "That was so awesome. He was dancing his ass off."

"I guess we have 'our song,' at least."

"Yes, I'd say we do." She grins at him. "And I still think you owe me a wedding dance."

He only shakes his head.

"Come on, if Elvis and his pot belly can put on the moves, so can you. I won't judge."

"You don't know what you're asking."

"Just one wedding dance?"

Luckily, he's saved from this conversation by the waiter coming over to take their drink orders. Giovanni tells him he'd like a vodka neat while Lindsay asks for a martini.

"At least you seem calmer now," she says, once they're alone again. "I take it you've accepted the horrible fate of being married to me?"

He grins with embarrassment. "Not so horrible."

"Why were you so terrified earlier? I can't figure it out."

He shrugs. "Aren't all grooms nervous on their wedding day?" He knows he can't discuss this with her, and if she pushes him, he'll have to shut her down. He's never discussed his relationship with Olivia—and he doesn't intend to start.

Lindsay considers him in that shrewd way of hers, a bloodhound hot on a scent. He can tell she's relentless when she puts her mind to something, a trait he recognizes because he's the same way himself.

He acts indifferent as he takes in the view outside but knows she isn't fooled. In the short amount of time he's spent in her company, it's clear she's fooled by very little. He suspects it's the reason she was so upset when he left her in Berlin.

If only things were different.

The waiter brings their drinks, and Giovanni notices Lindsay still has that bloodhound look on her face.

"So listen." He leans forward. "I want to discuss the situation with that check."

"What do you mean?" Her expression changes. "There is no situation. It's simple. I've decided I don't want your money."

"We had an agreement."

"And I've changed it. I don't want to be paid to help with the adoption anymore."

He takes in her earnestness. "I wasn't trying to guilt you when I had you Skype with Joseph and Sara."

"I know that."

He wonders how best to phrase this, as it's obvious she's touchy about financial matters. "I want you to take that check back."

"Why?"

"Because I know you need the money."

She picks up her martini. "Why would I need money? I just married a handsome and successful surgeon. My life is set."

"How are you going to pay for college? I assume you still want to get your teaching certificate."

"I'll sell some art, or I'll play poker. Whatever." She waves her hand in the air as she takes a sip from her glass. "I always find a way." Her eyes flicker with something, an emotion he doesn't recognize, but then it's gone.

He takes a drink of his vodka but realizes he isn't in the mood for it after all and puts it down. Judging by how quickly she's tossing back her martini, it's probably best he keeps a clear head anyway.

"I'm giving that check back to you," he informs her. "Consider it a loan if you want to."

She rolls her eyes. "Please don't start being an asshole about this, okay? I don't want your money. It's as simple as that. You should be relieved."

"I'm not."

"Twenty thousand dollars for a bride. You really want to pay that?"

The waiter comes by to take their food order, and Lindsay asks for another martini. They both order a steak, though she barely eats any of hers. She tells him how she used to come here with her dad when she was a kid.

"You did?" He's enjoying his meal and has to admit this is one of the best steak dinners he's had in years.

She pulls out a martini olive and sucks on it, and he can't resist watching her mouth. Her lips are full and sensual. He tries not to think about how talented she is with that mouth, but it's difficult. The glow of light coming through the window makes her skin appear luminous.

"After playing poker all day, my dad would bring me up here for dinner sometimes." She holds her drink, leaning back in her chair as she looks out the window. "It always made me feel special."

Giovanni glances around the restaurant again. The lighting is dim, and it's become more crowded since they arrived. He tries to imagine Lindsay as a little kid eating dinner here after watching her dad play cards all day. It doesn't sound like the best life for a child, but then he's seen children manage in all sorts of unusual environments.

By the time they finish their meal, she seems tipsy, and he decides it's best they go back to the hotel.

After paying the bill, they take the elevator down and make their way through the crowd again. She stops walking and tells him there's a picture of her father on the wall here. "Do you want to see it?"

He looks at her with surprise. "Sure."

"It's the Gallery of Champions," she explains. "They used to hold the World Series here every year before it moved to the Rio."

Lindsay takes his hand and leads him through all the tourists and people gambling. The casino is older and has definitely seen better days. It smells like years of buildup from smoke and sweat. Eventually, they come to a red wall with a bunch of framed photos on it—the words 'Gallery of Champions' above it in gold letters.

"There he is." She points to a picture of a guy who looks to be in his early thirties with dark hair. "These are all the Main Event winners who played here."

There's a name below the photo—Jack 'Handsome Jack' West.

Giovanni leans in to get a closer look and right away sees the resemblance to Lindsay. He's never considered himself much of a judge of whether another man is handsome or not, but he can see why her dad had the nickname. He reminds Giovanni of a young George Clooney. When he glances over at Lindsay, she's left his side and has wandered a short distance away, gazing out at the busy poker floor.

"Are you okay?" he asks, coming up beside her.

She nods. "It's just so strange being here after all these years. I don't know why I brought you. We should have gone someplace else for dinner."

He glances around. Like most casinos, the place is noisy and crowded, not really his scene. He senses memories are weighing heavily on her and takes her hand. "Come on, let's get out of here."

As they drive back toward the Bellagio, he figures they'll go up to the room and relax. They both still have jet lag, and he's certain it's contributing to all the heightened emotions today.

"Wait," she says. "There's one more stop I have to make."

He looks at her questioningly. "I was thinking we'd just head back up to our room."

There's a strange expression on her face—determination, but something else he can't quite place. He noticed it earlier.

"I need to do this," she tells him. "Just one more."

She directs him to a part of town away from the main tourist area. It's a bit seedier, with mostly strip malls and liquor stores.

"Over there." She points at a diner called Birdy's with a yellow sign that's obviously meant to look like another famous chain of diners. It's lit up, and there're a few cars parked out front.

"Are you still hungry?" he asks.

She ignores him, her large brown eyes fixated on the diner.

"Maybe you do need more food." He eyes her with concern. She drank those martinis but ate so little. He hopes her blood sugar isn't low. "Let's just get you something at the hotel."

"Park in front of that diner," she tells him. He starts to protest, but she cuts him off. "Just do it!"

He does as she asks, pulling into a space right out front. He shuts the engine off then turns to her with a frown. "What's going on here, Lindsay? Talk to me."

She's staring out through the windshield and appears to be trying to calm herself. He reaches for her hand, but she pulls away from him.

"Come on, we're going inside."

Before he can stop her, she swings the car door open and gets out. He follows her. Her actions have him on alert, and he's not quite sure what to expect when they enter.

A young waitress appears and leads them both over to a nearby booth. Lindsay points to the far end and tells her she'd prefer to sit over there. The waitress complies, and soon the two of them are sitting alone in a booth overlooking an unused parking lot on the side of the building.

"What is this place?"

Lindsay stares at the parking lot, her jaw tense. "I worked here during one of my summer breaks from college."

"Really?" Giovanni glances around. His first thought is she could do better.

As if reading his mind, she explains how it was the only job she could find at the time, how she was too young for anything else.

The waitress comes over, bringing them both a glass of water. She has a pad out, ready to take their order, but neither of them has even looked at the menu.

Giovanni is about to tell her to give them a minute when Lindsay starts asking her about some of the people who used to work here. The waitress doesn't seem to know any of them though, and after a short discussion, it's clear all of them are gone.

"How weird," Lindsay says, after the waitress leaves. "I've thought of this place so many times, always imagining it exactly the same, but it's different."

"Did something happen here?" Giovanni asks, a sick feeling in his gut.

"Everything has changed," she murmurs, ignoring his question, glancing around.

Her face is pale under the bright lights of the diner. He wants to reach for her, but senses she'd pull away.

"You know what? Let's go," she says abruptly. "Let's get out of here."

"Sounds good to me," he replies with relief.

They head outside toward the car again, but just before they reach it, Lindsay suddenly turns in the opposite direction. She walks over to the side of the building near where they were sitting, and he follows her to the small deserted lot.

The air is stifling and greasy smelling from the diner as they stand there together. Sweat dampens the inside of his suit. He's spent a lot of time in hot climates, but most of them cool down at night. Here, because of all the concrete, it's relentless.

There's traffic on the next street over and party music plays in the distance. Lindsay stares at the empty lot with a bleak expression.

Finally, she turns to him. "I'm ready to leave now."

She's quiet on the drive back to the hotel. He tries to talk to her, draw her out, but she doesn't want any part of it. When they get up to their air-conditioned room, the first thing he does is strip out of his suit jacket, yank off his tie, and roll up his sleeves. Lindsay goes to the minibar and pulls out a couple small bottles of vodka. She takes them with her into the bedroom but leaves the door open behind her.

He takes off his socks and dress shoes then walks barefoot to the open doorway to find her sitting in bed, heels kicked off, long tan legs crossed in front of her at the ankle. She's drinking from one of the little bottles.

"Are you sure you don't want to talk about it?" he asks, trying again.

She shakes her head but holds up the second bottle. "Do you want one of these?"

He enters the room and sits on the end of the bed, a sense of helpless anger coursing through him at what he's starting to suspect happened to her. "I'm sorry I made you come back to Las Vegas, Lindsay. If I'd known something bad took place here I wouldn't have asked you to come at all. We could have gotten married elsewhere."

She puts the bottle down, the one she offered him and smiles wearily. "It's not what you're thinking. That's not what happened to me."

"It's not?" He's confused a little but doesn't say anything, figuring if she wants to tell him she will.

"I have a lot of secrets." She pulls her knees up close, hugging herself. "I don't know why, but it's been this way my whole life."

He nods slowly. Unfortunately, he knows a thing or two about secrets himself.

"That summer, when I worked at the diner, there was this customer who used to come in. This older guy who was always looking at me." She takes a swig from the vodka then licks her lips. "A lot of the guys who came in looked at me—leered was more like it—but I knew how to handle them."

Giovanni imagines Lindsay as a young college student, the kind of attention she must have received, and he wants to punch every one of those assholes.

"This older guy was always nice to me though, always left me a big tip." She holds up the second bottle to him again. "Are you sure you don't want it? There's nothing like overpriced booze from the minibar."

"No, I'm good."

"Suit yourself." She shrugs and takes another drink from the bottle in her hand.

"What happened?" he asks, keeping his voice calm.

"Even though my dad made over a million dollars playing poker, there was nothing left when he died. Can you believe it? Nothing. My mom, Natalie, and I lived on welfare and food stamps." She gives him a penetrating stare. "Have you ever been poor like that?"

He doesn't say anything, just thinks about the cushion of money his family has always provided him. "No. I've been very fortunate."

"It can lead you down some strange alleyways, let me tell you." She sways a little and puts her legs back down, a slight slur to her words. "The summer I worked at that diner, there was no money at all. None. My mom drank away the little we had, and that shit job paid hardly anything. I was lucky to get free meals at work."

"I'm sorry, Lindsay."

She cuts him off with her hand. "The irony is that it happened on my dad's birthday. The day he died."

Giovanni is confused. "Wait a minute. Your dad died on his birthday?"

"Yeah." She takes a breath. "He had a heart attack while he was in bed with one of his girlfriends, celebrating. Natalie and my mom tried to hide it from me, but of course, I found out. That was the first time I realized he'd been lying to me." She shakes her head. "I still loved him though. Just like my mom, I loved him despite everything."

"Kids are supposed to love their parents."

She nods slowly. "It's like that old guy knew I was having a rough day.

The worst ever. That fucker. I must have been putting out waves of desperation."

There's a prickle of unease in Giovanni's gut as he tries to guess where this conversation is going.

"He waited for me after work." She closes her eyes for a second. "I worked a night shift, and he must have been out there for a long time . . . waiting. He approached me when I went to my car, and do you know what he said?"

Giovanni shakes his head, his eyes on Lindsay. Beautiful Lindsay. *My wife*.

"He offered me money." She fiddles with the small bottle in her hand. "A hundred dollars if I'd have sex with him."

"What did you tell him?"

"I told him no, that I wasn't a prostitute." She looks at Giovanni, searching his face. "And then he offered me two hundred. I said no again. And then he offered me five hundred dollars."

His throat goes tight, the muscles in his body clenching. He can barely breathe, trembling with fury that someone would do this to her. The only thing that calms him is the thought of finding that sick bastard and ripping his heart out.

Lindsay shakes her head and gives a bark of laughter. "Five hundred dollars was more than I made in a week at that shitty job—even with tips!"

"What did you do?"

She doesn't reply right away, drinking the last remnants from the bottle instead. She stares down at it for a second, but then looks up and meets his eyes straight on.

"I earned five hundred dollars."

Chapter Sixteen

~ Sometimes, you must face the thing you fear the most. ~

"IT WAS DISGUSTING." Lindsay shudders. Unfortunately, she remembers every detail of that nauseating experience. "I made him wear a condom though he didn't want to. I was so young and dumb. I told myself maybe it wouldn't be so bad, you know? I'd been doing it with boyfriends. I was sexually precocious, in fact."

"Did he take you somewhere?" Giovanni's voice is steady and she sees compassion on his face, but there's something else too. Anger, but she can tell it's not directed at her.

"We went to his car. It was parked on the side of the building in that small lot. It was dark and private. I thought he might want to go to a hotel, but I guess he used up all his money."

"Goddammit, Lindsay." He's shaking his head. "Anything could have happened to you. Do you know that? He could have hurt you or worse."

"I know." She runs her thumb over the empty bottle in her hand. "But he didn't." Her thumb presses down and her voice hardens. "Except for turning me into a whore."

"That's crazy. You're not a whore."

"I called Natalie afterward, hysterical." She smiles without humor. "You probably don't know me well enough yet, but trust me, I don't get hysterical."

"How old were you when this happened?"

"Twenty."

He shifts on the bed so he's closer. "Listen to me. That fucking scumbag preyed on you. He saw your moment of weakness and that's when he took advantage."

She stares at him, thinking she's never heard him swear so much. She picks up the second unopened bottle of vodka. "Well, that fucking scumbag paid five hundred bucks to take advantage of me." She gives a laugh and it sounds crazed. "In fact, Werner was right about how much money I could make giving blow jobs in the alley."

"We all make mistakes, especially when we're young. You *can't* let them define you or ruin your life." There's an odd note in his voice, and it catches her attention.

"It sounds like you speak from experience."

"I do."

Their eyes stay on each other and Lindsay sees something in his. It's only a momentary flicker, but the depth of it astonishes her. He's been hurt. Badly. She quickly realizes all those tales of Giovanni's coldness are false.

If anything, she's guessing he feels *too* much.

"What happened when you told Natalie?" he asks.

She chokes up. Even after all these years, what her sister did for her still moves her to tears. "She bought me a plane ticket so I could fly to Seattle the very next day." She smiles at the memory. "It must have cost a fortune. Natalie told me if I wasn't on that plane she was coming out to get me herself."

He nods with approval.

"She was seven months pregnant with Chloe at the time, but believe me, she would have figured out a way."

He grins a little. "I see why my brother fell so hard for her."

Lindsay leans her head back against the wall and closes her eyes. The rooms spins. She's not drunk, but definitely getting there. "The irony is I never even spent the money—the five hundred bucks. I couldn't touch it. I put it on the kitchen table for my mom before I left."

Giovanni remains silent.

She opens her eyes and looks at him. "You're the first person I've ever told this story to."

"What do you mean?"

"Natalie knows, and now you. No one else."

There's surprise on his face. "What about your two marriages? Your husbands never knew?"

"No, it's like I said—I've always lived with secrets." She fingers the bottle in her hand. "So many secrets . . . always."

She thinks back to her marriages. She probably should have told Josh, her first husband. Despite all her trust issues, she realized years later that he did love her, but by then, it was too late. She met him right after it happened and she worried he'd think less of her, that he wouldn't understand.

"Why did you tell me?"

"Because maybe I'm tired of secrets." She closes her eyes again for a moment and lets the room spin, her heart spinning with it. A roulette wheel. "Or maybe I want you to know me."

The air around them changes at her words. She senses it. The way it's stirred up, the way it brushes her skin light as a feather. When she opens her eyes, Giovanni is gazing at her like he recognizes her, like he *does* know her, and it takes her breath away.

"You don't have to sleep on the couch tonight," she whispers, moving closer to him on the bed. "Stay with me." She reaches out and takes his hand.

He doesn't answer right away. Instead, his expression changes to that tense one, the one she's come to know so well.

Uh-oh.

"I can't, Lindsay," he tells her quietly. "Not tonight."

"I see." Though she doesn't see at all. Since when doesn't he want her? A prickle of unease rises within her. She can't believe he's turning her down. Men never turn her down. A part of her is tempted to seduce him, to bend him to her will, because she could.

But then she stops herself.

I don't want him like that.

Her whole life it's been this way. The same thing. Men want her. They want this particular set of bones and skin, but that's all it is.

I want him to accept who I am beneath the mask.

But then another thought comes to her, and her unease grows worse. Much worse. A black pit ready to swallow her. Maybe he isn't happy to discover he's married a whore. She only did it once, but some people would say once is all it takes. Despite his words of sympathy, he is a man, and any man would see her differently after hearing she had sex for money.

How could I have been so stupid?

The air changes again. Only this time, it's fear settling on her skin, sticky and unwanted as spider webs.

She takes a shaky breath, trying to brush them off.

He pulls his hand away and rises from the bed. "I should let you get some sleep. We'll talk more tomorrow."

Lindsay doesn't sleep. She just lies there in the dark for the next hour, kicking the covers around, her mind racing. It's all come back again, dragging her down into those dirty waters. How many times has she wished she could go back in time and change that night? In her darker moments, she wishes she could find that old guy who paid her, who reduced her to nothing but a fistful of cash, and shove that five hundred dollars down his throat until he choked on it.

She thought she'd put this behind her, but it turns out it's only been waiting in the shadows, so patient, like that guy waited for her.

She thinks about Giovanni in the next room. If any man could handle the truth, she could have sworn it was him. Her dad was an expert at reading people. It's one of the reasons he was such a great card player because he could always tell when someone was bluffing. It's a talent she inherited herself.

How could I have been so wrong?

Finally, she can't stand it any longer. She shoves the bedding out of her way and gets up.

I need answers. Now.

She strides barefoot to the door and jerks it open. It's quiet in the living room and she figures he's asleep.

The lights are off, but it's not completely dark. He's left the curtains open on the huge floor-to-ceiling window, and the reflection from the fountain shines through.

It's spectacular, and she pauses.

When her eyes find Giovanni, she's surprised to discover he's not asleep after all. She can see him well enough, lying awake in bed with one arm tucked under his head. He's shirtless, and the shadows accentuate the muscle beneath his skin. So beautifully made. Even in her anger, there's a stirring of desire for him.

He was gazing at the fountain outside, but his head turns when he notices her walking toward him. He remains silent, his face unreadable.

Lindsay's heart pounds.

She's not used to taking the weaker position. "I know why you didn't stay with me tonight, but I just want to confirm it's who you really are."

"Huh?" He's still lying with his hand tucked behind his head. He wasn't asleep but appears to have been deep in thought.

Her hands go to her hips. She was so crazed and distracted earlier she never even changed, is still wearing the black dress she was married in. "You're full of shit. All your words about not letting it 'define me.' All lies, apparently."

"I don't know what you're talking about."

"I'm talking about *you*. Or is it an accident that after telling you what I did, you no longer want to sleep with me?"

"*What?*" Giovanni suddenly comes to life, sitting up on his elbows in bed. "Lindsay, you've got it all wrong."

"Don't act like you don't fucking know what I'm saying." She grits her teeth, her muscles tensing with fury. "Because you *do*."

"No." He sits up all the way now. He's very awake and it occurs to her he hasn't slept either. "That has nothing to do with it. I'm glad you told me what happened."

For a long moment, she doesn't reply, just stands there trying to catch her breath. Her throat's so tight she can barely breathe. Tears burn her eyes. After years of holding in her anger, telling herself it doesn't matter because she's stronger than that—the dam has burst and she's filled with rage. The kind that makes you want to scream and attack someone. Rage at that motherfucker who did this to her, who changed her from a normal woman into a whore in less than thirty minutes.

Giovanni's eyes are intent on her, assessing. The eyes of someone who knows how to deal with trauma. "Lindsay, listen to me. I didn't leave you alone tonight because of what you told me."

"I'm marked." Her voice trembles as she paces around the room. "That motherfucker marked me!"

"That's not true. You were in a desperate situation, and that pervert took advantage of you."

"You don't *know*. It changed me. Turned me into something I'm not!"

"Come here, Lindsay." His voice is low and firm.

She grinds her palms into her eyes to stop the flow of tears. There's movement on the bed, but she puts her hand out. "No, get back. Stay away from me."

Her body shakes, and she wants to hit something, punch someone, anything. Do damage, because maybe it'll release the damage inside. Instead, a sob bursts free and then another, until finally she can't stop them all and she's sobbing without end.

This time, when Giovanni moves off the bed and Lindsay puts her hand out to stop him, it doesn't work. He strides over and drags her close, even as she's pushing him away. Her cries turn jagged with hysteria, hurting her, and yet he holds her tight.

The pain is terrible and goes on for a long time until her stomach aches, and her throat turns raw. A wild tempest in a dark sea, but he never lets go of her. Never.

"It's all right," he murmurs, each wave crashing, his strong arms anchoring her.

At first, she hugs herself, but somewhere in the storm, she hugs him fiercely, letting him hold her steady above the churning waters.

"It's going to be okay," he tells her repeatedly, and he sounds so certain.

"But how do you know?" she finally asks, her voice hoarse from crying. "How do you know it'll stop hurting? That it hasn't ruined me?"

"I just do. You're tough, Lindsay. A survivor."

Tears run down her face again. "Do you want to know why I told you?" she asks. "The real reason."

"Why?"

She pulls back to look at him. "It's because I thought you could handle the truth. I thought you could handle *me*."

He grows still. His eyes stay on hers, absorbing every word.

"I told you my worst secret," she goes on. "The worst I've got. Do you understand?"

"I understand." His hand comes up to stroke her hair. "And you weren't wrong."

"I wasn't?"

His eyes are still on hers. "I can handle your worst. Your worst and more. Don't ever doubt that."

She can't speak and so she cries, tears streaming down her cheeks. His mouth moves close and then he's kissing her, the taste of salt on both their lips.

Relief pours through her as her fingers grip his neck and then his soft curls. She believes him. The storm pulls back, though the waters are still dark and chaotic below.

"Why did you turn me down tonight?" she asks. "Why?"

"It's not what you think."

She takes a deep breath. A wave of exhaustion hits her, and she leans against him. "Tonight of all nights."

"Come on." His arm's around her, and he pulls her along with him over to the sofa bed. "You're obviously wiped."

They lie down together with Giovanni on his back and Lindsay beside him, her head on his shoulder. The fountain outside sparkles with a cascade of light. She turns her body a little and lifts her head to face him. "Tell me the reason. If it's not because you don't *want* me." She nearly chokes on the words. "If you don't find me beautiful anymore."

The hand stroking her back stops and grips her tight. "I want you," he says heatedly. "Everything about you is beautiful to me."

"Then why?"

"I don't know how to say this." He licks his lips. "I didn't want to take advantage of you again."

She stares at him with confusion.

"I feel guilty about what happened in Berlin. What I did was wrong."

"Well, you should feel guilty. You never should have left me there alone."

He looks pained. "I know, but that's not what I'm talking about. I took advantage of you that night. I wanted you so badly, and you were in an emotionally vulnerable state." He touches her face. "I couldn't stop myself, but I can tonight."

"Are you kidding?" And she can see by his expression he's not. "You didn't take advantage of me."

"You'd just been robbed. All your savings stolen. There's no way you were making clear decisions."

She shakes her head. This wasn't at all what she expected. "That's not true. I mean, it's true I was upset, but I knew what I was doing."

He merely looks at her, and she can tell his mind is made up.

"I know I said some things to you that night." She thinks back to how she told him she was in love with him. *Maybe I was out of my mind.* The problem is she still has feelings for him—probably not love, but *something*. "I guess I was swept away," she admits.

"So was I, but I should have been stronger."

She trails her fingers over his muscular shoulder then up to stroke his jaw. Giovanni was clean-shaven earlier for the wedding but is scratchy with stubble now. She can't decide if she's touched or infuriated by his attitude. "You're a complicated man," she finally says.

A smile tugs on his mouth. "You're complicated too."

They gaze at each other, the fountain glows through the window, creating both light and shadow.

"This has to be the weirdest wedding night ever, and it's your first. You must be disappointed." She tries to say it lightly, like a joke, but she can't quite pull it off.

"I'm not disappointed. I know this is just an arrangement, but I've never met anyone like you."

"You haven't?"

"No." He slips his hand beneath her hair, his eyes soulful. "You disarm me in so many ways."

Lindsay doesn't know what to say. She can barely breathe. There's an energy pulsing through her, unlike anything she's ever experienced. Giovanni strokes her neck, and her eyes fall shut, his touch stirring places deep within. "What are you doing to me?" she whispers.

In reply, his hand slides down her arm, his fingers leaving a trail on her skin. When she opens her eyes, he's still gazing at her.

He pulls her in close. Their mouths meet, tangling with each other. Tongue kisses that warm her inside, warm her all over. She reaches out to hold him steady for her. He tastes like all the possibilities in the world are hers. Like doors and windows flung wide open.

The kiss grows hotter and she's all in, but then she senses it. Hesitation from him.

"Please don't say no," she pleads.

He draws back, and it's obvious he's struggling with it.

Lindsay shifts position, sits up a little more so she can address him fully. "That night in Berlin, a lot happened. It's true I was upset, but we both know you were the one in trouble." He blinks at her description. "I wanted you, but you *needed* me. And I was glad to be there for you."

He doesn't reply, only listens intently.

"But tonight is different." She tries to catch her breath as tears fill her eyes. "Because tonight it's me—I'm the one in trouble. You may want me, but I *need* you."

"Baby," he whispers, putting his hand up to her cheek. His expression softens with understanding.

She tries to smile even though she's crying again.

"Come here." This time there's no hesitation as he pulls her to him, brings her close again. He feels so familiar, so right, she has the surreal sense she's been waiting for him her whole life.

He rolls her onto her back, gazing down, and her sense of familiarity only deepens.

She reaches up to touch his face, lightly trails her fingers over his features. She knows she's emotionally raw, that all this confessing has rubbed her tough outer skin away.

"Kiss me," she whispers.

He does so gently at first, their tongues sliding over each, but it isn't long before the energy between them changes. Turns electrified. Giovanni shifts position again, so she's fully under him. Pressing her into the mattress, his mouth hot. She wraps her arms around his neck, inhaling the faint scent of cologne from earlier.

It's all so good. She's glad to be alive in this moment.

"What is it?" he murmurs.

"It's you," she says. "Just you."

He lifts up, meets her eyes, and nothing more needs to be said.

Giovanni runs a hand to her hip. He looks down as if noticing her clothes for the first time. "You're still wearing the dress you had on earlier."

"I know." She stretches her arms overhead and gives him a sexy grin. "You should take it off me."

His eyes go dark, hungry. "Roll over."

She does as he asks and feels the zipper slide down her back. Then he's pulling the dress off her shoulders, down her body until it's tossed aside. Next, it's her bra, and then her panties. She squirms with anticipation, waiting for the feel of his hands everywhere.

"What a view," he murmers as his hands stroke her shoulders then all the way down to her ass.

Her eyes drift shut with pleasure.

His mouth moves to the center of her back, kissing her Queen of Hearts while he cups her breasts. And then he slides lower to the base of her spine, kissing there too.

"So beautiful." He moves down to her ass. When he gently bites her left cheek, she lets out a moan. He bites the right one too, and another moan escapes her.

Passion floods her veins, running through her like a river, and she can't stay still as he continues caressing her with those amazing hands. When he stops and climbs off the bed, she turns and watches him over her shoulder as he takes off his pants, mesmerized by his naked body, all that muscular perfection. It makes her think of the classic sculptures she studied in college.

"You should model for me some time," she says, still watching him.

"Model?"

"Let me sculpt you. It'd be wonderful."

There's a grin on his face, and he seems embarrassed. "I doubt I'd be a good subject."

"You'd be a great subject. Plus, I'd get to stare at you for hours."

Giovanni gets back on the bed. All he does is touch her ankle, trail his fingers lightly up the back of her leg. By the time he reaches the top of her thighs, she's already whimpering with need.

"What do you want?" he asks softly, but he doesn't wait for an answer and lets his fingers slip between her thighs. A moan escapes her as she lifts her hips.

His breath grows harsh as he caresses her, plays with her while she pushes against his hand the whole time.

"*God*," he says. "You're incredible."

Lindsay's trying to control herself, but between the emotional need and now the physical one, she's not exactly doing a great job. "How do you say 'fuck me' in Italian?"

His fingers continue to stroke her, his thumb playing with her ass. When he speaks, his voice is rough. "Do you want to learn the nice way or the dirty way?"

"The dirty way, of course."

But he doesn't tell her either way and instead, changes position. He grasps both her hips with purpose and tells her to turn over. "Lie on your back."

"No, I want it like *this*," she insists.

He pauses, though she can hear him breathing hard. "You're sure?"

"Yes." She turns to look at him over her shoulder, and when their eyes meet, she sees his are hot with arousal.

"Then get on your knees."

She follows instructions and brings her hips up, her hands gripping the sheets in anticipation. It's hard to believe only a few weeks ago she'd lost her sexual mojo because now it's overflowing.

He moves behind her, caressing her ass and hips then down to her breasts as her eyes fall shut.

"Never doubt I want you," he says hoarsely.

He starts out slow and gentle, giving her body what it needs to accept him fully. Giovanni's large, but he doesn't rush it, takes his time. "Oh, God," Lindsay gasps when he finally takes her all the way, moving inside her, because it's the best ever. The perfect fuck. There's no other way to describe it.

She bites her lip with her head down, still moaning as he brings his fingers to where they're joined. The waves of her first climax rise up from nowhere and overtake her. She sobs at the intensity, riding it out long and hard.

He soothes her the whole time. With his hands, but with his voice too, telling her she's safe, that he's taking care of her. "It's okay, baby," he murmurs in a low rumble. "I've got you."

After she comes a second time, he's panting, hands tight—one on her shoulder, the other grasping her hip, his movements hard. She knows he's been holding back, but can't any longer. It's intense. All-consuming. She wants it that way, wants to lose herself, wants to put the past back into the past.

"Wow," she exhales afterward. "Just what the doctor ordered."

He collapses on his back beside her, still breathing hard.

She rolls toward him and slides her hand over his chest. "And you're definitely not taking it for granted."

"Taking what for granted?"

"That big cock nature's blessed you with."

Giovanni's brows go up before he breaks out laughing. Lindsay enjoys watching him. When he eventually calms down, and turns to look at her, it's with such affection it takes her breath away.

Neither of them speaks for a long time as they gaze at each other, the glow from the outside fountain illuminating them in a way that seems magical. And when he finally does speak, what he says rocks her to her core.

"With you," he whispers, "I know it would be forever."

Chapter Seventeen

~ Don't ignore the voice of your heart. ~

IN THE MORNING Lindsay wakes up in surprisingly good spirits. Last night wore her out both emotionally and physically, but it helped her too, and she's feeling more like her normal self again.

What a relief.

She rolls over on her side. They moved themselves to the king-sized bed during the middle of the night, and now she's ready to take her new man out for a nice long test drive. Unfortunately, Giovanni isn't there. The bed is empty.

She blinks, opens her eyes all the way, and her relief vanishes like smoke. With the exception of the air conditioner running, the room is quiet around her, and she doesn't even have to sit up, doesn't need to search the bathroom and the closet to know he's done it to her again.

"Motherfucker!"

She hears chuckling. "Good morning to you too."

"What?" She pushes herself up onto her elbows with surprise. "You're still here?"

Giovanni is sitting in the easy chair across from the bed. He's leaning back with his legs crossed at the ankle. His fingers laced across his chest. He's completely dressed, wearing black straight-legged cords that hug his thighs and a gray T-shirt with the words 'Las Vegas, Nevada' on it and a picture of dice.

Lindsay's eyes travel the length of him and when they reach his face, she sees something's wrong. She doesn't say anything for a long moment. "My God, you were going to leave again, weren't you? That's why you're dressed."

He doesn't reply. His eyes touch on hers, but then he looks down at his hands.

She sits up straight, bringing the sheet with her. Any anger she felt a moment ago is long gone. She doesn't even feel angry about the way he abandoned her in the past. All she feels is despair for him because whatever it is he's struggling with has to be bad.

"Somebody really did a number on you, didn't they?" she says quietly.

His eyes flash back to her. He's wearing his usual tense expression. "Something like that."

"Who? This woman who died?"

He nods and looks across the room toward the open bedroom door like he's ready to flee.

"Who was she? I already know you were in love with her."

But Giovanni only shakes his head. "I can't talk about it. It's not something I can discuss." He takes a breath. "Do you want to go out for breakfast, or should we order in?"

"Why can't you discuss it?"

"Because I can't." He gives her a look. "And don't press me on it."

Lindsay recognizes that tone, the finality. But she's never been good at taking orders from anybody, including him. "What happened? You were in love with her, and she died? Is that it?"

He shakes his head, his voice hard when he speaks. "No, that's *not* it. And I just told you I'm not discussing it."

"I see." She nods. "So you have your secrets too."

"In a word, yes. I didn't push you last night, so don't push me now."

"Why did you stay then? Why didn't you just leave like you normally do?"

He closes his eyes and rubs his forehead, but doesn't say anything.

"Whatever it is that happened to you, don't you think I'd understand? After everything I've told you?"

His eyes open and something flickers on his face, but then it's gone. "This is different."

"Did you whore yourself to somebody?"

"No."

She snorts. "Then how bad could it be?"

"Lindsay, I know you don't want to hear this, but from everything you've told me you were a victim." He sits up, then leans closer toward her. "You're blaming yourself, but that's classic behavior."

"A victim?" She laughs without humor.

"Yes, that's right."

"I'm nobody's victim."

He only looks at her with sympathy.

"Do you want to know why I called Natalie in hysterics afterward? It wasn't just because I'd whored myself. It's because despite how disgusting the whole thing was, I was terrified I'd do it again."

He listens but doesn't say anything.

"If I were desperate enough," she lowers her voice. "If I had no options left, I was scared it might *become* an option."

There's compassion on his face. "It doesn't change anything about what I said. We both know that scumbag took advantage of you."

She wants to believe him but knows it's only partly true. She scoots further down on the bed, closer to where he's sitting. "Tell me what happened to you," she presses. "Please, just tell me."

His expression turns to stone. He looks away, but not before she catches a glimpse of what's beneath it, how something ugly has sunk its teeth into him and doesn't want to let go. It's damaged him, and it hurts her to see it.

She pushes the sheets off. He looks up at her with surprise when she goes to him, his eyes dropping lower to her naked body. He makes room for her to sit on his lap and her arms wrap around his neck, drawing him close.

Neither of them says anything as they hold each other. She can feel his heart beating through his chest. Finally she pulls back and strokes his cheek. "Tell me," she whispers.

"I can't." He licks his lips. "But I can tell you why I stayed."

"Why?"

He looks into her eyes. "For you."

She smiles softly. "I guess that's a start."

Giovanni closes his eyes again, still holding Lindsay in his arms. She's relentless, and he's certain this won't be the last of it. She wants to know everything, but there are some things better left alone.

When he woke up early this morning, he had every intention of leaving. It was the same old impulse, the same compulsion to hit the open road, free and unencumbered. He got dressed, but he never made it to the door. He just couldn't do it. Instead, he sat there for a long time as she slept. He thought about his recent assignment, how he's still coming off the adrenaline. Then he thought about the last time he saw Paul, the two of them having a drink together after a long day of work. He sat questioning himself, his life and the choices he's made.

Until finally he heard her wake up with a loud curse. Right away, he knew he'd made the right decision.

So damn glad I stayed.

He's never believed in miracles, but he's starting to wonder if Lindsay coming into his life is exactly that. Because today, for the first time in a long time, he broke the mold and saw the open road for the lie it really was.

She's still sitting on his lap, stroking his cheek. "If you're not going to tell me your secrets then come back to bed. Let's have a nice *long* morning romp."

The huskiness in her voice is going straight to his dick. He was already half-hard by the time she sat down, so it doesn't take much to get him there. He caresses the small of her back then glides over to her hip. The cobra within him coils and his first instinct is to fight it, but then he realizes he doesn't have to. Lindsay isn't some one-night stand he has to feel guilty about later. Arrangement or not, she's his wife, and to his surprise the thought brings a sense of peace.

"When are we flying to Seattle?" she asks. "It's not today, is it?"

"Tomorrow."

She smiles. "Good." She reaches down for his hand and brings it to her breast, pressing it into her flesh.

His pulse quickens as he touches her, running his thumb over her dusky rose nipple until it pebbles.

She sighs, and that goes straight to his dick too.

"Listen, we need to have a talk first," Giovanni says, trying not to let this beautiful soft woman in his lap turn his brain to mush.

"About what?" She shifts position. Putting her mouth to his neck, she starts kissing him, then licking where she's kissed. His eyes close involuntarily, giving in to the sensation.

"Protection," he mutters.

"Protection from what?"

"Pregnancy . . . for starters."

She stops kissing his neck and looks at him.

"I've never been this sexually careless," he admits. "Ever."

"And you being a doctor and all . . ."

"We haven't discussed it, but I assume you're using some type of birth control? The pill or an IUD?"

There's a peculiar flicker on Lindsay's face, but it's gone so fast he figures he imagined it. "No worries, I've got it covered."

"Covered how, exactly?"

She shrugs. "Do you really want to know the details?"

"Yes, I do actually."

"Well, I haven't been on the pill since my early twenties." She slides her hand beneath his shirt. "So . . ."

He nods. "All right, so you have an IUD."

"Are we done yet?" she murmurs. Her hand strokes his stomach then moves lower to where his erection is straining against his zipper. Her mouth goes to his ear, and she bites him lightly. "Because I want you to take me to bed."

He tries to breathe. "We have to discuss this, Lindsay. I don't even know your sexual history."

"There's not much to tell."

"Somehow, I doubt that." He reaches down and pulls her hand away from where she's trying to unzip his pants. "Seriously, have you had a lot of lovers? And have you been safe about it?"

She looks up to meet his eyes. "I haven't been with anybody since I broke up with my last boyfriend."

"And when did this breakup occur?"

"A couple months before I went to Germany. We were together about nine months."

Giovanni pulls back and looks at her with surprise. "You're telling me you didn't sleep with anyone while you were in Berlin?"

"Only you."

"What about that guy I got into a fight with, the one who wanted to marry you?"

"Dieter? I never slept with him." She shrugs. "I never slept with any of them."

"He wanted to marry you and you never even slept together?"

"I kissed him once." She rolls her eyes. "A mistake, obviously."

He tries to decide if she's making this up, but he can't see any reason why she would. "What do you mean by 'them'?"

"The other guys with their proposals." Her hand slips beneath his shirt, pushing it up this time.

"*Marriage* proposals?"

Her fingers start to pluck and play with his left nipple. "Mmm . . . hmm," she murmurs, and then gives him a sly smile. "I hope this conversation is almost over."

The nipple thing is starting to make him sweat. He's still trying to wrap his mind around what she's telling him though. "You had other marriage proposals in Berlin. How many?"

"Three."

"Three including mine?"

"No, four including yours."

"Jesus." Giovanni stares at her. Her long brown curls fall over her shoulder like an ethereal beauty from a renaissance painting. She's certainly as lovely as a painting. Her brown eyes take him in with what appears to be growing understanding. He's always had a weakness for brown-eyed brunettes, though Lindsay's appeal goes far deeper than that.

Apparently, I'm not the only one who sees it.

She puts her hand to his jaw. "Don't worry about those other guys. It was nothing."

He wonders what he's gotten himself into here and how many men are currently in love with her. The truth is he's half in love with her himself.

He closes his eyes for a moment, and his head swims.

I sure can pick them.

"Seriously, don't worry about my history either," she tells him, moving around on his lap a little. "I get tested at every checkup. Plus, I haven't been sexually careless in years."

He nods, still in a daze.

Suddenly, there's music coming from his phone. *Tosca.*

"Oh, shit," he mutters.

"What's that?"

"My mom calling." He shifts position to try and reach his phone. "It's in my pocket," he tells her.

She lifts her body so he can reach it, and he can't stop staring at her breasts. His hard-on hasn't gone anywhere. Even the phone call from his mother isn't managing to deflate it.

He pulls the phone out, but only studies the display.

"You're not going to answer it?"

The spirited aria from *Tosca* plays a few more seconds then stops. Giovanni has a sick feeling in his gut. "She knows."

"Knows what?"

"That we just got married."

Lindsay shrugs. "Is that so terrible? You have to tell her sometime."

Giovanni doesn't say anything.

"You weren't planning to tell her?"

"I was hoping to put it off for a while. Possibly forever."

"Maybe she's calling about something else. You don't know for sure."

He rubs his brow, trying not to get stressed. "Maybe."

She grins. "No offense, but I have to admit having your mom as a mother-in-law is one thing I've never envied Natalie. Francesca is kind of a handful."

He smirks. "Actually, she's *your* mother-in-law now too."

"What?" Her eyes grow wide as realization dawns on her. "Oh, *shit*!"

He laughs at her panicked expression. "At least it's only temporary." He rubs his forehead again. "Christ, neither of my parents are going to be onboard with any of this."

"We got married for a good cause though. You don't think they'll understand?"

"A fake Vegas marriage? Are you kidding?" He takes a deep breath. "No, this is way too out of the box for them. They're more inclined to hire lawyers and throw money at a problem."

He notices there's a message on his phone, but doesn't listen to it. "How the hell did she figure it out? I don't get it." He thinks back to when he spoke with his mother a few days ago, and he's certain he didn't give anything away.

"I think it's my fault." Lindsay appears chagrined. "I told my sister and Anthony we were getting married last week. I didn't know you wanted to keep it quiet. He probably told your mom."

"No, I spoke to Anthony." Giovanni was having lunch with some friends at one of his favorite restaurants in Rome when he got a phone call from his irate brother giving him the third degree. "I asked Anthony not to say anything, so it isn't him."

She's watching him with his phone. "Aren't you going to listen to the message she left?"

"Maybe later."

She smiles. "Do you want me to call her for you and explain the situation?"

"No, that's okay. I think I'm man enough to deal with my own mother."

Lindsay raises an eyebrow, and Giovanni laughs.

She takes the phone from his hand and puts it down, and then she unfolds herself from his lap. She stands in front of him and stretches her arms overhead, arching her back.

His mouth goes dry as his eyes roam over her. "What are you doing?"

"I was just getting a little cramped and needed to stretch."

She's tall and lithe, with legs that go on forever. He's never seen Lindsay naked in full daylight, and it's a sight to behold.

"Come back here," he says, reaching out for her, but she moves out of his grasp.

"I think I'm going to take a shower now. Maybe spend the rest of the day in one of the poker rooms. We *are* at the Bellagio, so I should at least checkout Bobbie's Room." She gives him a coy smile. "Unless you have something better in mind?"

He rises from the chair and moves toward her, but instead of waiting for him, she quickly goes into the bathroom and closes the door.

He rattles the knob. It's locked. "What the hell are you doing?" he growls.

"Girl stuff," she tells him from the other side.

His brows rise, but then he sighs and goes over to sit on her side of the bed. Her suitcase is open nearby with various items of clothing shuffled around. The heels she had on last night are tossed on the floor. Her laptop and phone are sitting on the nightstand, along with the gold hoop earrings she wore yesterday, a tube of red lip gloss beside them.

He stares at the minutia of her life and is struck by how much he likes having it all here. It isn't just her fox that relaxes him, but Lindsay herself.

The bathroom door opens, and she emerges wearing nothing but a smile.

"I was worried you might have gotten dressed," he says with a grin.

"Me?" She laughs. "You've yet to learn this about me, but I'm the original nudist."

He takes her in with appreciation as she climbs onto the bed beside him.

"The question is why are *you* still dressed?"

His eyes continue to roam as she comes closer, and he grows more aroused at the sight. She pulls on his shoulders until he's lying over her, looking down into her face. She smells like mint, and he realizes she must have brushed her teeth.

"I'm not the original nudist," he confesses.

"Don't tell me you're shy."

He nods. "A delicate flower. I hope you're gentle with me."

She chuckles in a way that tells him gentle is the last thing she'll be. "Of course, I'll be *very* gentle. Don't worry."

"Thank you." He's smiling at her, and he can't stop. He's certain he looks like an idiot, but he can't remember the last time he felt this happy.

"Now, where shall we begin?" she breathes and then pulls him in for a kiss. And all he can think is *so damn glad I stayed.*

They doze for a while, and when Lindsay wakes up, she discovers Giovanni is still asleep. She remains still, watching him beside her. All the normal tension on his face is relaxed and he looks younger, peaceful for a change. She wishes she knew who or what happened to him. Part of it's the stress and sadness over losing a good friend and then trying to help Paul's family, but there's obviously more going on. She's fought her own demons, and clearly he has some he's been fighting for years too. If only he'd tell her what they are.

As she's thinking all this, he blinks a little and opens his eyes. It's late afternoon so the room isn't dark, the Vegas sun shining through the gaps in the curtain.

He doesn't speak as they gaze at each other. Kindred spirits.

"Wow, look at you," she whispers, reaching out to stroke his cheek. "Your eyes are as blue as the skies of Norway."

He chuckles then closes those blue eyes for a few seconds. "Thank you. All my Viking relatives will be pleased you think so."

"You're very welcome, Olaf."

He groans with contentment then pushes the covers back to get out of bed. "I need to take a leak."

He gets up and she watches him walk, that ass and those thighs all moving in perfect concert. "Hurry back," she tells him. "I have more plans for you."

"Plans? Christ, woman you've already worn me out." He looks at her over his shoulder. "In fact, I may have to start charging you."

"Oh? And what's the going rate?"

"Let me think about it." A few seconds pass and then she hears him in the bathroom pissing. "Twenty thousand," he calls out.

She rolls her eyes. "I'm afraid I can't afford you," she mutters.

There's water running in the bathroom sink, and a minute later he emerges, still naked. She takes him in from head to toe. He's muscular all over and beautifully proportioned, including that cock—currently flaccid, bouncing gently between his thighs.

On the way back, he stops at the cart with the leftovers from the room service they ordered earlier. "Do you want anything?"

Lindsay sits up in bed, shoving some pillows behind her back. "Maybe. What's left?"

"Mostly fruit," Giovanni says, popping what looks like a piece of melon into his mouth.

"No, that's okay."

He brings a plate over with him and sits in bed beside her. She can't resist helping herself to one of the strawberries. "I was thinking about what happens when we get back to Seattle tomorrow. I'll probably stay with Natalie and Anthony while I look for a place."

He turns to her with confusion still chewing. "What are you talking about? You're going to live with me as my wife."

"Do we really need to take it that far?"

"Yes, we do. There's a good chance we'll have to meet with someone from the adoption agency, and they'll need to see that we're an actual couple."

She puts the leafy part of the strawberry back on the plate. "But how? Are you going to rent an apartment? We can't just live in a hotel."

He shakes his head. "I've got it covered. I already bought a house in Seattle."

She goes still. "You did what?"

"I bought a house last week."

"How?"

"Online."

Her eyes widen.

"It's close to the hospital where I'll be working, but also looks close enough to the university for you."

"You bought a house off the Internet? I've never heard of such a thing."

He shrugs, still picking at the fruit on his plate. "We needed someplace to live and besides, I start work soon." His expression turns officious. "I don't like loose ends."

She doesn't know what to say. "I still have a small studio I rent. It's in a warehouse with a bunch of other artist's studios."

"Like the place in Berlin?"

"Sort of, but nobody lives in the building. Not on a permanent basis, anyway. I could probably stay there for a couple of weeks if it doesn't work out with my sister for some reason."

He puts the plate down on the nightstand then reaches over and takes her hand. "I just told you I bought a house. You're living with *me*. I'm your husband, remember?"

"Are we going to share a bed?"

"Probably." He pauses. "Don't you want to?" He's studying her now.

She feels a little uneasy. "It's just that we barely know each other, and yet we'll be living together."

Giovanni considers her. "It's a four-bedroom house. You could pick out one of the rooms as your own. Would that make you feel better?"

She nods. "I guess so."

He's still holding her hand, looking down as he plays with her fingers, examining them. Lindsay, who dislikes her hands, tries to pull away.

"This arrangement between us has obviously gotten more complicated," he says.

"It has. All the more reason I need my own space."

He doesn't reply and she senses he's a little wounded, although she's not sure why. "I'm not saying I want to stop having sex or anything," she clarifies. "Or stop exploring things between us." In truth, she's so attracted to him they probably could share a bed in his house, but then it would seem too much like an actual marriage. *And I definitely can't deal with that.*

He grins a little, still playing with her fingers, starts kneading them. "Glad to hear it."

As always, his touch feels amazing, but she still tries to pull her hand away. "Let go."

"What's the problem?"

"I don't know. I don't really like my hands." She can't believe she's admitting this. Over the years, she's learned if you don't point out faults to men, they rarely see them on their own.

"That's nuts." He's still holding her hand, examining it now. "Why don't you like your hands?"

She shrugs. "Everybody has to have something about themselves they don't like." In truth, she knows her hands are too rough-looking, and they're hardly dainty. "They're too big, and because of the various media I work with my skin is always dry."

"Your hands aren't big." He holds his up against hers to measure, and they're noticeably larger. Despite their size, Giovanni's hands are elegant with long, tapered fingers. It's easy to imagine him using them for the intricate work he does.

Her hands look like a peasant woman's, though she's certainly not admitting that out loud.

He's still looking down, and he laces their fingers. "We have something in common too. We both work with our hands."

Her brows go up. She's never thought of that. "True," she murmurs. She watches his handsome face, tries to imagine what his work is really like. So much responsibility. "What made you decide to become a pediatric plastic surgeon? I'm guessing you'd make more money working on adults."

He doesn't answer right away. "I went through a bad time when I was an undergrad in college. I was already pre-med, but everything in my life basically fell apart." His thumb caresses the top of hers.

Lindsay wants to ask what specifically fell apart, but doesn't.

He continues on his own. "My dad finally intervened and got me a job working at a children's hospital. Just grunt work, mostly volunteer stuff, but I really enjoyed it. I've always enjoyed being around kids." His expression goes tense as he remembers the past. "It was smart of him to do that. It made me realize how selfish I'd been."

Giovanni shifts position and lies down to get more comfortable. "That's partly why I'm indebted to Paul. He was my roommate at the time, and when things started to go bad for me, he's the one who went to my parents and told them what was happening."

"What *was* happening?"

"I moved out of the dorm and into a party house, started working at that strip club as a bouncer."

"Were you still taking classes?"

"Barely."

Lindsay lies down too. "And your parents didn't know? Didn't they see your grades?"

"No, they didn't check. I'd always been a good student until then." He reaches for her hand again. "Despite my acting like an asshole and telling Paul to mind his own business, he still managed to get in to see my father—no easy feat in itself. He told my dad how I'd moved out of the dorm, how my life was turning to shit." He grows quiet. "At first, I was seriously pissed at Paul for meddling, but later I realized he'd done me a favor. We became really good friends after that."

"Did your father ask you why you went off the rails?"

"No. I think he made some assumptions, but he didn't know the real reason."

She keeps her breath steady. "What was the real reason?"

He studies their joined hands, and for a long moment, he doesn't say anything. Finally, he whispers, "I fell in love with the wrong woman."

Chapter Eighteen

LINDSAY'S HOUSE RULES

~ The craziest ideas sometimes become the best adventures. ~

IT'S A SHORT flight back to Seattle the next morning, and Anthony picks them up from the airport with baby Luca in his arms. Lindsay already knows Natalie has to work half days at the bakery on Saturday but is delighted to see Luca, who has grown quite a bit in the last three months. He's chubby and bubbly, with a head of curly dark hair and big brown eyes.

"My God, he looks just like *you*," she exclaims, taking Luca from Anthony's arms. Luca studies her with an alarmed expression, but doesn't cry—his curiosity apparently stronger than his fear. "Who's your favorite auntie?" she coos to him.

On the way back to Seattle, she sits in back with the baby, while Giovanni takes the passenger seat up front. Anthony has a lot of questions about their marriage, but Giovanni tells him it would be easiest to explain the whole thing with Natalie present as well.

"Mom phoned me twice yesterday," Anthony tells him. "You need to call her like immediately. The last I heard, she was thinking about flying up here."

Giovanni finally listened to those voice messages last night—three in all. Apparently, Francesca learned about the wedding from Sophia, his cousin in Rome, the one who helped him pick out that suit he wore.

"Yeah," he mutters. "I'll call her when we get to the house."

Lindsay doesn't add anything to the conversation but instead, looks out the window at the city she's come to call home for more than ten years. It looks the same, but different too. There's a sense of comfort being back here again, to a place she knows so well.

Oddly, it was cathartic going to Las Vegas, and she doesn't have the same dread of the city she had before. It helped her to see how the places she has bad memories of have changed. Not that she plans to go back. Although, before leaving, she saw a sign advertising next year's World Series of Poker and it keeps sticking in her mind.

When they arrive at the house, her sister comes out of the front door dressed in jeans and a T-shirt, her hair pulled back into the ponytail she usually wears to work. Natalie is shorter than her and quite curvaceous, with a stubborn streak a mile wide. She's also solid and dependable, the kind of person you want on your side when the chips are down. Natalie went through a rough time a few years ago when her husband left her for another woman, but in the end, it wound up being the best thing that could have happened.

"Hey, stranger!" Natalie grins, pulling Lindsay in for a hug when she gets out of the car. "I'm so glad you're back. I missed you."

"I missed you too," she says, immediately surrounded by her sister's familiar vanilla scent.

When they pull apart, she can see the way Natalie is looking her over, a million questions on the tip of her tongue.

"Before you ask, I'm fine."

"You look great, but you always do. Is everything really okay?" Natalie glances over at Giovanni, who's holding Luca and speaking Italian to him in a sing-song voice. Unlike most guys still single in their thirties, who are awkward with babies, he's completely at ease.

Of course he would be.

It occurs to her how he must not only love children but probably wants a large family of his own someday.

Not that I could ever give him that.

"I'm fine," she tells Natalie, feeling a familiar hollowness. "Let's go in the house and Giovanni and I can explain the whole thing to you guys."

They head inside, the men following.

"Where are Chloe and Serena?" Lindsay asks Natalie, referring to her two nieces. Chloe is Natalie's daughter from her first marriage, and Serena belongs to Anthony.

"Serena is at a friend's house and Chloe is at her dad's, but she should be home soon. Both girls wanted to be here today when they heard you were flying back."

Lindsay smiles. She loves Chloe as much as if she were her own daughter, and she's grown to love Serena as well.

After asking Giovanni and Lindsay if they'd like anything to eat or drink, the four of them—along with Luca, who's being held by Anthony again—have a seat in the living room.

"All right," Anthony says, taking the bottle Natalie hands him to give to the baby. "What the hell is going on?"

Giovanni and Lindsay glance at each other. They're sitting on the couch together, though they aren't touching.

"It's complicated," Lindsay says, watching Luca's eyes drift shut as he drinks.

"It concerns what happened to Paul a few months ago," Giovanni tells Anthony, who's apparently already familiar with the situation, judging by the solemn expression on his face.

Giovanni leans forward on the couch, his forearms resting on his knees as he explains everything, filling in some of the details about Paul's death for Natalie.

Lindsay is silent, listening, but speaks up when he's finished. "I met the kids online," she tells her sister. "I couldn't *not* help them after that."

"Have you heard anything yet?" Anthony asks. "About the adoption?"

Giovanni shakes his head. "No, it's too soon. I just faxed the paperwork to the lawyer a couple days ago. I talk to Phillip regularly, and we're all hoping it works. They've been trying some other things through the embassy, but so far there's been no movement."

Anthony's face is grim, nodding as he glances down at Luca. "All I can say is I hope you get them out. How long do you think you'll have to stay married?"

Giovanni glances over at Lindsay. "I don't know. Six months, maybe?"

The four of them talk a little more about the situation and about their Elvis wedding in Las Vegas, which both Natalie and Anthony find quite amusing.

Eventually, Giovanni stands and tells everyone he should call his mom. Natalie points him in the direction of the family room for some privacy. Lindsay can't help laughing to herself at the dread on his face.

After he's gone, and Anthony has taken the baby upstairs for his nap, Natalie tells Lindsay she's set up the guest bedroom for her to sleep in. "Is that all right?"

"That sounds great. I appreciate it."

"Should we put Giovanni on the couch downstairs?"

"No, he can sleep with me."

Natalie nods, her expression searching. "So, it's like that, is it?"

"Yeah, it's like that."

"I appreciate what you two are doing here, and I'm all for helping those kids, but I have to admit I'm surprised you agreed to marry him so easily."

Lindsay doesn't say anything. She knows she needs to tell Natalie about the poker, but this doesn't seem like the right time.

"Did he talk you into it somehow?" Natalie asks. "I'm having trouble picturing this."

"I didn't say yes right away. But then later, I changed my mind."

"After you started sleeping with him?"

Lindsay lets out her breath. "No, some other things happened. There's more to the story, but I don't want go into it right now."

"I had a feeling there was more." Natalie eyes her steadily. "I hope you know what you're doing."

"I can take care of myself."

"Normally, I'd say yes, but this whole thing is complicated by the fact that this is Anthony's brother we're talking about. He's not just going to disappear when you're done with him."

They go into the kitchen where Natalie checks the food she has in the oven. She's making a large dish of lasagna, along with fresh bread from the bakery. It smells divine. Lindsay realizes she's hungry after all and pulls a banana from the bunch in a nearby wooden bowl.

"Giovanni's not what you think," she says, looking down at the banana in her hand, not peeling it yet. "There's a lot more to him. He's got depth. I think something happened to him in his past that's messed him up."

"Anthony's never mentioned anything. Do you know what it is?" Natalie puts the bread on a wooden cutting board and gets out a knife.

"No, he won't tell me."

Natalie starts slicing the loaf into thick pieces to make garlic bread but doesn't say anything.

"I told him about what happened to me in Vegas," Lindsay says, her voice quiet.

"You *did?*" Natalie looks up at her with surprise. Lindsay doesn't have to elaborate, as her sister already knows what she's referring to. "How did he respond?"

Lindsay tells her the things Giovanni said about it not being her fault, how she was a victim.

Natalie nods. "I can't believe you told him. But you should listen to him about this. He's right."

"Maybe." Lindsay peels her banana, takes a bite, and chews for a while. "I don't know if I agree with everything." She takes a deep breath. "I'm starting to make peace with it though. I don't think I ever really have before."

The conversation between them stops because Anthony comes into the kitchen. He turns on the baby monitor they keep nearby then pours himself some coffee from a warming pot.

"Where's Giovanni?" he asks, adding cream to his coffee. "Is he still talking to Mom?"

"He hasn't come out from the family room yet."

Anthony leans back against the counter, chuckling as he sips from his coffee. "I don't envy him this conversation. Both our parents sounded freaked out."

Lindsay tries not to be offended about the fuss being made, but it's starting to get on her nerves a little. "All because he married *me?*"

"I don't think it's so much you, but the situation. They're very conservative about stuff like this." Anthony shrugs. "And let's face it, this whole thing is unusual."

She nods, remembering what his parents were like when she met them at Natalie and Anthony's wedding. Conservative, wealthy, and living in their own affluence bubble—at least that's how Lindsay saw them. To his parents' credit though, they do love Natalie—especially now that's she's given them another grandchild—so Lindsay can't be too harsh on them.

"Do you think you can fill in at the bakery this week?" Natalie asks her, smearing garlic butter onto the slices of bread. "I know you just got back, but as always we're shorthanded on the register."

"Sure." Lindsay takes another bite of her banana. "I can watch Luca in the mornings too now that I'm back."

"We're okay for the moment," Natalie says. "Anthony has him before work, and I've found a daycare during the day. I need to start interviewing nannies soon though so we're covered when he leaves on his next observing run."

"That reminds me." Anthony puts his coffee down on the counter and gives Lindsay a look. "I understand you have some concerns about us hiring a nanny?"

Lindsay takes in his annoyed expression. She can hear her sister laughing as she finishes with the bread, wrapping it in foil.

He crosses his arms. "You're worried I'm going to fall under something called the 'nanny spell'?" He makes air quotes with his fingers. "Seriously?"

Lindsay shrugs and tosses her hair over her shoulder. "Hey, it's nothing personal. I'm just trying to protect you both. Haven't you ever seen *The Hand that Rocks the Cradle*?"

He's staring at her in amazement, and it looks like he wants to say more, but Giovanni comes into the kitchen with the phone at his ear, speaking Italian in a frustrated voice. It sounds like he's still talking to his mother, and clearly the conversation isn't going well.

He pulls the phone away for a moment and looks at her. "She wants to speak with you," he says quietly. "You don't have to."

"I don't mind." She reaches for the phone.

His mother, Francesca, is a beautiful, wealthy Italian woman who knows her mind and typically gets whatever she wants. It's clear she loves her family and would do anything for them, but it's also clear she has high standards and expects a lot.

She puts the phone to her ear. "Yes."

"Lindsay, you must talk sense into Giovanni," Francesca says in her heavy accent. "It is not too late to get the annulment!"

"Hello, Francesca," Lindsay says, in a dry voice. "It's good to speak with you again too."

"You must do this right away. Do not wait! I already have all the information for you and where to go."

Lindsay thinks back to yesterday when she and Giovanni basically consummated their marriage all day long. "Um, I'm pretty sure it's too late for any kind of annulment."

"No, it is not too late." Francesca sighs dramatically. "You must listen to me. Ever since he was a little boy, Giovanni wants to save the world, but there are better ways to handle these matters."

Lindsay glances at Giovanni, who's standing over by the fridge with Anthony. He's watching her with a tense expression that says he's ready to take the phone back at the first sign of trouble. She tries to imagine him as the little boy Francesca is describing and she sees it clearly. Serious and with a big heart, he would have definitely wanted to save the world as a kid. In fact, he still does.

"As a woman, you and I must have more common sense," Francesca continues. "That is often our role with men because marriage is not so frivolous."

"We're trying to do some good here, and hopefully, we'll succeed."

"This is not the way. Are you listening? I do not want you to get into trouble!"

"I'm not worried about it. I want to help."

There's a string of Italian words and then, "You are behaving as stubborn as him!"

"Look, no offense, but Giovanni is a grown man who can do whatever he thinks is right. Plus, I happen to agree with him."

Francesca, obviously upset, starts carrying on in Italian. Lindsay doesn't understand a word and finally goes over to Giovanni to give the phone back.

He puts his beer down. "What's happening?"

"I don't know. She's speaking Italian."

"Uh-oh." He takes it from her and puts it back to his ear. "*Si, Mama . . .*" He nods, and then starts talking to her again. Lindsay reaches for his bottle and takes a sip. *What have I gotten myself into here?* Anthony only shakes his head with amusement. Luca cries in the monitor, and they both hear Natalie asking Anthony to come upstairs through the speaker, so he leaves to go check on them.

Giovanni talks to his mother for a short while longer, eyeing Lindsay and wearing a funny little smile the whole time. Finally, he puts the phone back in his pocket.

"What did she say?" she asks, taking another swig of his beer.

"She says she likes you. That you have spirit."

Lindsay nearly chokes as she starts to laugh. "I'll bet. What did she really say?"

He gives a weary sigh then turns his head. "You don't want to know."

"Oh, well." She shrugs and takes another sip from the bottle before handing it back to him. "It's not like she can stop us."

His eyes are on hers, watchful. To her surprise, he leans down and gives her a kiss on the mouth.

"What's that for?"

"Just you," he whispers, wearing that funny little smile again. He rubs his nose playfully against hers. "For your spirit."

Chloe and Serena both make it home in time for dinner. There are hugs and kisses, and Lindsay is happy to see them, amazed how they look older even though it's only been three months. She notices Serena is happy to see Giovanni and, after listening, is surprised to learn he Skypes with her regularly. Lindsay knows Anthony's family is close-knit, but she hadn't realized Giovanni was involved as much as he apparently is. She's never really heard Anthony talk about his brother and is starting to wonder now if the reason had something to do with the one-night stand she shared with Giovanni years ago.

They sit down at the dinner table, and there's a lot of good-natured banter, as well as a fair amount of Italian thrown around, especially between the brothers who use elaborate hand gestures and facial expressions when they speak it. Serena keeps laughing, so their conversation must be quite amusing.

"I get why you're learning Italian," Lindsay tells her sister, who has started taking a class recently. "Can you tell what they're saying?"

Natalie has Luca on her lap and is feeding him some pureed vegetables. She tilts her head. "I'm not sure. Something to do with a pig, I think?"

"Really?"

"*Mi dispiace*," Anthony says to her and Natalie, still laughing about whatever it is they're talking about. "It's just great to have my brother here. We were talking about one of our cousins in Rome who's always trying different jobs. Now he's gone into business with someone who owns a small sandwich shop, but apparently he was complaining to Giovanni about the customers and how it's all too much work."

"Porca miseria," Giovanni says, chuckling. "It means 'pig misery,' but in Italian, it's a common way of saying a word like 'dammit' when something goes wrong."

Lindsay tears off a piece of garlic bread. "I'm pretty sure I could find a use for *that* phrase."

"Me too," Natalie says with a laugh.

After dinner, the brothers go out and bring in the luggage from the car. Both Lindsay and Giovanni have gifts for everybody. Hers are mostly T-shirts and various items from Berlin.

"These are so cute!" Chloe says, holding up some *Ampelmann* earrings she got both girls.

Lindsay explains how *Ampelmännchen*—the little figure of a man walking—are used at crosswalk lights. "But only in East Berlin, which is where I was living. After the wall came down, people were so fond of them they took on a cult status."

All her gifts are a hit, though it turns out they don't generate anywhere near the kind of interest and excitement as those Giovanni's brought from Africa.

"Ew!" both Serena and Chloe exclaim after examining a packet of some kind of snack food that he's handed each of them. "Yuck!"

"We can't eat this, *Zio Giovanni!*" Serena says, laughing. "This is like *so* gross!"

"Of course you can," he says with a smile. "I eat them all the time."

"You do not!" Both girls are gawking at him. "No way!"

"What is it?" Lindsay asks, looking over with curiosity at the variety of colorful bags he's pulled from his suitcase. He hands one to her and immediately Lindsay sees why they girls are freaking out. "*Bugs?*" Her eyes go wide as she stares at the blue bag in her hand, filled with what are clearly dried insects of some kind. "You don't really eat these, do you?"

"Let me see," Natalie says, and Lindsay watches her sister grimace as she examines a bag of some kind of dried worms that Giovanni's handed her.

Anthony, who's sitting on the couch with Natalie tucked into his side, shakes his head and makes a face when she holds the bag up for him. "Dude, seriously?"

"I want to see you eat one," Serena says to Giovanni, dancing around with excitement. "I don't believe you eat them!"

"Sure." He reaches for a red bag and opens it. "The curry-flavored crickets are my favorite."

Everyone is silent, holding their breath as they watch him reach into the bag for a few crickets. He pops them into his mouth, and as soon as he starts chewing both girls are shrieking with delighted horror.

"Mmm." He licks his lips. "These are great. Are you sure you don't want to try them?" He holds the open bag out toward Serena and Chloe, who are both laughing and shaking their heads. "What about you?" He turns toward Lindsay. "You're usually up for any adventure."

She meets his eyes and can see how much he's enjoying himself. She peers down into the bag filled with what look like small dried grasshoppers. "I don't know." Finally, she shrugs. "What the heck."

She reaches inside for a cricket, feeling everyone's eyes on her as she puts it in her mouth and starts chewing.

"Yuck, Aunt Lindsay!" Chloe moans. "What does it taste like?"

Lindsay chews up the cricket, trying not to think about what she's actually eating. It's crunchy and surprisingly not that bad. "It tastes all right," she admits. "It's kind of nutty and salty, with a kick of curry flavor."

"Are you going to eat more?" Chloe asks. "Did you like it?"

"I'm not sure." While it tasted okay, she has to admit it's hard to get past the fact that she's eating an insect.

She sees the way Giovanni is grinning at her, almost like a dare. "Go on, have some more."

"Oh, why not." She reaches into the bag for another cricket, much to Chloe and Serena's delight.

"Don't eat them all though," he tells her. "Save some for the rest of us." And both girls start giggling.

He stands and goes over to Natalie and Anthony, offering them the open bag. "Would you two like to try some curried crickets?"

Lindsay watches the way her sister and Anthony are eyeing each other.

"Ladies, first," Anthony says, tilting his head toward the bag, and Natalie laughs.

Finally, she reaches in and pulls one out, staring at it. "I don't know if I can do this."

"We'll do it together," Anthony tells her. He gets a cricket for himself. The two of them are studying each other again. "On three," he says. "One, two, *three*."

Both of them pop the cricket into their mouths. Lindsay can't help laughing at the panicked expression on both their faces as they chew. Giovanni is cracking up as well. And, of course, the girls are grabbing each other while shrieking with glee.

Lindsay glances over at Luca, who's sleeping peacefully on a blanket, oblivious to all the noise.

"Would you like another one?" Giovanni asks, still chuckling after they've both finished.

Anthony, who looks like he's just eaten a cat turd, shakes his head. "That was *disgusting*."

"I've had enough as well." Natalie tries to smile at Giovanni. "Thank you though."

Giovanni chuckles, grabs a few more crickets from the bag and then tosses them into his mouth like peanuts as everyone groans with amazement.

By now, the girls are coming around and deciding they want to try them after all. Serena goes first and then Chloe, both of them chewing with trepidation. Afterward, they agree the crickets are not as gross as they thought, "but they're still pretty gross." They each want to take a bag to school to share with their friends to get their reaction.

"It can be an acquired taste," Giovanni says. "Many people all over the world eat insects though." He tells them how, ounce per ounce, grasshoppers have more protein than beef. "They're very nutritious."

"I'll stick with beef," Anthony mutters. "I don't think I could stomach another one of those things even if you paid me."

"That's because you haven't tried the chocolate-covered ants I brought back just for *you*," Giovanni tells him with a grin, rubbing his hands together, and the whole room laughs.

Chapter Nineteen

~ It's okay to let a man surprise you. ~

THE NEXT DAY, Lindsay and Giovanni head over to meet with the realtor at the house he bought online. They take her car—a red Mini Cooper convertible—that Natalie and Anthony were nice enough to store in their garage while she was in Berlin. Lindsay hasn't driven a car in three months but has no trouble navigating the streets of Seattle as Giovanni gives her directions with his phone.

When they finally arrive, she parks in the driveway, and they both get out. She notices he's wearing a peculiar expression.

"Is everything okay?" Lindsay asks, glancing over at him as she grabs her purse.

Giovanni stands next to the passenger door staring at her with amazement. "Is that how you *always* drive?"

"What do you mean?" She tosses her car keys inside her bag.

"Nothing." He shakes his head, chuckling. "Forget it."

It's a sunny Sunday, and the realtor is already inside waiting for them. After walking them through the house and having Giovanni sign some papers, she leaves him with a set of keys.

"I'm afraid to ask what you paid for this place," Lindsay says, wandering over to look out the window at the backyard. She can't explain it, but for some reason, the house is having a powerful, visceral effect on her. It feels like she's been here before, even though she's certain she hasn't.

He shrugs. "I have money saved, and I figured it was time to finally use some of it. Plus, I've never bought a home before."

It's a nice Tudor-style older brick house in a swanky neighborhood and is exactly how Giovanni described it—close to the hospital where he'll be working while still being close to the university for her.

"What about your apartment in Rome?"

"I inherited that from my grandfather when he passed away."

"I didn't know that." She studies the backyard, which is fenced in and mostly just dried grass with a tangle of neglected trees in one corner. "I've never bought a home either."

"You should pick out which room you want as your bedroom. Did you see one that appealed to you?"

She thinks about it. The house has four bedrooms—three upstairs, including the master, and then one more on the first floor. "Probably the one downstairs."

"Really?" Giovanni comes over and stands behind her, sliding his arms around her waist. "You can have the master bedroom if you want," he says softly into her ear. "I don't mind."

"You're just saying that because you want an excuse to sleep with me."

He chuckles.

"You should take the master," she insists. "You're going to want to make that your own space. In fact, I'm not sure why you included my needs in any of this."

"What do you mean?"

She leans back against him and slides her hand over his. "It was nice of you to choose a house that also happens to be close to the university, but it wasn't necessary."

His only reply is to brush her hair aside and kiss the back of her neck. Lindsay's breath goes shaky. She's been trying not to let herself get turned on by him so much, but if anything, it's getting worse.

"Are you complaining?" he asks.

"No."

"Good." He kisses her neck again then nibbles her ear. Her eyes drift shut. Giovanni's been very affectionate with her since the phone call with his mom last night. She's not sure why, since she's certain his mother wasn't pleased with a single thing Lindsay said during their short conversation.

She turns around so they're facing each other. "You're the nicest arrogant prick I've ever met."

He grins and reaches down for her hand. "I want you to treat this like your home."

"But it's not really."

"It *is*," he insists. "Neither of us knows how long this whole thing will go on. I want you to be comfortable."

She considers this, glancing around at the bare white walls. "The first thing I'd do is add some color."

"And the first thing I'd like to do is christen this room." He pulls her in and brings his mouth down, kissing her in that slow, luscious way he's so good at. Lindsay wraps her arms around his neck, already wanting him, already knowing she'd let him take her right here on the hardwood.

"You feel incredible," he says, his hands kneading her ass.

"Of course I do."

He chuckles then pulls away. She watches as he goes to the front window to yank the curtains shut.

"Doctor Novello, I believe you have something dirty in mind."

Giovanni comes back toward her, his blue eyes aroused. And she sees he does indeed have something dirty in mind. He takes her hand and pulls her over next to the fireplace, so her back is against the wall.

"I can't stop thinking about you," he whispers, moving in close. "I'm obsessed."

"Glad to hear it."

"Are you?" He looks at her, and she can tell he's serious. "Are you glad?"

She doesn't say anything for a long moment, but then nods. "Yes."

He sucks in his breath, and it's shaky when he exhales. He doesn't say anything more, only brings his mouth to hers again, kissing her with real desire. A warmth spreads through her as he pushes her against the wall. The need coming off him reminds her of their first night in Berlin, that erotic perfume. Except this time, it's mixed with her own because there's a stirring deep within her, like the first notes of an instrument when it's played, vibrating all through her body and down her spine. She lets her eyes fall shut, lets herself enjoy it.

She wants him so much. It isn't even smart to want a man this much, and she knows it. A crazy memory flashes through her mind of her mother, and the way she used to go after her father's girlfriends. She remembers her mom once slapping a waitress during a poker tournament, knocking drinks to the floor, and then yanking Lindsay up from the chair where she'd been sipping her Shirley Temple. She and Natalie both thought their mom loved their dad too much.

Lindsay's eyes open.

That will never be me.

Giovanni's hands slip under her shirt, under her bra—soothing hands that lull all her fears. She moans when he lightly pinches her nipples, a spark of pleasure running straight between her thighs. His large hands are all over her now, but then he's moving lower, his mouth on her stomach, sliding down so he's on his knees. She knows what he's planning and is already squirming in anticipation.

She watches him unfasten the leather belt she's wearing, and then her jeans. He tugs them off her, lifting each foot to help her step out of them.

He leaves her black lace thong on and snakes his fingers inside the scrap of fabric, her hands gripping his wide shoulders to steady herself.

"No dirty talk from you?" he asks, his voice rumbling through the empty room, echoing.

He's looking up at her, touching her gently, gauging her reaction. He slides through to her center, where she's already wet and moving her hips in a mindless way.

She swallows, tries to catch her breath. She's so turned on she can barely think, much less string words together. "Make me come," she whispers. "Please." It's all she can manage, and she sees understanding on his face. His eyes are soulful as he takes in how exposed she's grown with him.

Instead of shying away from the emotional intimacy, he seems to welcome it, and she has a revelation. For him, it has to be all or nothing. There's no in between. And she suspects it's been nothing for a very long time.

"I want you," he says, his voice rough. "In every way."

Lindsay's only response is a soft moan, gripping his shoulders harder.

He glides his fingers from one hand down her thigh then up to her waist. With the other, he pushes her thong aside and brings his mouth to the place she needs it most.

She whimpers. Pulling his hair with pleasure. So perfect. As always, he's thorough and patient. Lindsay watches him the whole time through slitted eyes. Perceptive too. He's figured her out, what she likes and doesn't. Her own rhythm.

His head moves, first nodding, then back and forth. She tries to hold back for a while, lingering on the edge of bliss. When ecstasy arrives, it floods her mind and body, her knees nearly giving out, but his hand on her waist steadies her. He keeps going because he knows she'll come again, and she does, crying out as she grabs his head with both hands. She's breathing hard and feels invigorated, pulling him up to her.

"*Now*, I need you to fuck me," Lindsay says with a grin, resting her arms on his shoulders.

Giovanni isn't smiling, and she sees he's far past it. His cheeks are flushed, his expression hot with need. He fumbles with his pants, shoving them down, and then his hands are on her ass, pulling her in tight. "Hold onto me."

She does as she's told and he lifts her up, pinning her against the wall. Both of them groan when he slides home. She watches his face—his mouth open, teeth bared. Giovanni at his most primitive self. She loves seeing him like this, all the trappings of civility stripped away.

She bites his neck, digs her nails into him. In the same way he's figured out her rhythm, she's figured out his, and he likes a sting of pain with his pleasure. She pulls his mouth onto hers, and he kisses her in a reckless way, tongues and teeth clashing, then biting her chin.

When he breaks the kiss, his movements grow hard, fierce, reaching for it. He's close to climaxing, and when it's almost on him, she puts her mouth to his ear, and gasps the truth. "I want you all the way too."

"Lindsay," he growls, gripping her ass, his muscles tense as he fills her, pushing deep.

Afterward, they stay joined for a long while. He hugs her tight while she keeps her legs wrapped around his waist. His heart pounds through the hard wall of his chest, and she's awash with tenderness.

Finally, she releases her legs, and he lowers her to the ground. The two of them remain close as they come down from the sexual high.

Giovanni kisses her again and smiles. The smile she loves, the one that somehow checkmarks every box in her heart. "I don't think I could ever get tired of doing that with you," he murmurs.

She strokes his face. "Me either."

They gaze at each other.

She continues to stroke his face. "I should tell you though, I'm expecting some action soon."

"Action?" His brows go up in amazement. "Christ, woman, you're insatiable. What do you call *this*?"

Lindsay shakes her head slowly. "No, I'm talking about our bet in Las Vegas. You never seduced me in that horrible car, so now you have to answer all my questions."

He puts his forehead to hers and lets out his breath. "You know how to pick your moments, don't you?"

She doesn't reply because, of course, it's true.

"If you ask me, that bet is null and void," he tells her.

"Oh?"

"I never had a chance to seduce you in that car. We were hardly ever in it."

"There was the ride to the airport."

He snorts. "The ride where we left a half hour late and nearly missed our flight to Seattle?"

"That's the one, but it doesn't matter because you would never have been able to seduce me."

He chuckles. "Hey, I've got moves. Panty-dropping moves."

"You sure do." She smiles and meets his blue eyes. "I've told you more about me than I've ever told anyone."

"I know you have." He grows quiet as the tenor of the conversation changes. "And I'm glad you told me, but this is different."

"How?"

"It's far worse."

"What could be worse than me whoring myself to some dirty old man?"

Giovanni's eyes grow pained. He brings his hand up to her cheek then leans in and kisses her softly. "Don't let that hurt you anymore, baby."

She meets his gaze, and then nods. "I'm trying."

"Good."

"Tell me, though, what's worse?" she whispers.

He lets out his breath. "Damn, you're relentless." She thinks he's going to shut her down again, but surprisingly doesn't. "Lying to all the people you love for years. Every day. Straight to their faces." He looks at her. "That's worse."

"What did you have to lie about?"

He shakes his head and turns to the side. "An affair. One I never should have had."

She tries to picture why he'd have to lie, and it isn't difficult to guess the reason. "She was married. That's it, isn't it?"

He nods.

"But you weren't, so who were *you* lying to?"

"Family, friends, everyone. Nobody knew." There's such a bleak expression on his face it makes her heart ache.

"Sometimes affairs happen in secret." She tries to imagine it going on for years, and can see how that would be difficult. "Why didn't she just leave her husband?"

"It wasn't like that."

"What was it like?"

But Giovanni doesn't answer. Instead, he steps back and pulls his jeans up, not looking at her. Lindsay does the same, refastening her belt. The moment between them is slipping away. She wants to bring it back but doesn't know how.

Her phone chirps in her purse, and she goes over to check it, wondering if it's from Natalie. Instead, there's a text from Dagmar. She's only spoken to her friend once since she left Berlin, but they've been texting regularly.

She gasps as she reads it.

"What is it?" He turns to her with concern. He's standing by the window looking out at the backyard.

"Werner has been picked up by the police, and it turns out he had eight thousand euros on him!"

His brows slam together. "Do they know where it came from?"

"Dagmar says he told the police he won it playing poker, but she says she doesn't believe him." She shakes her head and glances up at him. "Well, no shit!"

"What else does she say?"

Lindsay reads the rest of it. "Apparently, Werner got caught cheating at Spielbank Europa, and Varik threw him out and banned him for life. When he snuck back in, they called the police." She shakes her head. "Dagmar says she's going to try and get what's left of my money back to me. She says she's sorry she didn't believe me, and that she's come to see now how wrong she was about Werner." She puts her phone down. "Well, damn."

Giovanni walks over to her. "I hope you do get your money back."

"So do I. Even some of it would really help."

"You could let *me* help you."

She looks up into his face, so earnest. She knows he wants to be her hero. "I can't take your money."

He seems ready to argue but then stops himself. "All right." He sighs in a resigned way. His eyes roam the space of his new home. "I need to buy some furniture as soon as possible. There's not even a bed to sleep on here."

"I have furniture."

He looks at her with surprise. "You do?"

She laughs. "Of course I do. Unlike you, I haven't spent the past four years roaming the Earth like a vagabond."

"Do you have a bed?"

"Queen-sized."

He nods, but then gives her a sly grin. "That'll do."

They spend the next week getting settled in Giovanni's new house. Lindsay even goes to the hardware store and buys paint. She figures if she's not working on art she might as well do as Giovanni suggested and make the house feel like home. She's picked out all sorts of bright colors—emerald green, teal blue, and of course, dark red for her bedroom.

She also starts working at La Dolce Vita, her sister's bakery, a few hours every morning, filling in at the register. She's done it many times in the past, and it's great to hang out with the regular crew, along with Blair—one of her besties, who bakes wedding cakes and is co-owner of the bakery.

"We need a girls' night now that you're back," Blair says, hugging Lindsay on her first day of work. "And I can't believe you got married!"

"I know. It's sort of a complicated situation, though."

Blair nods. "Natalie filled me in on some of it earlier, but I want to hear more."

"It happened really fast. Hopefully, we'll manage to do some good."

"I know it's only an arrangement, but Natalie says you guys are living together as man and wife, with all the fringe benefits?"

Lindsay stirs her iced dirty chai latte with a straw, taking a break after the morning rush. "Pretty much."

"I can't believe it's Anthony's brother. Is he as handsome as Anthony?"

"Please." Lindsay sweeps her hair over her shoulder. "Are you kidding? He's *way* hotter than Anthony."

Natalie, who is standing only a few feet away, flipping through the pages of one of her master recipe books, lets out a loud laugh when she hears this. "As if *that* were possible."

"Oh, it's possible," Lindsay tells Blair. "In fact, it's the reality."

Natalie glances up from the book she's taking notes from. "You seriously think Giovanni is better-looking than Anthony?"

"Of course he is."

"I hardly think so."

Lindsay puts her hand on her hip. "Giovanni may not be as pretty as Anthony, I'll give you that, but what he lack in prettiness he makes up for in *many* other ways, trust me."

Natalie appears dubious.

Blair fidgets with what appears to be embarrassment. "Um, I think you guys are getting into sort of a *weird* area here if you don't mind my saying so."

Lindsay and Natalie both look at Blair, then at each other.

"She's right," Lindsay says to her sister, laughing a little. "I think there's a certain 'ick' factor here we're skating awfully close to."

Natalie nods. "Yes, let's just agree they're *both* handsome and leave it at that."

After working at the bakery every morning, Lindsay usually goes back to the house to find Giovanni playing handyman. He bought a shiny set of new tools at the hardware store, so every day it's something different. Typically, as soon as she walks through the front door, he's dragging her over to show her his latest project. Recently, it was installing new light fixtures in the downstairs bathroom.

He pulls her inside the bathroom door, flicking the lights off and on as if it were some kind of miracle.

"What do you think?"

"Very nice."

"It's quite an improvement, isn't it?" He flicks the lights ten more times. "Look at that. Fantastic."

"It's great."

"I think I'll do the ones upstairs next," he tells her. "Do you think I should stick with the same design?"

Lindsay opens her mouth but doesn't get a chance to speak.

"I believe I will," he says in his usual decisive tone. He's still studying the new fixtures. "These were an excellent price, plus they remind me of my favorite opera house in *Roma*. Very elegant." He flicks the lights some more, grinning like a little kid. "How about that? Isn't that something?"

She smiles. "When do you start work at the hospital?"

"Not for another week, but I'm going in tomorrow for a few hours to get acquainted with everyone. Why do you ask?"

"No reason." She glances around the bathroom. "I wonder if I should paint in here too."

"Absolutely. Choose whatever color you like."

She arrives home from the bakery next Friday to discover he's in the backyard pruning the tangle of neglected trees. He's wearing a pair of faded Levis she's never seen before and a gray short-sleeved T-shirt. Classical music plays from the new speakers attached to the iPod docking station he bought a couple days ago.

"What's all this?" Lindsay asks, walking outside after changing into flip-flops. It's a warm day, and the air smells like fresh-cut grass. She's carrying two glasses of iced water and hands one over to him.

"Thanks." He takes it from her, his throat working as he drinks half of it down.

"You're getting these trees into shape?"

"Yes." He nods, wiping his mouth with the back of his hand. "It turns out they're fruit trees. Isn't that great? I've always wanted to own my own. As far as I can make out, there are two apple and two plum, and those are blueberry bushes over there." He points to them like a proud parent.

The trees have obviously been neglected for a while, and she doesn't see much in the way of fruit growing on them. But with Giovanni involved in their care now, she imagines they'll be flourishing in no time.

He hands the glass back to her and continues pruning. She goes to sit on the back patio, looking around the yard and wondering if she should add flowers out here. Her inside painting projects are coming along nicely, and many of the rooms have at least a spark of color. It's already brought more life to the interior.

Lindsay puts the glasses down on the ground and relaxes as she watches Giovanni work. He's sweating through his T-shirt, and his cheeks have a healthy flush. Those soft jeans are hugging his ass and thighs in a way that's almost indecent.

"Do you think you'll be pruning much longer?" she asks, a hopeful note in her voice.

"Probably. I read it's best not to cut too much in summer, but these are so overgrown I'd like to remove the dead wood."

Nice.

She leans back on her arms and continues to watch, sipping her iced water, feeling like a voyeur. Classical music drifts out from the house's open patio door.

It turns out Giovanni is into opera, of all things. She loves music, but has never listened to opera and has certainly never thought it was something she could enjoy. Oddly, she doesn't mind it. There's real passion in some of the singing—the *libretto*, as he calls it.

Only a couple weeks have passed since they arrived, but somehow the two of them have fallen into this peculiar domestic life together. Lindsay doesn't remember ever feeling so at ease with either of her previous husbands and definitely none of her boyfriends—whom she always kept at what you might call an emotionally healthy distance.

Very ironic.

All her stuff is here too. They managed to get most of it moved from her storage unit with little fuss since Anthony was nice enough to help. She told Giovanni she had plenty of guy friends who could help bring her stuff over, but his face turned nearly apoplectic at the suggestion. Her queen-sized bed is in the downstairs bedroom, as she requested, and of course, he's been sleeping with her every night. Despite all his new purchases, she's noticed a bed for himself hasn't been one of them.

Not that I'm complaining.

She's comfortable—too comfortable—and a part of her is starting to get nervous with all this domesticity, though she's mostly been ignoring that part for now.

He walks over, and she eyes him with appreciation.

"Why do I feel like a piece of naked bacon?" he asks.

Lindsay gives him a lascivious grin. "Because I'm undressing you with my eyes?"

"That must be it."

"You look awfully hot. Are you sure you don't want to take your shirt off? I'd be willing to make it worth your while."

He chuckles. "But I'm a delicate flower, remember?"

"I promise we'll keep it just between the two of us."

"Well." He pretends to consider it. "As long as you promise."

He moves closer, and she pushes her sunglasses to the top of her head. "Speaking of delicate flowers, I think I might plant some along the border out here. What do you think?"

He reaches for his water and sits down beside her. "Sounds great. I like everything you've done with the house so far."

She slips her arm through his. "Thank you. It's been sort of fun, really." She's not sure why, but she has a strong desire to leave her mark on this house.

He finishes the rest of the water in the glass and puts it down. "It has been fun, hasn't it? I've never experienced anything like this before."

"Me, either."

Lindsay's eyes go to the way their arms are linked, taking in the ease of them together. All this domestic bliss. And what's crazy is a part of her wants it, wants this life with him. She's even looking forward to having Joseph and Sara stay here before they go to their uncle. She tries to imagine her and Giovanni together as an actual married couple, and it's not that hard.

"Oh, I went by the hospital again this morning," he says. "I almost forgot to tell you."

"How is it going there?"

"Good. I'm looking forward to starting work." He turns to her. "Listen, how do you feel about coming in and teaching an origami class to some of the kids sometime?"

Her brows go up. "At the hospital?"

"I think it's something many of them would enjoy, but only if you want to."

Lindsay is quiet, considering this. "They'd let me come in and teach a class? They don't even know who I am."

"Well, I told them you were my wife and a professional artist." He grins. "I gave you a glowing endorsement."

"You told them I was your wife?"

He nods. "Yes, Lindsay. We're married, remember?"

"I know."

He's watching her, appears to be measuring her reaction. "You don't have to do the class. I'm not trying to put you on the spot or anything."

She thinks it over. She's taught classes to kids in the past. Not at a hospital and not origami, but she knows she could do it. "That's okay. It sounds like fun, actually."

"There's one other thing I should mention." Giovanni considers her for a long moment.

"What is it?"

But then he shakes his head. "It's nothing. Forget it."

"Are you sure?"

He nods. "Yeah."

She leans into him, already getting excited about teaching the class. "I have tons of origami paper. Lots of colors and designs. It should be a blast."

"That's great. I'll let them know."

"Oh, wait. Except I can't do it on Monday." She sits up suddenly, remembering. "I'm helping Natalie interview potential nannies."

He chuckles. "Yes, I heard all about it from Anthony—who's not too pleased, I might add." He gives her a look. "You're seriously trying to help them avoid something called the 'nanny spell'?"

"Excuse me, but it's a real thing," she informs him. "You're just blind to it because you're a man."

He gives her an amused look. "You know I was raised with a nanny, right? And trust me, my father never slept with her."

"What did she look like?"

He shrugs. "I don't know. Like a normal woman."

"Was she young and hot?"

"No, she was older. Kind of plain." He pauses. "Now that I think about it, I'm pretty sure she was a lesbian."

Lindsay nods with approval. Francesca was no dummy. "See, your mom understood."

"So is this how you'll be if we ever have to get a nanny?"

She goes still, the breath knocked clear out of her. She tries to recover quickly before he notices. "Why would you ask that?"

He shrugs. "I don't know. What if it worked out between us?" He searches her face then lowers his voice. "Stranger things have happened."

She imagines the kind of life she's certain he wants—big and messy with a house full of kids. It's a life she'd love too, but she knows it's not something she could ever give him.

She turns her head and looks out at the currently barren fruit trees. *Just like me*. She never tells any of the men she's involved with about her infertility. She figures they don't need to know, and what's more, she doesn't want anyone's pity.

Another secret.

And one she has *no* plans to share with Giovanni.

Chapter Twenty

~ Men don't always know what's best for them, but luckily you do. ~

"I HAVE A whole list of potential candidates lined up for us to speak with today," Natalie tells her, sipping from a glass of ice water with lemon. "Hopefully, one of them will work out."

They're in her sister's dining room. Lindsay picks up the stack of nanny résumés Natalie printed up and flips through them. "None of these have photos."

"I know. The agency didn't forward any for some reason."

Lindsay spreads the résumés before her on the table and studies them with a keen eye. From what she can tell, the nannies are all older women, which is good. They appear to have plenty of experience, and it looks like they've been vetted since each one has a page of outstanding references. Unfortunately, it's not enough. "These are completely worthless to me without a photo."

"I wouldn't say *worthless*. I'm more concerned with what kind of experience they have." Natalie glances over at Luca, who's currently sitting in one of those baby saucer contraptions with all sorts of amusements attached. He's grinning and drooling as he uses his fist to bat a fuzzy bumble bee. "Although, what I mostly want is someone Luca feels comfortable with, and I can trust."

"I know. And that's what I want too. Just think of me as your guard dog. I'm here to sniff out any potential problems."

"You know Anthony is fairly insulted by this whole thing."

Lindsay nods. "I don't blame him. I would be too if I were him. He's a great guy, but he's still a guy, and I imagine he doesn't read trashy magazines, right?"

Natalie laughs. "No, I wouldn't say he does."

"So he has no idea how common the nanny spell is."

Her sister sighs and picks up her glass.

"Hey, no worries." Lindsay shrugs. "Just blame the whole thing on me. I don't mind. I'm happy as long as I know in the end you guys are safe."

"Just to be clear, I *trust* Anthony. I explained to him though how I *do* think you have good instincts about people." Natalie considers her. "You're just like Dad that way."

Lindsay's eyes flash over to her sister. She wonders if she should tell Natalie about the poker. It would be a relief to finally get it out there, but she decides this isn't a good time. *I haven't hit a single card game since I've been back anyway.* Her money is getting low, though. Of course, she doesn't have a bankroll to play cards with either. *Hopefully, I'll sell a sculpture soon.* Her agent, Emily, e-mailed her this morning and said the gallery in San Francisco was delighted by the piece that arrived from Berlin recently. It sounded like they were pretty certain they could find a buyer.

The doorbell rings.

"That must be the first one!" Natalie gets up to answer it.

Lindsay smiles over at Luca, who grins back. He's quite a friendly little guy. "Don't worry," she tells him. "Your Auntie Lindsay is on the case. And you're going to have the best damn nanny in the whole world if I have anything to say about it."

"Come on in and have a seat." She hears her sister's voice from the other room. "I thought we could sit in the living room and just talk a bit."

Lindsay stands as Natalie comes back into the dining room to get Luca.

"Would you mind carrying his saucer?" Natalie asks, reaching in to pull him out of it.

Lindsay grabs the saucer and the résumés and follows her sister into the living area. The women all take a seat while Natalie holds Luca on her lap. He's squirming and reaching for the fuzzy bee again, so Natalie puts him back into the saucer. He immediately starts batting at it, laughing.

"What a sweet boy," the potential nanny says. "What's his name?"

Natalie grins. "His name's Luca, and he's six months old." She motions toward Lindsay. "And this is my sister, Lindsay."

The nanny introduces herself, and Lindsay leans back on the couch, studying this woman like Columbo. The nanny is heavyset and has short, wavy salt-and-pepper hair. Natalie chats about what she's looking for, going down a list of questions. The nanny responds to all of them with ease.

The conversation goes well and after about forty minutes or so, they conclude the interview. Natalie tells her how she has a few more people to speak with, but that she'll be in touch.

"What did you think?" her sister asks coming back into the living room after walking the nanny to the door. "She seemed all right."

"Absolutely not."

Natalie's brows knit together. "Why? What's wrong with her?"

"That nanny was *way* too attractive."

"She's sixty-eight years old."

"I don't care." Lindsay holds Luca in her lap. She blows on his face as he giggles and tries to grab her mouth. "I'm your guard dog, remember?"

"You honestly think Anthony would have an affair with a woman old enough to be his mother?"

"And did you check out her rack?" Lindsay shakes her head. "Forget it. No way."

Natalie laughs. "You're completely insane!"

Lindsay motions toward her sister's ample bosom. "Hey, we *know* what your husband's tastes are like. The last thing we need is a nanny with a pair of double D's—or worse—running around here."

"You realize how offensive all this is, don't you? You can't just judge people like that or not hire someone for a job based on their body type!"

"Sure, you can. I'm doing it right now."

"My God." Natalie lets out her breath, still laughing as she sits on the sofa beside her. "I'm glad there's no one around to hear this conversation. I'd be mortified."

"Look, she was too strict anyway."

This gives Natalie pause, and she appears to be thinking it over. "She *was* kind of strict, wasn't she?"

"I thought so."

"All that business about schedules for this and schedules for that." Natalie looks down at Luca, who's happily chewing on a cold teething ring Lindsay gave him. "Anthony and I both prefer to just feed him whenever he's hungry."

"I agree, so let's move on. When does the next one arrive?"

Natalie and Lindsay spend all afternoon interviewing nannies—five in all. The youngest was sixty-seven, the oldest eighty.

"Jesus, are there *no* hags left in this world?" Lindsay says with disgust as Natalie comes back from walking the last candidate to the door. "Every one of those women was *far* too attractive."

"I'm exhausted." Natalie flops down on the couch. She reaches over for

Luca, who's starting to get fussy, taking him from Lindsay's lap. "And you truly are insane. You know that, right?" She settles back down on the couch, adjusting her clothes to nurse the baby.

"I'm not insane. I'm just trying to help you find a suitable nanny."

"That last one was eighty years old, and you thought she was too hot?"

Lindsay snorts. "Trust me, she's still got game."

"Come on." Natalie rolls her eyes. "She was a totally nice grandma type."

"Oh, really? How many times did she mention how she thought Anthony was handsome?"

During their last interview, the grandma nanny walked over to the fireplace mantel to look at some of the family photos. She kept staring at the pictures of Anthony, commenting on them even after she sat back down again.

Natalie opens her mouth then tilts her head. "Huh."

"Exactly. Grandma had the hots for Anthony."

"I don't know."

"I'm telling you. Plus, we need to see photos of these women in advance. This whole thing is a waste of time otherwise."

As they're discussing this, the front door opens, and Anthony comes inside, home from work. Lindsay wonders if his ears are burning. He's wearing a white *Star Wars* T-shirt with an X-Wing fighter on it and the Death Star in the background. Anthony is a professor of astrophysics at the University of Washington. He's also six years younger than Natalie. Lindsay's never seen two people better suited for each other.

"Hey," Anthony says, walking over to them in the living room. He leans down and kisses Natalie hello. "How is everyone today?" he murmurs.

"We're fine." Natalie smiles up at him.

Anthony takes his leather satchel off and sits down beside Natalie on the couch. He reaches over to gently stroke Luca's hair, as he's fallen asleep in Natalie's arms.

Lindsay watches the two of them together. Such a beautiful family. It squeezes her heart. She's so happy her sister found a love like this. Anthony truly is a good guy and definitely enough man for her sister.

He turns his attention toward her now, his dark eyes flickering with a mixture of bemusement and annoyance. "So, how did the interviews go? Are you going to be able to save me from the nanny curse, or am I doomed?"

Lindsay doesn't bother to correct him that it's 'spell' not 'curse,' instead brings her shoulders up with chagrin. "I'm sorry, but I'm afraid it's not looking good."

"What do you mean?" He turns to Natalie, and his voice softens. "You didn't like any of them?"

"None of them were quite right," Lindsay tells him, though Anthony is still looking at Natalie.

"What did *you* think?" he asks her.

"I have to agree with Lindsay. I just didn't feel a connection with any of them. Not because of the curse or spell, or whatever." She gives Lindsay a look.

He nods. "That's okay. We'll keep looking. I'm sure we'll eventually find someone."

"I hope so." Natalie sighs. "This whole thing is already tiring."

"It'll be worth it in the end, though." Anthony offers to take the baby from her to lay him down for his nap. As he heads upstairs, Lindsay follows Natalie into the kitchen.

"It's kind of early for dinner." Natalie goes over to the stove and lifts the lid on a pot of chili she has cooking. "But do you want a sandwich? I'm going to make one for Anthony."

"No, thanks, I'm not hungry. Plus, I'm making dinner for Giovanni tonight." Lindsay leans against the counter. "It's his first day of work at the hospital, and I thought he'd enjoy coming home to a hot meal."

"That's nice of you." Natalie flashes up at her. "How's it going over there anyway?"

"Weirdly okay."

Her sister nods. "I have to admit, I wasn't too thrilled about Giovanni at first—or any of this, really. He's one of those larger-than-life kind of men I've always found sort of intimidating."

Lindsay considers her sister's description and realizes there's truth in it. He *is* kind of like that. She smiles to herself thinking about him. He's serious in so many ways, but you can't deny his passion is big.

"He's really grown on me," Natalie continues. "Plus, he's amazing with the girls and Luca. They're all crazy about him."

"I know." Lindsay is still smiling. "He's all right."

"I noticed something else when you guys were staying here." Natalie gives her a sideways glance as she stirs the chili. "He's very affectionate with you."

"I guess." Lindsay shrugs and pretends to act indifferent. She picks up one of Luca's baby toys and slides the rings around.

"I think he has real feelings for you. Of course, I shouldn't be surprised." Natalie turns down the heat on the stove. "They all fall in love with you in the end, don't they?"

Lindsay doesn't bother answering and continues to fiddle with the baby toy. What Natalie said is mostly true. Men fall in love with her easily, and they always have. But she's not so sure about Giovanni. "I don't know. Giovanni is a tough nut to crack."

"I'll bet. Plus, I think you have feelings for him too."

She looks up. "What do you mean?"

"You giggle quite a bit when he's around," Natalie says with a grin.

"I do not."

"Yes, you do. It was fascinating to watch. Every time he came near you, it seemed like you were giggling."

Lindsay scoffs. "Please. I do *not* giggle."

"I don't think I've ever seen you act that way around a guy before, not even when you were in high school."

"I like him. So what? I already told you that."

Natalie laughs, but it's a knowing laugh. "I didn't realize you liked him *that* much. Are you in love with him?"

Lindsay puts the baby toy back down on the counter and decides to be completely honest. "I don't know. It's crazy, but I think I might be."

"*Really?*" Natalie's eyes widen.

"Don't tell Anthony, okay?"

Natalie doesn't have a chance to answer because Anthony walks into the kitchen. "Don't tell me what?" he asks, turning on the baby monitor. "Is it more bullshit about the nanny curse? Because I have to tell you, Lindsay, you're skating on thin ice with all this."

"I'm only trying to help," she says sincerely. "I mean well. You know that, right?"

"That's what I keep telling myself." Anthony takes a seat at the kitchen's center island. "But do you really think I'm going to have an affair with our nanny?"

"Of course not. I'm just heading off any potential disasters."

Her sister sets a plate with a sandwich on it in front of him. He reaches out and puts his arm around her waist, drawing her close. "Thank you, Miss Natalie."

She grins at him. "You're welcome."

"This looks almost as delicious as you," Anthony says in a teasing voice.

Natalie leans down to kiss him, and the two of them go at it for a few seconds.

Lindsay feels like a third wheel. She clears her throat. "Hello? I'm still standing here, remember?"

The happy couple breaks apart. Natalie gives him one last kiss before she goes back over to the fridge and starts putting the sandwich ingredients away.

Anthony takes a bite of his food, chewing for a bit. He looks over at Lindsay. "You know, I grew up with a nanny, and there were no disasters."

"Yes, I heard *all* about your nanny from Giovanni." Lindsay tries not to roll her eyes. Francesca was obviously smart enough not to explain her hiring decisions to anyone.

"If you're really that worried about this, why don't you two just look for a male nanny?" Anthony says before taking another bite of his sandwich.

Lindsay's mouth opens with astonishment. "A manny! My God, why didn't I think of that?" She puts her hand to her forehead. "It's genius!"

Natalie comes back over to the island, eating a piece of apple she just sliced up. "There were some male nannies listed on the referral site. It didn't even occur to me to look at them."

"As long as I don't have anything to be concerned about." Anthony's eyes go to his wife with a little grin. "Just promise me you won't hire some kind of hot stud muffin."

Natalie laughs. "I don't think you have anything to worry about." She leans down to him and lowers her voice. "You're the hottest stud muffin around."

"A manny . . ." Lindsay nods slowly. "That's the perfect solution." She glances over to where her sister and Anthony look ready to rip each other's clothes off. "Okay, I'm leaving now. It's clear you two aren't getting enough alone time."

Lindsay stops at the store on the way home to pick up groceries. She's decided on Mexican-style burgers slathered with guacamole and grilled onions for dinner, along with a big green salad. She grabs fresh strawberries and whipped cream for dessert.

By the time she expects Giovanni home, she's already made the guacamole and grilled the onions. She's in the middle of making the salad, humming along to *La Bohème*—the most beautiful opera she's heard so far, and definitely her favorite—when she hears him come through the front door.

"Hey, what's all this?" He enters the kitchen with a grin, putting his stuff down on the counter—a computer case along with his phone, pager, and some paperwork. "It smells incredible in here."

"I thought I'd make dinner to celebrate your first day at work. How did it go?"

"Great." He peers around at the ingredients. "I met with a few new patients and their families. It's going to be fantastic having access to so many resources for a change." He reaches for a tortilla chip and pops it in his mouth, and then he reaches for her. "Come here."

"Hey, watch it." Lindsay gives a girly laugh. She puts down the knife she was cutting tomatoes with as he pulls her in close. Her butterflies are fluttering as usual, and she suddenly remembers what Natalie said about her giggling.

Am I giggling?

He puts his mouth to her neck and his hand on her ass. He nips her, and she lets out a little shriek.

Holy shit. "Have I become a giggler?"

He moves his mouth up to hers and kisses her, tasting like corn chips. "I like all the giggling," he murmurs, squeezing her ass. "I like everything about you."

"What?" She pulls back from him. "You've noticed it too?"

"I've noticed you seem happy." He kisses her again and keeps his face close to hers. "Are you happy? I hope so."

"Yes, I'm very happy."

He grins, that beautiful smile and her heart nearly bursts from happiness. She knows right then what she told Natalie earlier today is true. *I'm in love.* As crazy as it sounds, she's been in love with him since Berlin, and every day it's only gotten stronger. There's no point in denying it to herself any longer.

The two of them gaze at each other, and she wonders if he feels it too. She's not sure, though, as there are parts of himself he's still holding back.

"I have to ask you something important," he says.

"What's that?"

He rubs his stomach. "Is the food almost done? Because I'm starved."

Lindsay rolls her eyes. *Men.* It figures. With guys falling at her feet all these years, the one guy she wants is still standing upright. "It's almost done. I just have to fry up the burgers." She moves to do just that but he stops her, and she looks up at him.

"I'm happy too," he says, taking her hand. "I haven't felt this good in a long time, and it's because of *you*, Lindsay."

She raises an eyebrow and gives him her best sultry expression. "Of course it's because of *me*. I wouldn't expect anything less."

He chuckles and draws her close again. Putting his face down near hers, he kisses her, then does that nose-rubbing thing he likes. "*Ti adoro, fragolina mia.*"

"What did you say?"

"I said, 'I adore you, my little strawberry.'"

Lindsay giggles. "I do like strawberries."

"I've noticed."

She giggles some more and decides what the heck. *I'm going to giggle as much as I want.*

Lindsay starts on the burgers, heating up the frying pan while Giovanni takes his computer and paperwork from the counter and goes into the living room.

"And you're playing *La Bohème*," he calls out to her. "My favorite opera of all time."

"Really? I think this is my favorite so far too."

She hears him turn the music up louder and smiles to herself. Whoever thought she'd be happy living in an arranged marriage with a surgeon who likes comic books and opera? Bizarre. She opens the freezer to grab the frozen burger patties.

When she takes them to the counter, she can hear Giovanni actually singing with the music. "Olaf sings opera," she murmurs. "How about that?" She grabs the large knife she used for the tomatoes and starts trying to cut the frozen burgers apart.

Giovanni is still singing when he enters the kitchen. "I'll have to take you to see this sometime. It's incredible. You'll be crying your eyes out."

"Is that—Ow!" There's a sharp pain as she cuts her finger.

"What is it?" His face changes to concern.

She looks down. With horror, she sees there's blood coming from her finger. A lot of blood. "Oh, my God." Her stomach drops and her vision goes dark around the edges. The last thing she sees before it all goes black is Giovanni running toward her.

Chapter Twenty-One

~ There's nothing sexier than a real hero. ~

WHEN LINDSAY COMES to, she's disoriented. Flat on her back. A golden-haired Viking hovers over her.

"Thor?"

"Look at me, Lindsay," Giovanni says, and her eyes go to his. She feels his fingers checking the pulse at her throat. He nods. "Good."

Music is playing—*La Bohème*—and she realizes she's lying on the kitchen floor.

"How many fingers am I holding up?" he asks.

"Two."

"Does your head or chest hurt?"

"No."

"Do you feel any kind of numbness or tingling anywhere?"

She mentally scans her body. "No, I don't think so."

"When was the last time you ate?"

She blinks. "I'm not sure." She tries to remember. "I think I ate some chips and salsa while I was cooking."

"You just fainted." He studies her. "Has that ever happened to you before?"

"Yes." She nods and swallows, closing her eyes. "Once—when Chloe was born. I was there for the birth, and there was some . . . blood afterward." Suddenly, she notices the pain in her hand, remembers cutting herself. "My finger!"

She tries to get up, but he stops her. "It's fine. Keep your head down."

"Is it bad?" She lifts her hand and catches a glimpse of it wrapped in a clean dish towel, sees a hint of red before he gently puts her hand back.

"No, it's not bad. I'm going to get you some juice. Stay right there, and don't move."

Lindsay continues to lie on the floor. She watches Giovanni grab a glass and fill it halfway with orange juice from the fridge. He comes back over to her.

"I'm fine now," she says, starting to feel a little silly on the floor. "Really, I can sit up. Like I said, it was just seeing the blood that got to me."

"No, I want you to stay like this for a little longer. I'm going to have you take a few sips of juice, though." He comes over to her and has her lift her head up enough to drink a bit.

"How long was I out?" she asks, putting her head back down.

"Not long. I'd say ten seconds." He places the glass on the floor and sits next to her, picking up her injured hand. "So you've fainted before at the sight of blood?"

She nods. "I'll bet that sounds really dumb to someone like you."

"No, not at all."

She laughs a little. "I could never do your job. Can you imagine? I'd be a disaster."

He smiles kindly. "It's not for everyone. Some people have difficulty with blood or certain kinds of pain too. It's called vasovagal syncope, and it's not uncommon."

"Really?"

He nods. "I've seen plenty of it over the years. Some people faint during a needle stick every time."

"Did I hit the floor? What happened?"

"No, I managed to catch you." He gently unwraps the dishtowel on her hand. "I'm going to examine your finger now."

She watches his face with his regular tense expression. He's gentle, but it doesn't change the fact that she's in pain. "It hurts, but it kind of tingles too," Lindsay tells him.

He's still inspecting her finger. "I think you've cut into the nerve."

"Is that bad?"

"You may find your sensation is different once it's healed." He looks at her. "It needs to be sutured."

She doesn't like the sound of that. "Sutured? What's that? Will it hurt?"

"It'll be fine," he reassures her. "I'm talking about stitches. Just a few. It's not a big deal."

"Not to *you* maybe."

He considers her. "The question is do you want to go to the ER and have them do it for you, or have me do it here?"

"Can you?" She studies him. "I'd rather not go to the ER."

"Sure, it's not a problem. I have my medical bag." He wraps the towel around her finger and instructs her on how to hold it firmly but gently with her other hand. He also tells her not to look at it. "When was the last time you had a tetanus shot? Do you remember?"

She thinks back. "A couple years ago. I smashed my thumb while I was working at my studio." She remembers how one of the other artists in her building took her to the emergency room. She didn't faint, but there wasn't as much blood either. "They gave me one at the hospital."

"Are you allergic to any kind of medication?"

"No."

He glances over toward the living room. "Let's move you to the couch."

"Are you sure I need stitches? I'd rather not. I mean, I've never had them before."

"Yes, I'm sure."

"Maybe you could just bandage it up. That's probably good enough."

"No, Lindsay. That's not good enough." Giovanni instructs her to wrap her arms around his neck, says he's going to carry her.

"This is silly. I can walk. Seriously, you don't have to carry me!"

But he's already lifting her. She has to admit she's sort of enjoying it, though she'd be enjoying it a lot more if she hadn't filleted her finger.

He carries her over to the living room couch—a maroon sectional they pulled out of her storage unit last week. He places her down on it so she's lying flat. She tries to tuck a pillow under her head, but he stops her.

"Just lie flat for a little longer." He stares at her legs for a moment like he's considering something but then seems to change his mind. "I'll be right back. Let me get my bag." He looks at her pointedly. "And don't get up."

"Yes, Doctor."

She watches him turn the volume down on the music before he leaves the room.

Lindsay sighs and waits patiently, holding the towel with firm but gentle pressure just the way he showed her. Her finger not only hurts but is throbbing. "Porca Miseria," she mutters.

When he returns, she suddenly remembers how she left the frying pan on the stove turned on. "Oh, shit!" She starts to sit up.

"Hey, lie down." He comes over, carrying his bag and some clean towels. "What are you doing? Just take it easy."

"I left the frying pan on."

"Don't worry, I already took care of it."

"Oh? That's good." In truth, she did feel a little woozy when she tried to get up, though it's mostly because she looked down and saw the blood from her finger soaked into the cotton.

He places a brown leather doctor's bag on the floor. It's beat up, and she recognizes it from when they flew into Seattle. He scoots the coffee table over, arranges some things, and then moves one of the sections from the couch close to her, so he's sitting beside her.

"All right, let's see that finger again."

Lindsay gives him her left hand with the cut middle finger on it and tries not to look as he unwraps it. She hisses. Giovanni has set up some of the things he'll need on the table, and soon she feels him gently cleaning her wound.

"It hurts," she tells him. "It's throbbing."

"I know, baby. I'm sorry. I'm going to numb it for you in a second."

"What?" Her eyes grow wide, staring at him. "Numb it for me how?"

"With lidocaine."

"Like a *shot?*" She moans with outrage that this is happening to her. She kicks her legs around. "I don't want a shot! I fucking *hate* shots."

"You're going to be fine, but you need to stay still. Would you like a comic book to look at?"

"How about some vodka? Do you have any vodka in that doctor's bag of yours?"

He chuckles. "I can't say that I do."

She snorts. "Not much use then, is it?" Finally, she agrees to the comic book, and he hands her an issue of something called *Laser Man*. "What the hell is this? Don't you have any *Thor*?"

"No, how about *Spiderman?*"

"Forget it. Unless it's *Thor*, I don't give a shit."

She whimpers and wails when he gives her the shot in her finger, letting loose with a stream of curse words. She then pouts as she tries to manage the stupid comic book with one hand, waiting for the numbing agent to kick in. They spend the next fifteen minutes with Giovanni tending to her wound, admonishing her to stay still. Despite her bad behavior, he's gentle and patient with her—not that this stops her from complaining endlessly.

"I hope you know what you're doing," she tells him. "I don't want to end up with some kind of fucked-up mutant lizard finger."

His eyes flash to hers, and they're filled with humor. "Christ, Lindsay, I'm a plastic surgeon."

"So what? You could still give me a fucked-up lizard finger! In fact, shouldn't you have laid me down on the dining room table? Wouldn't that be more like what you're used to?"

He keeps his eyes focused on her hand. "What are you talking about?"

"Like for surgery! So you can stand next to me. For fuck's sake, I shouldn't have to tell you that!"

"I don't necessarily stand when I'm in the OR. It depends on the procedure, but often I'm sitting."

"You are?" Her brows shoot up with surprise. This was new information. She's always imagined him standing next to a table with a bunch of bright lights shining from above.

He tilts his head as he examines her finger. There's a gentle tugging sensation, but that's all since it's completely numb otherwise. "For the more delicate surgeries I perform, I'm always sitting," he explains. "It's easier to focus."

Lindsay watches his handsome face as he tends to her wound. For the first time, what he actually does sinks in, and it takes her breath away. Giovanni repairs the faces of children. Of beautiful little babies. It's incredible.

"What's it like?" she asks, overwhelmed with awe. "To do what you do."

"I love my work. It's a privilege, and one I never take for granted."

"What if you make a mistake, though? Does that ever happen?"

He shakes his head. "No." She feels mild pressure on her finger. "There's no room for mistakes in my life."

"How's that possible? It sounds too stressful."

He shrugs. "I'm used to it. That's why I don't like surprises. I prefer to have a plan before I begin anything."

She wonders where she fits into all this. Their relationship was hardly planned. She suspects it's been as much of a surprise for him as it has been for her.

"I guess that explains why you're such a control freak," she mutters.

"Probably."

"You can't control everything though."

"No," he agrees, then glances up at her with a wry smile. "You certainly can't."

She wants to ask him more questions but doesn't get the chance.

"Okay, I'm finished here," he says in an officious tone. She feels light pressure again and can tell he's wiping her finger with something. "I don't have a splint with me, but I'll grab one for you at the hospital tomorrow. Try not to bend the finger. And don't get it wet."

"Can I see?" Lindsay looks over at her hand.

"I haven't bandaged it yet."

"It's okay. I think I can handle it, as long as it's not bleeding."

He lets her take her hand back, and she examines the perfect row of small stitches he's put in for her. Four in all. "I guess it's all right. Though it does look mutant."

"Here." He holds his hand out for hers. "Let me bandage it for you."

She sighs and doesn't say anything more as he finishes up. She knows she's acting horribly.

Later, when he's all done with her and has cleaned up, he comes back over to where she's still lying on the couch with a pillow tucked under both her head and hand. She scoots back to make room for him so he can sit next to her.

"Thank you for taking care of me," she says, feeling embarrassed about how awful she's been behaving. "I didn't exactly make it easy for you."

Giovanni reaches down and strokes her hair with affection. "What an unpleasant patient you are."

"I know. I'm sorry."

"*Exceptionally* unpleasant, even."

"I try to be exceptional in everything I do."

He chuckles and lets his hand slip beneath her hair, so he's rubbing the back of her neck. It feels so good, her eyes drift shut.

"It's okay, I'm a terrible patient too," he admits.

"Are you?" She opens her eyes.

He gives her a pointed look. "What do *you* think?"

She laughs. "I think you're probably worse than I am."

Giovanni fries up the burgers and assembles them following Lindsay's instructions. He's never been much of a cook but has always wanted to learn. With the exception of the most rudimentary dishes, he's never really had much opportunity.

Maybe that will change now.

Moving into this house with the knowledge that he'll be staying put in one place for a while has been a revelation for him. He didn't realize just how ready he was to stop living like a 'vagabond,' as Lindsay so aptly put it.

And, of course, she's been the biggest revelation of all. He never thought he'd get to this point with a woman. Deep down, he worried Olivia had destroyed something within him, something fundamental.

But it turns out that isn't true.

For the first time in a long time, he's seeing possibilities for his future. In fact, his life has become all about possibilities.

They decide to eat dinner on the large couch in the living room. Lindsay has her plate balanced on her lap with a pillow. Her brown eyes wander over and catch hold of his. They do this a lot, and every time he can't stop himself from grinning like an idiot.

"Would you mind adding more pepper to my salad, please?" she asks.

"Sure." He reaches for the mill and grinds more for her since she can't do it with her injured hand. The pepper mill is a black king of spades and has a matching queen for salt. They're hand-carved by an artist she knows. It's just one of the many little touches she's added that's been turning this into a home. She recently put a doormat out front that says, 'Actually, there is a doctor in the house,' and he laughed with approval when he saw it. He's probably laughed more with her than he has with anyone his entire life.

"Thank you, Olaf." She bats her lashes at him and then prongs some lettuce with her fork.

He enjoys watching her eat. Lindsay is a sensualist, and he takes pleasure in all the little things that seem to delight her.

Of course, she can be headstrong at times too. Temperamental, even. She always speaks her mind—occasionally to a fault. She's not a planner like he is and seems allergic to even the idea of a schedule. She's bold—especially in bed, not that he's complaining about that.

Most of all, though, Lindsay has become the sun, bright and lovely, bringing him out from the shadows, from that steel prison where he's been living far too long. Every day he's more grateful than the one before that she's come into his life.

Thank God.

He only wishes now he'd seen it when they first met years ago, but he remembers how even then there was a spark of something between them.

I just wasn't ready for her yet.

Despite her sometimes irreverent exterior, he's noticed something else about her. She's soft-hearted beneath that outer toughness. Kind and surprisingly thoughtful. She tries to hide it, and he suspects she worries it makes her appear weak, though nothing could be further from the truth.

He can't believe he ever thought she was anything like Olivia. From the outside, Olivia was also beautiful and passionate, but inside she was cold and ultimately self-serving. *Just the opposite of Lindsay.* If only he'd understood that sooner, but then he was too young to really see it.

More and more, he's grown to love Lindsay's unusual slant on the world. She doesn't see things in black or white, or even in shades of gray. She sees them in color. Vivid color. Just like the walls she's painted and the flowers she's planted around the house.

"How's your finger?" he asks. "Do you want something for the pain?"

She shrugs. "It's okay." And then she gives him a wicked grin. "I know something that might help me later though."

"Sexual healing?"

"With strawberries and whipped cream, if you please."

Giovanni chuckles a little, puts his empty plate on the coffee table, and shifts position so he can lie back on the couch and be closer to her.

He rests his hand on her thigh. Whenever he's near Lindsay, he can't stop touching her. "Do you want me to cancel your origami class at the hospital?"

"I don't think so." She appears to consider it as she studies her bandaged finger. The class is scheduled a few days from now. "I mean, it's the middle finger on my left hand, so it should be okay. Plus, I would hate to disappoint any of the kids."

He nods, not surprised she doesn't want to cancel. "Oh, and by the way, I saw my credit card statement recently."

She sticks her fork into a cherry tomato on her plate and looks at him questioningly.

"From that card I left you in Berlin?"

Her eyes widen for a microsecond, but then she shrugs and opens her mouth to eat the tomato. "What about it?"

"You donated a thousand dollars to UNICEF?"

She continues to eat her salad. "I was pissed at you for abandoning me in that hotel room. You should be grateful."

"Grateful for what?"

"Grateful I didn't buy the mink coat and diamond ring I had my eye on."

Giovanni doesn't say anything. For some reason, his own eyes flash to the plain gold wedding band she's wearing, and he feels a peculiar embarrassment. If he could do it over again, he knows he'd buy her something with far more panache.

She smirks. "So you see? You actually got off cheap. Plus, it's for a good cause."

What in the hell is he supposed to say to that?

"Maybe you'd like to send them my paycheck too," he mutters, though in truth he doesn't really care. He regrets abandoning her after that night in Berlin. It pains him to even think of her waking up alone in a hotel like that now.

"You pull that shit on me again and I just might."

His hand is still on her thigh, and he gently squeezes it. "That won't ever happen again. I promise."

She considers him for a long moment. "It better not."

A few days later, Giovanni spends his morning in the OR repairing a cleft lip on a three-month-old. The surgery goes smoothly, and after speaking with the parents in the recovery room, reassuring them both and explaining some of the post-operative care, he checks the time. He realizes Lindsay is probably still at the hospital teaching her origami class and decides to stop by and say hello.

Not bothering to change out of his scrubs, he finds the classroom and sneaks in the back, nodding a greeting to some of the parents who are there along with a couple of the nurses.

The kids are all sitting at a table as Lindsay goes around to each one, helping them. He sees a number of colorful origami animals and stars they've already made spread over the center.

She doesn't see him yet, and for a long moment, he simply stands there watching her, enjoying the sight. Her hair is pulled into a low ponytail, with a few strands falling loose around her face. She's wearing a long blue skirt and a short-sleeved T-shirt, along with a colorful beaded necklace. As always, she looks lovely, and he enjoys seeing her as an outsider, as others do.

Beautiful and vivacious.

When he initially asked her if she wanted to teach this class, he worried whether she could handle dealing with children who were ill, since it can be difficult for some people. But in the end, he decided she'd be fine.

And he sees now how correct he was. She's completely at ease, and obviously having a great time as she teaches the kids in that unflappable way of hers.

Eventually, she looks up and notices him. "Hey, what are you doing here?" She smiles, her eyes taking in his scrubs.

"I had a moment and just thought I'd stop by."

"That was nice of you." She turns to everyone in the small group. "This is my husband, Giovanni, or Dr. Novello."

He nods and murmurs "Hello" to everyone, and they all return the greeting. Inside, he's stunned. He's never heard Lindsay refer to him as her husband before and has to admit he likes the sound of it.

She takes in his scrubs again. "I've never seen you . . . dressed like this."

"I've been in surgery all morning."

Her eyes still linger on him, but then she turns to the kids. "He's the one who repaired my Godzilla finger." She holds up her bandaged middle finger, which now has a splint on it, and has apparently been under discussion.

"Did it hurt when he fixed it?" one of the kids asks.

"A little," Lindsay admits. "But I've discovered a silver lining to having this Godzilla finger."

"What's that?" another child wants to know.

"It's easier to flip people off in traffic when they're driving like jerks." Lindsay's brows go up as she realizes what she's just said.

Though everyone in the room laughs, including the kids.

"I think *I* could use one of those," one of the nurses comments, and there are nods of agreement.

Lindsay meets his eyes. He's still chuckling because he knows firsthand that she drives like she's being chased by terrorists.

"I'm glad it's come in handy," he says in a dry tone. "You might as well make the most of it."

One of the kids asks her a question about the origami elephant he's making, and she goes over to help. Giovanni stays and watches for a moment longer, only because he can't pull his eyes away. In truth, he's completely mesmerized by her and he's certain the whole room can see it, not that it matters.

She's my wife, after all.

He leaves the classroom and, after checking on his patient from this morning and a couple of others, he grabs a sandwich and a bottle of water from the lunch room. While he's eating, he gets his phone out and surfs the Web for a few minutes, reading more about fruit trees and how to care for them.

On a whim, he thumbs in a name he's been meaning to look up for a while, and that's when he discovers something that takes him completely by surprise.

Lindsay, it turns out, has her own Wikipedia page.

Chapter Twenty-Two

**~ Sometimes with men, as with life,
you have to break your own rules. ~**

GIOVANNI DOESN'T GET home until late. Lindsay is in bed, sipping a glass of wine and reading through her e-mails, when she hears the front door. There's still no word on whether the gallery in San Francisco has sold her mask yet. No word from Dagmar about her money either.

I need to do something soon.

Mostly though, she needs to get back to work. She opened her studio the other day but hasn't started any projects yet. School will be starting in a few weeks. If only she had a bankroll she could at least earn some money playing poker. When Giovanni comes into the bedroom, he looks exhausted.

"I thought you'd be home hours ago," she says. "Do you want me to heat up some food for you?"

He sits down on the edge of the bed and kicks his shoes off. "They needed me in the ER. A dog bite came in—a bad one." He flops down on his back and closes his eyes. "The little boy's going to be okay, though."

She moves over so she's closer to him and caresses his face. There are shadows beneath his eyes, stress lines on his forehead. "Is there anything I can do for you?"

He opens his eyes and looks up at her, his face softening as they gaze at each other.

"Do you want a glass of wine?" she asks.

"No."

"A hot shower with me going down on you?"

He smiles faintly. "You're not allowed to get your finger wet."

"It's not a problem. Unlike you, I'm right-handed, remember?" She holds up her right hand and wiggles her healthy fingers.

He doesn't say anything, only considers her. She senses there's something else bothering him and soon discovers she's right.

"Why is it you never told me you have a Wiki page?"

Lindsay manages to hide her surprise, though she knew this was coming eventually. She moves away from him and reaches for her glass. "How did you find it?"

"I Googled your father and it led me straight there."

She sips her wine, knowing what's next. It's not the first time she's had to deal with this. "You Googled my dad?"

"Why didn't you tell me about your first husband? All you ever said was he's a musician."

"It's true. He is a musician."

"But the lead singer for East Echo?" Giovanni frowns like he's still processing it. "I don't listen to rock music much, but even *I* know who they are."

Lindsay looks down at her bandaged finger. She's still wearing the splint. "It was a long time ago."

"And that famous song they had, 'Queen of Hearts,'—it's about *you*." He looks at her. "That tattoo on your back. The one I've kissed so many times. That's what he's singing about, isn't it?"

She grips her glass but doesn't say anything. She hates that Wiki page, and she hates that song even more. It's about a woman who collects hearts and refuses to return them. *If only Josh had never written it.* The Wiki page has been a plague as well, and she has no idea who created it. It would be one thing if it focused on her career as an artist, but it barely even mentions her art—all it talks about is how she was once married to Joshua Trevant and how he wrote that song about her. "Look, it was an unpleasant breakup, but it was ages ago. More than ten years. They weren't even famous yet."

"I can't believe you never told me about this." His eyes stay on hers. "I thought you didn't want to keep secrets anymore."

"It's not a secret. I was going to tell you eventually. Is it really that big of a deal?"

"It is when I have to find out about it from a Wikipedia article."

She feels her temper flare. "What does it matter? It's not like you tell me everything." She puts her glass down. "In fact, you won't tell me *anything*."

They stare at each other, and both of them know what she's referring to. He closes his eyes again but doesn't reply.

"I got an e-mail from the children's coordinator who set up your class at the hospital," he says. "You were a hit. They want you to come back and teach it again, possibly even set up something regular."

She nods. *Of course, he'd change the subject.* In some ways, he's as impenetrable as Fort Knox.

"They'll pay you." He looks up at her.

"Great."

His eyes stay on her, not looking away.

"What is it?" she asks.

He doesn't speak right away, and she senses he's choosing his words carefully. "You've become incredibly important to me, Lindsay. I *need* you to know that."

She nods, wonders if she should tell him how she's in love with him. One of her rules has always been to let guys say it first, and it's been easy until now because they always did.

"Come here." He puts his hand out to her, and she takes it, moves over so she's directly beside him again. His fingers slide into her hair, drawing her close. "Kiss me," he murmurs.

Lindsay obliges and puts her mouth over his. He tastes vaguely like spearmint as she breathes in his essence, already wanting him. *Always wanting him.* She's not sure how she's let herself become so vulnerable with a man, but somehow it's happened. Somehow, all her rules have been stripped away. It makes her nervous, but there's a part of her that's exhilarated.

"Let's go take a shower," he says, smiling with his mouth still against hers.

They go into the bathroom and Giovanni turns on the water. The room smells fresh and sweet, like the fig candles she's been burning lately.

He helps pull her camisole off and then her little shorts.

"I can't believe I'm saying this," she tells him, "but I think your scrubs are kind of hot."

"Do you?" A grin pulls on his mouth.

She reaches out and puts her hand against the solid wall of his chest, the cotton material smooth beneath her fingers. Part of it was seeing him at the hospital today wearing them. If that hospital were a field of battle, Giovanni would be one of their most capable commanders.

Once she's naked, he reaches for the clear plastic bag they've been putting over her hand to shower with. He gently slips it on and then ties it closed around her wrist.

He strips his blue scrubs off next and leaves them in a pile on the floor. Her eyes wander the length of him. He's healthy, fit, and very male. Every inch of him. And some of those inches are currently jutting out in a way that can only be described as magnificent.

He follows her into the shower. Hot water streams over them both as they wash each other. Mostly he washes her since she can't do much with her injured finger. He's been showering with her every day since it happened, patiently washing her hair for her and then her body. And then making love to her. *That's always the best part.* She smiles to herself.

He soaps up next and she can't resist sliding her uninjured hand down his powerful back, and then to his front, stroking his cock as he cleans himself.

When he's done, Giovanni turns around and pulls her into his arms, wrapping her in his large body, still mindful of her hand.

His mouth comes down on hers, and he kisses her, wet kisses mixed with shower water. She senses something exposed about the energy coming off him tonight. Something raw. But then maybe it's just that he had a long day, or maybe she's confusing it with herself because she's unraveling in so many ways.

His hands slide down her spine and then lower, kneading her ass before they move up and grasp her hips, his erection pressing against her.

"Let me go down on you," she tells him, wrapping her hand around his hard length. "I know it's been a while." Lindsay lowers herself, but he stops her.

"Not right now."

She looks up into his face and discovers his eyes are needy on hers. It's sexual, but she sees there's more to it than that.

He brings her up and presses her back against the cool tile of the shower, kisses her again until they're both breathless. His hands mold her breasts. Their bodies slide against each other, and it's all so good.

"Let's go to bed," he rumbles low in her ear. "I want to be in bed with you tonight."

He turns the shower off, and they both get out. Giovanni dries her off, patiently helping her remove the plastic bag from her hand. "I should change the bandage on this."

"Do it later," she says. "It can wait."

He pauses, considering. "Okay."

Once they're in bed, he pulls her into his arms. They kiss for a long while, his mouth like velvet. Eventually, he rolls her beneath him, his cock hard and pressing against her thigh. Lindsay strokes his cheek, bristly after a full day without shaving.

It's late and the room is dark, but they've left her bedside lamp on, casting a mellow glow over them both.

As always, he's gentle when he takes her, giving her time to accept him. She enjoys it at first, but then she doesn't need any more time. She reaches around to grab his back and then his ass, urging him deep.

"Lindsay," he gasps, groaning as he invades her to the hilt, pushing up on his elbows.

She curls her fingers around his neck and lets her breath out in a rush, already intoxicated with desire. A moan escapes her and then another as she arches into him, wrapping her legs around his thighs as he moves inside her.

He captures her mouth, and they kiss, deep and lush, restoring all the places that need tending, that have ever been wounded.

"I see you," he whispers, his words thick with emotion as he gazes down at her. "I see *all* of you."

Her heart beats like a wild thing because she knows it's true. He does see all of her. Not just her surface, but everything beneath it as well. Her true face.

"I love you," she says, unable to stop herself. Her breath shakes, but she forges ahead, breaking all her rules. "I love you, and I think you should know that."

His movements slow, his eyes searching hers, and then his expression turns to one of quiet amazement. "Baby," he whispers, cupping her cheek with his hand. "My beautiful Lindsay."

He brings his mouth to hers again. Gentle at first, kissing her softly, but then there's heat, and it's doing crazy things to her. His body thrusts hard. She gasps because it's like a roller coaster plunging down from a great height. Her throat goes tight, and her eyes sting as she trembles all over, hugging him fiercely.

That's when she realizes he's trembling too, and she understands they're on this ride together.

Afterward, Giovanni is lying quietly beside her, breathing deep. She senses he's not asleep, though, which is surprising considering the long day he's had.

The bedside lamp still glows, both of them too lazy to reach over and turn it off.

Lindsay closes her eyes. Her mind tumbles over what she's just told him, giving up her trust like that. But she doesn't regret it. In fact, she's glad she told him.

"Her name was Olivia," Giovanni's deep voice cuts through the room's silence. "We had an affair. It lasted nearly four years."

Lindsay opens her eyes. She's on her side facing him and can see his profile clearly. She puts her hand on his chest, and he takes it, lacing his fingers through hers. "And you loved her?"

"I did." He licks his lips. "It was a mistake, though, and one I deeply regret." He turns his head and looks at her, his eyes filled with emotion. "I've never told anybody about this. Not my parents or my brother . . . friends, lovers. No one."

She squeezes his hand because she understands what he's saying. He didn't return the 'I love you,' but he's doing it now. He's showing her.

"Why?" she asks softly. "Why the big secret? Just because she was married?"

"Yes." He nods. "That was part of it. Olivia always insisted we keep it quiet, said no one else needed to know. That is was just between the two of us."

"Did she love you?"

He doesn't answer for a long moment. "In her own way, I believe she did. But it was complicated."

"How?"

He doesn't reply though. She sees this is difficult for him, but senses he needs to talk. That it will help him to release it, the same way it helped her to share her secret.

"How did you meet her?"

"Her husband worked at the hospital with my dad. He was a cardiac surgeon. The first time I met her was at a party, but it was just briefly."

She tries to make sense of this, and a prickle of unease settles over her.

"After that, I ran into her at a pizza place in our neighborhood and then at the park." He snorts. "Later, she admitted she'd followed me. She was very attractive, and I took it as a compliment at the time."

"Wait a minute." She sits up on one elbow. "How old were you when this happened?"

Giovanni doesn't say anything but then meets her eyes. "I was seventeen when it started, a senior in high school."

"And how old was she?"

"In her thirties."

"My God." Lindsay's stomach turns. She had no idea it was something like this. "She was a predator."

He frowns. "I don't know if I'd go that far. Like I said, at the time, I took it as a compliment. In fact, I was interested in her."

"She stalked you when you were seventeen years old."

"I know how it sounds, but that's not how it felt. And it's not like I was a virgin or anything." He lets out his breath. "I didn't look seventeen. Hell, I was nearly as big as I am now. I basically looked like a man."

"But you *were* seventeen." She stares at him with amazement and is surprised he doesn't see what's so obvious.

"I wanted her as much as she wanted me," he insists. "I blame her for a lot of things, but I don't blame her for that part."

She rolls over so she's on her stomach facing him, taking his hand again. "What if it were a seventeen-year-old girl with some guy in his thirties? Would you say the same thing?"

"No. I'd say nail the bastard to the wall."

"What about another seventeen-year-old boy—let's say our nephew, Luca. Would you want that for him?"

Giovanni scowls. "Of course not. But that's different."

"How?"

"I don't know. It just is." He rubs his forehead. "I understand what you're saying, but it didn't feel like that to me. I fell totally in love with her."

Lindsay meets his eyes, and she sees he believes it.

"I grew to hate her though," he says, his voice hard. "Because of the lies. All the secrets. I'd see her husband occasionally, and I'd feel sick knowing what we were doing behind his back."

She doesn't say anything, only watches the pain on his face.

"I hated lying to my family the most." He closes his eyes when his voice shakes. "I'm ashamed that I lied to them for so many years."

She could see how it must have been terrible for him. That kind of subterfuge is hardly in his nature. In a way she's surprised this bitch Olivia convinced him to do it, but then manipulating a hormone-driven seventeen-year-old probably wasn't that difficult.

It occurs to Lindsay how she and Giovanni have something in common. They were both preyed on when they were younger, but hers was only one night, while his lasted for years.

She moves closer to him and strokes his jaw, kissing him. What happened to him hurts her deeply. She now sees the kind of monster that's sunk its teeth into him, and how it's far uglier than she imagined. How it stole part of his youth.

His eyes are drifting shut from exhaustion.

She continues to strokes his handsome face. "You should go to sleep, Olaf."

He nods slowly. "I think I have to." He looks at her. "I promise I'll tell you more about it later."

"Okay," she whispers, and it breaks her heart.

"There's something else." His eyes are still on hers. Despite everything he's told her, there's something joyful in his gaze.

"What?"

He smiles. "I love you too."

Early the next morning, Lindsay wakes up groggy to the sound of Giovanni speaking on his phone to the hospital. She hears him talking about his patient from the OR last night and about a few others. He sounds like his normal self—completely in command with a dash of control freak thrown in for good measure.

After he hangs up, he turns to her, noticing she's awake. "Sorry if I woke you. I need to go in for a few hours, and then I'm on call tonight."

"It's okay. I have to get up soon, anyway." She's working at the bakery this morning, and when she gets home wants to plant some more flowers in front of the house.

He moves closer to her on the bed. He's still naked beneath the covers and wraps his warm body around hers, grinning. "I don't have to go in right away. I could probably carve out a few minutes first."

She raises her brow. "A few minutes? That's all I get?"

"All right, maybe ten."

"They better be an incredible ten fucking minutes."

"I assure you, they will be," He kisses her then nuzzles her neck. "Are you still in love with me?"

"Of course."

"Say it again."

She looks at him, tenderness coursing through her. "I love you."

He takes in her words, and she can tell he's pleased. He runs his thumb lightly over her brow. "I want you to stay that way forever."

Her breath catches. "Maybe I will. But only if you do the same."

"Don't worry," he whispers. "I already know I'll love you forever."

And with that mind-blowing statement out of the way, he pulls her close and proceeds to show her just how incredible ten fucking minutes can be.

Afterward, as she lies there in bliss, letting her fingers trail down his back, she smiles. Ten minutes turned into twenty, and they were certainly incredible. He kisses her again, but then pulls away reluctantly and gets out of bed. Morning sunlight streams through the window, allowing her to admire him walking naked across the bedroom.

"I can't believe you don't have a single tattoo." She rolls onto her side and props herself up on her elbow as she studies his body. Those thighs and that fantastic ass. "Not even one."

He opens the closet to pull out a shirt. "That's okay. You have enough for the both of us."

Her brows go up. "Did I hear you correctly? Are you complaining about my ink?"

"I'm not complaining," he says, reaching in for a pair of slacks. "But don't get any more."

"I'll get more if I want to. In fact, I've been thinking about getting an *Ampelmann* from Berlin on my shoulder, or possibly my ankle."

"You have beautiful skin, Lindsay. It doesn't need to be adorned."

"It's my body, and I'll adorn it if I please." She goes quiet, trying to understand his resistance. "Is this about the 'Queen of Hearts' thing? Is that still bothering you?"

Giovanni comes over, carrying his clothes before he goes to take a shower. He sits on the bed next to her. "I admit, that did bother me, but only because I felt like you were keeping another secret." He takes her hand. "Let's not have any more secrets between us."

Lindsay nods, but her stomach clenches because, of course, she does have another secret. A big one. Her infertility. She wonders if he'll still love her 'forever' if he finds out she could never give him children.

Maybe it won't matter.

"What's wrong?" he asks with his usual perceptiveness. Sometimes she wishes he were just a little bit dumber.

She shakes her head. "It's nothing." She knows she needs to tell him, but it has to be the right moment, not when he's running off to the hospital. "Would it really bother you if I got another tattoo?"

"No, of course not. I just think you're beautiful the way you are, that's all."

He leaves to get ready for work, and she decides to put this whole thing out of her mind for now. She's learned that sometimes worrying about something too much creates a problem where there is none.

They're both busy the next couple of days. He's at the hospital a lot, and she works at the bakery in the mornings and then goes to her studio in the afternoon. She finally goes online to register for classes at the university—though she still has no idea how she's going to pay for them.

There's a party at Natalie's on Friday. It started out as a girls' night, but turned into an 'everybody is invited' sort of thing, so she and Giovanni go together. After they arrive, she learns Natalie has already found a manny. It's the brother of Anthony's assistant from work.

"You're going to like him," Natalie tells her, as Lindsay helps set up the buffet of food for everyone in the dining room. "He's a great guy. Married and in school right now to become a kindergarten teacher."

She nods with approval. "I still want to meet him, but I have to agree, he does sound perfect."

Blair is there with her husband, Nathan, and she comes over to give Lindsay a hug. "You weren't kidding about Anthony's brother," she says. "He's really handsome and kind of intense too. Plus, he's a surgeon—how hot is that?"

"Very fucking hot." Lindsay grins and glances over to Giovanni, who's talking to Nathan across the room. It occurs to her that they'd probably get along as they're both well-traveled. She sees Tori, another friend, and they both wave hello.

"I have to ask, though." Blair leans closer. "Does he pass the Bandito Test?"

Lindsay glances over at Giovanni again. The Bandito Test was this test Blair and Tori came up with to test a guy's worthiness. The basic scenario is this: If you were kidnapped by a group of banditos, would the guy rescue you, even if it meant putting his own life in great danger?

"Of course, he'd pass," Lindsay says. Hell, knowing Giovanni, he'd rescue her then go back and rescue everybody else who'd been kidnapped too.

He senses her perusal because his eyes go to hers and stay there. Neither of them can look away. It's been like this all night. Eventually, he pulls her into Natalie and Anthony's guest bedroom, the one they stayed in, which is now filled with coats and purses.

"Let's get out of here," he murmurs, pushing her against the closed door. "I'm going nuts. I want to be alone with you."

She wraps her arms around his neck. "We haven't been here long enough. Don't you want to be social?"

"No." He kisses her then trails his mouth down to her neck. "I want to take you home and do all manner of dirty things to you."

"We have to stay a little while longer," she tells him, to which he grumbles and growls.

They go back out and join the party, though he stays by her side, holding her hand and whispering in her ear as he nuzzles her some more. All the while, Lindsay giggles like a teeny bopper.

When she goes into the kitchen to grab some paper towels to help clean up a spill, Anthony is there. "I don't know what's going on between you and my brother," he says with amazement, "but I haven't seen Gio this happy in a long time."

Later, she sees Natalie watching them with a little smile. By the time they announce they're leaving, her sister whispers to her in the doorway, "You two look like you're married for real."

That comment stays with Lindsay and unfortunately, not in a good way. Despite how happy she's been, a part of her is still nervous. She never wanted to marry again, to set herself up for that kind of pain, yet somehow this arrangement is turning into an actual marriage, and she doesn't know what to do about it.

Over the weekend, Giovanni tells her more about his relationship with Olivia. It hurts her deeply to hear how he was used—not that he sees it that way, but she certainly does.

After he explains how he lied to his parents by telling them he was involved in various sports and other after-school activities, when instead he was with Olivia, she asks how they managed it.

"Where did you go to be together? Her house?"

"Sometimes," he says.

They're sitting together on the couch after having dinner. He was at the hospital all day as usual, but it turns out finally has tomorrow off. "I take it her husband was gone a lot for work?"

"He was, and occasionally we'd meet at her house, but mostly we'd meet at other people's houses."

"What do you mean?"

Olivia apparently owned her own interior design firm and had access to numerous empty houses while her clients weren't around. Lindsay's sure they would have been seriously pissed to discover how much she abused their trust.

"Were you ever caught?"

He nods. "A few times, but I think she liked it. Olivia enjoyed the rush. She was kind of a thrill seeker. She'd lie and tell them I was a design student, or if we stayed at a hotel, she usually told people I was her nephew."

"And they believed her?"

"No one ever questioned it."

She shakes her head. "I'm surprised her husband never figured it out. After all that time how could he not have suspected anything?"

He takes a swallows from his beer. "Sometimes I wondered if he knew. Not about me, but that she was with someone. She admitted to me at one point how there had been other guys before me." He reflects for a moment. "There was someone after me too, I think."

"Young like you?"

He nods. "That's the impression I got. Olivia always seemed most concerned my parents would find out."

"I'll bet." She tries to imagine what his parents would have done if they knew the truth. Olivia had good reason to be scared. She's sure they would have gone after her with everything they had.

"I tried to break it off with her in the beginning." He licks his lips. "I tried a couple times."

"What happened?"

"She convinced me to stay." He looks at her. "I once yelled at her and told her how I wanted to be a normal teenager and date teenage girls like I was supposed to."

She reaches for his hand and squeezes it.

"In the beginning, she used sex to convince me, and it was difficult to resist. Then later, I fell in love with her." He stares down at the beer bottle. "I'm ashamed to admit it, but at that point, I didn't want to leave. I chose to stay with her, despite all the lies it involved."

"Being manipulated like that isn't really choosing," she says, but knows he doesn't believe her.

"For a long time afterward, I didn't want to be with anyone else, and when I finally gave in to my own needs, I couldn't give anything emotionally."

He closes his eyes and leans his head back on the couch. There's anguish on his face, and she feels it too, along with a deep rage toward Olivia. *If she weren't already dead, I'd go after her myself.*

"We don't have to talk about this anymore," she says. "Not if it's hurting you."

He opens his eyes and looks at her. "No, I want to tell you. It's weird, but I think it's helping me. It's like for years I've been frozen in a long winter, and now it's finally spring." He smiles and draws her in closer. "You're my spring," he says quietly. "My new beginning."

She touches his face, her heart in her throat. "You're mine too."

Chapter Twenty-Three

~ Be careful. Even fake marriages are complicated. ~

THE NEXT MORNING, as Giovanni changes the bandage on her finger, checking for signs of infection, Lindsay tells him how she thinks he should consider talking to somebody about his past.

"What you do you mean? Like a professional?" he asks.

"Yeah, like a therapist or counselor."

He gives her a wry look. "I don't need therapy." And then he leans down and kisses her on the mouth. "All I need is you."

She disagrees, thinking it might be good for him. "You should consider it. I know you don't believe this, but from everything you've told me, Olivia didn't just fuck your body. She fucked your mind too."

He pauses. "I'm fine. Look at my life. I'm not exactly struggling here."

"It's true that, professionally, you're successful, but your personal life was a mess for years."

"*Was* being the operative word." He finishes cleaning off her finger with some kind of antibacterial spray and throws the cotton in the garbage. "I'm happy to say your finger is healing well, and I don't see any sign of infection. We can leave the bandage off."

She nods. "Okay, thanks."

He goes over to the sink and washes his hands. When he's done and drying them on a towel, he tells her how he's going to buy some more fruit trees for the backyard soon, how he wants to plant some apple trees along the fence.

"We should finish setting up the rooms for Joseph and Sara too," Lindsay says, thinking it over. She's done some painting, but they haven't bought beds yet. "Have you heard anything about the adoption?"

"I spoke to Phillip briefly the other day, and we're still in a holding pattern. He's worried, though. It sounds like things are growing even more politically unstable."

"Can we do anything?"

"Not really, but I feel like I'm letting Paul down somehow."

"That's crazy. It's not like you have control over any of this."

"I know." Giovanni gazes out the kitchen window. "I just wish I could do more."

She goes over and wraps her arms around him, resting her head on his shoulder. "You're an amazing friend. Most people would never go to such lengths."

He hugs her in return, and they stay that way for a while.

When she finally pulls back, she sees he's smiling down at her. "What is it?"

"I was just thinking about you in that origami class the other day. You're really great with kids."

"Thank you."

"Do you think you'd like to have kids of your own someday?"

Her eyes widen as adrenaline spikes through her. She knows she needs to tell him about her infertility before things get even more serious in their relationship. *I should do it now. I can't let this go on.*

"My mom called me at the hospital yesterday," he says. "It was only a short conversation, but I think she's changing her mind about all this. Our arrangement."

"Really?" She blinks with astonishment.

He nods. "It turns out my dad has reconsidered, and he's been talking to her about it." He smirks and rolls his eyes. "She said something crazy too."

"What was that?"

"That you and I would make beautiful babies together."

Lindsay's throat goes tight. She tries to smile, but it feels like she's doing it from a million miles away. "Why would she say such a bizarre thing?"

"Because I told her about us." His blue eyes go to hers. "That we're involved, and that I'm in love with you."

She tries to take a breath. "I can't imagine she was too pleased. I don't think she likes me."

He shrugs. "Apparently, she approved of the way you handled that nanny business with your sister, although I thought the whole thing sounded nuts."

She knows she has to tell him the truth, how they will never make beautiful babies together, how that particular hand will never be played.

But somehow she can't find it within herself. *Not yet.* It's such a lovely fantasy that, for a little while longer, she wants to live it, wants to pretend she's seeing it from his point of view.

Giovanni studies her. "Is everything all right?"

Lindsay licks her lips. "This is happening so fast. I'm the one who swore I'd never get married again, remember?"

"Hey, we're just taking things at our own pace. Don't worry about anything else."

"I'll try." She does feel nervous though. In truth, she's way past the point where she would have left any other relationship.

"There's one other thing I wanted to tell you about." He gets a mischievous grin on his face. "I'm not sure what you'll think of this, but it turns out Seattle Children's is participating in an upcoming fundraiser. Its theme is the Roaring Twenties. There's an auction and a poker tournament."

"You're kidding."

He's still grinning at her. "I think you should enter. People can stake you, and all your winnings will go to whichever hospital you're playing for."

She considers it. "I don't know if I can afford it. What's the buy in? I still have school to pay for."

"Don't worry about that. I'll stake you. It's for a good cause, after all."

She gives him a long look. "You don't care if everybody knows your wife plays poker? Some people might think that's weird."

"Are you kidding?" He chuckles. "It'll be great. They'll *never* see you coming."

She nods. "That's true." They typically never do. It's always been one of her advantages.

His hands slide to her hips, and he pulls her in close. "You should teach me how to play sometime."

"You don't know to how play *poker?*" Her mouth opens with astonishment.

"No, not really. I played a couple times in college, but I barely remember it."

"I didn't know that." It's difficult for her to even imagine such a thing. It seems like she's always known how to play. She remembers her dad teaching her card rankings when she was very young. "Sure, I could teach you."

"But I want to play *strip* poker." He waggles his brows, and she laughs.

They spend the next few hours each doing their own thing. It's a warm Sunday, and Giovanni is outside in the backyard with his beloved fruit trees. Lindsay calls a few friends she hasn't spoken with since she's been back from Germany. Afterward, she goes out to talk to him.

"Listen, I just spoke with a friend of mine." She stands next to where Giovanni's building some kind of wooden trellis. "He's going to come by today and drop off some of my stuff."

"Okay."

She doesn't move, and he glances at her. "Is there something else?"

"He's the guy I was living with before I went to Berlin. I just thought you should know that."

His lips come together in a flat line. The hammer in his hand goes still as he appears to be taking in her words. "Why is he coming here exactly?"

"Because he has some things of mine. Some jewelry and some clothes. Plus, we're still friends." She gazes at the house and yard for a few seconds. "You told me to treat this like my home, and I have been, in every way except one."

"What's that?"

"You probably haven't noticed, but I haven't had any friends over."

He shrugs. "I don't mind if you have friends over. In fact, I've had invitations to socialize with colleagues recently, but I wasn't sure how you'd feel about that sort of thing."

"I'm fine with it." Lindsay looks down at her flip-flops. She recently painted her toenails dark blue. "Look, a lot of my friends are men." She glances up at him. "I just get along with men. Don't get me wrong, I have women friends too. But I've always had both."

She can see Giovanni trying not to struggle with this news and doing a poor job of it. "I understand. You should invite your friends over, even if they're . . . *men*." He nearly chokes on the word.

She eyes him dubiously, but nods. "Okay, good."

While she's waiting for her ex-boyfriend to show up, she sits at the dining room table with her laptop, updating her artist blog and some of her other social media pages.

Giovanni's already come inside the house twice, scowling and territorial. An alpha dog ready to stake his claim. Any second now, she expects him to start pissing on the furniture.

"It's really no big deal," she explains again. "I'm just friends with him still. That's all."

He nods with a grave expression. "Of course, I understand. No problem." Though it's obvious there *is* a problem.

By the time they hear a motorcycle roaring into their driveway, Lindsay's worried. She's dealt with enough men fighting over her that she already knows the signs beforehand.

"You know, maybe I'll just get my stuff from Dylan out front," she says in an offhanded way as she gets up. "That's probably easiest."

"Dylan?" Giovanni's scowl deepens. "That's his *name?*"

She nods.

He grumbles and says something in Italian, which she's certain isn't a compliment toward Dylan. "Tell him to come inside. I told you I don't care. I'm going back out to work on the trellis."

She watches him walk out the back door. He's wearing those soft Levis she loves and a fitted blue T-shirt that says 'UCLA Medicine' on it.

Lindsay goes out front and finds Dylan there, just getting off his Harley. He unstraps his helmet, smiling when he notices her.

"Hey, Linds. It's good to see you." He comes over to give her a hug.

"You too," she says, breathing in his familiar scent. They lived together for almost six months, and she's glad they managed to stay friends. She's had plenty of ugly breakups over the years, but this wasn't one of them.

"You look good, sweetheart." His eyes roam over her as he gives her a rakish grin. "Real good."

"Thanks, so do you."

Dylan is handsome, with sun-streaked blond hair and hazel eyes. He's wearing torn-up jeans and a black biker's jacket. They moved in together at his insistence, but this was back when she had lost her mojo and wasn't feeling it with any guy. They tried to make it work, but the whole thing really never took flight between them.

"I've got your stuff." He walks back over to the bike to open one of his saddle bags and retrieve her things. He pulls out a plastic sack and hands it to her.

"Thank you, I appreciate you bringing it by."

"No problem." He looks around at the house. "Nice place. So, it's true? You really did get married?"

Lindsay nods. "It was kind of a sudden thing." She's not sure if Dylan is still in love with her, but she doesn't think so. The vibe she's getting tells her he's over it.

"Very sudden, I hear."

"We were swept away."

He nods, chuckling. "Don't worry, Linds. I'm happy for you."

"Do you want to come inside the house?" Part of her hopes he says no, but the other part of her thinks maybe she needs to test Giovanni. *I mean, how is this ever going to work between us if he can't handle me having friends over who are guys?*

"Okay, but I have to keep it short. I'm meeting someone."

She raises an eyebrow. "A hot date?"

"Yeah, basically. It's kind of new, but so far it's good."

They head inside, and she doesn't see any sign of Giovanni. She offers Dylan something to drink, and he accepts a glass of ice water.

"Really nice," he says, nodding as he looks around. "I've always liked these old Tudor homes, and this one is a beauty. It appears your new husband has good taste in more than just women." He winks at her.

"Do you want to meet him? He's just out back."

"Sure."

Dylan follows her out through the back door to where Giovanni is still hammering away at something near the fence. Lindsay doesn't know why she's bringing Dylan out and hopes this isn't stupid on her part.

As they get closer, Giovanni stops what he's doing. She can see the way he's taking Dylan's measure. He's still holding the hammer, and Lindsay is suddenly nervous.

Dear God, please don't let this turn into a homicide.

She can see the news story already: *A well-respected pediatric surgeon is accused of murdering his fake wife's ex-boyfriend in a fit of nonsensical jealousy. Fake wife hopes this doesn't ruin their adoption plans. Fake wife also admits she loves the accused and says their marriage is 'almost real'.*

Lindsay introduces the men, and they shake hands. Giovanni is wearing his usual tense expression and looks more like Thor than ever with that hammer by his side.

"Congratulations on your wedding," Dylan says. "And let me just say you have great taste in women."

"Thank you."

"And houses, as well. This is a beautiful Tudor. I'm guessing it was built around the early 1930s?"

"Thanks and yes, it was. 1934."

Dylan asks a few questions about the house. Giovanni seems guarded, but still polite.

"I see you're building a trellis." Dylan nods down at the wood frame Giovanni was hammering a few moments ago. "Are you planning to add some fruit trees against the south fence there?"

"I am." Giovanni is now looking at Dylan with interest. "Mostly apple."

Dylan nods, his eyes roaming the back yard. "It's an excellent idea. It makes perfect use of the space."

"I thought so," Giovanni agrees. "I'm still trying to figure out how many trees I can fit back here."

"There are a few varieties of plum you also might want to consider."

And before Lindsay knows it, the two men are discussing apple and plum trees and Giovanni's plans for his mini orchard. She had no idea Dylan knew so much about fruit trees but then remembers his parents run a plant nursery.

After a short while, Giovanni seems to relax, and by the time Dylan tells them he has to leave for his date, her husband appears almost reluctant to let him go.

"You should drop by my parents' store up in Shoreline," Dylan says. "Tell them I sent you and they'll give you a twenty percent discount."

"Really? Thanks, I'll do that."

Lindsay walks him back out front to his motorcycle. When she comes back, Giovanni is in the house grabbing a bite to eat.

"You did very well," she says, coming up and wrapping her arms around his waist. "I'm impressed."

"Thank you," he says in a dry tone. "You should have told me he was a master gardener. I could use one of those right now."

"It never occurred to me. He's an architect, but I forgot his parents own a nursery."

Giovanni cuts off a piece of salami and pops it in his mouth. "So, did I pass your little test?"

"I wasn't testing you." Her eyes go to the salami in his hand. "You know I haven't seen you eat a single insect since we've lived here. Not even one potato bug."

He smirks. "Don't change the subject."

"Okay, fine." She accepts the bite of salami he offers her. "I just wanted to make sure you could handle it when more of my male friends come around to visit."

"*More?*" He looks slightly queasy. "How many more are we talking about?"

"I don't know, less than a dozen." She laughs at his panicked expression. "Don't worry, they're not all ex-boyfriends."

"Christ." He shakes his head as he cuts off another piece of salami. "I'll bet they're all in love with you, though."

Lindsay doesn't say anything since she suspects a few of them are—not that she encourages it.

"Why didn't it work out with that guy I just met? With *Dylan*."

She shrugs. "I don't know. There was no sizzle."

Giovanni meets her eyes. "We've got sizzle." He gives her a sexy grin. "*Lots* of sizzle."

She steps closer to him and steals the piece he's just cut for himself. "We sure do, Olaf."

After Giovanni finishes attaching the two trellises he's built to the back fence, he drags one of the chaise patio chairs over and takes a seat. He won't be able to plant anything until the weather cools, but at least it's all prepared.

There's something about all this—a home of his own, laying down roots for the first time—that relaxes him in ways he never thought possible. He's been living on adrenaline for so many years he'd forgotten what it felt like not to.

"Admiring your handiwork?" Lindsay says, coming out to join him.

"Yes." He chuckles a little. "It's kind of crooked, but I'm still enjoying it. I can't remember the last time I built something."

She puts her hands on her hips, studying his trellis as he studies her. She's wearing a pair of cut-off shorts, which show off her long legs and round ass in a way that can only be described as spectacular.

"It doesn't look crooked to me," she says, turning around and catching him admiring her body.

"Come over here." He grins, reaching for her.

She walks closer, and he opens his thighs, making room for her to sit between them.

"I've worked with wood a little," she tells him, sitting sideways between his legs so they can still see each other. "I taught a class years ago where we sculpted using an axe."

"You sculpted with an axe?"

She nods. "It was this crazy technique a friend and I came up with. In fact, I threw the axe at my sister's door one night, and it got stuck. This was before she knew Anthony—though he's the one who finally figured out how to remove it."

He chuckles. "Damn, you're dangerous."

"Don't worry, I won't be throwing any axes at your front door."

"*Our* front door," he corrects her.

"Okay," she says. "Our front door."

"Don't you feel like this is your home? Because that's how it feels to me."

"I do for the most part. It's just that I'm not paying for any of it."

"You buy groceries," he points out. "Not to mention all the other ways you've added to the house. None of this would be the same without you."

"I feel like a kept woman though." She looks around at the yard. "I could never afford a place like this."

"I don't expect you to pay for any of it. That wasn't part of our arrangement." He slides his hand down her arm, enjoying the feel of her smooth skin. "I love taking care of you. It pleases me more than you can imagine."

She frowns. "Once I'm flush again, I'll help pay bills."

"You don't have to. In fact, I still wish you'd let me give you the twenty grand we initially agreed upon."

"Forget it." She rolls her eyes. "Don't even go there."

He doesn't say anything, knowing it's an argument he'll lose since he's already lost it a few times.

"Have you thought any more about what I said earlier?" she asks, laying her hand on his chest. She fingers his T-shirt. "About talking to a therapist?"

"Not really."

"Why not?"

He takes a deep breath. "I know you mean well, but I don't need therapy. I think you're mischaracterizing the relationship I had with Olivia. I wasn't a victim."

"That's the same thing I said about what happened to me, remember?"

His hand on her arm slows. "Do you accept it now? That you were taken advantage of by that scumbag?"

She goes quiet. Her lovely brown eyes seem to reflect on this. It's early evening, and the sky has turned orange and pink. There's a smoky scent in the air from one of their neighbors barbecuing. "I'm starting to see how what happened that night was like the perfect storm." Her expression turns adamant. "But I also understand how nothing that creep did could *ever* define me. I define myself."

Giovanni slides his hand into hers. "I'm glad to hear you say that."

She turns to him, and her expression is sympathetic. "In many ways, I think what happened to you is worse."

"All I did was fall in love with the wrong woman. It wounded me, but it turns out wounds heal over time." He glances down at her injured middle finger.

Lindsay scoots up a little so she can rest her head on his shoulder. He wraps his arm around her, kissing her hair before leaning his head back on the lounge chair and closing his eyes. Grateful a million times over again that she came into his life.

I've finally fallen in love with the right woman.

"You may not agree with my way of thinking," she says. "But I hate what she did to you. A part of me wishes I could have gotten my hands on her."

He opens his eyes.

"Can I ask you something? How did Olivia die?"

He takes a deep breath and lets it out, gazing up at the sky. "She was eaten by a shark."

Lindsay goes still. "What?" She raises her head from his shoulder and stares at him. "I'm sorry, but what the fuck?" A bubble of laughter escapes her.

"It's true."

"Eaten by a *shark?* No way." She laughs some more, incredulous. "You're making that up."

"I'm not." He shakes his head, chuckling a little. "It sounds nuts, I know. But she was attacked by a shark while scuba diving off the coast of Florida."

"Are you sure? A *shark?*"

"I'm sure. I even met with the touring company who took her out on their boat. Apparently, there were several shark sightings, but Olivia refused to listen to the warning. In fact, she nearly got one of their guides killed." He remembers talking to the owner of the boat, how they said she insisted on diving despite everyone trying to convince her otherwise. "She was always too reckless, and she hated the word 'no.'"

"How long ago was this?"

"About eight years."

"That must have made headlines."

"It did. It made international headlines." Absurdly, Olivia would have enjoyed all the media attention as she was quite vain.

Lindsay takes this in, and another small bubble of laughter escapes her. "Damn, I'm sorry. I know it's not funny."

"It's not," he agrees, though he can't stop grinning either.

They both look at each other, struggling to keep a straight face.

She bites her lip. "I'm a terrible person for finding humor in this."

He shrugs. "These things happen."

"Eaten by a shark? I've never heard of anything so crazy."

"She did love the sea."

Lindsay's eyes go wide and before he knows it, she bursts out laughing. He can't stop himself from laughing with her.

"We're going straight to hell!" she tells him before another wave of laughter hits her.

"Probably," he admits, still chuckling as he wipes his eyes. He was saddened when he heard about Olivia's death all those years ago, and he certainly wouldn't wish it on anyone, but he has to admit there was a ridiculous irony to it.

Finally, they get themselves under control, and Lindsay lays her head back down on his shoulder. "Unbelievable," he hears her still muttering. "Eaten by a motherfucking shark."

Chapter Twenty-Four

~ The truth doesn't always set you free. ~

A FEW DAYS later, Lindsay finally gets some good news on the financial front. Her agent, Emily, calls while she's at the bakery to let her know one of her masks from the gallery in Berlin just sold to a German business and they want to commission two more.

"That's fantastic!" She grips the phone with relief. "Do they have anything specific in mind?"

"It sounds like they want two pieces in a similar style, but are leaving it to your discretion."

"Love it." She grins. That's her favorite kind of commission.

"I'll forward their e-mail. I've already sent them the standard contract. You should be receiving the funds from the gallery in Berlin, minus their cut, within a week."

After they hang up, Lindsay dances around the cash register, doing a little bump and grind.

"Good news?" Carlos, their star barista, asks, pouring steamed milk into two large white mugs.

"The best ever." She tells him about the sale and the two pieces commissioned, and he agrees it's definitely good news.

She goes in back to share her news with Natalie and Blair and discovers Natalie's new manny is there with Luca. In an ironic twist, the manny is named Manuel and even goes by Manny as a nickname. She met him for the first time when he brought Luca by yesterday for a visit. Manuel is twenty-five years old. He's straight, married, handsome, slightly overweight, and Lindsay's approval of him is one thousand percent.

He's also a good guy, and Luca took to him right away.

"Hey, big boy. Come on out and hang with your auntie," Lindsay says to Luca, unstrapping him from his car seat carrier. His grin goes wide as he grabs a hunk of her hair and pulls hard. "Ow! Hey, I'd like to keep *some* of my hair." She dances around with him as he giggles and drools. "My goodness, you're light on your feet!"

"You're in a good mood," Natalie says, laughing as she turns to watch the two of them.

Lindsay tells them about the phone call from Emily, and both Natalie and Manuel agree it's fantastic news.

When she arrives home later that evening, after working in her studio all afternoon, she's surprised to discover opera on the stereo and Giovanni in the kitchen making dinner.

"Hey, what's all this? I thought you had to be at the hospital tonight."

"No, it got canceled."

"Really?"

"I was filling in for another surgeon, but she came in." He shrugs. "I'm still on call, though."

"Wow."

He chuckles. "I know."

Lindsay goes over to the fridge to grab a bottle of wine. "Well, I'm glad you're here because I have incredible news to share."

She notices he has a pot of water on the stove he's bringing to a boil, and he's also melting butter in a large pan.

"What news is that?" he asks.

She tells him about her sale in Berlin. "Can you believe it?" She uncorks the bottle. "Just in the nick of time too. I had absolutely no idea how I was going to manage tuition."

"That's great. Congratulations."

"Thanks." She pours herself a glass of wine and takes a sip, letting her eyes slide down his body. He's wearing tan cords and a fitted T-shirt that's fitting him very well indeed. "I want to celebrate."

He glances at her. "Should we go out?"

"No, let's stay *in*."

"All right," he murmurs and then gives her a suggestive look. A pleasant tingle runs through her veins, slipping down her spine. She watches him turn off the heat on all the burners, also moving the frying pan. Always thinking ahead. His approach to life is so different than hers. She's never been much of a planner, but she sees the benefit a lot more than she used to.

He moves closer to her, takes her wine glass and sets it on the counter.

"You know what?" She slips her arms around his neck. "I don't think you've ever fucked me in this kitchen."

Giovanni tilts his head as a grin pulls on those sensual lips. "You're right, I haven't." He bends down to kiss her. She thinks he's going to remedy the kitchen fucking situation, but instead he reaches around for her hand. "Come on, I have a little surprise for you."

He leads her into the living room near the stereo. She looks around the room but doesn't see any surprise.

"Close your eyes," he tells her.

She obliges and hears him turn off the opera. There are some clicking sounds of him manipulating his iPod. A few moments later, she hears a familiar rhythm guitar, a rolling drumbeat, and then Elvis singing.

"Burning Love!" She opens her eyes with a shriek of delight.

"Our song," he says in a dry tone. And then he leans in toward her. "I've decided to finally give you that wedding dance you wanted."

"Are you serious?" Lindsay claps her hands. "I finally get to see Frankenstein's monster?"

"God, help me," he mutters. "I hope I'm not ruining any chance of you ever sleeping with me again."

"What? Don't be silly." She's already rolling her hips to the music. She loves to dance and rocks out regularly with Natalie and her two nieces.

As the music pulls her in with its irresistible beat, he starts trying to dance too, teetering from one foot to the other.

She's already slipping into her groove, grinding her hips and swinging her hands overhead.

"Woohoo!" She laughs, dancing around him then trailing her fingers lightly across his chest as he starts bobbing his head. His foot-to-foot teetering seems to be increasing in intensity.

"I love this song," she says, letting her hair fly. She shakes her hips and spins a couple of times. "Nice!" She nods at him with encouragement.

His hands come up in front of him, and he starts shaking them like they're on fire. It's so bizarre that she's never seen anything like it. His teetering is still going strong and appears to have morphed into a stomp, while his head bobs up and down like a giant ostrich.

"Yeah!" She sings to him as she waves both her arms in the air, still dancing around him.

His expression is intense, but he's grinning at the same time. It appears he's in full Frankenstein mode. His arms are swinging all over as his whole body rocks wildly back and forth.

Lindsay is clapping and laughing as she gives him room to do his thing. She hopes he doesn't knock any of the furniture over but figures it's worth it to see this glorious sight.

By the time the song starts winding down, they're both laughing and out of breath.

Giovanni has stopped doing the Frankenstein and is grinning at her with affection instead. "Come here," he breathes, swooping her into his arms.

"And you claimed you can't dance," she teases as she presses herself against him. "That was incredible."

"Incredible is a word for it, all right."

She grins. "Well, I *loved* it. I sure hope you don't hide your light under a bushel anymore."

He rolls his eyes, the flush on his face going deeper as he laughs with embarrassment.

"What made you finally decide to dance with me?"

He gazes down at her, still grinning, and shrugs. "I don't know. I realized I can be myself with you, that you can handle it."

She nods, her heart ready to burst with joy. Their eyes stay on each other, and in that moment, she's completely and utterly in love. There's no other way to describe it. She's never felt like this before, never wanted so many good things for someone with her whole self. Never found anyone who moves her so deeply.

"I can definitely handle it," she says, stroking his jaw.

His eyes go soft before he bends down and brings his mouth to hers. "Forever," he murmurs before kissing her gently, licking her lips as he plays around. But Lindsay's breath is already coming fast, and she tightens her arms.

"I love you," he says, drawing back to take her in. "All the way, every day."

"I know," she whispers. "Me too."

And then they're kissing again, but it's not gentle and playful—it's full-on out of control. Reckless, with tongues and teeth. She whimpers into his mouth, gripping his neck because she wants him inside her now.

Giovanni reaches down and grabs her ass with both hands to hoist her up, and she immediately wraps her legs around his waist.

He starts making his way toward the bedroom, still kissing, bumping into the wall.

"Hurry!" she insists, her mouth pressed against his. "I can't wait!"

Somehow, they get through the doorway and make it onto the bed, both of them panting and pulling at each other's clothes, with Lindsay on her back as Giovanni hovers over her.

She grabs at his cords and then his bare ass when they're finally shoved out of the way. "What's taking so long?"

His breath is harsh and desperate as he tries to get her jeans off. He yanks one pant leg down and doesn't bother with the other because she feels him big and hard right at her center, pushing her thong aside.

"Oh, God," she gasps when he shoves his full length inside her, none of his usual preamble of trying to take it slow. It's intense, over-the-top, and incredible in every way.

He's already groaning and moving out of control. He grips her thigh. "Wrap your legs around me tight," he says coarsely. "Yes," he breathes as soon as she complies. "That's it."

It's all so hot she already feels the beginning of her climax. His mouth is smoldering on hers, and she's moaning into it, but then he breaks the kiss and pushes up her shirt, his hand under her bra. She claws his back, groaning and biting his shoulder through his cotton T-shirt as her release overtakes her like a storm.

Almost from a distance she hears him coming too, and then it's all up close. His body is relentless, his hand still on her breast as he shudders and groans low and long.

When he finally collapses on top of her, she tries to catch her breath, both their hearts still hammering.

"Damn," he says as he tries to breathe. "I think we've got sizzle."

She giggles then bites his ear. "We sure do, Olaf. 'Burning Love' is the perfect song for us."

Eventually, Lindsay pushes Giovanni off her. They both strip the rest of their clothes away and scoot up on the bed. He lies on his side with his head at her breast while she plays with his hair.

They stay this way for a while, both of them drowsy, until they fall asleep. When she wakes up, it's nightfall with the hall light shining through the open door. Giovanni shifts a little, and she senses he's awake too, though neither of them speaks. She thinks about the myriad of things that have brought them to this moment.

For some reason, her mind wanders back to what he told her last night about Olivia and the shark. *What a gruesome way to go*. She has a hard time finding any sympathy for her, though, not after what she did. *What kind of woman gets involved with an underage teenage boy?*

"Can I ask you something?" She runs her fingers through his soft curls.

He grunts then draws back from her. "Sure."

"What did Olivia look like?"

He takes in her face and hair. "She was a brunette with brown eyes." His gaze travels down her body to where the sheets have been kicked aside. "Tall and slender with long legs."

Lindsay watches the way he lingers on her own long legs, and a flicker of unease passes through her.

He shrugs. "To be honest, she was beautiful. At least on the outside."

Her unease gets worse because a queer sort of comprehension is dawning on her. "Do I *look* like Olivia?"

Giovanni freezes. His eyes widen and flash to hers.

"My God." Her head swims when she sees the alarm on his face, the mistake he realizes he's just made. She pushes away from him. "I *do*, don't I?"

"It's not how it sounds. I've always had a penchant for brown-eyed brunettes with long legs. That's my *type,*" he insists. "Before I ever met Olivia."

She swallows, tries to calm the sick feeling in her stomach, the fear that's started to take root. "When I first saw you in Berlin, you told me I reminded you of someone." Her voice gets stronger as she remembers it. "*That's* who you were talking about, isn't it?"

He sits up on one elbow. He doesn't answer her right away, and she can see he's being more careful now. "Yes, I admit you reminded me of her a little. But only in a very superficial way."

Her fear not only takes root but starts to bloom. She should have put this together much sooner. *Or maybe I didn't want to see it.*

"How did you and Olivia break up?"

He blinks at her then looks away, letting his breath out like he's accepted the inevitability of this conversation. "I asked her to marry me, and she said no."

"Was she cruel about it?"

He nods. "She laughed and told me I was just a kid. She said she didn't love me, how she was only having fun and I should do the same."

It hurts Lindsay that someone used him like that. It doesn't help her fear, though—just the opposite because now it's bearing fruit. "That's why you were so freaked out when you asked me to marry you, isn't it? Because I reminded you of her."

He doesn't say anything, but doesn't have to because she can see on his face it's true.

She sits up with a jerky motion and moves away from him. She can't move away from the fear, though. "Why is it you never told me I look like her? You should have told me."

"Because I didn't want this reaction. And as I said, it's only on the surface. You're nothing alike on the inside."

"Is it possible our relationship is just your way of reliving the whole thing with Olivia again?"

"*What?*" Giovanni's expression grows thunderous as he sits up too.

"That's absurd."

She reaches for the sheet to cover herself. She doesn't want to believe any of it. It's like poison, but she can't dismiss it either. "How do you know?"

"Because you're *nothing* like her. I fell in love with *you*." There's panic on his face.

Somewhere inside her, a voice is asking why she's so surprised. *You honestly thought you could fix him? Don't you know better?*

"Is it all just a lie?"

Giovanni moves closer to her on the bed. "Listen to me, Lindsay. I love you. How can you even doubt that? What's between you and me has nothing to do with anybody else."

"So it's purely a coincidence that you fell in love with a woman who looks like *her?*"

He tries to reach for her hand, but she pulls it away.

"I have a type," he continues. "So what? I already told you that. A lot of people do."

She doesn't reply as she tries to figure out if her fear is groundless.

"I want us to create a life together," he says. "I *love* you."

Her eyes go to his, and she decides maybe it's time to test that love. "I need to tell you something. It's something I should have already told you."

"What is it?" He seems frustrated. "Another secret? I thought we were past all that."

"Do you remember when your mom said we'd make beautiful babies together?"

He nods, and she can see he's confused about where this is going. "Yes, of course."

Lindsay closes her eyes for a moment. "That won't happen. Not with me, anyway. There won't ever be any babies."

"What are you talking about?"

"I can't have children."

His eyes widen with surprise. It's only for a second, but she sees it. "Why do you assume that?"

"Because I tried years ago with both of my husbands. I finally went to a doctor and discovered children are not in the cards for me."

Giovanni goes quiet. She's doing her best to read him but is having difficulty. "So you lied about having an IUD?"

"I didn't lie. I just . . . evaded your question." She takes a deep breath and lets it out. "I'm infertile. Does that still fit in with your plan to love me 'forever'?"

He doesn't answer her and instead appears to be deep in thought.

She studies him, her heart sinking. "I didn't think so."

"Christ, give me a minute here, will you? Let me take this in." His brows furrow. "Why *exactly* do you think you're infertile?"

"I had an infection when I young, probably in my teens, and it left a lot of scar tissue. I can't conceive."

"That doesn't sound impossible. There are probably ways around it."

Her eyes sting and her chest goes tight. She's not having any difficulty reading him now. He wants children of his own. Of course he does. Why wouldn't he?

"Maybe," she says. "But maybe not. They weren't too encouraging years ago." She thinks about how she tried to get pregnant in the past, and as difficult as it's been, she's had to accept the truth.

"It doesn't matter," he says, finality in his tone. "I don't care. I still want you."

She studies him, and she can see he wants to believe it, but she knows it *does* matter. And that's when she realizes this isn't about testing his love—it's about testing *hers*. Because she could never force him to give up having children for her.

"Talk to me, Lindsay." His blue eyes look worried. "What's that expression? You're scaring me."

"This is all so complicated between us, isn't it?"

"No." His voice is deep and adamant. "It's very simple. We belong together. It's changed both of our lives."

Lindsay takes in his handsome face. And it's true what he's saying—her life has changed. Giovanni's strength has helped her, and she's helped him too. *But that doesn't mean it's forever.*

Suddenly, there's a beeping sound from the other room. It's his pager going off.

"Dammit." He turns his head toward the sound then looks at her again. "I'm going to have to go in." He heads out to the other room, and she hears the beeping noise stop.

When he comes back into the bedroom, she's still sitting on the bed with her back against the wall. He picks up his clothes from the floor and gets dressed.

"You should have told me about the infertility sooner," he says quietly. "But I understand why you didn't." His eyes go to hers, and they're filled with compassion. "I imagine it was a terrible blow, especially for you."

She doesn't say anything. He's right. She's not surprised he gets it, that he understands how terrible it was for her. But she's already shed a million tears over this and doesn't want to shed a million more. That's exactly what this would be.

When he bends down to kiss her good-bye she doesn't move, so he kisses her forehead. "We'll talk about it some more when I get back."

After he leaves, she sits there for a long time. Finally, she lies down on the bed filled with despair. It's all so familiar. With two failed marriages behind her, she's been in this exact same spot before.

She had a lot of good reasons for not getting married again.

And it's time I start remembering what they are.

"Fantastic news. Seriously, I'll tell my parents too." Giovanni's voice awakens Lindsay from a deep sleep.

She was up most of the night, trying to talk herself out of her fears. The truth is she loves him so much it's clouded her judgment. *I let things go too far this time.*

"What is it?" she asks groggily, sitting up. "Has something happened?"

He's still talking on his phone. "That's wonderful." He comes over and stands near her, already dressed. "I can't tell you how glad I am, and Lindsay too. Yes, I'll tell her you said so."

"What's going on?" she asks, after he ends his conversation.

"Great news. Joseph and Sara are on a plane to New York as we speak."

Her mouth opens with astonishment. "Wow! That *is* great news. I take it that was Phillip?"

He nods. "He's at the airport right now, ready to board a flight. The kids flew to Frankfurt last night and now they're headed to the States. He and his wife have gotten custody."

"How did he manage it?"

"Greasing the right palms, it sounds like." He stares down at his phone. "I'm happy it worked. He's been talking with the embassy here, and they were able to help too."

She grins. "I'm *so* glad!" She pictures Joseph and Sara coming to the States finally and is filled with relief.

"Me too. Oh, and Phillip told me to thank you for everything. Obviously agreeing to adopt a couple kids you'd never even met was incredibly kind."

She nods. "Of course. I still hope I get to meet them in person."

"You will. We'll figure something out."

She takes this in. It occurs to her the reason for their arrangement is over. *We don't have to stay married anymore.*

"Is something wrong?" he asks, slipping the phone into his front pocket.

Lindsay looks up at him. She's always thought Giovanni would make a terrible card player. He's too easy to read. But it occurs to her his perceptiveness might make up for it.

"It's nothing." She doesn't want to spoil his happiness right now. "We can talk about it later."

"Are you still upset about last night?"

"Let's not talk about it now. I'm just glad everything worked out for Joseph and Sara."

But he doesn't budge. "I do want to talk about it now. Let's get this out in the open and discuss it."

"No. I'm going to take a shower, and I can manage it alone."

"I know what you're doing," he says. "I thought it over while I was at work. You're purposefully sabotaging things. This is your pattern in relationships. No one ever leaves you, because you always leave them first."

She clenches her jaw as she gets out of bed. "Don't presume you know my motives for anything."

"You don't want to believe something this good could be real, but it *is*."

She tries to walk past him, but he's blocking her way.

"Don't do this, Lindsay," he says. "Don't *ruin* it."

She looks up at him and sees the apprehension on his face. "Look, we've had a great time together. But I can't give you everything you want and let's face it, the fact that I look like Olivia is fucking creepy."

He rolls his eyes with exasperation. "Not this again. Should I find you a photo of her to prove that your resemblance is minimal at best?"

"That won't be necessary."

"This is insane." He rubs his forehead. "You're not even older than me. You're four years *younger*. Plus, I'm telling you that you're *nothing* like her."

The voice inside Lindsay, the one that always tells her when it's time to leave, is whispering in her ear. She tries to block it out, but can't. "There's too much going on here. Don't you see? I can't possibly ask you to give up having children."

"I told you it doesn't matter!"

She sucks in her breath at such a bold lie. Her heart races. "But it *does* matter." She tries to push past him again, but his hand is on her arm, holding her back.

"Please, Lindsay. This is the best thing that's ever happened to either of us, and you know it."

"Let go of me." Her voice shakes. There's terrible pain in his eyes, but she steels herself against it. She knows it's possible to love someone too much. She's witnessed it firsthand. "Just let me *go!*"

Chapter Twenty-Five

LINDSAY'S HOUSE RULES

~ Love hurts, but not forever. ~

I WORRIED THIS day would come.

Giovanni wanted to trust the happiness between them, and he did, but he always worried that eventually Lindsay would rip his guts out.

When he came home last night, her things were already gone. Not the furniture, but her clothes and jewelry. That cheap gold wedding ring he bought her in Las Vegas was sitting on the kitchen counter.

He's devastated—there's no other word for it—but he has to function. People are counting on him, and that's no small thing. Compartmentalizing his life is something he's always excelled at, and thank God for it now, because it's serving him well.

The next few days are long and arduous. It feels like he's swimming through lava. He tries to reach her during his breaks in surgery, and then between patients during his clinic hours. Of course, she doesn't answer her phone or texts, and he wonders if she's even listening to all the voice mails he's left. If he had to guess, she's deleting them. He finally drives to her sister's bakery during one of his longer breaks on the off chance she'll be there. The smell of espresso and baked goods surrounds him when he enters.

"Do you know where Lindsay is?" he asks Natalie, who judging by the sympathy on her face, already knows what's happened. "I've been trying to find her."

Natalie shakes her head. "I'm sorry, I really don't. You could check her studio. She hasn't been to the bakery for a couple of days and hasn't talked much about what's going on, not even to me."

"All right." He nods. "I'll check there again." He turns to leave, but she stops him.

"I'm sorry things turned out this way. For what it's worth, I know she loves you." Natalie studies him with compassion. "Unfortunately for Lindsay, that might not be enough."

When Giovanni gets back late that night, he sits on the couch in the living room with her wedding ring in his hand. He's been carrying it in his pocket. The house is so quiet around him. His chest tightens as he pulls in a deep breath. The last time he cried was when he heard about Paul's death, and that was a dark day.

He thinks back to the Wikipedia article he read about Lindsay. He was in medical school when that song "Queen of Hearts" came out. They were playing it everywhere on every radio station. It was about a woman who stole hearts and kept them under lock and key.

Little did I know my own heart would someday be one of them.

After he initially saw the Wiki page, he searched the internet for pictures of her first marriage out of curiosity. To his surprise, he found photos of an achingly young Lindsay with her rock singer husband. Candid shots of the two of them together, showing how much they were in love.

Those pictures bothered him, but it was the ones he saw of the rock singer taken after Lindsay left him that bothered Giovanni the most. The guy was *wrecked.* Completely crushed by the divorce, and you could see it in every photo

For days afterward, he couldn't get those images out of his mind. They disturbed him. He wondered if he was looking at his own future.

Well, now I know.

It was a surprise to hear about Lindsay's infertility, and he wishes more than anything she'd told him sooner. He dislikes surprises and couldn't hide that fact from her. He'd be lying if he said he didn't wish they could have kids together someday, but he always knew he'd adopt as well. There are too many children in the world who need a good home.

A few days later, his brother convinces him to go out for dinner. The truth is he's practically living at the hospital. With Lindsay gone, there isn't any reason to go home.

"Dude, why didn't you tell me about all this?" Anthony asks. "I had to hear about it from Natalie."

They're sitting at an Italian restaurant in an area not far from the university. He and Lindsay came here a couple of times on Anthony's suggestion, and the food was good.

"I know. I've been working a lot."

Anthony shakes his head and switches to Italian, asking him exactly what's happening between him and Lindsay.

“I don’t know. There’s not much to tell.” Giovanni looks out the window onto the busy street filled with traffic. “She left me.”

“Yeah, I gathered that. She stayed with us last night.”

“She did?” His eyes flash back to Anthony. “How is she? Is she all right?”

“She looks okay. I wish I could say the same for you. No offense, but you look like shit.”

“Did Lindsay say anything?”

“Not to me.” Anthony chuckles. “There’s plenty of conversation, but it all stops as soon as I enter the room.”

“She probably feels uncomfortable since you’re my brother.”

Anthony picks up his beer. “I imagine so.”

Giovanni’s glad he at least knows where she is and that she’s okay. “I need to talk to her again. This whole thing is crazy.”

“What exactly happened? To be honest, the way things were going I figured you two were going to stay married.”

Giovanni leans back in his chair. He wonders how much he should say. “It’s complicated.” He takes a deep breath and leans forward again. “Part of it concerns something that happened to me a long time ago, back when I was a teenager.”

“What do you mean?”

And before Giovanni can stop or second-guess himself, he decides to tell Anthony about Olivia.

When it rains, it pours. Lindsay’s money arrives in her bank account from Berlin just in time to pay tuition. The same day, she gets a call from Dagmar, who tells her she’s recovered some of the stolen cash from Werner and is going to figure out a way to wire it to her.

“I appreciate that,” she says. “I could really use it right now.”

“I am so sorry I ever got mixed up with that *drecksau* Werner and that he stole from you. You were right about him all along.”

“I’m sorry, too,” Lindsay says. “I know you cared for him.”

“He was a liar and a thief! How could I have been so blind?”

“Sometimes love blinds us to the truth.”

“At least he will pay for what he did to you.”

Apparently, Werner got caught red-handed during a burglary and is currently in jail.

“Yeah, that’s something at least.”

They talk a little more, and Lindsay tells her about what happened with Giovanni and how she’s moved out.

"Are you sure you know what you are doing?" Dagmar asks. "It sounds like a big mistake to me."

"It's time for me to move on."

"But why? You love each other."

Lindsay tries to find the right words to describe this pressing need for her to leave. She lets her breath out. "Love isn't everything."

She's been staying with Natalie and Anthony. After she left Giovanni, she went to her studio, but she was going crazy there. He kept calling, and she kept deleting his messages. She knew he'd come looking for her, and that's one of the first places he'd check. She wasn't sure if she could resist Giovanni if he showed up in person, so she stayed with an artist friend for the first week before going to her sister's, just long enough to get onto more solid ground.

As soon as the money from Dagmar comes in, she'll start looking for an apartment.

She thinks about Giovanni's house, the flowers she planted there, his beloved fruit trees, and that shiny red toolbox.

She misses all of it more than she can even put into words.

She misses how he was so intense at times, but then she'd surprise him into laughter, and he'd reveal that beautiful smile, how he wore his heart on the outside for everyone to see—and what an amazing heart it is.

The nights have been the worst, and not just because she misses his body or the feel of those incredible hands. She misses *him*, his essence. That solid strength. She felt safer with Giovanni than she's ever felt with anyone in her life.

It will pass, though. It always does.

The blur of men she's known over the years is a testament to that. Eventually, they all fade. The trick is to keep moving forward—and most importantly, don't look back.

"I told you this would be different," Natalie says as they sit in the living room together watching a movie. Some chick flick, though Lindsay is so distracted thinking about Giovanni she isn't following any of it. Anthony is out having dinner with him, and she keeps wondering what they're talking about.

Probably me and how evil I am for breaking his heart.

It's for the best and eventually he'll see that. *Someday, when he's married to another woman and has children with her, he'll look into their faces and be grateful I did this.*

"It's not different." Lindsay tries to act nonchalant. "It's just another breakup. So what?"

"I don't believe that." Natalie is watching her. "You're obviously in love. Plus, it's different because this is Anthony's brother we're talking about. I told you before, he's not going to conveniently disappear when you're done with him."

Lindsay picks up her glass of wine, wishing it were something stronger, something that could knock her unconscious until this was all over. "Whatever." She takes a swallow. "I know what I'm doing."

Natalie only shakes her head. "For once, I don't think you do."

Lindsay tries to go back to watching the movie. Part of the problem is she can't tell her sister the whole story. Not the part about Olivia, since that's Giovanni's secret and she would never break a confidence like that. Natalie, of course, knows about her infertility, and she could see her sister was torn on it. Because how do you take away someone else's choice to have children? And they've both seen firsthand how much he loves kids. Natalie still thinks she should talk to him some more, but Lindsay doesn't see the point.

Later that night, when Anthony comes home, Lindsay's still watching television though her sister has fallen asleep. The baby monitor is turned on, and she's been checking on Luca.

"Hey," Anthony says, coming into the family room, standing behind the couch where Natalie is lying. He grins and motions with his head. "How long did she last?"

"A few hours, though she started babbling a bit toward the end."

He chuckles. "Baking recipes?"

"Yeah, I think it was some kind of chocolate cake this time."

Her sister has this sweet habit when she's drifting off to sleep where she gives baking instructions.

Anthony is still grinning affectionately at his sleeping wife. Lindsay senses something from him, though, and only hopes it's not animosity toward her over his brother.

When Anthony looks back to her, his expression is solemn. "Gio told me about Olivia tonight."

"He did?" Her brows go up. It's not at all what she was expecting. "I'm surprised he told you, but I'm glad. Is he going to tell your parents?"

"No." He shakes his head. "We discussed it, but it would only hurt them at this point." He rests his hands on the couch where Natalie's still sleeping. "I have to tell you, after hearing about that relationship, it explains a lot."

"It does?"

He nods. "There was always something off about things back then, you know? I once overheard part of a phone conversation he was having with someone who I thought was a woman, and when I asked him about it, he completely flipped out on me, yelling his head off about privacy."

"He blames himself." She looks down at her wine glass. "I told him I thought he should talk to someone."

"I think you're right."

She glances up at him.

"I don't know if he will. In fact, I doubt it. My brother tends to think he's invincible."

She can't help her smile. "That's for sure."

Neither of them speaks for a long moment, but she senses he has more to say.

"You know, I met Olivia a few times." He meets her eyes. "I remember her quite well."

She fiddles with her glass but doesn't reply. Obviously, Giovanni told him the rest of it.

"You don't actually look like her. It's never occurred to me in the whole time I've known you."

"I want to believe that."

His voice is emphatic. "I hope you *do* believe it because it's true."

The next day, Lindsay gets an e-mail from the person who set up her origami class at the hospital, asking if she'd like to teach another. At first, she hesitates. Classes at the university are starting soon, plus Giovanni might decide to drop in, and then what? She knows she has to see him eventually, but she's not sure if she's ready yet.

But then she thinks of the kids and how much fun she had teaching the last class. This is what she wants to do with her life, and she can't let a guy stand in her way.

On Monday, her classes at the university begin and right away she discovers college life has changed quite a bit in the past ten years. The biggest change being that all the guys look way younger.

"I'm getting old," she complains to Natalie and Blair, stopping by the bakery on Friday after her classes are done. "I'm like the grandma now. I'm not the hot babe I used to be."

Natalie rolls her eyes and laughs. "Give me a break."

"It's true." Lindsay sinks her fork into a piece of caramel cake—her favorite. "You should see how young some of these kids are. I'm surprised nobody's asked me to buy them beer yet."

Blair laughs. "Well, just tell them Granny doesn't approve."

Lindsay swallows a bite of cake. "I'm going to have to seriously up my game. I've only had four guys ask me out since school started, and it's been a whole week."

"Do you want to go out with someone new?" Natalie asks.

Lindsay shrugs and looks down at the fingernails of her left hand. She painted them black recently in the never-ending battle to glamorize her ugly hands. "Not really, though I probably should." In fact, she knows she should. The best way to wash the taste of one man out of your mouth is to start tasting another.

"You're probably not ready," Natalie says. "It hasn't been very long since you broke up with Giovanni."

"Of course I'm ready." Lindsay licks the back of her fork and grins. "Baby, I was *born* ready." Unfortunately, her little joke makes her think of Elvis, and then her mind goes to Giovanni and their wedding. Everything in her life lately circles back around to him, and she doesn't know how to make it stop.

Blair stirs her iced coffee with a straw. "I'm with Natalie on all this. You were too hasty breaking up with him."

Lindsay rolls her eyes. She's already heard plenty from her sister. Even Dagmar's been texting her still going on about how she's making a mistake.

"You even admitted Giovanni would pass the Bandito Test and rescue you," Blair reminds her.

"I don't need anybody to rescue me." Lindsay pushes her plate aside. "Hell, I'll rescue *myself*."

Blair appears skeptical as she sips her coffee through a straw. "That's not the point."

"It is in my mind."

"You two seemed so right together at Natalie's party," Blair insists. "I've never seen you like that with anybody."

Lindsay's eyes go to the two women. "I don't know why you're giving me such a hard time all of a sudden. Normally, you guys couldn't care less about my breakups."

"That's because you were never in love with any of them." Natalie scoops chocolate chunk cookie dough onto a large baking sheet. "This time, it's different."

"We only want you to be happy," Blair adds.

"I *am* happy."

Both women look at her, and Lindsay has to admit the words sound false even to her own ears.

"Or I will be," she mutters. "Very soon. If everybody stops giving me shit."

Blair only sighs and shakes her head. "I have to get back to work. I have a meeting with a bride in a few minutes." She gives Lindsay a long look. "Don't take this the wrong way, but sometimes you're kind of a mercenary about men."

Lindsay raises a brow. "So now you two are against me?"

"We're not against you," Natalie says after Blair leaves. "We're on your side."

"It doesn't feel that way. I'm doing Giovanni a favor, trust me." Lindsay goes quiet. "I'm doing what's best for both of us."

Natalie glances over at her but doesn't reply. Anthony recently told her about Olivia. Apparently, Giovanni said it was okay. "I've been thinking about something," her sister says, scooping the last of the cookie dough out. "Have you tried doing an internet search for Olivia?"

"No. Why would I do that?"

"If she died from a shark attack and it made headlines, I'm certain you could find the story online." Natalie puts the scooper down and looks at her. "I'll bet there's a photo. You could see what she looked like."

Lindsay goes still.

"It might help you," Natalie says. "You could see it and decide for yourself."

"Maybe." Lindsay watches her sister as she rolls the baking sheets with dough on them over to be loaded into the oven. She considers this. *The question is, do I really want to know?*

"Also, what's all this I hear about you playing poker?" Natalie asks, coming back over to her, wiping her hands on her white apron.

Lindsay's pulse jumps, but she keeps her expression flat. "Um, what?"

"Anthony said there's a fundraiser for the hospital that includes a poker tournament, and you're playing in it. Is that true?"

"Oh, that." Lindsay waves her hand. "Giovanni signed me up for it a while back, but I don't think I'm still playing in it."

Natalie seems mystified. "Why would he do that? You haven't played poker in years."

Lindsay takes a deep breath and realizes it's time to finally tell her sister the truth. She only hopes it doesn't upset her. "To be honest, that's not entirely true."

"What do you mean?"

"Let's go talk about this in the office."

Natalie's brows go up, but she nods, and Lindsay follows her into the bakery's back office.

"What's going on?" her sister asks, closing the door. "I have a feeling I'm not going to like this."

It's now or never.

"I didn't know how to tell you, but I've sort of started playing cards. In Seattle last year, and then in Berlin too."

"What?" Natalie stares at her. "You've been playing poker?"

"I supported myself with it in Berlin. It's crazy, but I made twenty thousand in only a couple of months playing cash games." Lindsay smiles helplessly. "It was unbelievable."

Natalie looks pale. "But where is all that money? What happened to it?"

"Somebody stole it. Remember I was robbed?"

"All of it was stolen?"

Lindsay nods. "Pretty much." And then she tells Natalie the rest of it, how Giovanni stepped in, and about their initial arrangement.

"My God." Natalie sits down in one of the office chairs. "I always knew there was more to that story. Why didn't you tell me?"

"I'm sorry," Lindsay says quietly. "I know I should have told you everything. I never mentioned I was playing cards last year because I didn't want to worry you while you were pregnant, and then things just snowballed from there."

Natalie nods slowly, but Lindsay can see her sister is upset. She still looks pale.

Lindsay pulls up the other office chair and sits down, leaning forward. "I'm not like dad. I don't blow my winnings. Believe it or not, I run a tight ship."

"It's a slippery slope though," Natalie points out.

"Not for me." Lindsay takes a deep breath. "When I first started going to some of the local poker rooms, I didn't even play. I just watched the action. And you know what it felt like?"

Her sister shakes her head, her expression wary.

"Home."

Natalie blinks.

"I felt so comfortable. I spent most of my childhood around card games." Lindsay licks her lips. "That's one way I am like Dad. There's something about it that calls to me. I enjoy testing myself."

"I have to admit you always were drawn to it." Natalie takes a deep breath. "I shouldn't be surprised you're good at it. You were a good card player, even as a kid."

"I still have a lot to learn. I don't know if I could ever be on a world-class level like Dad was or anything." She reaches for her sister's hand. "Please don't be angry with me. I hated not telling you."

"I would have tried to talk you out of it. You know that, right?"

"I know, and I think that's the *other* reason I didn't tell you." Lindsay gives her a wry grin.

"Twenty thousand, huh?" Natalie considers this. Finally, a smile tugs on her mouth. "Who were you playing against? A bunch of fish?"

"No." Lindsay chuckles and pretends to act offended. "All right, I admit occasionally, but plenty of real card players too." She tells her more about the poker scene in Berlin. “I haven’t played cards since I’ve been back, but I think I might check out some of the local games soon. Are you going to be okay with that?”

“As long as I know you have a handle on it.”

“I do. Absolutely.”

Natalie leans back in her chair and seems to reflect on all this. “Maybe you should play in that hospital tournament. I can’t believe I’m saying this, but I think it might be kind of fun to watch you play poker.”

Chapter Twenty-Six

~ There are plenty of both fish and sharks in the sea. ~

TEACHING THE ORIGAMI class the second time turns out to be just as much fun as the first. The children are enthusiastic, and Lindsay brings a wide mixture of samples to work from. She chats with a few of the nurses who were there last time as she walks around helping all the kids.

The problem is every time the door opens, her heart stops—and she's not sure whether she's relieved or disappointed when it isn't Giovanni.

After the class is over and the kids have all left, she stays to clean up the scrap paper and to pack all her stuff away. She brought plenty of colorful paper and some of her favorite origami books. When she's nearly finished, the door opens again.

The air in the room changes.

Her pulse jumps and when she turns, Giovanni's standing there wearing light blue scrubs, breathing fast like he ran to get here.

She doesn't say a word, though she can't stop herself from drinking him in.

"I'm glad I caught you," he says, still catching his breath as he walks toward her. When he moves closer, she sees a strain on his face, the lines around his mouth have grown deeper. His eyes appear to be taking her in too, and when he's directly in front of her, they're both silent, gazing at each other.

A long moment passes.

She knows exactly how to act, how to put the right expression on her face, the exact pitch her voice should be. She's dealt with enough ex-lovers over the years to have perfected her technique. Except with Giovanni it's different.

"A surgery day, I see." She motions at his scrubs, trying to stay calm.

"Yes." He nods, still keeping his eyes on hers. "How was the class? I'm sorry I missed it. I was hoping to get here sooner."

"It was great. A lot of fun." She looks away. "I'm just gathering all my supplies. I need to head out since I have homework." She turns and shoves the last two origami books into her backpack.

"That's right. How is school going?"

"It's good." She zips up her bag. "I really should get going."

He steps closer, and she freezes. She can smell him—clean sweat with a hint of adrenaline. It's so familiar that, for a second, it overwhelms her. Her breath catches, and she's surprised by the rush of desire she still feels for him.

He leans toward her, but he's only reaching for her backpack. "Come on, I'll walk you to your car."

They take the elevator to the parking lot. "I got some of my stolen money back from Dagmar," she tells him on the way down.

"Really? That's great. How much did you get back?"

"About eight grand." She glances at him. "I plan to start looking for an apartment soon, and then I'll be able to get my furniture out of your house. I can move it sooner if you need me to."

He blinks, looking like he's forgotten she even has furniture there. "Sure, there's no rush."

When they arrive at her red Mini, they both stop by the driver's side door. She takes her backpack from him and gets her keys out. "I'd better get going."

"How's your finger?"

She glances down at her left hand. "It's okay. Kind of itchy, actually."

"May I see it?" He holds his hand out.

Lindsay hesitates, but then gives him her left hand. He takes it and lifts it closer. Her wound is a fresh pink scar at this point since he pulled the stitches out for her a while ago. His touch soothes her, even now.

As he gently examines her finger, she examines him. Her eyes roam over his handsome features, that sensual mouth, the little dip in each corner she's always enjoyed licking so much.

A wave of intense longing comes over her. She misses stroking his jaw and the feel of those soft golden curls. The pleasure of touching him whenever she wanted to.

"It looks fine," he tells her, still inspecting her finger. "I don't see anything to worry about. How's the sensation?"

"It doesn't hurt, but it's numb and tingles sometimes."

He nods. "That's normal. It takes a while for nerves to regrow. This time next year you'll have a better idea of where you're at."

"There's something I've been meaning to ask you. Why did you tell Anthony I was playing in that poker tournament for the hospital?"

Giovanni looks at her with surprise. "Because I assumed you were. I've already written a check to stake you."

"You have?"

"I wrote it right after I asked you about it. Before you . . . moved out."

Lindsay considers this.

"You should play in it," he says encouragingly. "It's for a good cause."

"Let me think about it."

He looks down at her hand still in his, and his voice grows quiet. "I've decided to take your advice about talking to someone." He runs his thumb gently across her knuckles. "A counselor."

"I'm glad to hear that. I'm glad you told Anthony about everything too."

"It felt strange to talk about it, but I've learned secrets can destroy you."

She nods, but doesn't say anything, her gaze dropping to where his hand is still absentmindedly caressing hers.

Neither of them speak.

"I should go now." She tries to pull her hand back, but he still holds it.

"How are you?" he asks quietly. It's not a casual question. She knows him better than that.

Lindsay licks her lips. She wants to tell him everything is wonderful, just perfect, but he's too perceptive, and he'll see right through it. "It's been harder than I expected," she admits. "But I'm doing okay." She tries to smile.

"It doesn't have to be this way."

"Unfortunately, it does."

"No." The blue in his eyes goes darker, so they're almost violet. It looks like he's struggling to say something, and when he finally does his voice is rough. "Just come back to me. Please come back *home*."

Lindsay's throat closes up. She knows how much it's costing him to be this vulnerable. "I can't," she finally manages to say.

He jerks his head to the side, looking out at the parking garage.

"It's better for both of us. You'll thank me someday."

"No." His eyes flash back to her. "You're wrong about that." His voice is stronger now, certain. "I'll never thank you for this."

She pulls her hand away, and he releases it readily this time. "I know what I'm doing. And you *will* thank me."

"No, and we both know this isn't about your infertility or about whether or not you look like Olivia. It's about your *fear*. That's why you're running, and that's why you *always* run." Giovanni snorts. "Remember? I've been there myself."

A strange panic grips her, squeezing the air from her lungs. "I want a divorce," she says, shaking inside. She feels him go still. "You said we'd divorce once our arrangement was no longer necessary."

The emotion on his face is so raw it slices through her. Sharp and painful. *I stayed too long.*

His expression hardens . "I've said over and over again how you're nothing like Olivia."

She clutches her car keys, ready to flee.

"But it turns out there's one way you're *exactly* like her."

Giovanni doesn't wait or watch Lindsay drive off. Instead, he turns and walks back toward the hospital, heading straight to his office. He's waylaid by one of the nurses, who updates him on his patient from this morning's surgery. His chest is tight, but he manages to bring it under control, manages to put everything back in its proper place.

Hiding a broken heart from the world.

It won't be like last time, where he went off the rails and nearly wrecked his life.

I'm not a kid this time.

Seeing Lindsay again today was a shock. His feelings for her haven't diminished one bit. He's not used to feeling helpless. Begging her to come back. Hell, he'd have fallen to his knees if he thought it would do any good.

I've survived this before and I'll survive it again.

Ironically, Lindsay's taught him how to not fear the very thing she's running from herself. If only she'd learn it too.

He saw the panic in her eyes and knows she isn't there, maybe never will be. For all he knows, she'll be like that song for years to come—collecting hearts, but always afraid to offer up her own.

He spent so many years hating Olivia, hating her for all the lies, for the power she had over him. He hated her for ruining his life once, and then more recently he hated her for ruining it again. But that was a waste of time.

I'm done with that.

Lindsay owns his heart. And despite everything, he knows he could never hate her. It saddens him to think of all the years they could have had together. Incredible years. Because he already knows one thing with absolute certainty.

He'll love her for the rest of his life.

"You sure are pretty."

"Thank you." Lindsay tries to act interested in the guy sitting across from her at the coffee shop.

Since seeing Giovanni last week, she's gone on what you might call a dating binge. A bender even. This is the eighth guy she's gone out with in seven days. After that meeting at the hospital, she decided it was time to move on, take back her life, and so she's determined to get back in the saddle whether she likes the horses or not.

The current guy is named Dustin. He's tall and lanky with a bleached blond goatee and plenty of ink. She met him while she was waiting in the return line at the university bookstore. He's a photography major with high hopes of transferring to film school next year. As a result, he took her to see an art house movie that was so pretentious with its flashing lights and crazed cinematography that it nearly burned her eyeballs.

"For an older woman," Dustin continues. "How old are you anyway?"

"What?" Lindsay blinks then stares at him in amazement. "How old are *you?*"

"Nineteen."

Her eyes widen, and she nearly chokes on her dirty chai latte. Upon closer inspection, she realizes he does look awfully young. *What in the hell was I thinking?*

In an effort to block out all thoughts of Giovanni, she's been saying yes to every guy who made an effort. She hasn't paid much attention to any of them, since it's more about quantity than quality.

"But I think you're hot," he says with a grin. "That's why I asked you out."

"How nice," she murmurs in a dry tone. *My God, when did I sink to this level?*

"*Really* hot."

"Look, I'm sorry, but I'm going to have to cut this evening short," she announces, reaching around for her purse. "I have a test to study for tomorrow."

"Oh, yeah? That's too bad." Dustin strokes his sprinkling of chin hairs and leans forward in his chair. "Say, listen. Can I ask you a favor before you go?" His baby blue eyes are beseeching on hers. "Do you think maybe you could buy me some beer?"

Despite the dating binge—or maybe because of it—Lindsay's sexual mojo has taken a nosedive. Not that she's slept with any of these guys, or even kissed them. She'd never admit it to anyone, but the thought of another man touching her is repellent.

In the past, she would have already slept with someone new, would have already forgotten the last guy's name even. She knows it's going to be difficult finding someone who can match Giovanni's intensity. Plus, all these guys seem like boys. Of course, it doesn't help that the last one actually *was* a boy.

So it's a little different this time. So what? Eventually, I'll find my groove again.

In the meantime, during the long nights, she's back to hanging out with her temperamental old friend—her trusty vibrator.

Geez lady, not you again.

Yes, I'm back, so just deal with it.

You're killing me here.

Luckily, between school, the commission for those two masks, and hitting some of the local poker rooms, it's plenty to keep her occupied. She barely thinks about Giovanni, or so she tells everybody who asks.

The truth though is she thinks about him a lot. Never one to linger or get too sentimental, she finds these memories of him creeping up on her like some kind of ninja attack. Out of the blue, she'll suddenly remember the way he smells or tastes. The way he loves to kiss and, of course, that magnificent cock.

Mostly, she remembers the way he looked at her, and how she knew he was seeing *her*.

In her darker moments, she stares at the photos of him on her phone. The early ones from Berlin and then the ones she took of them more recently at the house. Giovanni with his toolbox and that delighted grin, or working outside in those soft jeans.

It's only in her blackest moments that she imagines the children they might have had together. In a different world, one where she could actually give him those beautiful babies.

But that smartens her up, a splash of ice water bringing her back to reality. She wants him to have those babies someday, even if it's not with her.

Plus, there's the whole Olivia mess. *Did he really only fall in love with me because I look like that demented bitch?* Most of her says no, but there's a small part that still can't dismiss it.

A week later, while Lindsay's working in her studio, she gets a phone call from an unknown number. She ignores it at first, but when it rings three times in a row she finally answers.

"Lindsay, I am so glad to find you!" a familiar woman's voice says with a thick Italian accent.

She only knows one woman with a thick Italian accent.

"Francesca?"

"Yes, of course. We must discuss this terrible situation with you and my

Giovanni."

Lindsay is quiet, trying to make sense of this phone call. "I'm sorry, but how did you get this number?"

"It does not matter. What matters is you are wanting a divorce from my son. Is this true?"

"That's right. Our arrangement is finally over, so you should be pleased."

There's a soft snort across the line. "But I am not pleased. Why do you wish to divorce?"

"Look, I'm sorry. I know you wanted an annulment, but we'll never get one. I think Giovanni's already told you that we were romantically involved."

"*Sì*, he is telling me this. I also know he loves you, and that is why you must not divorce. You must stay *together!*"

Lindsay's mouth opens, stunned into silence.

"Of course, we will have to have another wedding," Francesca clarifies, in a matter-of-fact voice. "Not this Las Vegas. That is just . . . *No*."

"Maybe Giovanni hasn't mentioned it to you, but one of the reasons we've broken up is that I can't have children."

Francesca doesn't speak right away. When she does, her voice is softer. "He has told me this, and I am very sorry to hear it. But what he has told me of your condition does not sound so impossible. You should not lose hope."

There's a sick feeling in Lindsay's stomach because she can't hang her future on a bunch people hoping for something that might never happen. "I'm sorry, but it's best for us both if we end it."

"Do you love Giovanni?"

Lindsay goes quiet. "That's not the point. It will never work in the long run. Believe me, I know."

"No, you do not know." Francesca lets out a frustrated breath. "Giovanni was always so serious as a boy, and now he is the same as a man. This is it for him. He loves *you*, Lindsay."

"And eventually, he'll love somebody else."

Francesca tries to convince her, and she's relentless, but Lindsay can be relentless too. She even tries to lighten things with a joke. She appreciates what Francesca is trying to do, fighting for her son's happiness—or so she believes—but she's not cut out for marriage.

Plus, Francesca doesn't know about Olivia.

After the two of them hang up, Lindsay tries to put the conversation out of her mind. Oddly, in many ways she understands Francesca and suspects they're probably more alike than they are different.

That evening, when she gets back to Natalie and Anthony's house, she sits on her bed in the guest bedroom. She's been so busy she still hasn't found an apartment. Luckily, neither Natalie nor Anthony has complained yet. She tries to be helpful around the house but knows she's pushing it and needs to move out soon.

Tucking some pillows behind her back, she opens her laptop and brings up Google, the conversation with Francesca replaying in her head. She's been thinking about it all afternoon, that along with Natalie's recent suggestion.

She doesn't know Olivia's last name, but figures how many women have been eaten by a shark in the past ten years?

There can't be that many.

Amazingly, it only takes her a few minutes to find a news video with details of a shark attack on a woman named Olivia Cruz.

Her heart races as she pushes Play on the video. There's a blonde news anchor discussing the attack on a female diver off the coast of Florida. They show a boat from the diving company, and then suddenly there's a picture onscreen of Olivia.

Lindsay sucks in her breath and immediately hits the space bar to pause it, staring at the image.

Olivia has long wavy brown hair, brown eyes, and Giovanni was right—she's very attractive. Beautiful even. It's a casual shot from the shoulders up and looks like it was taken outdoors.

Does she look like me?

Lindsay manages to enlarge the paused video a bit and then finds herself studying it for a long time. Olivia is smiling as she looks off to the side, a confident smile, almost a smirk really, and all Lindsay can think is, *This is the monster that sunk its teeth into Giovanni, the one who wouldn't let go.*

She keeps staring at the image. Finally, she climbs off the bed, decides to find Natalie and ask her opinion. Her sister is downstairs helping Chloe with homework at the dining room table.

"Can I show you something on my computer?" Lindsay asks.

Natalie looks up. "Sure, can it wait a minute?"

"No problem." Lindsay wanders over to the living room where Anthony is sitting on the couch working on his computer as well. Luca has started crawling recently, so they have everything gated off.

"Did you by chance give your mom my cell phone number?" she asks Anthony from across the room.

He glances up at her. He's wearing thick black-framed glasses, which always remind her of Clark Kent. Her brother-in-law is very handsome, but he's also a serious geek. "No. Did my mom call you or something?"

She leans against the door frame. "It was no big deal. I was just curious how she got my number." She wonders if Giovanni gave it to her, but can't picture him doing that.

"What did she want?"

"She wants me to stay married to your brother."

Anthony looks at her with astonishment. He takes his glasses off. "Seriously?"

She nods. "I was surprised. I always thought she didn't like me."

"I don't think that's true." He studies her. "What did you tell her?"

"I told it's over between us. That I want a divorce."

Anthony takes this in. She knows he speaks to Giovanni regularly and wonders what they've discussed. Except for that one night where they talked about Olivia, he's said very little to her concerning the breakup.

And clearly he's still not saying much.

"How is Giovanni doing?" She can't resist asking. "Is he okay?"

"He's all right." Anthony puts his glasses back on and turns toward his computer again. "Last I heard, he was putting the house up for sale."

"*What?*" Lindsay goes still. "He's selling the house?"

"It's a lot of house for one person."

She knows it's irrational, but she loves that house and doesn't want him to sell it.

Her sister comes over. "Okay, I'm ready. What is it you want to show me?"

"It's upstairs." Lindsay leads the way, her head still reeling over the news of Giovanni selling the house. She doesn't want to imagine someone else living there. *What if they replace the new light fixtures he put up, or tear down the trellis he built for his fruit trees?*

"I heard you asking Anthony about Francesca," Natalie says once they enter the bedroom. "I thought you should know I'm the one who gave her your number."

She spins around. "Why would you do that?"

"Because even *she* gets what's obvious to everyone except *you*."

"Not this again. I already told you, I know what I'm doing." Lindsay glances over at her. "I can't believe you gave Francesca my number without warning me. Are you nuts?"

Natalie laughs. "I figured you could handle her."

Lindsay grumbles. "That's not the point." She sits on the bed, scooting over to make room for her sister. "I found a news broadcast about the shark attack on Olivia. There's a picture of her."

"Really?" Natalie's eyes widen as they go to the computer screen. "What does she look like?"

"See for yourself." Lindsay taps the shift key to bring her computer out of sleep mode. The large image of Olivia is still paused on the screen.

Natalie leans forward, turning the computer toward herself a little. "So *that's* her." Her sister studies the image.

"What do you think? Does she look like me? And be honest."

Natalie glances up at her. "I think she has the same coloring as you, and her hair is kind of like yours, but beyond that . . . No, I don't see much resemblance."

Lindsay lets out her breath. She thought the same thing.

Natalie's eyes go back to the screen. "It's weird to look at her, isn't it? She was attractive enough that I'm guessing she could have had an affair with any guy she wanted. Why go after a seventeen-year-old kid?"

"She obviously had issues. Giovanni told me he wasn't the first one or the last."

Natalie shakes her head. "I know it sounds terrible, but I don't feel sorry that she was eaten by a shark."

"Me either. In fact, I'm surprised it didn't spit her out in disgust after the first bite."

Chapter Twenty-Seven

~ With men, as with poker, you must use every advantage. ~

"AS I'VE ALREADY said, I think you should do it."

"I don't know." Lindsay looks down and wiggles her toes, which are currently soaking in a basin of hot water.

She's getting a pedicure along with Natalie and her two nieces. It's Chloe's fourteenth birthday, and Lindsay decided to treat everyone. She and Natalie are discussing the fundraiser poker tournament happening next weekend.

"Your winnings would go to help Seattle Children's," Natalie points out. "And you said Giovanni's already staked you, so why would you hesitate?"

Lindsay glances over at Chloe and Serena, who are sitting next to each other giggling over something on Chloe's phone.

"You're worried he'll be there, aren't you?" Her sister gives her a shrewd look.

Lindsay shrugs and tries to appear indifferent. "Not at all."

Natalie laughs. "I hope your bluffing skills are better than that. Anthony and I want to stake you too, but that's worrisome."

"For your information, I just won fifteen hundred bucks last night."

"See," Natalie says. "All the more reason you should play in this tournament. You'll probably clean up, and all that money goes to charity."

"Yeah." Lindsay lets out her breath.

As far as her game goes, she's feeling pretty good, and winning that big pot last night didn't hurt. She's been keeping a notebook, hitting some of the local action, plus she and Dagmar have started analyzing their poker hands again.

Her classes are going well and her grades are holding up. She's nearly done with the second mask to send off to the buyer in Berlin, so she'll be getting another nice check from them. She even found an apartment recently, though she can't move in until the beginning of next month.

Everything is going surprisingly well.

So, why do I feel like shit?

It's like she's sleepwalking through her life. The same chronic dissatisfaction that plagued her before she left for Berlin has returned. And to make matters worse, the ninja memories are still attacking her.

"I've already found a 1920s-style dress," Natalie says, as the pedicurist pulls her feet out of the water and dries them off. "So you have to play in the tournament because I want to wear it."

"You went shopping without me?" Lindsay lifts her own feet out too.

"Just online. I'll show it to you. I found a website that has a bunch of clothes styled from that era."

"You and Anthony can still go to the fundraiser even if I'm not there."

Natalie sighs. "I know, but it'll be more fun with you. I want to cheer you on. Plus, it'll be exciting to watch you kick some poker ass."

"And to think I was actually *afraid* to tell you I was playing poker," Lindsay says in a dry tone.

"Now that I know you're not gambling away your winnings, I'm all for it." Natalie goes quiet and looks over at her. "And I think you're right. Something about all this does feel like home. It's like we've come full circle, haven't we?"

She nods. "I'm not nearly as good as Dad, so don't get too excited. And I've played in very few tourneys so far." The action is faster in cash games versus tournament play, but her sister already knows that.

"Don't worry. I'll be cheering you on, even if you're knocked out in the first round."

Lindsay cringes. "God forbid. Let's hope *that* doesn't happen."

Lindsay finds the perfect dress—scarlet red, sleeveless with a black fringe on the bottom. It's too gorgeous to pass up. Plus, if she wears a push-up bra, it'll be low-cut enough to distract the weaker male players. Her dad always told her to play ruthless. The best card players are the ones who use every advantage they have.

"Are you nervous?" Natalie asks after Lindsay does her sister's hair and makeup in the master bathroom.

"Yes, a little," she admits.

For some reason, this poker tournament has been all over the local news lately. She's not sure why it's become such a big deal, but it has. It sounds like everybody who's anybody in Seattle is going to be there tonight.

"I know what will help." Natalie grins at her. "Let's rock out to that poker playlist. I'll bet the girls will be up for it too."

They head downstairs to find Anthony in the kitchen with Luca talking to Manny, who'll be staying with the kids tonight. Anthony's wearing a black tuxedo, his hair gelled back, and when Lindsay sees the way he smiles at Natalie, it makes her heart hurt. For just a moment, he looks a bit like Giovanni.

"Miss Natalie," Anthony says. "I'm liking this dress on you."

Her sister grins. "Thank you." Luca reaches his arms out when he sees Natalie, and she takes him from her husband. "Do you want to rock out with us, honey bunny?" she coos to him.

"You guys are rocking out?" Anthony asks, an innocent note in his voice.

Lindsay smirks to herself. Since she's been staying here, she's noticed every time they rock out Anthony manages to be in the vicinity, and every time Lindsay looks at him he's trying to hide the fact that he's staring at his wife's body while she dances.

"We thought it would help calm Lindsay's nerves," Natalie tells him.

"Good idea," Anthony says in quick agreement.

Lindsay goes to ask Chloe and Serena if they want to join, and both girls immediately jump up.

"Of course!" Chloe says.

"Are we doing the poker playlist?" Serena asks, following her back into the living room. Natalie is already there with the baby.

The playlist is something Serena found online, and they've been listening to it all week.

Pretty soon, Lady Gaga's "Poker Face" is blasting through the speakers and the four of them are dancing around the living room. The girls are laughing and jumping up and down, Natalie is doing a bump and grind with Luca still on her hip, and Lindsay's swinging her hair around, getting into her groove.

Sure enough, she sees Anthony from the corner of her eye, hovering in the doorway. He's talking on his phone with his gaze locked squarely on Natalie's ass.

Lindsay laughs. In truth, she thinks it's sweet the way he ogles her sister.

She glances at him again and suddenly the phone to his ear registers. She wonders if he's talking to Giovanni. The music is loud, but she strains to hear, trying to tell if he's speaking Italian.

She hasn't seen him in almost three weeks, not since that day at the hospital when he begged her to come back. She keeps wanting to ask Anthony about him but has managed to muzzle herself. She even drove by the house in stealth mode when she knew he wouldn't be there. The lawn is overgrown, and the flowers she planted are all dead. It saddened her to see it. There was a For Sale sign in front.

The truth is she's probably more nervous about seeing him tonight than she is about playing poker. Just the thought of it has her pulse racing.

Not that anything's changed.

Except he was telling the truth about Olivia.

Prince's "U Got the Look" comes on next, and everyone adjusts their moves to the different beat. Lindsay dances over to Natalie and reaches for Luca, figuring she'll give her sister a break.

Luca grins, putting his arms out, and Lindsay's heart melts. She's fallen completely in love with her little nephew. His brown eyes go wide, and she manages to stop him just in time before he grabs her earring. "No, I don't think so, baby boy."

"Gah!"

Lindsay spins him around and Luca squeals with laughter. But as soon as she starts dancing again, a ninja attack sneaks up on her. And it's a bad one. The worst ever.

She's dancing in a different living room than this one, "Burning Love" coming through the speakers. Giovanni is flailing his arms around with all his wild Frankenstein moves, letting his freak flag fly just for her.

God, I loved him.

Lindsay stops dancing. Her throat closes up, and her eyes burn as she tries to breathe, tries to pull it together. She needs to calm down, knowing this is no way to go into a tournament. If this keeps up, she'll be playing on tilt.

"It's okay," she tells Luca, who obviously senses her mood change. His little brows furrow as he studies her. "It's *all* good, no worries."

Clearly, he doesn't believe her, because his furrowed brow doesn't go away and his mouth opens with a wail as he starts to cry.

Natalie comes over. "Is everything all right?" She reaches for the baby, but when she looks at Lindsay her expression turns to concern. "Hey, are you okay?"

She nods and tries to smile. "Don't worry about me. I'm fine."

Pocket rockets.

Nice.

The very best hole cards a person can have in Texas Hold 'em is two aces, and Lindsay's staring at a pair right now. The odds of a hand like this are only two percent.

She remains calm. Indifferent even. It's always been her strength. Most people get excited when they see these kinds of cards and immediately start raising, but she was taught better than that.

Instead, she puts her cards back down and glances around the table. So far, she's made it through the first grueling round of play tonight, and after a short break is finally near the end of the second round. Whoever makes it past this hand will go to the final table. Since it's only one evening of play, the action has been fast, which suits Lindsay just fine.

She was nervous going in, but as soon as she sat down with her glass of mineral water and her stack of chips in front of her, she felt her usual poker calm come over her.

Just like home.

The flop is laid out, and it's the ace of spades, two of clubs, seven of hearts.

Very nice.

She pretends to look at her cards again—all part of the show.

So far, most of the games have been fast and loose as the inexperienced players fall away. She's been playing it close and tight, though, and it's serving her well. She hasn't had to do much bluffing yet, but knows the players who've been paying attention have already noticed her style.

"Are you in?" the guy to her left asks.

She nods, but only calls.

Unsurprisingly, most of the players competing are amateurs doing it for fun, plenty of doctors, nurses, and other hospital workers. There's a lively quality to the event with lots of jokes and laughter, and Lindsay's been joining in.

Some of the men have been checking her out—their attention wandering from their cards to her pushed-up cleavage as they try to flirt with her.

But then there are the experienced players. The ones who don't check her out or flirt with her. The men are definitely straight, but they're here to win.

It took her a few hands at each table to spot them, but she's narrowed it down. The most formidable player so far has been this short, middle-aged guy everyone calls Dr. Bill. He's already outplayed her during a few hands and is winning a lot of money. There's also an Asian woman named Kimmy who's been killing it. Lindsay's not doing too badly herself, though, and has a sizable stack of chips in front of her.

There's been no sign of Giovanni. During the short break after the first round, she casually searched the crowd but didn't see him.

There's no reason for him to show up here tonight.

Except her spidey senses say otherwise.

The turn is laid out, and it's a jack of diamonds. Lindsay decides to raise, but nothing too extreme. Happily, one of the other players is building up the pot for her anyway and, from what she can tell, he's just made his pair.

When the river reveals an ace of diamonds, Lindsay doesn't even blink. She's got the nuts with four of a kind, and her goal now is to get that pot as large as possible.

When it's her turn, she raises again but pretends to hesitate slightly. She can feel Mr. Pair of Jacks trying not to smirk as he raises to the maximum. They go around the table once more, with what appears to be a lot of confident people putting in plenty of chips. Dr. Bill already folded after the flop, and with the way he's been eyeing her, he knows she's got it.

It's the showdown and Lindsay reveals her four pips. The guy with the pair of jacks' mouth falls open. There are a few more groans around the table. Dr. Bill nods with approval, smiling at her, and Lindsay can't help smiling back. He's obviously been trying to figure her out all night.

She gathers her chips and lets out her breath.

I did it.

She made it to the final round. The main event. It's not exactly the World Series of Poker, just a fundraiser, but at least she's made it far enough she doesn't have to go home in shame.

Natalie and Anthony both congratulate her during the break.

"This is fantastic!" Natalie hugs her tight. "See, I knew you'd kick some poker ass tonight."

"Thanks." Lindsay grins. "I've had some good cards, which has helped."

"Maybe you'll win the main event! Wouldn't that be great?"

Lindsay laughs. "I don't know. That Dr. Bill guy has been outplaying me. Who is he? Between him and that Kimmy woman, it's some fierce competition."

"It looks like Dr. Bill is a vascular surgeon," Anthony says, reading from the evening's program." He scans further down the list. "And Kimmy appears to be a midwife."

"Really? Wow. Well, they're both wicked-good card players." She looks at Anthony. "What does it say about me in there?"

"Lindsay West, Sculptor and Teacher."

Lindsay takes this in. Giovanni must have given them that information. She tells them she's going to grab a bite to eat. "Just something light to keep my stamina up. I'll be back."

On her way over to the buffet, Dr. Bill, of all people, comes up to her. "I wanted to formally introduce myself," he says, putting his hand out. "How long have you been playing poker?"

Lindsay shakes his hand and tells him she's only been playing seriously the past year or so but has been around card games all her life.

Dr. Bill fishes something out from his pocket and hands her a business card. "I won't keep you long. I just wanted to invite you to a regular game that I'm a part of. We play weekly, and it's whoever shows up."

She looks at the card in her hand. It's his business card, and on the back, he's written his cell phone number, along with the name and address of a restaurant downtown.

"It's a private game," he continues. "Some of the local grinders play, as well as some of the more talented amateurs. A few of us participate in the World Series every year. We're always looking for exceptional players to join our group."

"Thank you, I'll check it out."

"Please do." He grins. "It's a good place to sharpen your skills, and I think you'll discover you're among friends."

After he leaves, Lindsay slips the card into her purse, buzzing with excitement. She's heard about some of these private games.

She's about to head over to the buffet but stops. The hairs on the back of her neck stand up, and when she turns around, she discovers why.

It's Giovanni.

He's right across the room talking to some woman, a tall, attractive brunette wearing a dark blue flapper-styled dress. They're close together and he's smiling.

Her heart pounds as she takes in the scene, trying to make sense of it.

Did he bring a date?

Her first instinct is territorial. That's *my* man. The two of them are laughing about something, and Lindsay stands there frozen in some kind of bizarre fight-or-flight mode.

Just as Giovanni turns his head and sees her, some man walks up beside the brunette, putting his hand on her arm, and Lindsay realizes she's misread the whole scene.

That's not his date.

Giovanni starts walking toward her. He's wearing the blue Armani suit, the one he picked up in Rome for their wedding. He's not dressed for the 1920s at all, but it doesn't matter because he looks incredible. *My God, did I actually forget he's this handsome?*

"I see you made it to the final table," he says with a grin. "I can't say I'm surprised."

She nods, still recovering from her near heart attack when she thought he was here with someone.

"Maybe you'll win this thing."

"Maybe." She takes a deep breath. "There are actually some good players here."

"Are you enjoying yourself?"

"I am."

His blue eyes are focused on hers and he feels so familiar, so right. *If only things were different.*

"Are you really selling the house?" she can't help asking. "It's what Anthony told me."

He nods, his expression changing to the tense one she knows so well. "Yes, I don't see any point in keeping it now."

"That's too bad. You put so much work into it."

He considers her. "Lindsay, we both know that house is nothing to me without *you* in it."

She turns her head to the side and pretends to study the crowd.

"Which brings me to the main reason I came here tonight. I need to talk to you."

She looks at him again.

"I'm leaving," he says. "I've decided to take another assignment overseas. I just wanted to tell you in person. I have a lawyer handling the paperwork for the divorce."

"What?" Her eyes grow wide as her pulse shoots up. "Why?"

"It's for the best. I can't stay here anymore."

"So, you're running away again?"

He shakes his head. "No." He glances around. "Come on, let's find someplace private to talk."

He leads the way, and she follows him out of the main area into one of the corner alcoves. There are still some people walking around, but not as many.

"I'm not running from anything," he tells her. "I just don't see the point in staying."

"I saw a picture of Olivia," she blurts out. "I looked her up online, and you were right."

"What do you mean?"

"I don't look like her. I was freaking out over nothing."

Giovanni nods slowly. "I'm glad you finally believe me, but I don't want to talk about Olivia. She's taken up too much of my life already." He goes silent and then his expression softens as he takes her in. "I admit I'm not immune to your outer beauty, Lindsay."

She goes still at his words, her back pressed against the wall.

He moves closer. "How could I be? I'm still a man."

His clean scent drifts over her. His nearness is having a powerful effect on her, making her want things she shouldn't. Her breath catches. "Don't do this. Not now."

"But it's *you* I fell in love with. It's everything about you. I fell in love with how you swear so much I want to call an exorcist. With how you'd rather be bled by leeches than plan ahead." A smile tugs on his mouth. "Even with the crazy way you drive."

"What?" she scoffs at him. "There's nothing wrong with my driving."

"You drive like you're behind the wheel of a getaway car after a bank robbery."

"I do not!"

He chuckles softly. "You do."

"There are just too many damn people in my way," she mutters.

"As beautiful as you are, your appearance isn't what matters the most to me."

Her breath shakes. He's telling her everything she's ever wanted to hear. Except it isn't enough.

"I know you don't believe me, but I don't care about your infertility." He pauses. "That's not what I meant. I care, but I'd be just as happy if we only ever adopted."

Her eyes go to his, skeptical.

"You still don't believe me?" He shakes his head. "Look at my life. Who knows more than I do about how many children there are in this world who need a good home? Why do you think I agreed so readily to adopt Joseph and Sara? It wasn't a stretch for me."

"But you'll want your own someday too," Lindsay insists. "I can't take that from you."

"You think you're so good at reading people. Well, then tell me if I'm lying about this."

She opens her mouth then closes it. She's spent the last three hours doing just that—searching for weaknesses, searching for whatever it is the other players were trying to hide.

He stands before her and she studies him. It only takes an instant to see the truth as plain as day.

He's not lying.

"I have to go," she whispers. Her pulse has started to race because there are no more barriers. No more reasons to run. The voice that usually tells her when it's time to leave is silent.

"You're always on to the next one, aren't you? Just like your tattoo, just like that song."

Her breath shakes. "I have to get back."

He nods. "I understand your panic. I've been there myself." His eyes are sympathetic. “Ask yourself something, though. Is this the life you really want? Always running from love?”

Chapter Twenty-Eight

~ If you're smart enough to find a good man, don't be stupid enough to lose him. ~

LINDSAY'S GAME HAS turned to shit.

She keeps waiting for her usual poker calm to come over her, but it's not happening.

She's sitting at the final table with her mineral water and her stack of chips, all the familiar pieces in place.

Except she's losing badly. Making one foolish move after another. Playing loose and reckless, trying to steal the blind or bluffing with rags when she should be folding. She might even have gotten away with this nonsense if it were a different set of players who didn't know better.

But not this group. They see every mistake.

"Are you all right?" Dr. Bill asks her at one point.

"Sure, no problem."

Kimmy has been eyeing her with a mixture of sympathy and curiosity.

Lindsay takes a deep breath and lets it out. She tries to get her head back in the game, tries to stop her heart from spinning out of control.

I'm not running away from anything.

Giovanni is wrong. What the hell does he know anyway?

How dare he throw that song at her. That fucking song which has been plaguing her for years.

And there's nothing wrong with the way I drive. I drive great. Perfect even, motherfucker.

Two more players are knocked out during the next hand, and things grow intense. Despite all her mistakes and shrinking stack of chips, Lindsay's still in the game.

Time to quit screwing around.

The cards are dealt and, with annoyance, she catches herself chewing on her bottom lip as she studies her hole cards, both of them diamonds.

What in the hell am I doing?

The flop brings two more diamonds and Lindsay smiles. Well, what do you know? *Hallelujah, it's raining diamonds*. One more is all she needs to make a flush.

She notices everybody around her raising, but to be honest, she hasn't been paying much attention. She needs to start thinking about this game, but all she can think about is Giovanni. Their conversation playing itself over again in her mind.

The part where he said he loved her. And then the part where he said he was leaving.

Dr. Bill raises the maximum bet and Lindsay calls, figuring why the fuck not? The odds of hitting her flush on the turn are only about one in five. She knows her game is off, and her stack of chips is dwindling, but if she hits her flush, it's all good.

The turn brings a king and it's not a diamond. A black card. A spade.

She frowns. *Dammit.*

The other players are all hovering like vultures, waiting for the kill. She can feel them closing in, searching for any weakness. You can't let emotions get involved in a poker game.

For some reason, she remembers Cockroach Breath from Berlin. The way he lost it all, a grown man playing on tilt because of love.

Lindsay snorts to herself. *As if I'd ever do that.*

But then her throat goes tight when she remembers what Cockroach Breath said.

Love is everything.

It was an odd sentiment coming from a guy like that.

When she thinks about Giovanni leaving, her heart aches. Has she ever loved anyone this much? The voice that usually whispers in her ear is back. Only this time, it's saying something different.

Are you really going to let him go?

Dr. Bill is raising the maximum again and Lindsay decides to go all in. There's nothing left for her anyway. It's hard to believe, but that's what it's come to. If she doesn't hit her flush on the river, she's down to the felt. Busted.

And that's when a queer realization comes over her. She glances around the table at the other players. They're all looking at her with knowing eyes like she's an easy mark. *What the hell?* She blinks a few times and then it finally dawns on her.

I've been playing on tilt this whole time!

She sucks in her breath. *I've lost everything.*

More than a game of poker. Because suddenly she sees it all as clear as the meaning of that horrible song, how she's been on tilt much longer than a single card game. She's been living her life that way.

And it's been obvious to everyone except me.

She shakes her head with amazement.

It turns out Cockroach Breath was right.

Love *is* everything.

She waits for the river, the final card. And when it's played, Lindsay starts to laugh because she's ruined, taken down by none other than . . . the Queen of Hearts.

Giovanni knows he should buy a winter coat soon. He hasn't owned one in years, but it's fall now and cooling down enough to where it's become obvious he needs one.

Not that I'll be needing one for long.

It's night, but he's sitting outside in the backyard, staring at his fruit trees. They're doing well, and after removing the deadwood a while ago, he's pleased to see they've grown some new foliage. The trellis he built is still there against the back fence.

Maybe the next owner of this house will make use of it.

He came back from the fundraiser tonight and changed out of his suit, figuring it was time to start work on that resignation letter to the hospital.

Instead, he's been sitting out here in the cold staring at his trees.

They won't be mine much longer.

The house hasn't sold yet, but there's plenty of interest. Two couples have already made offers. He should be glad. Soon, this will all be behind him, and he'll be back overseas again, living like a vagabond.

Maybe that's the life I'm meant for.

He hasn't decided where yet. Not Africa though. Possibly Southeast Asia, or maybe South America. Everybody needs doctors.

It was difficult seeing Lindsay tonight, though it's been more difficult not seeing her. She's left a gap in his heart that's impossible to fill. After all these years, he's finally learned what it's like to honestly fall in love—not the manipulation he experienced when he was younger, but the real thing. A part of him was still hoping he could change her mind, get her to see what she's giving up.

As he's thinking all this, he notices movement from the corner of his eye.

He turns his head and sees it again. There's someone inside his living room.

Giovanni goes still, certain he locked the front door.

He unfolds himself from the chair and starts making his way cautiously toward the house. Unfortunately, he left his phone inside.

Suddenly, he sees someone near the French doors, but the lighting is dim and he can't tell who it is. One of the doors opens. His eyes widen when he hears music coming from the house. It takes him a moment to realize what it is, but when he recognizes the song, his heart hammers.

Elvis Presley's "Burning Love."

Lindsay steps outside. When she sees him, she stops, her hand on the door handle.

Giovanni stops walking too.

Neither of them move.

His heart pounds, unsure what to make of her presence here.

He opens his mouth to speak. But in an instant, it all changes because Lindsay is running toward him, running in her flapper dress and high heels. Before he knows it, she's thrown herself into his arms.

Relief floods his veins, so powerful it makes his head swim, rocks him to his core because he finally understands.

She's come back to me.

Their mouths are on each other, kissing crazily. It feels like a million years, and it feels like one long day. The longest day of his life.

He picks her up and carries her back to the house, holding her tight, not wanting to let go.

"I thought I knew what I was doing . . ." The words tumble out of her mouth. "But I was wrong . . . I was wrong about so many things."

"You're here now. That's all that matters."

Inside the house, the music still plays. Their song. He takes her to their bedroom downstairs, the one he still sleeps in. Her fox still on his nightstand.

He lays her on the bed and she pulls him down on top of her.

"Touch me," she pleads. "I want to feel your hands everywhere."

He slips his fingers beneath her flapper dress to her soft skin and discovers stockings with garters. "Damn," he groans with approval. "You're keeping these on."

She smiles up at him. "I knew you'd like them, Olaf."

"Don't ever leave me again," he says, his voice hoarse with honesty. "I don't know if I could survive it."

Her eyes go soft as she reaches up and strokes his jaw. "I won't, I promise. This time, it's forever."

"I lost the final round in a big way tonight," Lindsay admits. She's lying naked beside Giovanni, her head on his chest, enjoying the solid beat of his heart. She tells him how the final card played was the Queen of Hearts. "The perfect symbol of my downfall."

He lightly strokes her back, trailing his fingers over her tattoo. "You can't be the Queen of Hearts forever."

"I know." She sits up partway and meets his eyes "For years, I thought it was a strength to own my own heart, to keep it locked away and separate."

"And now?"

"Now I realize I was wrong because I've given my heart to you and it's only made me stronger."

"We've made each other stronger."

She nods, knowing it's true. "I do feel bad for losing that game, especially since you staked me."

"It all goes to charity so there's nothing to feel bad about. I'm surprised you lost though."

She tells him how she was playing on tilt after their conversation. "Now that I think about it, it's *your* fault I lost."

He chuckles. "I guess I'll have to make it up to you."

"You better." She slides her fingers lightly across his chest, enjoying the familiar feel of his skin. "In fact, I hope you don't have to be at work soon because I expect you to make it up to me all night long."

"Christ, I'd forgotten how insatiable you are." He tucks his arm under his head and lets out a satisfied grunt. "Lucky for you, I'm man enough to handle it. Despite my being a delicate flower."

Lindsay gives him a wicked grin. "Don't worry." She leans in close, her mouth at his ear. "I'll be gentle."

She can feel him smiling, and when she pulls back, discovers his gaze is full of affection. "Baby," he says softly. "I *missed* you."

"Me too." She blinks back tears, before leaning in to kiss him again. Long and luscious. She takes her time, licking the sensual dip in each corner of his mouth. His eyes drift shut, a whisper of a smile on his face.

She reflects back to that game tonight and has never been so glad to lose a hand of poker in her life. Although, she's already thinking about doing something crazy next year, something her dad would even approve of. Playing at the World Series in Las Vegas. It turns out he was right. In some ways they are made of the same stuff, but Lindsay's decided that's okay.

The truth is she likes some of that stuff.

She never would have considered it before she met Giovanni, but he's helped her heal and move past what happened to her.

I'm ready for anything now.

His eyes open and he sees the way she's watching him. "What are you thinking about?" he asks.

"I'm thinking about how much I love you. And how I'm sorry for everything I put you through recently."

He doesn't reply, his gaze intense on hers.

"You didn't deserve it."

He takes a deep breath. "You want to know what I've learned from all this, and from Paul's death?"

She shakes her head. "What?"

"People are always saying life is short, so you need to live for today, but I did that for years. I don't want to live for today anymore." He laces his fingers through hers. "I want to live for tomorrow."

She absorbs his words.

"I want to build a life," he says. "With you."

Her heart fills with joy. "I want that too."

He caresses her neck as his eyes roam her face. "So beautiful," he murmurs. "*Fragolina mia.*"

She sighs and lies down with her head on his chest again, hugging him tight. "You know, your mom called me a couple weeks ago."

"She did?"

She lifts up to look at him. "She tried to talk me out of divorcing you, said we should stay married."

He goes silent, clearly stunned. "You're kidding. What did you tell her?"

"I told her I'd do it on one condition."

"And what was that?"

Lindsay grins. "She'd have to agree to change your name to Olaf."

Giovanni nearly chokes before he bursts out laughing. She loves seeing him this way, all the normal tension on his face relaxed.

Finally, he manages to calm down. "You didn't really say that, did you?" But then his brows go up when he sees her expression. "Holy shit, you *did?*"

"I only meant it as a joke!"

"What was her response?"

"She laughed mostly, but I couldn't understand the rest of it." Lindsay considers him. "I think I need to learn some Italian curse words."

He grins. "Don't worry, you *will.*"

Epilogue

The Golden Rule
~ Love is everything. ~

"YEAH, BABY, TAKE it off," Lindsay says with a grin. "Take it *all* off."

Giovanni grumbles as he strips his jeans down and kicks them aside, his hard chest and those muscular thighs on full display for her.

Nice.

"I've only got one piece of clothing left," he complains, looking down at his blue boxer briefs. "What the hell."

She chuckles. "Hey, you're the one who wanted to play strip poker."

"This isn't exactly what I had in mind." He points to her sitting across from him at the dining room table with all her clothes still on. "You fully dressed while I'm over here buck naked."

"I'm not fully dressed. I did lose my socks, after all." She sticks her foot out and wiggles her toes around provocatively. "And my earrings." She motions toward the center of the table.

Giovanni rolls his eyes and laughs. "Give me a break."

They've been playing cards for the last hour or so, and she's won nearly every hand.

"Those books are all worthless," he growls, motioning to the stack of poker books he was studying earlier. "They're not helping me at all."

She tilts her head and smiles at him with affection. It's become clear he hates to lose. "I think it's really cute you were reading poker books."

"I don't know why I bothered."

The books are hers and she's read them many times. "They're helpful, but you have to already know what you're doing. You just learned how to play."

His only response is another grumble.

In truth, she's impressed with how much information he managed to retain. He learned the rankings quickly and memorized a number of the statistical odds. What Giovanni doesn't realize though is he has a massive tell. Every time he gets a good hand, he bounces his left leg. He'll stare at her with his best poker face while that left leg is going crazy.

She figures she'll point it out to him later. After she gets to see him naked, of course.

She leans back in her chair, glancing around the house at the way things are shaping up. They bought some new furniture recently and have hung the tribal art Giovanni picked up during his travels. His parents were storing it for him. In fact, they flew up for Christmas recently and announced they're planning to sell their home in LA and move to Seattle.

God help us.

Lindsay worried she'd clash with Francesca when they visited, but it was better than she expected. Yes, her new mother-in-law is a force to be reckoned with, but it turns out she does have a sense of humor. In the same way Lindsay can surprise a laugh out of Giovanni, she discovered she could do it with Francesca too.

They decided to renew their vows again and have another wedding this summer. It seemed silly to Lindsay at first since they're already married, but Giovanni changed her mind.

"That crazy Las Vegas wedding will always be ours, and I'm glad we did it, but I want to claim you in front of everybody. All our family and friends. Maybe it's just an Italian thing, but it matters to me."

How could she not agree with that? They decided to make it a big party and invite everyone. In fact, Phillip and his wife have already said they're looking forward to flying up with Joseph and Sara, who are both adjusting well to their new life in the States.

"And I'm buying you a new ring," Giovanni told her.

She looked down at the cheap gold wedding band, which she'd grown oddly fond of. "I can't believe I'm saying this, but I kind of like this one."

"You don't want a diamond? The only reason I haven't bought you a new ring yet is I figured you'd prefer to design your own"

"You're right, I would. I guess I'd like to keep this one too."

"Wear them both. I just want to spoil you." He leaned down to kiss her playfully. "I can't help myself."

They've started a new weekly ritual. Every Friday night, when Giovanni comes home from work, they push all the furniture out of the way, put on

Elvis Presley, and the two of them dance their asses off, him stomping and swinging those arms around.

She doesn't know how it's possible, but she falls more in love with him every day.

He also took her to see her first opera last month, *La Bohème.* And he was right, she cried her eyes out. It was beautiful and sad and passionate. She held his hand tight the whole time as tears streamed down her face. They've already signed up for season tickets.

"It's your turn to deal." He pushes the cards her way.

She takes them and feels his eyes on her as she expertly shuffles the deck. She figures this will be their last hand of strip poker tonight. They're playing the Texas Hold'em version. If they both make it to showdown, the loser sheds a piece of clothing.

She deals out the cards and they begin the game. She nearly folds after the flop but decides to stay in. Right after the turn, which is an ace of diamonds, his leg starts bouncing, so she figures he's just made his pair. She nearly folds again but waits to see what the river brings. Happily, it's a third seven.

"No way!" His mouth falls open when he sees her three sevens at showdown. "I had a pair of aces. I should have won!"

She leans back in her chair. "I'd like to claim my prize now."

"This is unbelievable," he mutters. "I don't know what I was thinking playing poker with you."

"Why don't you come on over here, Olaf." She gives him a lascivious smile. "And I'll help you take off that pesky underwear."

He shakes his head, laughing in disbelief. Finally, he gets up and moves to where she's sitting. She runs her hands down the length of his muscular body, enjoying herself. When she slowly slides them over his thighs, he lets his breath out. There's definitely something stirring beneath those boxers.

"You want to know what I think?" she asks, looking up at him.

"What?"

"We're *both* winners."

He grins at her with that beautiful smile. The one she gets to love forever. "I think you're right."

THE END

A Note from the Author

Thank you so much for reading *Some Like It Hotter*. I loved telling Lindsay and Giovanni's story. I hope you enjoyed spending time with them too.

If you haven't read the other books in the series, but would like to, you can grab the first book, *Year of Living Blonde* (Natalie and Anthony's story). All the books in this series are standalone titles and can be read in any order. The next book in the series is *Object of My Addiction* (Tori's story. You might remember her from *Return of the Jerk*. She's Nathan's sister and Blair's best friend.) Find out what happens when Tori, who's family is usually on the wrong side of the law, falls for a lawman...

If you'd like to hear about future books, be sure to join my mailing list for updates. You can join at andreasimonne.com.

And lastly, if you enjoyed reading about Lindsay and Giovanni, please consider leaving a review or rating to help get the word out.

Thank you and happy reading!

Andrea

Books by Andrea Simonne

<u>*Sweet Life in Seattle*</u>

Year of Living Blonde, Book 1

Return of the Jerk, Book 2

Some Like It Hotter, Book 3

Object of My Addiction, Book 4
Too Much Like Love, Book 5

<u>*Other*</u>

Fire Down Below

About the Author

ANDREA SIMONNE GREW up as an army brat and discovered she had a talent for creating personas at each new school. The most memorable was a surfer chick named "Ace" who never touched a surf board in her life, but had an impressive collection of puka shell necklaces. Eventually she turned her imagination towards writing. Andrea still enjoys creating personas, though these days they occupy her books. She's an Amazon bestseller in romantic comedy and the author of the series Sweet Life in Seattle. She currently makes her home in the Pacific Northwest with her husband and two sons.

Some of the places you can find her are:

www.andreasimonne.com

https://www.instagram.com/andrea_simonne/

https://twitter.com/AndreaSimonne

https://www.facebook.com/andrea.simonne.author

https://www.goodreads.com/author/show/8557240.Andrea_Simonne

http://www.amazon.com/Andrea-Simonne

authorsimonne@gmail.com

Acknowledgements

THERE ARE SO many people who have helped me on my journey to publishing each book in this series. As always my first reader and sister-friend Erika Preston read the first draft and had great ideas, especially about handling Giovanni's story. Thank you, Erika! Hot Tree Editing has edited all the books in this series, and I'm grateful for their wonderful editors and support. My friend Susan Gideon proofread the final manuscript and as always I'm thankful for her incredible eye for detail. Christine Borgford at Perfectly Publishable has done the beautiful interior formatting & design for all three books in this series. Writing is fun, but can get lonely sometimes. I'm lucky to be part of a group of very talented writers. The awesome Plot Princesses—Amy Rench, Haley Burke, and Pattie Frampton—thank you ladies for all the laughter and encouragement. Lastly, I want to thank my amazing husband, John, and both our boys for always cheering me on. And, of course, for all the research hours where we played countless games of Texas Hold 'em!

Made in United States
Orlando, FL
09 January 2022

13206744R00171